PRAISE FOR VENATORS

"*Venators: Promises Forged* is a darkly spirited young adult novel that prompts eager anticipation for the next book in the series."

—*Foreword Reviews*

"A dynamic, intriguing, and magical world with interesting characters and a story that will engage teens. The world building is fascinating and well developed, and Walls has done everything right to create a solid series opener. Readers will be begging to see what happens to their heroes. The intense action sequences, hinted-at romance, and entertaining dialogue make this book a first purchase."

—*School Library Journal*

"Fast-paced plotting will appeal to readers searching for a thrill . . . Recommend to older fans of fantasies like Cassandra Clare's Mortal Instruments series."

—*Booklist*

"A thrilling, beautifully written book about all things supernatural. This start of the series makes readers want more, and the powerful feeling of fantasy completely takes over while reading this book. Fans of Cassandra Clare's Mortal Instruments series or Laini Taylor's Daughter of Smoke and Bone series will surely appreciate *Venators*."

—*VOYA* (*Voice of Youth Advocates*)

"A deftly crafted, impressively original, and inherently fascinating read from first page to last."

—*Midwest Book Review*

"Devri Walls brings to life a gritty world with twists on well-known monsters and a sense of bloody danger that's often terrifying while also weaving in a calmness and wonder that finds the beauty of it all."

—*Seattle Book Review*

"Devri Walls has stunned us again! Her first book set the bar sky high, and the second leaves us clamoring for more! The Venators books are must-reads."

—Genese Davis, author, *The Holder's Dominion*; video game writer, *Omensight*

"A worthy adventure—full of excitement, passion, and intrigue. Perfect escapism reading, with plenty of wit, drama, and derring-do. Walls creates an immersive world with fresh takes on classic themes, all without sacrificing pace and entertainment."

—Allen Johnson, screenwriter, *The Freemason*

"Yes! The Venators series is back. Maneuver through a minefield of politics . . . Battle one of the darkest fae villains around . . . Dive through the arch with Rune and Grey . . . You won't regret it!"

—Dani Eide, PerspectiveOfAWriter.com

"It's so rare to find all my favorite things in one book, but Venators definitely delivers! Devri's characters are the kind you root for and think about long after you've finished the story. This one gets shelved under 'Favorite'!"

—Heather Hildenbrand, best-selling author, the Dirty Blood series

"Walls does it again. *Promises Forged* is a magical source from start to finish, and you won't want to put it down until you're done."

—Troy Lambert, best-selling thriller author

VENATORS

LEGENDS RISE

VENATORS

LEGENDS RISE

DEVRI WALLS

BROWN BOOKS
PUBLISHING GROUP

Venators: Legends Rise

Brown Books Publishing Group
16250 Knoll Trail Drive, Suite 205
Dallas, Texas 75248
www.BrownBooks.com
(972) 381-0009

A New Era in Publishing®

Publisher's Cataloging-In-Publication Data

Names: Walls, Devri, author. | Walls, Devri. Venators series ; bk. 3.
Title: Venators. Legends rise / Devri Walls.
Other Titles: Legends rise
Description: Dallas, Texas : Brown Books Publishing Group, [2020] | Interest age
    level: 014-018. | Summary: "In the third installment of the Venators series, Rune,
    Grey, and their companions Beltran and Verida have set off together to save their
    mentor Tate from the gladiator games. As their group struggles to stay together
    under the strain of their situation, Rune's twin brother Ryker is falling more
    surely into the clutches of Zio the sorceress, who has her own plots for the future
    of Eon, and the Venators"--Provided by publisher.
Identifiers: ISBN 9781612544427
Subjects: LCSH: Supernatural--Fiction. | Good and evil--Fiction. | Gladiators--
    Fiction. | Imaginary places--Fiction. | Transgenic organisms--Fiction. | LCGFT:
    Fantasy fiction.
Classification: LCC PS3623.A4452 V463 2020 | DDC 813/.6--dc23

ISBN 978-1-61254-442-7
LCCN 2019915834

Printed in the United States
10 9 8 7 6 5 4 3 2 1

For more information or to contact the author,
please go to www.DevriWalls.com.

Somewhere within these pages lies a small piece of my soul.

To my fellow soul droppers: chin up and carry on.

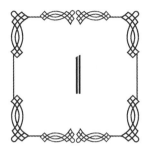

The meeting with the Venators would be starting within the hour, and tensions in the council house were at an all-time high. Beltran should've been summoned by now. He walked from one end of the bedroom to the other, staring at the door and worrying that Dimitri would choose *today* to do something completely unpredictable. And worry was not a look he particularly enjoyed wearing.

Pacing wore grooves in his floorboards.

When a piece of parchment finally slid beneath the door, Beltran leapt on it, breathing a sigh of relief as he unfolded it to find Dimitri's impossibly thin penmanship and unmistakable tact: *Come. Now.* The terse order was followed by a list of dos and don'ts for the meeting that would've been glaringly obvious to any shifter with half a brain. The vampire had also forgotten to say *please*.

Beltran smiled, tapping the parchment against his fingers. *Please.* He chuckled to himself, trying to imagine that coming from Dimitri's mouth. The day Dimitri uttered the word *please* was the day he should be well and truly worried—a clear indication that the vampire knew something he shouldn't.

It would be an obvious warning, but not the only one. If that vampire uttered so much as a *syllable* of nicety in Beltran's direction, it would, without question, be time to flee. Which would mean admitting to the resistance that he'd burned his council bridge and kissing his goal of safely gaining access to Zio goodbye.

Dropping the note on his bed, he straightened his shirt and headed for the door.

The halls of the council house were well lit this morning, but sparsely occupied, and as he navigated their lengths, he pondered just how close he'd come to being exposed in the past. The last time he'd been in a situation similar to the one he fully intended on jumping headlong into this morning, he'd been forced to offer Dimitri intelligence to keep his trust. It had been a painful choice, but in the end, there had been only one secret the right size and shape to safely share without endangering the resistance . . . or the detail's of Verida's *other* endgame.

Given the choice, he was sure that Verida would've chosen to reveal the same secret he had. But she wasn't given a choice, and he'd betrayed her, offering up to Dimitri the one secret she'd whispered across his pillow in a rare, heartfelt bid to open herself to him. In truth, he'd protected them both. Yet he'd lost Verida's trust forever. Completely destroying a relationship with someone he'd loved.

The pain of that moment had *not* dulled with time, and as he prepared to turn the final corner, he dropped it, leaving it pulsating on the plush council house rugs. And not a moment too soon. As expected, at the end of the hall, Dimitri was waiting. He was facing the door to the ballroom, hands clasped behind his back, not a single wrinkle in his perfectly crisp white shirt or freshly pressed slacks.

Once Beltran had strolled within reach, Dimitri flipped on him with vampiric speed. His hand whipped out, gripping Beltran's upper arm and squeezing until it hurt.

"You will not be seen or smelled during this interrogation." Dimitri leaned in, exposing thin white fangs—the telltale mark of the genetically superior species he laid claim to. "Am. I. Clear?"

The tips of Dimitri's well-groomed nails were digging into his skin. Beltran struggled to keep from flinching, his smile tight and thin. "Perfectly. You want me to observe the council without being detected. I understand the stipulation."

In order to secure this summons, Beltran had shared with Dimitri a heavily edited story of how he'd witnessed Ambrose's magic deep within Feena's territory, knowing the information would cause Dimitri to demand that he attend and observe. While the habit of suspecting fellow council members of nefarious actions was universal amongst the group, it would be completely unacceptable to be caught openly evaluating one another to verify said suspicion. Dimitri would need Beltran to watch from the shadows and interpret initial reactions and ill-disguised expressions that Dimitri was unable to properly observe socially, shedding light on any devious undercurrents.

The vicelike grip continued to dig into Beltran's bicep. The pain was wearing on both his patience and his tightly clenched jaw muscles. "Did you have a preference as to what form you'd like me to use?"

"Come now, Beltran. Surely you can think of something."

Not a single thing he'd admit to.

"Perhaps with time and planning . . ." He dragged out his words, offering a crafted illusion of newly formed thought. "Avoiding both your and Silen's sensitive smell and hearing is a difficult challenge, given the parameters. We're working in an enclosed space. I don't have any of the natural disguises afforded by the outdoors."

Dimitri hissed in disgust and released his arm. "It is unwise to treat me as if I am a common fool."

"On the contrary." Beltran dipped his head. "I was deferring to your intellect. I truly hope you have a suitable idea that might enable—"

"—you to use it in the future?"

He cut his eyes up from their lowered station, smiling thinly. "I'm not sure exactly what you'd like me to say. No matter which way I step, you're waiting to pounce."

Dimitri sneered, his disgust thick as a winter fog. "I find it unfortunate that you haven't mastered the ability to turn yourself into a nice brooch." He shaped his thumb and forefinger into an oval and held it against his lapel.

"Alas, the lack of oxygen and functioning organs does deplorable things to a body. Perhaps an insect?" Beltran rubbed his chin in thought. "Or a small rodent? If I stood in the back corner of the room, perhaps I could avoid detection."

His straightforward suggestion pulled Dimitri from his fantasies of seeing Beltran turned into a decorative bauble. "You think my senses so weak, do you? That simply lingering in the back of the room would be sufficient?"

The vampire's senses were anything but weak. But this was about angles, drafts, choosing the right places to hide. These were skills Beltran had mastered, the depths of which Dimitri didn't need to know. What few realized was that shifting was less a gift than the arduous *potential* of a gift. If you learned how to use it, you could become a formidable adversary. Or you could live as a mere shadow of your true capacity. Beltran never was one for ease.

Why anyone would choose to live beneath his capabilities was unfathomable.

"If you have a better suggestion," Beltran said, "I'm happy to oblige."

"A rat seems appropriate for you. Don't you think?"

"I certainly can try it, if that's what you'd like. It's a bit larger than I would've chosen."

"A mouse, then." Dimitri waved his hand in an imperialistic flip. "Small as you can. I'll take care of the rest."

Beltran did as he was told—without the usual irritation at being commanded. He desperately wanted in that room, and if submission was the entrance fee, so be it. He set to work—shrinking, growing fur, a tail, repositioning ears, reshaping his skull. When he was finished, he measured no more than a finger's length from tip to tail—the smallest mouse he could achieve while remaining anatomically correct.

Nature was a precisely designed wonder, and every form had its limits. If Beltran stretched or decreased in excess, bodily systems stopped functioning properly. A quick trick, such as flattening himself to slide through the bars of Rune's cell, was the exception—much like holding your breath to swim underwater. But for shifts of any length, both physiology and consistency were important. As it was, he was straining his ability to properly reduce his size. The blood vessels were losing the uniformity required to sustain life.

Dimitri leaned down, picked Beltran up by the tail, and proceeded to place him on the palm of one hand. He brought his other hand over the top and began vigorously *rubbing* Beltran's furry little body from top to bottom.

Seven. Hells!

Dimitri was scenting him.

Hands moving in both directions, Dimitri jerked and tugged his fur, smashing Beltran's sensitive whiskers between his fingers. The small, scaly sections of his tail kept catching on the vampire's thumb and pulling up like a fingernail bent backward. He squeaked once in pain but otherwise endured the humiliating procedure without audible protest.

Once Dimitri was satisfied, he lifted Beltran to eye level, peering at him with those pale-blue eyes. "Stay close enough to me, and the scent will be disregarded." He lowered his hand with shocking speed.

The ground dropped out from underneath Beltran. Air rushed by as he free-fell from Dimitri's chin to his waist before reconnecting with the vampire's cool, pale skin. He'd barely rebalanced his weight before Dimitri tipped him into his *pocket*. Swear words spattered uselessly against the back of his teeth in a failed transfer from his brain to this inferior mouse anatomy, its long, thin mouth incapable of creating the sounds necessary to let Dimitri know what he thought of this particular choice.

The vampire threw open the doors and strode into the ballroom. Beltran bounced helplessly around the pocket until Dimitri took his council seat, at which point he found himself crushed between the wooden arm of the chair and the thigh of one sadistic ass of a vampire.

He gasped for air, struggling to free himself. These ribs had not been designed for this kind of pressure. He could try to thicken the bones or opt for padding by adding a layer of fat between him and the chair . . . but he dared not. Though the odds were small that anyone else would notice, Dimitri would feel the change of shape. Given the vampire's current mood, the breadth of assumptions he could jump to would be wide. Instead, Beltran kicked with his hind legs and clawed at the inside of the pocket with his front paws.

Dimitri shifted, releasing the pressure.

Beltran glared at the slice of light streaming in from the pocket's opening and snapped his teeth. Bloodsucking bastard, he'd done that on purpose.

"Dimitri, so good of you to join us."

Beltran identified the speaker as Ambrose.

"My apologies. I was dealing with some council business."

Beltran wouldn't be observing anyone from in here. Using his claws, he climbed up the pocket lining and carefully poked the top of his head out. He was unsurprised to find that Dimitri had already positioned his arm in a way that blocked Beltran from the view of both Rune and Grey, who stood facing the council and ready to report.

"Let us begin," Dimitri said. "We have all heard the claims the pair of you made upon your return. Are you *sure* you saw Feena using bodies to feed her plants? If we attack on hearsay, the damage to the council's reputation and our relationship with the fae will be irreparable."

Beltran slid down Dimitri's finely pressed pants and landed on the seat of the chair. He'd stolen every second he could to coach both Rune and Grey on navigating potential questions from the council today. Now all he could do was hope it paid off.

"I can promise you it's not hearsay," Grey said.

"A promise doesn't go very far in this world, Venator." That was Shax—and an already annoyed Shax, at that.

"It's more than a promise. I'm a witness." Grey's voice trembled. "Feena fed off of *me* as well."

Dimitri's chair was last in the line of council seats, and Beltran had been placed in the pocket facing the side door. He inched toward the front of the seat.

"How did you manage to get out of Feena's courts when so many have failed?" Tashara asked.

Rune responded, "I'm certain we wouldn't have made it out alive had it not been for Omri's assistance. The thanks and recognition go to him."

Thatta girl. Formality of speech and nothing to suggest she'd planned the answer beforehand.

"I was unsure it would be sufficient." Omri's voice slid across the room like unbroken water. "I'm pleased to hear that one simple orb was enough to get you both out alive."

Beltran rolled his beady eyes. *One* orb. That pretentious, conniving elf. What the hell was he up to? And how had he contained some of Ambrose's magic in the same type of orb he'd trapped his own in? Not knowing the how or the why was driving Beltran mad!

"Yes, that *one* orb made all the difference. We can't thank you enough." The slight emphasis let Omri know that Rune was choosing to support his lie.

Dimitri shifted to the side so his knee rested against the center of the chair while his ankle leaned against the leg. Beltran leapt from the seat and landed on the back of Dimitri's calf. His needlelike claws dug into the tightly woven fabric of the pants. He pulled one foot out and lowered it, then the other.

"We did some heavy damage trying to get out," Grey said. "The repairs will require a lot of energy, and Feena will be looking for more victims to help power them."

"Feena survived, then," Silen said. "Isn't this a familiar situation? Another unsanctioned trip outside the council house, another job unfinished."

Beltran dropped to the floor and ran behind the chair leg, peeking out at Rune and Grey. The two Venators stood close together, hands behind their backs, feet spread shoulder width apart. Their markings were solid black and their faces impassive. Now if he could only see the council.

"The mission was to rescue Grey," Arwin reminded Silen. "They were given no orders to harm Feena, as we had no cause to do so. You cannot expect them to both follow orders and act of their own volition."

Silen growled under his breath.

"We assume Feena survived," Rune said, "but she was severely injured. It's possible she didn't."

"*Possible*," Dimitri snapped, "is one of my least favorite words, and you're all too cavalier about throwing it around." His sneer flavored the statement, painting a picture so clear it was as if Beltran had eyes on him. "That said . . . Taking into consideration that the Venators have survived Feena, werewolves, and a dragon, I propose we send them back in to eliminate Feena while she remains in a weakened state."

"I concur," Ambrose said. "They have proven themselves capable, and now would be a perfect time to rid ourselves of that fae-blooded abomination."

How convenient.

Ambrose certainly wanted Feena out of the picture, but she was also after the key to Kastaley. She would benefit if possible threats to that end were suddenly eliminated. Beltran would wager a rather large sum that she was also holding on to hope that a second trip across the river would prove to be . . . less than survivable for at least one of their *capable* Venators.

"If we're in agreement that the Venators are ready for missions," Silen said, "then I would remind the council of their other priorities."

"He's right," Rune said. "We promised Silen we'd make the werewolves' needs a priority and clean up the mess we made. Every day we waste is another day that Beorn moves farther away while his pack continues to grow. If we don't stop him, he'll return for vengeance. We would like to request that we be allowed to keep our word to Silen and protect this council from further attacks by Beorn's pack."

"And what of Feena?" Tashara asked.

Given the attention the succubus had paid Grey when she thought no one was looking, Beltran guessed she was addressing him, but Rune answered. "Feena was badly injured and her courts nearly destroyed. Were a council-sanctioned army to attack now, we believe the outcome would be drastically different than last time."

"Do you?" Shax cooed. "Do you really? In *all* your human experience dealing with fae, you feel now would be a prime time to attack? Well, then. That's really all the proof we need, isn't it?"

"Shax, darling," Tashara said, "I realize your ego is wounded because Rune refuses to allow you in her bed, but really, they have managed to accomplish what we have not. Wait to argue until there is actually something to argue about. Or is this simply an opportunity to express your jealous disdain?"

Beltran needed to get to a better vantage point. But how to get off this dais without being seen?

Ambrose tittered at Tashara's reprimand of Shax.

"Besides," Tashara continued brightly. "Rune's resistance to you makes the rest of us like her all the more."

Saints and demons, what was going on? He'd known Tashara to reprimand Shax for minor things, but he'd never seen her set out to humiliate him. There was a commotion. Beltran peeked around Dimitri's shoe. Shax was on his feet, red faced and tugging at his vest. The spectacle pulled the attention of every member in the room.

Now or never. Beltran leapt and sprinted across the tile floor as fast as his very small legs could carry him, aiming for the cover of a serving hutch that squatted against the wall.

"I will not be insulted by the likes of you," Shax snarled. "Any of you!"

Beltran skidded around the furniture leg, his claws scrabbling for purchase. It didn't matter what form you were in—there was always *something* that was ill suited to the task at hand.

Dimitri, now within Beltran's sight, rubbed at his temple. "Shax, sit down. Unless you'd like to permanently vacate your seat on the council."

Shax sputtered, "Permanently vacate—"

"I agree with Rune," Arwin said brightly—as if there weren't a furious incubus still standing next to him. "Silen's claim does precede the need to send the Venators back into Feena's territory."

Shax's mouth gaped, and his hands shook.

"Shax!" Silen shouted. "Now!"

The incubus clamped his jaw shut and sat.

Arwin leaned forward so he could look to both the right and the left, addressing the group equally. The tip of his white beard dropped over his knees. "Send the Venators where we cannot go. If Feena is injured, now would be a perfect time to launch our own attack. Let the people see that the council is not in need of the Venators to do our work."

"He has a point." Tashara pushed her blonde hair over one shoulder. "The rumors have spread with a fury. Many are questioning why we reintroduced the Venators if not to shore up our weaknesses. Let them see that the council is quite capable of handling problems as they arise on our own."

"And if they're wrong?" Ambrose said. "And we walk into a fae court at full power?"

"They're standing here, aren't they?" Arwin pointed out. "You think Feena would've sent them back to us alive?"

"As spies, perhaps." Ambrose's eyes narrowed, the green markings around them flickering darker. "That's a possibility."

"With all due respect—" Grey began.

Rune stiffened. Beltran's body responded in kind. Grey wasn't supposed to say anything besides what he already had. *Anything.* Beltran could not have been clearer. If Grey lived out the remainder of the year, it would be a miracle.

"Feena uses both soul and body to feed her underground courts," Grey continued. "She hooked me into her plants, and . . ." The *and* dangled like a worm on a hook. The room leaned forward, anxious to hear what was fighting to come out of Grey's mouth. ". . . into her mind."

Rune's head turned, her eyes widening before she checked herself. Beltran was reeling. The possibilities were . . . picked up by Ambrose immediately. She flexed her long, thin fingers around the curled front of her armchair. "*What* did you say?"

"Feena linked to my mind. She pulled out my memories and my pain, taking pleasure in the worst moments of my life. She gagged me with roots, fed parts of my soul to her plants, and left me hanging by my skin in a wall of flowers. There is nothing, *nothing*, she could say or do that would ensure my loyalty once she released me. I want her dead more than anything I've ever wanted in my life. If you don't accomplish the mission while we're away, I'll be looking forward to shoving a dagger through her heart myself when we return."

His voice was ice, and there was an edge beneath it that chilled Beltran's blood. So that was Grey's Venator.

Ambrose's arms shook. "But could you see *her?* Could you see inside her mind?"

"No," Grey said. "When Feena linked with me, I couldn't even see what she was looking at." He swallowed. "I only knew because I had to relive all the emotions while she watched."

Disappointment rolled over Ambrose's face, flickering through her fae markings like lightning in one of her storm clouds. She peeled her hands from the arm of the chair and clasped them in her lap. "How unfortunate."

Dimitri drummed the fingers on his right hand against his leg. "Beorn's rogue wolf clan is cutting a swath of destruction. The people are suffering, and the council is bound to honor the agreement between the Venators and Silen. We will send a decree out with the Venators demanding that Beorn appear before the council and that his pack be banished to the other side of the Blues for their part in the unsanctioned attacks. Let it be shown that the council will not allow such actions to go unchecked."

"Are we all in agreement?" Arwin was ready to push a vote.

"Nearly."

"Nearly?" Omri looked down his nose at Silen. "You have everything you've asked for. What else could the wolves need?"

"Ransan had already made an alliance with Cashel to unite against us and the Venators. Even if Ransan decides not to reunite under Beorn's rule, the treason has already been committed. *Both* packs must be held responsible."

"Very well," Dimitri said. "Both will be summoned, and the packs will suffer the same fate. Will that suffice?"

Silen gave one succinct nod.

"And what of Feena?" Shax asked. "Are we allowing *her* actions to go unpunished?"

Dimitri's lips thinned. "As both Arwin and Tashara pointed out, if we want the people to be confident in our strength, we'll need to handle Feena ourselves. As you are so interested in justice against the fae, perhaps you'd like to lead the first wave of attacks at my side?"

Silence stretched, pregnant with the palpable amusement of the rest of the council. Beltran leaned against the buffet leg, his mouse body shaking with laughter. Shax despised anything that wasn't glamorous, fun, or sexual—the latter wrapping up all of his favorites in one lovely package. But interestingly enough, the incubus held his composure.

Shax loosed a glare designed for Rune alone and held it as he spoke. "I would be honored to fight by your side, Dimitri."

Tashara snorted with a shocking lack of delicacy. Shax whirled, twisting in his chair to address it. Beltran braced for the most undignified fallout to ever be displayed in a council meeting with guests. Unfortunately, the incubus was interrupted by a flare of light.

A small, sparkling orb appeared in front of Omri, who narrowed his eyes at the intrusion. It flashed like a star, rays of brilliance rotating with intermittent bursts. Beltran had heard of this before, but he'd never actually witnessed this particular form of elven communication.

"Well, well. What's this?" Ambrose crossed her pale-green legs. "And after so many lectures on controlling my magic use within the council house. What emergency has come up that was important enough to justify interrupting the council's proceedings?"

Omri's face was hard to read, his expression barely changed. He snatched the ball from the air and pressed it to his temple, closing his eyes. Whatever the message was, it wasn't good; the dark elf's eyes snapped open, and his fist closed over the orb, which vanished immediately. He surged to his feet. "I must go."

Ambrose tilted her head, carefully watching. "What's the matter?"

Omri's gaze washed up and down the council members, settling momentarily on Ambrose with a questioning look barely betrayed by a subtle quivering of his brow. "There's an emergency at Kastaley I must attend to. I'll message when I know more. Keep me abreast of the developing situation with Feena." He stepped off the dais, his shoulders tight beneath his robes of silver and gold brocade.

An emergency at Kastaley . . . Such as a missing key, perhaps?

Beltran's connections made him more aware than most of the extreme pressure that had been building on Eon. Constant threats, approaching wars, a never-ending stream of plots and schemes, some of them realized and some not. Zio's hand was the most visible, and she was the most unpredictable player. But there were many others functioning in the shadows, waiting to reveal themselves until the game had been played and the victor declared. Things were changing at a pace not seen for some time. They must examine the possibility that the reintroduction of the Venators had tipped some vital piece of this delicately balanced scale.

2

When Omri left, Grey hoped the meeting would finally be over, but they weren't done yet. Rune still had to spin the rest of the lies and half truths they'd concocted to get them out of this place. Yes, tracking down Beorn would be their first priority. Yes, Tate had already gone ahead to ascertain the pack's direction and where they might find the alpha. No, there was nothing more they could tell them about Feena's court. Yes, they were in good health, fully recovered, and ready to face a pack or two of werewolves.

Because who wasn't ready to go to battle with a couple of werewolf packs on a moment's notice?

The second the council agreed to release them on a mission, electrified anxiety had hijacked him. It rolled in an ever-circling loop through his extremities until he could hardly stand still. But then there were more words spoken, additional platitudes offered. When the meeting finally concluded, Dimitri descended from the dais and asked to speak with Rune. Grey took the opportunity to quietly slip from the ballroom, but as he left, he overheard the vampire asking her to more specifically describe the damage that Omri's magic had done to Feena's court.

The foyer was quiet. Grey strode to the main staircase, where, in anticipation of a favorable decision, Verida had stacked a pile of weapons for both him and Rune. He loaded up everything he could carry—crossbow, sword, daggers, throwing stars, and more. He slipped some of them into the pockets of his Venator pants, slung the bow and sword over his shoulder, and tucked anything he couldn't carry in a large leather bag. They needed to be far, far away before everything came crashing down around them.

He hurried across the mosaic floor and approached the towering double doors in the main foyer. Though the doors were magnificent, the knocker—a small, inconspicuous mallet attached to the wall on his right—felt out of balance. He grasped the handle and swung it downward. The sharp rap sounded loudly, and he stepped to the center to wait, bouncing from the ball of one foot to the other. The movement elicited clangs from the bag over his shoulder.

Some of the weapons he'd packed he still didn't know how to use. In Tate's absence, he was counting on Verida to teach him.

Tate.

Grey missed him fiercely. Tate had stayed behind in Feena's court to buy Rune, Verida, and himself time to escape. A characteristic choice for the Venshii, but Grey blamed himself. At the end of the day, he'd willingly walked into the fae queen's trap, and now he had to live with the memory of the strongest, most proud man he'd ever met holding on to him and *begging* Grey to save him from being permanently returned to his past life as a slave in the gladiator games.

Every night since, as he lay half-awake with his inner demons, he'd felt the memory of Tate's fingers digging into his arm.

A creak sounded, and the hinges on the doors began to twist, pulled from the other side by Stan and Bob. The two wooden slabs separated and light streamed in, splashing over the tiled floor and illuminating the paintings of former council members that hung in rows across the far wall. The painted eyes of those long dead flared to life beneath the brilliance and stared at him with piercing gazes. He looked away.

Upon seeing who'd knocked, Stan and Bob both shouted desperate hellos and promptly pressed themselves against the walls, trembling in fear.

Damn it. They'd been getting better.

Grey attributed the change to Verida having already passed through. No doubt she'd reterrorized the two enormous guards, insisting that Venators were, in fact, giant eaters. He was too distracted to soothe them again and too tired to be angry at Verida. Grey offered what little emotional energy he had left—a halfhearted wave—and stepped into the outside air.

Overhead, the sun shone brightly, and he looked up, squinting. Without a single cloud in the sky, the light flowed uninterrupted across the land. It colored everything golden, lifting the spirit and suggesting that all was well.

His expression soured.

The sun, as it turned out, was a liar.

Grey followed the line of the hulking castle's perimeter toward the stables. Despite its size, its gargoyles, and the stone balconies hanging off its walls, not one shadow survived the sun's direct onslaught. He was halfway to the stables when Rune jogged up next to him, weapons jingling. She slid her arm through his and pulled him tight to her side. The hilt of the dagger sheathed at his thigh pressed into his hip bone.

Rune ducked her head, tucking a stray piece of hair behind her ear. "That's how you did it, isn't it?" she muttered under her breath.

His stomach lurched. "Did what?"

Rune raised a brow.

Yes, he knew what she was asking, and no amount of eyebrow coaxing was going to convince him to talk about it. He'd strategically revealed a few details of what had truly happened in Feena's court to bury the suspicion that they might be spies, but it had been a risk . . . and probably a mistake.

The gravel crunched beneath their feet, and Grey pretended not to notice the glare Rune was drilling through his jaw.

"Fine," she huffed. "*I'll* talk. Why didn't you tell me Feena went into your mind?"

"Because it was horrible, and I'm trying to pretend it didn't happen."

Rune waited for more. When none was forthcoming, her arm grew tighter around his. Grey stared desperately at the corner, hoping for Verida to materialize. It was only a matter of time before Rune—

"When Ambrose asked if you could see into Feena's mind, you lied, didn't you?"

Grey cringed. And there it was. "No."

"You saw something, Grey! I'm not stupid. That's how you got us out. That's how you knew all the things you knew."

He jerked his arm free and grabbed her by the shoulders. "I don't know what you're talking about," he hissed, as quietly as he could. "And *you* don't know what you're talking about."

"What . . . ?" She leaned away, pulling against his hold. "What is the matter with you?"

There was fear on her face. It caught him off guard. Why would she . . . ? Grey recognized the aggression in his stance and could feel the anger etched between his brows. The realization of how tight his grip was sucker punched him with acute and visceral memories.

He recoiled.

Sucking in a mouthful of air, Grey shook his hands at his sides, as if he could shake off the action. "I'm sorry," he said. "Rune, I'm sorry. I . . ." He stumbled, desperately grasping for words that would help her understand while keeping her safe.

In that brief moment when Ambrose thought Grey had been privy to information she wanted, the hunger in her eyes had been ravenous. There would be no protection where this was concerned. If *anyone* discovered how much Grey knew, Feena's people would be just the beginning of his problems. There was no possible safety except in silence.

"Listen, you need to forget whatever you're thinking. You can't . . ." Grey's tongue was thick and unmanageable, and he could see that stubborn set to Rune's chin emerging. "Just forget it! I didn't see anything, and I don't want to talk about what happened down there." His voice hitched. "*Ever.*"

Verida, leading three horses, packed and ready, stepped around the side of the council house. There she pulled up short, looking bewildered. "What are you two just standing there for? Get your asses over here, and let's go before anything changes."

"Anything changes" was Verida's—severely understated—way of reminding them that they were running from a number of imminent disasters. A messenger announcing that Feena was, by all accounts, dead. A report that Tate had not been sent ahead, as Verida claimed, but was on his way to fight in the games. Or an emissary with news of war between Feena's people and Ambrose's. It was Ambrose's magic, after all, that had enabled the Venators' survival and Feena's death—a fact Ambrose was ignorant to.

Rune's face had finished its transition to stubborn determination. The lips, the jaw, the small lines around her eyes.

Grey jerked his head toward their transportation. "You heard Verida. We need to go."

She humphed and crossed her arms. "What did I say?"

"Nothing. I'm still just a little . . . off."

"Rune! Grey!" Verida shouted. "Now!"

His body moved toward Verida and escape even as he twisted at the shoulders to look back at Rune. "I'm sorry I scared you. I am. But we've got to go."

"Grey, wait—" She lunged forward, her fingers wrapping around his arm.

His breath caught, and he yanked free. "I said forget it!"

"Fine!" she shouted at his retreating back. "What the hell is wrong with you?"

"Nothing!"

Nothing but the *buts*.

But if Rune found out what he'd actually seen in the faery court, someone would kill her for it. *But* he'd felt intrinsically different since Feena had stolen some piece of him that he couldn't identify. There were the strange nightmares, *but* those weren't his, for they revealed things he couldn't possibly know. When he woke from those nightmares, his body throbbed from head to toe like he'd been fed through a meat grinder. *But* the other dreams were his. Those left him sweating and gasping for breath. *But* every time he looked at Rune, all he could think about was how she'd kissed him. Rune Jenkins had kissed *him*. *But. But, but, but . . . But* he'd then watched her visibly regret it. He'd like to forget that kiss, *but* the memory of it was seared onto the back of his eyelids.

In the larger scope, none of it mattered. Which left only one consistent and simple answer for what was wrong with him: nothing. Such an easy . . . *monumental* lie. Grey didn't know if it was the guilt of lying to everyone or the weight of the truth locked inside him, but something was smashing around his insides like a wrench in an engine. It clanged and banged until it cut the circuit between Grey Malteer— the boy he used to be—and his cool, collected Venator persona. He ducked his head and pulled his shoulders forward, sinking into his habitual turtle shell. He didn't realize he'd slowed to a stop under the mental recitation of his current circumstances until someone took his wrist and slapped reins into his palm.

Grey blinked, looking up.

Verida stood in front of him, a black horse's muzzle over her shoulder. Her smile was sickeningly sweet as she cooed, "I don't know where you are at the moment, but I need you to get on this horse before I throw you over its back. Think you can do that?"

"Yes."

"Great!" Her face fell. "So do it." She pointed at a white and brown horse standing behind Grey's. "Rune, that one's yours." Verida walked around Grey's mount, doing a quick double check on the cinch. "The crossbows go here." She patted a strap that ran over the top of the pack. "All other weapons can be looped through wherever they fit. Make sure that everything's secure and you aren't banging anything against the horses' flanks while you ride. Always keep a weapon within reach."

Verida went to work checking the cinches and knots on all three horses while Rune and Grey secured their chosen weapons. They were nearly done when a fourth horse whinnied. Verida's head snapped up as Beltran came around the corner, leading a saddled horse with a full pack and what looked like several blankets thrown over his shoulder.

"No!" Verida slapped down the end of the leather strap she'd been working with. "I smelled you, but I figured you knew better than to pull something like this. You are *not* invited."

Beltran waved, his expression bright and not the least bit concerned with the angry vampire. In fact, Grey was fairly sure he was enjoying her tantrum. "Come now, let's not start this off on a bad foot."

"A bad foot? I'll show you a bad foot." Verida stormed at Beltran, head lowered and shoulders squared.

"My pack is full of gifts from Arwin for you and the Venato—"

"We don't need them."

"You don't even know what they are. Maybe we should ask Rune and Grey what they think."

Verida roughly poked one finger against Beltran's sternum, using the motion to punctuate her words. "I. Don't. Care."

"*Ouch!*" Beltran curved inward, rubbing at his chest. "Seven hells, Verida!"

"I am not about to set off on some merry adventure with you."

"I don't think you have a choice, but I am rapidly tiring of vampires not withholding their strength when it's unnecessary."

"It felt fairly necessary, and I *was* holding back. Your sternum isn't broken, now is it?"

"With one finger?" Beltran twisted his head to the side. "I think you're exaggerating your strength just a bit."

"Shall we see?" Verida moved in further, eating up the little space between the two.

"Listen, darling, I'd stay here if I could. I detest sleeping on the ground. But Dimitri has ordered me to come along. You know how he gets when someone disobeys him. Which means . . ." Beltran smiled widely and sidestepped Verida with a flourish, like a magician stepping magnificently out of the way before a rabbit jumped out of a formerly empty box. "Unfortunately, there is nothing I, or you, can do about it."

With a satisfied pep in his step, Beltran led his horse past Verida to turn his enthusiasm on Rune and Grey. "With that nasty business out of the way"—he pulled a blanket from his shoulder—"I come bearing gifts. These were specially made for our two Venators." He tossed one to Grey.

Dark gray wool with maroon trim. Grey held it at arm's length. "A blanket?"

"Better. Your official council cloaks." Beltran took the second one between both hands and snapped it so it fell straight. He held the cloak out toward Rune as if it were made of fine silk and he was the gentleman of the evening. "May I?"

To Grey's delight, she scowled. "Not today."

She snatched it from Beltran's hands and rolled it around her shoulders, fastening the cord at her neck. The cloak fell to midcalf and was embroidered on the right breast with a four-pointed red star—the symbol of the council.

"Hmmm." Beltran's eyes danced over Rune. "Still upset at me, I see."

"Ohhh, we passed that a while ago. Upset doesn't cover it."

"Love—"

Rune's fists balled at her sides, and Grey thought she was going to slug him. "Stop calling me that!"

Verida sauntered to her horse. "It appears I'm not the only one who doesn't appreciate being spied on."

Grey twitched as the memory of Beltran's smug face smiling down from a tree flashed in his mind. It had been one of the more mortifying moments of his life.

"She told you?" Beltran grimaced. "Isn't that just wonderful."

"No, she didn't." Verida took hold of her saddle horn and threw Beltran a smirk that was a cross between a strutting peacock and a cat with a mouse's tail dangling between its lips. "You're just ridiculously predictable. I'm looking forward to Rune and I having more things to discuss on the journey."

Grey pulled his cloak on and gathered up the reins. "We're wasting time."

Beltran grunted some sort of agreement and pulled himself onto his horse. Verida followed suit, still chuckling about gaining the upper hand.

Rune looked at Grey.

Grey looked at Rune.

Both their feet remained firmly planted on the ground.

Verida sighed. "Neither of you knows how to ride, do you?"

Rune put a foot in the stirrup and reached for the saddle horn. "How hard could it be?"

"Mother of Rana!" Verida exploded. "Why do I keep making assumptions about what you two know. From the moment you showed up with Tate at that inn, you've known how to use a . . . a . . . *fork*, and that's about it!"

"What did I do now!" Rune snarled.

Beltran cleared his throat. "Try your other foot, love."

Rune took a closer look at the angle she'd placed herself in, blushed, and reset her stance. She then pulled herself up and threw one leg over the horse's back, coming down hard in the saddle. The horse jolted forward. She let out a yelp but managed to get a hold of the reins and pull her mount to a stop.

"She didn't get thrown off," Verida said to no one and everyone. "It's more than I expected."

"You know what, Verida? I would really enjoy watching you on the other side of the gate. Just one day on our side"—Rune lifted a finger—"that's all I'm asking for. So I could stand back and make comments about how clueless *you* are."

"What could there possibly be to learn in a world such as yours?"

"You wouldn't even know how to open a car door."

Grey smiled to himself. *That* he actually would like to see. Her vampiric condescension would melt within an hour. Of course, it would most likely be replaced by hostility, so on second thought . . .

Verida's face went still. She turned her horse in a tight circle, trotting past Grey and addressing him alone. "Hurry up." She snapped the reins and tapped the horse's side with the back of her boot, thundering away.

"I don't think she appreciated that, Rune." Beltran flicked his reins and galloped off, leaving both Venators in the dust.

"Well, isn't that funny!" Rune shouted at his back. "I didn't appreciate her attitude. So there's that. Do either of you even know what a car is?" She shook her head and cracked the reins.

As the others' hoofbeats melded together, Grey was left alone. He patted his horse's neck. "That didn't look so bad. You aren't going to buck me off, right?"

He'd never been on a horse in his life. Imitating what he'd seen, Grey managed to mount without feeling like too much of a buffoon. With the higher vantage point, he looked for the others. Verida had already vanished from view over the lip of the plateau the council house sat on, and Beltran and Rune were disappearing fast. Grey resituated in the saddle, took a breath, and dug his heels into the horse's side.

The horse whinnied, reared, and bolted. Grey's arms flailed. One foot came out of the stirrup, and he was nearly jerked clean off the horse's back. He frantically let go of the reins with one hand and grasped the saddle horn instead, trying to balance himself without accidentally jerking the horse to a stop. Flying over the animal's front end instead of the back didn't seem like an improvement to his situation.

Riding had looked smooth from a distance. It was not.

Grey jostled and bounced as his horse raced after the others. It wasn't until they dropped over the first dip on the descent from the council house that the animal settled down and Grey started to feel the rhythm of the gallop. Understanding dawned, and he settled in, allowing his body to move *with* the horse instead of against. But he was still bouncing around as though on the worst roller-coaster ride of his life. Up ahead, Beltran seemed to be hovering just above the saddle. Grey imitated his stance, pushing up and using his legs like a pair of shocks.

Verida reached the bottom of the cliff first—the same place where Tate and the carriage had been waiting for them on that first night—and turned her mount north.

The four horses thundered through the forest on a mission to put distance between them and the council house. The landscape blurred together—trees, bushes, vegetation—until Rune couldn't differentiate one mile from the next. Verida led, residual irritation rolling off her back in waves and washing Rune in a stifling haze.

It wasn't until they emerged in front of a small canyon and waterfall that Rune realized she'd been here before. It had been their second full day in Eon. She, Grey, and Verida had run for their lives from a pack of werewolves, and the chase—or at least the first half of it—had ended here.

"We'll let the horses rest for a few minutes," Verida announced. "Then we move on."

Rune walked her horse to the edge of the canyon wall, breathing in air weighted by the waterfall's mist. As her mount nibbled at the grasses along the rim, Rune evaluated the distance from one side to the other. She still couldn't believe she'd made that jump only minutes after accessing her Venator abilities for the first time.

Grey rode up next to her. She hadn't heard the sound of hooves over the roar of the falls. It was warm enough that he'd pushed his cloak over his shoulders. The short sleeves of his shirt cut in tightly, displaying his biceps and exposing the thick Venator marks that ran down his arms.

"How long ago were we here?" she asked.

"I don't know. Two weeks? Three? I've lost track of the days."

She sat with that for a moment, trying to reconcile the timeline. "Why does it seem like forever ago?"

"Because it was." Grey rested his forearm across the saddle horn, face pensive. "We've lived a lifetime since then."

Rune carefully watched from the corner of her eye, determined not to let him catch her staring. He never reacted well to that, and she suspected that now, after their kiss and the utter disaster that followed, he'd react even worse. But she couldn't stop herself.

Despite the days of rest and rich food in the council house, there were dark circles under Grey's eyes, and his cheeks were sunken—maybe even more so than when she'd found him in Feena's lair. But there was something else, something more that she couldn't put her finger on. It was like a . . . strange, unexplainable sense of years added.

Grey jerked his head, motioning away from the canyon. "It looks like Verida is leaving us. Again."

Rune rolled her eyes. "Of course she is. What is *she* so pissed about?"

"I have a hunch." His smile was barely there. "Maybe don't mention earth?"

"I concur." Beltran rode past, barely sparing a glance for either of them. "Thanks to you, Rune, she seems to be a tad bit irritated this afternoon."

"Thanks to me?" She twisted in the saddle. "Did you stop to think that Verida might be pissed off at *you*?"

"Ah—" Beltran slowed his horse and straightened, throwing his shoulders back with exaggerated pride. "This is a rare day indeed. I can honestly say that I haven't done a single thing."

Grey snorted. "You're here, aren't you?"

He looked over his shoulder, that twinkle in his green eyes, and winked. "Well played, Grey. Well played."

Irked that she'd noticed the stupid twinkle in the first place, Rune clutched the reins.

Grey chuckled as Beltran rode away. Once the shifter was out of earshot, he added, "To be fair, it was probably both of you."

"Probably. But we don't need to tell Beltran that. He's already impossible to deal with. Seriously, though, how sensitive can Verida get? I didn't even say anything that offensive."

"You implied that she wouldn't be able to open a *door*."

"I didn't—" Realizing how that must've sounded to someone who didn't know what a car was or how doors on earth might differ from the ones here, she laughed. "Fine, but you know it's true. The auto-locks alone would do her in."

"Maybe." He put his hand to the side of his mouth in a conspiratorial whisper. "Or maybe she'd just rip it off the hinges like in the movies."

"Movies." Homesickness rushed at Rune like a Mack truck . . . complete with autolocks. "*Movies*." She sagged. "I miss movies. And popcorn. And Milk Duds. Why are Milk Duds so amazing? Don't answer that. That's a dumb question. They're chocolate and caramel. How could they not be amazing?"

Grey's expression was tender, but he didn't participate in the reminiscing. When he spoke, it was melancholy. "Earth seems like a lifetime ago too."

"Yeah." She sighed. "You know what's strange? It's starting to feel like that life was the dream, and this one's reality."

"That's not strange. It's the truth. Eon is where we should've been, where our bodies wanted to be." He stared across the canyon at something Rune couldn't see. "In some ways, I feel like I was wishing my whole life away, waiting for this one. And now—" Grey blinked, hard. "Now I wonder if that was a mistake."

There was an uncomfortable beat of silence, filled by the pounding of the falls. She opened her mouth, not even sure what she was going to say, but Grey abruptly cleared his throat and pulled the reins to the right, turning his horse and riding after Verida and Beltran.

Grey's words froze Rune, left alone, to the saddle.

Wishing my whole life away . . . was a mistake.

On earth, she'd been pulled toward something she didn't understand. Living life with a perpetual sense of wrongness, always caught in a desperate search for more. It was why she'd never kicked back against her mother's expectations like Ryker had. She was so wrapped up in the belief that if she just tried harder, she would find what was missing. It never occurred to her that the *more* she needed wasn't even *on* earth.

Rune closed her eyes, pulling in a long, slow breath. Being here, in Eon, she felt whole and at ease. But there was a sadness that went beyond missing her brother. She hadn't understood . . . until now.

Oh my God, I wished my whole life away!

The air in her lungs imploded, pulling her sternum toward her backbone. She'd missed out on so much. What if she'd just enjoyed the movie? Or savored the Milk Duds? Studied a little less and gone out with friends outside of sports practices? But no; she'd lost it all looking for more.

Rune wiped at her eyes as Grey's figure disappeared around the bend. With no choice but to follow, she packed up her sorrow, slowed her breaths, and reluctantly directed her horse in the same direction. She would unpack this another day, when her wounds were no longer raw.

The line of their small group stretched out, leaving large gaps between each rider as they traced the route Verida had laid along the canyon ridge. It was several miles before Verida finally turned her mount onto a treacherously thin path straight down the canyon wall in a gambit for the floor below. Rune was the last to follow.

When her horse stepped obediently down, she pitched forward. Pressing her hands into the saddle horn, she pushed back, swallowing a yelp and resituating her weight to help counterbalance the angle. The path cut back and forth to smooth the angle of the descent, but even with the switchbacks, the trail was dizzyingly steep and thin enough that the horse could barely fit all four hooves. It was slow going, and by the time she reached the bottom, Verida, Grey, and Beltran had already rested, had let their horses drink, and were mounted and ready to ride. Rune stayed in the saddle, letting her horse dip its muzzle in the cool water.

The river was wide, quiet, not more than two feet deep, and crystal clear. No signs of fae or nixies—just brown river rocks and small orange fish that darted from one hiding spot to the next. They rode straight through. Water droplets splashed up her boots and pant legs and sparkled in the sunlight.

Verida trotted up the opposite bank and veered hard left, cutting into the forest and setting the speed. They alternated between short bursts of running and longer sections of trotting. When she finally stopped, she called back, "Markings on from here on out. Use them unless the situation demands otherwise. I don't want to be caught unaware. Ever."

"Do we have to wear these cloaks?" Grey ran his finger over the embroidery of the council's symbol with a grimace. "Everyone is going to associate us with them the moment they see us."

As a general rule, people were either terrified of the council or hated them.

"Unfortunately, yes." Verida scratched around the base of her horse's ears. "If the council doesn't get at least a report or two as to our whereabouts, they'll grow suspicious."

"She's right," Beltran said. "We need the occasional rumor to wing its way to Dimitri."

"But that means the council will know where to find us." Grey dropped his hand from his cloak, panic filling his voice. "Once they figure out what happened—"

Verida interrupted. "Are you referring to anything in particular?"

He sputtered. "Take your pick!"

Her blue eyes gave him a cold warning. She clicked to her horse and trotted away.

Apparently, the conversation was over. Grey looked to the others in disbelief.

Rune urged her horse faster, riding up next to Verida. Grey and Beltran were close behind. "Won't the rumors also help Beorn's pack find us?"

"Maybe. And that should be avoided at all costs. However, between facing Beorn and his pack ahead of schedule or doing battle with the entire council, I'll gladly go head to head with a werewolf pack"—Verida tipped her head in thought—"or four."

"Only four?" Beltran said. "You do not want the council hunting you down. It's been some time since they've worked together, but the worry of rogue Venators would be enough to unite them. Facing all seven at once . . ." He whistled. "Not even Zio will attack them head on."

Rune's horse reared. She yelped and clenched her leg muscles around the saddle, grasping at the horn as the horse twisted its body in the air to change direction. Its front hooves smashed down, and the horse bolted, cutting a path between Beltran and Grey.

Rune pulled hard against the reins. "Woah, woah!"

The horse tossed its head in response and reared again, pawing at the air.

"Rune, move *with* the horse! No, stop—" Beltran dropped from his saddle. He ran and jumped in front of the horse with his arms up.

When the front legs came down, Beltran lunged forward, grabbing hold near the bit. "Saints, Rune! Loosen up on those reins!"

He took the slack she offered and carefully pulled the horse's head to him, pressing his forehead against the muzzle. "Shhh. Shhhh."

The horse steadied beneath his touch, its feet dancing slower and slower.

"There you go," he whispered. "Easy, girl. Easy."

When her horse finally came to a stop, Rune was gasping for air. "What happened?"

"Probably that."

Behind them, Grey pointed to the tree Rune had just passed. Hanging from one of the branches, as if it were one, was a large brown snake. It lifted its head and flicked out its tongue, tasting the air.

"That would do it." Beltran kept his eyes locked with the horse's. "Next time, you've got to relax. Your panic drove her higher."

Rune nodded a breathless understanding. "Is the snake venomous?"

Verida cocked her head, looking at Rune beneath raised brows as if she were the dumbest person she'd ever met. "Of course. Are there any that aren't?"

"Wha—?"

Grey saw Rune's temper flaring and quickly cut her off. "Yes. There are nonvenomous snakes on earth."

"Not venomous? What a waste of a species." Beltran ran a hand down the horse's muzzle and scratched under her jaw, muttering reassurances.

"It is *not* a waste of a species," Rune said. "I prefer my snakes without venom, thank you very much."

"I'm with Rune." Grey tried to urge his horse closer to look at the snake, but his horse was having none of it. It dug its back legs in and refused to move.

"You should try being one sometime." Beltran gave Rune's horse one last pat and turned for his own mount. "No legs, no arms, just a pair of teeth. I'm of the mind-set that small things should have a defense system. It's only fair."

She opened her mouth to argue, simply for the sake of arguing, but found she couldn't even do that. How do you debate the purpose of a snake's abilities and what it should or should not have with a shifter? And she had to admit, the thought of going through the world squirming on her belly did give her the desire to defend herself.

"Let's go!" Verida called.

As the adrenaline faded, Rune realized her wrists were throbbing. It was probably just strain, but the pain focused her attention on the exact spot she'd been ignoring all day.

When we call, you will come.

She ran a trembling thumb over the underside of her left wrist.

Don't delay, or that bubble will move to your heart.

Beads of cold sweat broke out across her forehead and down her back.

That bubble will move to your heart.

Don't delay.

Your heart.

Rune swore she could feel teeth. She scrubbed at the thin skin of her wrist, wanting to rid herself of the sensation and the horrible promise beneath it.

"You look deep in thought."

She jolted. "Hmm?"

Grey and Verida had already moved ahead. Beltran was waiting beside her with that slightly crooked slant to his mouth that was neither a smirk nor a smile. The slant that made her forget she was furious at him.

"Thought?" she repeated dumbly.

The slant deepened to a smirk.

"Oh! Uh, not really. No."

His eyes shone with preemptive amusement, and he leaned back in his saddle, evaluating. "When you forget to put effort behind it, you're a terrible liar."

She turned on an award-winning smile. "Beltran, my favorite shifter. I wasn't thinking about anything. In fact, I am doing fantastic! But thank you so, *so* much for checking on me."

"Mmm, no. There was entirely too much overcompensating happening . . ." He waved a hand over her general form. ". . . everywhere. That smile, for starters—"

"Oh, shut up!" Rune gathered up the reins.

"Wait!" Beltran lowered his voice, checking Verida's distance as he did. "We still haven't talked, you and I."

"About what?" If she could've employed more sarcasm, she would've. "Are you referring to how you sat in a tree and eavesdropped on things that weren't any of your business? You really want to talk about that?"

"Certainly. And then, when you're done yelling at me, we will discuss the *other* matter. You can come find me, or I can find you. Your choice. But we *will* talk."

The demanding tone raked up her spine, reminiscent of home. Demands from her mother, her brother, her coach. Rune's hackles rose. "And if I choose to keep my business my business?"

"Well, my love, under normal circumstances, I would respect that—however heartbroken your wishes might make me. But for this . . ." His arm whipped out, and he grabbed her wrist, twisting her hand palm up and pressing his fingers into the nixie bubble. "I won't take no for an answer."

Rune yanked free, her nostrils flaring with tight breaths.

"Until then." Beltran pressed his heels into the sides of his horse and trotted forward.

4

The sun was resting low in the sky when Verida finally stopped in a small clearing. "We camp here. The human village is a few miles away, and we can't approach at night."

Grey dismounted. Having ridden all day, his legs nearly collapsed under his own weight. "Human village?"

"Yes," she said. "Beorn nearly destroyed it after his father was killed. The Venators are to deliver restitution funds as a sign of goodwill from the council. But if we want to locate Beorn, we'll need to learn everything we can while we're there—about the attack and anything they might have overheard."

Verida ducked, loosing the saddle cinch and briskly giving instructions on how to care for the horses and their equipment. Everyone followed her orders as quickly as they could, though Rune and Grey were more waddling than walking after that ride. Once the saddles and packs were neatly lined up across the ground, Verida removed the bridles and set the horses loose to graze.

Grey watched them wander through the trees, freely nibbling at different grasses and plants. "They just . . . know how far they can go?"

"Generally." Verida shook her saddle blanket out. "Little magic, little training."

Having already finished everything he'd been asked to do, Grey stood awkwardly, looking at their surroundings for the night. It was strange; Beltran had disappeared, and Verida was acting as if they were out for a weekend camping getaway. All he could see was what had occupied every corner of Eon since he'd arrived: a shadow behind every tree and a demon beneath every bush, all waiting to jump out and slit his throat. "Are you sure we're safe?"

Verida snorted. "Of course not. But these are human lands, and the nearest bordering pack territory was Beorn's. Therefore, currently vacant." She set the blanket on top of her saddle to keep the dirt off, using the stirrup to weigh it down. "Beltran is flying over the surrounding area to make sure nothing followed us and all is as calm as it seems."

Rune stormed by, catching Verida's shoulder as she did.

Verida twisted to the side under the impact. "What's your problem?"

"I'm tired. And starving." She snatched a blanket as if it had personally offended her. "I thought Beltran was out getting dinner, but no, he's doing a flyby . . . or whatever. *You* obviously didn't notice, but the rest of us haven't eaten since breakfast."

"There's food in your pack."

"In my . . . The whole time?" Rune's arm went slack, and the blanket brushed the ground, accumulating a mess of dead leaves and dirt along the edge. "Why didn't you tell us?"

"Grown adults handle things by using words, or do they not do that where *you're* from?" Verida put her hands on her hips. "I figured you'd ask when you were hungry. That blanket is dirty . . . again." She pointed. "Shake it out."

Rune's lips were trembling. She was about to blow.

Although Grey was sure everything she said would be the truth, she'd regret most of it as soon as she got some food in her. He gently reached out and took the blanket. "Here, I've got it. Go get something to eat."

She reluctantly released it. Grumbling a thank you, she brushed her hands off on her pants and headed for her pack.

"I had the kitchens prepare a full meal for tonight." Verida sat down and leaned against a tree, stretching out her legs. "After that, we'll have to buy supplies where we can and hunt where we can't."

Beltran emerged from the forest, arms loaded with dried wood. "All right, Verida. Near as I can tell, we're alone. What's the plan?"

"I thought you'd have that all figured out by now."

He dumped the logs and crouched down to arrange them for a fire. "I was too busy talking with Dimitri to spy on anyone else. Apologies. Besides, it'd be best if we all knew what we were doing."

"I think I'll let Rune eat first—she has that crazed look in her eye." Verida smirked. "I'm worried she'll pull a dagger."

"It's a distinct possibility, and I happen to have one easily accessible." Rune yanked a large tin from the pack, holding it up in victory. "Found it! Grey, do you want me to grab yours?"

"I've got it." He chuckled. "Go sit down. Eat."

Rune was halfway through her dinner before Grey and Beltran sat down with theirs. The kitchens had sent an impressive spread of meats, fruit, cheeses, and bread. They ate in silence, too busy shoveling food into their mouths for conversation. Rune hadn't been the only one to feel their missed lunch.

Grey was nearly full when Beltran set aside his empty tins and addressed Verida. "We're fed, and Rune looks less maniacal, so let's hear it. You said you wanted to avoid the packs."

"Thought that would be wise. Beorn has a contract on both Rune's and Grey's heads."

"Agreed. But difficult, considering Dimitri sent us with the summons for Beorn and Ransan to appear on judgment for treason."

Rune choked on a piece of cheese. "Wait, what? They want us to just . . . walk into a werewolf camp and deliver a treason summons? As if they'll all be totally OK with this?"

Grey, Beltran, and Verida looked at her with matching raised brows.

"What?"

"You're the one who told Silen we'd take care of Beorn," Grey said. "And you heard the council. What did you think they wanted us to do?"

"I don't know," she grumbled. "Send it via bird or something. Nail it to a tree and run?"

"Actually . . ." Verida perked up. "That's not a bad idea. The summons must be delivered in person, but we just happen to have someone who could"—she wiggled her fingers in the air—"fly that parchment right in."

"Doable." Beltran nodded. "Although I think Beorn identified me when Rune and Grey attacked their camp. I won't be a welcome guest."

"So make sure you're not seen," Rune said. "You're good at that."

It wasn't a compliment so much an accusation, but Beltran took it as he took most things—however he pleased.

He winked. "Quite right."

"But what about Tate?" Grey asked, picking at the rest of his bread. "Where are we going after the village?"

"The games," Verida said. "Range Arena is close enough to the Blues, it'll look like we're going after Beorn. And with your cloaks on, any reports that make their way back to the council will confirm we're doing what they requested."

"How do you know Tate's fight will be at the Range?" Beltran asked. "Per my sources, the challenge hasn't been announced yet."

"I found Tate's wife and son. Ayla and Brandt were brought in weeks ago." Verida refused to meet Grey's eyes, staring blankly into the fire instead. She inhaled sharply and resituated. "Now we just need in. Beltran?"

"Range Arena is the most protected of any. I assume you weren't able to procure entrance."

"Not through official channels, and if I ask any more questions, I'll alert my father. If I haven't already."

"Are you serious?" Rune looked between Beltran and Verida as if they were joking. "Dracula? We're going to have to fight *Dracula*?"

"If . . . *once* he realizes Tate is fighting," Verida amended, "I have no idea what he'll do. Tate is still, by law, property of Dracula and on loan to the council. Hopefully I'll have a believable story concocted by the time we arrive, just in case."

"Oh," Rune snapped. "Just in case. That's wonderful."

"Wait, we're trying to get *into* the games?" Reality slowly sunk around Grey. "But . . . no! We can't let him fight! I promised—what if something happens, what if—"

"Grey . . ." Verida shook her head. "I should've explained, I . . . Well, by the time we get there, Tate will already be in the arena."

"So?"

"So"—Beltran picked up a rock and tossed it into the fire, watching the embers scatter and twirl—"once Tate is delivered to the games master, there is no way to get him out. The only vulnerable point in the security is when the fighters are actually in the arena—and that vulnerability isn't an easy breach, just accessible. Range Arena holds the top fighters and the largest spectator capacity—more betting, larger purses—and the owners of the gladiators demand top security and insurance. In order for the wizards to keep the assets safe and secure, they employ magic, wards, guards, and natural defenses. If you can think of it, they most likely use it. Our only hope is if we can get a ward down—and that is a very large *if*. Beyond that, we'll need the audience to provide enough noise and chaos for us to get Tate off that arena floor and out of the games master's reach."

Rune gaped. "You're telling me that our best plan to save Tate is jumping into the middle of a *live* gladiator match?"

"I'm looking for another way, but . . ." Verida took a deep breath. "I'm very familiar with the games and the accommodations. I'm not optimistic."

Beltran stretched back, leaning on his elbows and rolling his neck. "Without an invite, I assume we'll be gaining access through the Underground?"

Verida shrugged one shoulder. "We don't have a choice."

"My connections? Or yours?"

"Whoever's work."

"Mine would be better."

Verida scowled.

"Look, I know you don't like needing my help, but given the circumstances, you have to keep a low profile. The last thing we need is for word to get back to your father that you're nosing around for illegal entrance to the games."

"I know, I know." She groaned, rubbing at the bridge of her nose. "And if I reserve the family box, someone will send a bird winging to my father."

5

Zio and Ryker stood across from each other in the large training room. Over the last few days, Ryker had become intimately familiar with the pockmarked wooden floors and the aged, painted walls. It felt more like home than any football field ever had.

When he'd first arrived, Zio had worn gowns, but once they'd begun Ryker's training, she'd dressed them both in head-to-toe black. The material of the shirt and pants breathed like cotton and clung like leather. It hugged curves and highlighted musculature—both of which Ryker always took the opportunity to appreciate.

Zio faced him from across the room, her platinum hair pulled tightly away from her face. "Are you ready?"

The exertion of sparring made Ryker's endorphins spike, and he was aching for the high. Centering his balance, he readjusted his grip and raised his sword. "Let's go."

"Is your Venator ready?"

The beast scrawled its presence in the lines of a vicious smile that crept across Ryker's face. "You know it is."

An eerily similar smile crossed Zio's lips. Ryker nodded acknowledgment and charged. Their blades hissed across each other in passing.

He was still learning how to handle weapons and execute the intricate sequences of body movement. As always, Zio's blows came slow and rhythmic, easing him into the battle. But today, he was aching for more, and he pushed the pacing until time lost meaning and he was dripping with sweat.

Ryker dodged a parry and spun hard to the side, bringing up his blade. Zio moved left but her eyes cut right. Reading the tell, Ryker twisted at the waist to protect his left side as she pivoted on one foot, switching directions. He grinned. Even his mind was functioning at a higher level lately. He'd always been smart, but now he was constantly calculating—judging angles and distances with increased accuracy, deciphering moves and motivations based on minute changes in body language.

"Good." Zio gifted him a rare syllable of approval, then reset. "Tired yet?"

He smirked. "Never too tired for this."

He didn't know how to define this thing Zio referred to as his inner Venator, but he knew what it felt like. It was power and ease and a powerful hit. The more Ryker learned, the more he wanted. When he woke, training was the first thing on his mind. At night, he didn't want to quit. The downtimes between sessions grated on his nerves until he found himself pacing his room. Overnight, *Venator* had become his drug of choice.

Zio circled him, one foot crossing precisely over the other. Ryker stepped in response, keeping her in his sights as he watched for a tell. What he saw instead was a presence that made his inner warrior roar. It was an indefinable thing glistening beneath her skin, and he was drawn to it physically, mentally, even spiritually—if he believed in that sort of thing.

"What?" she asked.

"Just wondering how long you're going to keep stalling."

"You've gotten too comfortable." Zio exploded into motion, running at him with speed far above human capacity.

Ryker's eyes widened, but there was no time for him to process his surprise. He needed to act. He bent his knees, bracing for impact, but Zio veered to the side. Ryker pivoted to follow, hoping to turn the tables from defense to offense, but there was nothing in that direction. She was heading straight for a wall. Confused and unable to calculate her next move, his sword arm unconsciously relaxed.

Zio met the wall at full speed and took three steps *up*. By the fourth step, she was nearly horizontal to the floor. She brought her feet together and kicked off, flipping over him. He tracked her movements, his neck arching back as the tip of his sword dropped, scraping against wood.

Zio twisted her wrist as she passed. Instead of raking him with the blade, she rapped the hilt of her dagger against his temple, hard. Ryker's head spun, and he staggered. He hadn't even had time to think of raising his sword before she'd grabbed his shoulder with one hand and pushed the tip of her dagger beneath his chin with the other.

Breathing hard, he stretched up and away from the bite of Zio's blade. "That . . . was incredible."

"That was nothing. Stay with me, and I'll teach you more than you can imagine."

Ryker grinned, and his eyes cut to the side. "There's nowhere else I'd rather be."

A knock sounded against the main door. Zio flipped her blade around her fingers and sheathed it. "Enter."

Elyria's copper-colored ears poked through her long black hair. She stopped just inside the threshold, leaving the door open behind her. "As of an hour ago, I broke the fae we collected from Feena's court." Her nostrils flared at the edges, and she clasped her hands together at the waist. "You asked to be alerted immediately. Considering I don't have a choice, I came as soon as it was done."

Zio motioned for Ryker to follow as she headed for Elyria. Ryker glanced at his arms as they walked, noticing for the second time that his markings remained black when he was in the presence of either Zio or Elyria.

"I can't tell you how much I adore the constant commentary on your circumstances." Zio slipped her fingers under the obsidian pendant that always hung at Elyria's neck.

Elyria turned her face away at the physical contact.

"Perhaps," Zio said, "I should be more specific next time when I give orders. Demand a more demure slave?"

"I am at your mercy. I'll leave it to you to decide if you want to hear how this stone grates upon me or not."

"Your perceptiveness is always appreciated. We both know how I enjoy watching you suffer." She flipped her hand out, and the pendant landed heavily against Elyria's chest. "Speaking of suffering. Did you enjoy breaking our guest?"

"I rarely enjoy following orders, Your Majesty. Shall I tell you what Nuala said? Or would you rather hear what I had to do to procure the information? You're usually more interested in the latter."

Ryker had never seen anyone or anything talk to Zio as Elyria was now. His skin prickled, and he waited, expecting Zio to put a stop to this fae's disrespect. But her body was humming with amusement.

"Visit my quarters later, and you can regale me with all the salacious details. For now, we will hear the information."

Elyria's lips pursed. "Feena still clings to life. The Venators succeeded in mortally wounding her, and she was forced to take refuge in the form of a tree to survive. The fae have not been told how much of her is left, only that Keir is claiming to communicate with her."

"Interesting. And Tate?"

"Nuala was able to confirm that he was captured and is being held under guard and chain until the transport takes place."

"Very good. Who will be escorting him?"

"I don't know. The goblins snatched Nuala too early. The fae court was still embroiled with the transition to their new king, Keir."

Zio beamed. "Keir will make a delightful mess of things. He's young, impulsive, and burning with the need for revenge. Did our prisoner know anything of his plans?"

"No. It seems Feena kept her plans for Tate quiet. Nuala knew nothing of the plot you assisted in hatching. I suspect Turrin and Morean were aware, but Morean is dead. Killed by Tate. Turrin has been named head of Keir's guard, and I assume he will be involved in Tate's transport to the arena."

Zio circled closely around Elyria, brushing her arm against the fae's. "And you are sure she knew nothing of Feena's plans?"

"Very."

From behind, Zio leaned over her shoulder, setting her lips against Elyria's ear. "Has Maegon been fed?"

Elyria's flinch was subtle, but there. "It was as you demanded."

"Wonderful. And did the fae—what was her name . . . Nuala? Did she put up a fight?"

"No."

Zio made a sound of disgust in the back of her throat and pulled away. "It's been too long since this land has seen true war. The species are growing soft. Did she at least scream?"

"They all do."

"Not all." Zio absently brushed her fingers over the exposed skin on Elyria's neck, her mind elsewhere. "Some are delightfully silent."

"I am pleased to hear the voctorium is working," Elyria said.

Zio laughed, dropping her hand. She stepped around, waiting to face the fae before she responded. "No, you're not."

"No." Elyria raised her chin, holding more defiance in the gesture than Ryker thought possible. "I'm not."

Voctorium? Ryker was always listening—Zio had instructed him to—but he was struggling to keep up. He committed every strange name, place, and reference to memory, but the mental box he was filing them into lacked organization of any kind. It might as well have been a foreign language.

"You haven't answered the most important question," Zio said. "Did Feena deliver her message to Ambrose before she fell?"

"I wouldn't know."

Zio clicked her tongue in disappointment. "Oh, but you would." She pulled a dagger from the slim sheath built into the thigh of her pants.

Elyria kept her eyes focused over Zio's shoulder on the back wall. She didn't flinch as Zio pushed the tip of the dagger into her own finger and spun it. Nor did she look down as a large drop of blood bloomed just below Zio's nail.

Ryker couldn't tear himself away.

"Changing your form isn't the only thing you excel at." Zio pressed her finger against Elyria's temple, smearing a line of blood from the corner of her eye to her chin. When Zio was finished, she pulled back to admire her work, wiping her finger on the side of her pants. "Would you like to share your thoughts? Or should I force you?"

Ryker moved closer—he couldn't help himself. He was drawn in by Zio's show of power. He'd been raised in a world that touted equality as if it were actually truth, but Zio didn't subscribe to this belief. She was obviously superior to this fae and didn't try to hide it. In fact, every move she made spoke to his core desires—strength and superiority. Two things she flaunted without apology.

"Whichever you prefer, *Your Majesty*." A rivulet of blood separated from Zio's design and trickled down Elyria's neck.

He had never heard a title uttered with such contempt. That *she* would speak that way to Zio sent rage flooding through his body. He surged forward, ready to throttle this thing himself.

Zio stretched an arm between him and Elyria, pressing it against his chest. "By all means, exercise what little freedom you have left. Choose for yourself. Would you like to tell me your thoughts? Or shall I make you?"

Elyria took in a long, slow breath. "Feena would not have kid-napped Tate unless the message had been delivered. To do so would've shown her hand. Your plan appears to be moving forward, which suggests that the agreement has been struck and the key is in play. My guess is that the new king will move Tate within the next day or so to deliver him to the arena with as much time as possible for the Venshii to rest before the match. If you'd like me to predict the path the fae will take, there is only one obvious choice. King Keir will need to pass through the Dark Forest if they are to avoid multiple pack territories and march unseen until they're in proximity of the Blues." She bowed. "I will return when I hear from our spies regarding Tate." She turned to go.

"Her mind is a beautiful thing, isn't it?" Zio said to Ryker. "There's always just one little problem. I can't trust her." She raised her voice. "Elyria, was there anything else? I would hate to find out later that you'd withheld information from me."

Elyria froze with her back to them, one hand on the edge of the door. When she spun, her expression was impassive. "The Venators are out of the council house."

"Rune! Rune is out?" Ryker's pitch rose with his excitement. "Where is she?"

Elyria turned her attention fully to Ryker for the first time since she'd arrived. Her pale-green eyes were framed with long, dark lashes, and they roamed over him, heavy with disgust.

Zio's movements were a whirlwind. She backhanded Elyria so hard the force knocked her off her feet. The crack sounded throughout the room. Zio loomed over her prone form, boots pressing against Elyria's shins. "I tolerate your disrespect because, on the days it doesn't make me want to put a sword through your heart, it amuses me. But under no circumstance will your attitude bleed over to my guest. If there is further confusion on that point, I'll try my hand at conventional torture on a shifter who has been commanded not to shift. Now *get up!*"

Shifter?

Elyria pushed smoothly to her feet, the mark of Zio's palm staining her cheek. "Will there be anything else, Your Majesty?"

Zio exhaled laughter on puffs of air. "Ryker, did you see what she did there?"

The cogs in Ryker's mind, which had been so deftly turning, cranked to a halt. He had no idea what Zio was referring to. His cheeks burned with embarrassment.

"Elyria chose her offense carefully, knowing it would elicit a response from me. I suspect she hoped that in my anger, I would dismiss her instead of questioning her further about the Venators. Shifters excel at manipulation of every kind."

"She's not fae?"

"Not at all. Now, let's see if I'm correct. Elyria, who's traveling with the Venators? I know they didn't send them out alone."

"Verida."

"Anyone else?"

Elyria was silent.

"You see, Ryker? Always be on your guard." Zio slid her hand back under Elyria's pendant. "Tell me everyone who is traveling with the Venators, or I will utter a *portion* of the word that stops your heart. It's been a while since you've felt the pain of your heart contracting as it starts to die. Do you need a reminder?"

"Verida and . . ." Elyria closed her eyes. "Beltran."

"Beltran." Zio repeated the name with a deep sigh of satisfaction. "*Finally*. Is there anything else?"

"No. That's everything we know so far."

"Alert me the moment anything changes. You're excused."

Ryker waited until Elyria left the room and the door clanged shut behind her. He had so many questions—but only one that he cared about in this moment. "Rune is out of the council house. When do we leave?"

"The last time I heard the Venators were out, I sent my dragon—"

"A . . . a what? Who?"

Zio must've misread Ryker's expression as horror for her actions rather than the disbelief he was struggling with, because she proceeded to explain herself. "I didn't know Rune was your sister. I was simply trying to prevent the council from procuring two new weapons." She frowned in recollection. "It should've been an easy kill—two untrained Venators from earth, walking around Eon for the first time. But thanks to Beltran, Grey managed to take my dragon's eye."

Ryker shook his head, trying to physically clear the word *dragon*. It had to be a metaphor. Or a name for a warrior. *The Dragon*. He didn't know. The word landed in the unlabeled box in his head with all the other information he didn't understand.

He would worry about it later.

"What are you saying? We aren't going because she's with"—he fumbled for the name—"Beltran? I can't just leave her out there, captive to the council. She's my sister!"

"I know, Ryker. I know." Zio gently took him by the shoulders. "We'll find your sister, I promise. But we must be smart. We have to think. If Verida is with them, it's likely they're trying to retrieve Tate, which means they're heading for the games. My spies will watch, and if I'm right . . . we will have a prime environment in which to retrieve your sister. And Beltran."

"*Who* is Beltran?"

"The answer to everything. With Elyria and Beltran under my control, I could intensify my efforts to overthrow the council and rid the land of the abominations that cover it. The tides would shift. And you, Ryker, could stand at my side through it all." Her eyes lingered on his mouth, and she moved her hand up to cup his jaw, rubbing her thumb across his stubble. "Would you like that?"

Her touch was electric. Ryker's groin ached, and he croaked, "Yes."

Zio's breath washed over his lips. "Good." Her hand slid away, and Ryker's knees wobbled in its absence. "Now come. I have something to show you."

After such a long day and a full meal, Rune and Grey were both yawning. Beltran was feeling the exhaustion himself, but he needed Rune to be at least partially awake for the conversation he had planned for tonight. He got to his feet and brushed off his pants.

Verida eyed him from across the fire. "Where are you going?"

"I tried to explain before we left, but I was rudely interrupted." Grinning at Verida's silent glower, he crossed to the packs and started pulling out shimmering pieces of fabric. "I have gifts from Arwin."

Grey leaned back on the palms of his hands, craning his neck. "What is that?"

"Your tents." Beltran strolled behind Grey, separating one from the rest and dropping it in his lap.

"*This* is my tent?" The fabric whispered through his hand, sliding away like liquid silk to pool in his lap. Grey's face fell. "We're going to freeze."

"On the contrary." Beltran handed one each to Verida and Rune. "Tonight you will be warm, comfortable, and, most importantly, unnoticeable to anything passing through the area."

Given his ability to shift, Beltran didn't actually need a tent—he could sleep just about anywhere in a well-insulated form. But he was endlessly fascinated with Arwin's abilities and wasn't about to pass up an opportunity to experience the wonder of magic by instead volunteering to turn himself into a bear.

Besides, with Rune so nearby, he was particularly attached to this human form and would rather not be covered in fur in the middle of the night. Although, considering the cold shoulder she'd given him since the incident, an unexpected tent visit from Rune was probably a touch optimistic.

"How are we supposed to use this?" Grey asked. "Are there stakes or ropes or—"

"Grey." Beltran tsked. "We're dealing with a wizard. Arwin would be offended. Observe." He flipped the fabric outward the way Arwin had shown him, making it snap in the air. Then he gave it a sharp yank, pulled it over his head, and released. The fabric fluttered down around him and caught, puckering as if suspended by something and then draping to the ground.

At first, Beltran could only see the brightness of the fabric, but then a translucent circle appeared at the central point above his head. The effect grew larger, flowing down like rainwater until it appeared as though he were surrounded by nothing at all. The only sign of the tent's presence was the occasional shimmer that rippled across the inside.

Beltran could see everything, but to an outsider, he'd just become invisible.

Verida looked at the fabric in her hand like it was a viper, and Beltran stifled a laugh. She hated magic. The lack of control, understanding, and predictability ate her alive.

"Go ahead," he called. "Try it."

Rune's nose crinkled. "Not very soundproof, is it?"

"Intentional. I asked Arwin to leave it that way."

"Why would you have done that?" Verida took out her nervousness on the first thing she found, gesturing wildly with the delicate fabric. Clenched in her hand, it flipped and rolled. "What if Grey snores?"

Grey's head snapped up, his brow furrowed. "But . . . I don't."

"Well, Verida darling, that way, when you try to kill me in the middle of night, Rune and Grey will hear my screams and come running to my aid." He poked his head between the flaps and almost winked—he wanted to—but the look on Verida's face said she'd probably remove the offending eyeball.

"I'll speak to Arwin about the glaring flaw in his design when we return."

"I'll let him know to expect you."

"Hey," Rune said. "Why didn't we use something like this instead of nixie bubbles?"

Verida whirled, shouting and shaking the tent in the air. "Because I didn't know Arwin could do this, and we weren't walking around the *council* house openly asking for help to disobey the *council*!"

"All right, all right!" She held up a hand. "Sorry I asked."

"Don't worry, Rune, it's not you," Beltran said, stepping out from the tent. "Verida hates magic."

"Stop. Talking!"

He shoved his hands in his pockets and shrugged at Rune as if to say, *See?*

"I don't think I'm understanding," Grey interjected. "Did you really choose not to soundproof this because you were afraid she'd murder you in your sleep?"

"Would you blame me?" Beltran mimicked Verida's earlier flailing and grinned. "But no. Arwin said I could have invisibility or sound protection. I chose what I thought would be the most beneficial."

"It would've been nice to know you were bringing tents before I packed the regular ones," Verida snapped. "We could've done without the additional weight."

"We'll need both. Arwin gave me a very long speech loaded with copious amounts of wizardly terms that I wasn't completely familiar with, but it basically meant that fabric doesn't hold magic as well as earth does. He infused a stone—which he proceeded to instruct me no less than fourteen times not to lose—and then connected the rock to the fabric via another spell. It was very convoluted but amounted to the simple fact that the fabric can only hold so many hours of magic before it needs to be placed back in the pack with the stone. These should last until morning, but once the tents are depleted, they'll need to rest for at least a full day before they can be used again."

He smiled at Verida, who asked, "Then *why* are we using them tonight?"

"I thought it best to test out their capabilities."

"I see." She pulled in a tight breath through her nose. "And hope we don't need them tomorrow? Excellent."

"A better option than pulling them out when we desperately need them and discovering they don't work."

"Hold up," Rune interrupted. "Let me get this straight. Our tents have to . . . *charge?*"

Beltran looked at her blankly. "I have no idea what that means."

Rune rolled her lips in.

Grey burst into laughter, holding up the tent like he'd found the prize of an era. "Rune! Look! It's the new, upgraded iTent! The Bluetooth connection is nonexistent, but it's new, improved, *and* doubles as a shelter."

"But," she snickered, "how's the screen size?"

The two Venators continued, laughing hysterically and dropping one joke after the next.

"I have absolutely no idea what they're talking about," Beltran said dryly, glancing at Verida. "And I'm beginning to dislike how often that's happening."

"Agreed."

At least they agreed on *something*.

Grey held the edge of the tent fabric to his ear, and Rune laughed even harder.

"What's so funny?" Verida demanded loudly.

"It's just . . . something from . . ." Rune wiped at her eyes. "Earth."

"Oh." Verida's hands went to her hips. "Something *else* I wouldn't know how to use?"

They froze, their joy vanishing as rapidly as if it had been magicked out. They stared at Verida as though if either of them moved, she would blow. Which Beltran had to admit was a possibility.

He leapt to the rescue. "Go on, go on. Try them out like I showed you." Rune and Grey seized the offered escape, pulling the shimmering fabric over their heads and vanishing beneath. Beltran hadn't thought Verida's frown could cut deeper into her forehead, but it did. "You too," he urged.

Once they were all beneath their tents, Beltran scanned the clearing. Their supplies revealed someone was here, but the tents worked perfectly. Even the dirt and leaves beneath them appeared undisturbed.

"Woah!" Grey called. "This is crazy! I can see everything."

"And unlike in a regular tent," he pointed out, "you can see the assassins before they see you."

"Assassins. What a perfect thought to fall asleep to," Rune huffed as she dropped to the ground. "You always know just what to say to make a woman feel good."

Beltran smirked, rocking back on his heels.

Oh, Rune, you have no idea.

7

Though the night was cold, Beltran was right. Beneath the transparent drapes of his tent, Grey was as warm as if he were at home with an electric heater humming in the background. The sleeping pad he'd been handed was no thicker than a few pieces of paper. He'd expected it to feel like that, but when he lay down, the unexpected sensation of an overly cushioned mattress startled him so badly that he leapt to his feet.

Grey was exhausted. Now that he was feeling both warm and surprisingly comfortable, his eyelids grew heavier. Sweat trickled across his brow and slid into his ears as the power of each blink pulled him closer and closer to the abyss. His hands were trembling; he gripped the sides of his thighs.

For as long as he could remember, sleep had brought a certain measure of apprehension. Nightmares plagued him. They were unpredictable, but too often his dreams replayed the actions of his stepfather. He remembered once thinking—after a string of very rough nights—that it couldn't possibly get any worse.

He couldn't have anticipated how wrong he was.

After their first battle with the werewolves and subsequently watching Valerian burn to death by dragon fire, his feelings regarding sleep morphed. First to fear, then abject terror. Sleep ceased to be a place of rejuvenation and became the time he handed over control. When he lost himself, slipping headlong into the same nightmares that he strong-armed into submission during his waking hours.

Like a demon held captive by the sun, his subconscious would slip its restraints in the light of the moon and venture out to play.

He dreaded every second.

Yet every nightmare, no matter how horrific, was preferable to the excruciating dread he felt at the possibility of one of the unexplainable experiences Feena had referred to as his "visions."

Since he'd returned from the forest, it had only happened once—if a vision was really what it was. For a few moments, he'd been back with Tate's wife and son, Ayla and Brandt. Not only was the experience itself terrifying, but when he awoke, his body had hurt far worse than before. It felt like someone had cut him open, manhandled his organs, and shoved them back in without care or concern as to where they belonged. The aftereffects were taking longer to heal as well. The first time he'd had a vision, his aches had vanished within minutes. After the one two days ago, he'd spent half the morning trying to mask the pain in his midsection from everyone at the council house.

Grey's breaths came faster.

Think of something else—anything else.

But what else was there to think about? No matter where his mind jumped, he could see nothing but pain and suffering.

He couldn't stay awake forever.

Grey closed his eyes. The pressure freed a tear, which trickled down his cheek like a sparkling flag of surrender.

8

Zio took hold of the door handle in the sparring room and glanced over her shoulder. "Are you coming?"

Ryker hadn't moved from where she'd left him. He still had his sword in hand, still trying to process the information from Zio's exchange with Elyria, but now all he could think about was her hands on his face. "But . . . we are going after Rune, right?"

"Of course!" she said, as if surprised he'd felt the need to ask. "But we must be smart and careful. Once my spies return, we'll make a plan." Zio's body eased into fluidity, and the tone of her words changed. "Until then . . ."

Her eyes roamed over Ryker's chest with suggestion, then trailed lower. Slow, unabashed—excruciating. His body temperature soared toward boiling point; she met his building desperation with heavy-lidded coyness. Her lips pursed for a millisecond. Then she pulled the door open and slipped into the hall.

Ryker would've followed her anywhere, but after that look, he couldn't get to the door fast enough. He leaned the sword against the wall and hurried out behind. When he'd first arrived, Zio had always led, staying a few steps ahead at all times. Yesterday, she'd waited, allowing him to walk next to her. He was well aware that he wasn't her equal—he could feel her power more than he could feel his own. But being allowed to walk side by side down the dark stone halls of the castle . . . He couldn't help but feel like he'd won her favor.

"Your training is going well," she said abruptly. "After so many generations, I would've expected the inbreeding to have diluted your Venator blood."

"Inbreeding?"

"On earth. Humans with Venators."

"But"—Ryker frowned—"I *am* human."

"Mmm, in a way."

"In what way?"

"In the way a dog is not a wolf, despite the similarities. And a wolf is not a werewolf." She waved a hand. "It's complicated and not terribly important. All you need to know is that you've been trying to be something you're not, and the further you move from your human origins, the better you'll feel." As they walked, she reached over to trace a Venator marking that ran over his bicep. "Your blood is singing. Isn't it?"

Zio's touch was butter-soft electricity.

"My blood is, um"—Ryker tugged at the waistband of his pants, clearing his throat—"definitely doing something."

She smiled, but her fingers slid away and her pace increased, leaving him hurrying to catch up.

"Where are we going?" Ryker asked.

"It's a surprise."

They walked past the dining area and through parts of the castle he'd never seen before. As they walked in silence, he worked up the nerve to ask something that had been bothering him.

"If the Venators have been gone for so long, how do you know so much about us?"

"My history is long and sordid. Suffice it to say that I know a lot about a great many creatures."

"Are you a witch?"

"I am . . . unlike anything else on Eon. Perhaps someday I will tell you more, after you've proven yourself worthy. This way."

Ryker hurried to take the corner she'd just vanished behind and followed her down a winding set of stairs. "How do I do that?"

"That starts now." Her voice bounced against the tight stone walls of the stairwell. "I've chosen to show you something no one else knows of. I'm trusting you, Ryker, not to reveal my secrets. Not even to your sister."

"And if I do?" The words were an unconscious challenge, out of his mouth before he'd thought about what he was saying. He realized his mistake a split second before Zio twisted and shoved him against the wall. She stepped up from the stair below, pressing one knee into his thigh and her forearm against his windpipe. With her other hand, she held a dagger at his cheek.

"The *second* you betray me, I will use you until there is nothing left. And when you're of no more use to me, I will torture you in ways you can't even imagine. When you beg me to kill you, I will keep going." She ran the dagger down his face without breaking the skin, watching her own movements with delighted fascination. "And going, and going." She glanced up. "Don't make me threaten you, Ryker. I don't like doing it."

His fear abated, settling into a cold chill that lay just beneath the surface of his skin. "Yes," he said, low and husky. "You do."

Zio's eyes lit.

Ryker took the initiative, pressing forward, leaning into her and the dagger. The additional pressure on his esophagus cut off his air supply, and the blade she'd been so delicately wielding slid into the skin beneath his jaw. Hot blood trickled down his neck.

Zio eased the pressure on his windpipe and lowered her knife. "I enjoy watching you dip into the Venator you were always meant to be. It makes me want to push you harder."

"Why?"

"Because . . ." She straightened, dragging her palm down his chest and over his stomach. When she reached his hips, she pushed up the edge of his shirt and skimmed her fingers across the top of his waist-band. Ryker's stomach muscles quivered, and his breath shuddered. There was no mercy. She trailed her fingers back and forth. When she paused at the button, he nearly came undone.

Never had any woman affected him like this.

Zio lifted herself onto her toes, arching her body so that the only points of contact between them were her fingers against his stomach and the brush of her lips against his cheek. "Because, Ryker Jenkins, you remind me of me."

The amount of empty space between them was agonizing. Ryker wrapped his hand around Zio's waist and pulled her tight against his hips. They'd been this close before, but never in training gear. Without the fabric of her gowns padding the feel of her, Ryker moaned.

She nipped his ear with her teeth. "Later."

"Later?"

"When I think you can handle it."

He dropped his head against the wall, too distracted by the ache in his lower half to worry about the additional throbbing at the back of his skull. "Why do you torture me?"

"Because watching you squirm is delectable."

"I'm glad one of us is enjoying it."

"Stay with me, and I'll show you all the things you wish to know." She took the next step down the stairs. "And others you didn't know to wish for."

Ryker sagged, wanting to punch something with his rubberized limbs. Instead, he rolled his eyes and kicked off from the wall to follow her. "Now will you tell me where we're going?"

"I have some vampires imprisoned. We're going to pay them a little visit."

"You have vampires? Here?"

"I have many things here, and you are about to meet one of my favorites."

"A vampire?"

She laughed. "No. We're going to take one of the vampires to *meet* my favorite. Although I'm certain you're going to appreciate Maegon far more than the vampire will."

9

Rune had been dreading going to bed from the moment Beltran grabbed her wrist and demanded they have a conversation. But here she was, lying flat on her back with her arms crossed and staring at the sky instead of sleeping—stubborn enough to stay put, but not stupid enough to get undressed. If Beltran was so damned determined to talk, he would have to come to her, because she wasn't moving.

There was a rustle. Rune rolled her head to the side and watched through the clear fabric as Beltran emerged from his tent. His dark hair was rumpled, and when he'd straightened, he rolled his shoulders back and stretched his neck from one side to the other. He shook out his arms and bowed his head, his eyes fluttering shut as if he were deep in thought. Dark leather wings grew out behind him.

Rune's breath caught in her throat. She couldn't decide if he looked like an avenging angel or a demon. Regardless, the silhouette sent something fluttering in her stomach. Beltran lifted his head and waited, knowing full well she could see him. Fighting her feelings, she looked back to the sky and tucked her arms tighter around herself.

When she didn't emerge, he picked up a handful of dirt and tossed it toward her tent. Tiny bits of dust and rock fell across the top, marring the overhead view for her and marking the location of her tent for him. She scowled.

Beltran felt his way around the surface till he found the tent flaps. He poked his head in. "Ah," he whispered. "You *are* awake. I suspected."

"Are you going to haul me out of here kicking and screaming?"

"Mmm . . ." He mulled it over. "You're getting stronger. In my human form, trying to take you by force won't end well for me. No, I was contemplating just talking here—at full voice, of course—regarding the particular thing we need to discuss and seeing how long it takes before you come out all on your own, pleading for me to stop. At that point, I suspect you'll be willing to go anywhere I ask." His smile was brilliant—and irritating. "Not that I've given it all that much thought."

She sat up. "I'm starting to understand Verida's feelings about you a little better."

Beltran flinched. "I see. Well, then, I'll . . . uh, just wait outside." He ducked out.

A twinge of guilt flared. She'd meant to hurt him and had known exactly how to do it.

On the other side of the sheer tent fabric, Beltran rolled his shoulders forward, shoved his hands in his pocket, and kept his eyes on the ground. Given the posture, Rune half expected him to kick at a rock. She was almost ready to apologize when he cleared his throat in a not-so-subtle countdown.

Rune slapped her palms against the sleeping mat and rolled to her feet, storming out. "Fine, let's go."

"If you insist." He held out his arms, indicating how he meant to carry her. "May I?"

"Beltran." Verida's voice came from somewhere to their left—just a few feet away but completely invisible. "I don't know where you're taking her, but if something happens, you can trust that I will not stop until I have removed your head from your shoulders."

Rune cringed. She'd heard. Of *course* she'd heard. They were in the same clearing, and she was a vampire.

"I suppose we'll have to be careful," Beltran said to Rune. "I do believe she means that."

He stepped closer, reaching without grabbing. Despite demanding the conversation, he still waited for permission to touch her, his eyebrows raised in a question. Once Rune gave a curt nod, Beltran scooped her into his arms, bent his knees, and pushed up. His wings caught the air, and with one powerful stroke, they were airborne and cutting up through the tree branches. As they flew, the wind nipped at Rune's exposed arms with astoundingly sharp teeth. She shivered, cursing herself for not wearing her cloak. Beltran pulled her closer to his chest.

The next shiver had nothing to do with the cold.

Until now, Rune had refused to think through the ramifications of what she'd done that night on the river with Grey and the nixies. She hadn't cried about it—because crying would've meant thinking, and to avoid thinking, she hadn't allowed herself to feel anything. But there was no escaping the conversation now, and for the first time since that night, she relinquished the fight.

Her emotions exploded, and she shoved her forehead into Beltran's chest so he couldn't witness the break. The tears flowed in a constant, salty stream. They stung her eyes and dripped onto her lips, and every drop that slipped between them tasted like dread.

Through it all, Beltran didn't say a word. His arms tightened around her, but he held his questions. Enormously grateful for that small act of comfort and privacy, Rune let him cradle her in his arms as they flew and didn't move until her ability to cry was exhausted and the dampness had dried.

She pulled her head up and looked down at the dark sea of tree-tops rushing past endlessly below. "Where are we going?"

"Somewhere we can speak freely without the worry of being overheard."

"Does Verida know where you're taking me?"

"Absolutely not. Once Verida's senses are tuned in to something that doesn't smell right, she'll chase it until she finds the source. Today, we're the source."

"Sounds like someone else I know."

He glanced down at her and smiled. "Me? No. I rarely chase. I'm simply observant, which takes a certain degree of calm patience. Verida misses a lot always chasing down new leads that appear more promising. She's short on attention and temper because she believes she can pummel her way to what she wants. I, on the other hand, prefer to handle matters with more . . ."

"Delicacy?"

"Flexibility. Different problems require different solutions. Beating things into submission rarely yields the results I'm looking for."

"But it works for Verida."

"Does it?" Beltran pitched to one side and they descended rapidly.

Rune squeaked.

They dipped beneath the canopy, flying through a cocoon of leaves, where thick branches reached for them like giant's arms trying to rip them from the sky. Beltran glided easily back and forth between them. Up ahead she spotted a small break in the trees. Glowing blue mushrooms marched up the sides of trunks, lighting up the empty space like a landing strip. Beltran gently set Rune on her feet in the center, then came down beside her.

Aside from the bioluminescent mushrooms and flowers, Rune saw nothing about this place that made it different from where they'd just left. "If you were just looking for a section of forest, I'm sure we could've found one closer."

"Ah, but I wasn't." Beltran's wings withdrew, vanishing into his shoulder blades through one of the magicked shirts Arwin had provided. He marched around the area, peering through every split tree trunk.

"What are you doing?"

"Looking for the entrance. If it could move, I'd swear it had been relocated by the sprites. But since it can't, it appears I've forgotten what I'm looking for." He put his hands on his hips and slowly turned in a circle. "Which is out of character and a tad bit embarrassing."

"What are we searching for? Maybe I can help."

"A peephole that, when looked through, will reveal the entrance to the sprites' realm. There are multiple entrances across Eon, but unfortunately, I can't remember exactly what this one looks like."

Rune stilled. "Another realm? You mean like how I passed from my home to here?"

Something caught Beltran's eye, and he jogged forward. "Not exactly. But in a way." He leapt and pulled himself up onto a branch.

"Uh-uh," Rune said. "No way. I'm not making anymore dimensional . . . jumps, or whatever it is you call it. I already got stuck in this realm, and there is—"

"As long as you don't go breaking rules, you won't get stuck. I promise." He shimmied down to the end of the branch and peered though a Y-shaped split at the end. "Ah, found it! I forgot to account for the fact that this tree has grown since I last visited." He motioned with one hand. "Take six steps forward."

There was really no use fighting this. And . . . she *was* a little curious. "Now what?"

Beltran ducked, looking again between the two branches. "One more step. Good. Now reach your arm out . . . like you were grabbing a doorknob. Up. Good. Hold it right there."

Rune stood in the middle of the clearing, hand out, feeling like an idiot. "Do we have to say a magic word or something?"

"Not a word. Those are too easily spread around. This key was meant to be kept by the person it was gifted to." Beltran dropped to the ground and came up next to Rune. He pulled a small, silver token from his pocket and evaluated her arm. "Did you move?"

She gave him a withering look. "Can we please get on with this?"

"I'll assume that means no." Beltran brought his arm up until it matched the height of Rune's exactly and tossed the token. It vanished into thin air.

"What—?"

"Shhhh. Just wait."

The night shimmered, undulating like heat off a sidewalk on a hot summer day, until it took the form of a freestanding door. The wood was pale, almost white, with decorative hand-painted flowers around the face.

It was not the glowing portal Rune was expecting. "That's . . . quaint."

"The owner is quite fond of flowers." Beltran pushed the door open. "After you."

"Nooo, I don't think so. After you." They locked eyes. "I insist."

Beltran didn't even attempt to hide his hurt. "After all we've been through, you don't trust me?"

It took her back, the betrayal so clearly displayed on his face, until she remembered the moments they'd shared in the council house turret and the conversations in his room. There was a depth to Beltran that he never let her see when they were in a group—which made it easy to forget it was there. Especially when he made her angry.

"I trust you," she said, trying to soften the blow. "I just don't trust that." Rune pointed. "The last time I stepped through something like that, I was chased by goblins and werewolves and shoved into an alternate dimension."

"Fair enough. Together, then?" He reached out a hand.

Rune steeled herself, then slid her hand through his and allowed him to pull her through the open door. On the other side, the world around them faded into a ghost realm. The bright-blue mushrooms lost their luminance and sat like black lumps on trunks of paper white. An eerie fog washed the remainder of the forest in shades of gray.

"Just a little further."

Beltran's voice fell dead and flat against her ears. She shook her head to clear whatever was blocking the sound. But it wasn't her; it was this place. Their footfalls were muted against the darkened earth, and the spaces of silence buzzed with weight. Rune's markings came to life, glowing a rich teal that splashed across the desolate landscape.

Beltran glanced over his shoulder and stumbled. "Oh, no. Turn those markings off, love. The sprites will appreciate that even less than Dimitri."

Rune did as he asked.

"Thank you." He squeezed her hand. "One more step, and we're there."

Without warning, the ghost realm gave way to a new landscape painted in vibrant color and lit by the sun, which was shining brightly overhead.

Rune startled. "It's daytime."

They were still in the same area—she recognized the layout—but this realm was touched by magic. Branches twirled instead of bending; leaves were iridescent green instead of flat; and the trees dripped with trumpet-shaped orange blooms with whimsical purple stamens.

Beltran pointed to a little cottage at the edge of the clearing. "That's where we're going."

When they reached the doorstep, he gave her a small, reassuring smile and knocked. The door swung open to reveal what Rune assumed was a sprite.

"Hello, Sarena."

The female's skin and hair were a creamy white. She was adorned entirely in peach, from the flowers in her hair to the ruffles at the bottom of her skirt, which brushed against her bare feet. Though she lacked the pointed ears of fae and elves, her facial structure was similar: high, thin cheekbones, wide eyes, and full lips. But Sarena's eyes made Rune's skin crawl. The irises were milky, appearing white at one angle but tinged with a pale green when she turned her head. The effect was macabre.

"Beltran," Sarena said fondly. "It's been many years . . ." As she noticed Rune's markings, the pleasantries faded. Frowning, she pointed a long, thin finger at her. "What. Is. *That?*"

Beltran threw his arm between Rune and the sprite. "Let me explain."

"There is no need! You have shown a Venator the entrance to my home. Beltran of House Fallax, I revoke—"

"Wait, wait, wait!" He leapt forward and grabbed the sprite by her shoulders, shoving his face against her ear.

Sarena glared at Rune as he talked. When Beltran backed up, she pushed past him and snatched Rune's wrist, roughly twisting her arm to poke at the nixie bubble. "You've made a deal."

Rune's other hand clenched at her side. "I have."

"Of your own free will?"

"Yes."

"Is there anything you can do?" Beltran asked.

It was then that Rune understood. Beltran hadn't brought her here to *talk*. He'd come looking for help.

"No. My cousins followed the rules. Even the Venator admits the agreement was sound."

Sarena looked down her nose to search Rune's face. Seething disdain leaked from her eyes like poison. Rune knew what the sprite was looking for, because it was what they *all* looked for—the Venator. Sarena's eyes narrowed, and she began increasing the pressure on Rune's wrist, digging her thumb into the nixie bubble.

Rune winced. "You're . . . you're hurting me."

"I know." Sarena's head jerked several inches to the side in a sharp, birdlike movement. "Will you allow me to continue?"

"What are you . . . ? Sarena!" Beltran surged forward, reaching for Rune.

"Beltran, stop!" Although Rune desperately wanted out of this situation, her gut screamed that if he intervened now, there would be no recovering. With Beltran stilled—and looking like he'd swallowed a frog—she turned her attention back to Sarena. "What do you want from me?"

"To see what we're dealing with. Make that beast that lives inside of you known."

"No." Her wrist was throbbing, and it was everything she could do not to rip it away, but any movement she made now would be interpreted as aggressive. "I am not a monster . . . or an animal. And I choose who I want to be."

"A cornered dog will always bite. It is its nature." Sarena's voice became serpentine as she hissed the syllables. "And I have never met a Venator who cared very much for their ability to choose another path."

In Rune's peripheral vision, Beltran shifted his weight from one foot to the other. The nervous energy was unlike him, and she read it as clearly as a flashing neon sign: there was a very real danger here.

"You've never met us," Rune said. "We're differ—"

Sarena's head turned so fast that her hair spun, slapping across Rune's face. "There are more?"

Beltran was already raising his hands in apology. "Just one."

The sprite yanked Rune forward, throwing her off balance. She grabbed a dagger from the sheath on Rune's thigh, and before Rune knew what was happening, she had the blade pressed into her side.

"Tell me the truth, little girl. Does your Venator roar?"

A wash of white noise flooded Rune's ears. The Venator rose to protect itself against the unholy, abominable . . . *Damn it, damn it, damn it!*

"Rune . . ." Beltran murmured her name in warning.

Sarena leaned her cheek against Rune's. The sprite's skin was cool, the texture rougher than her own. "Tell me," Sarena urged again. "Is she roaring now?"

Rune squeezed her eyes closed.

"You foolish girl. You speak of choice, but I can see her. The Venator bleeds through your limbs, changes your posture, brightens your eyes." Sarena let the hiss of Rune's tight breaths hang between them—audible proof of the inferno burning inside. "I should kill you right now."

Rune was furious—at herself, at the situation. "I *can* choose."

Sarena's chest jerked in silent, derisive laughter.

"Please." Beltran inched closer. "Listen to her. These two Venators *are* different—I never would've brought her here otherwise. You must know that."

As Beltran pleaded with Sarena, Rune lifted her humanity, using it to quench the fires of hate and fury and the burn of her genetic predisposition. She untangled herself from the Venator with painstaking determination. Within seconds, her breathing had returned to normal.

Sarena loosed her hold.

"*I* choose my future." Rune pulled her chin high. "Me. And I will not be ruled by instinct."

Sarena pulled back, scrutinizing her with the strange, jerky movements of an owl. "We will see how much weight your words hold when the situation is more dire than the one I just placed you in." She tapped the flat side of the blade against her palm. "But you have surprised me."

"If I may . . ." Beltran reached over Sarena and delicately plucked Rune's blade from her hand. "The other Venator, Grey, offered himself up as a trade to Feena to free one of her pets."

"Did he escape, this other Venator?" Sarena's eyes tracked the dagger until Beltran handed it off to Rune, who returned it to its sheath.

"Yes. He and Rune managed to defeat Feena."

Sarena stared at Beltran as if she'd misheard. He nodded confirmation. "For many years, the trees have spoken of Feena's atrocities," she said. "The fae queen needed to be stopped."

"Are you certain there's nothing you can do?" Beltran asked. "For Rune."

"If this claim is true, it is surely worthy of something. However, I can not undo the agreement she made with my cousins." Sarena turned her attention to Rune, grasping her hands at her waist. "But if it was you who helped to defeat Feena, I truly wish I could. You're welcome to use my home for as long as you need this evening."

"Thank you."

"A warning. Know that if we see any signs of danger from the Venators, we will not hesitate to attack."

Rune sighed. "Get in line." At the confused look on Sarena's face, she explained, "Sorry, I just meant that there are others who feel the same."

"I'm sure there are." Sarena's smile was thin. "But how many can emerge from another dimension to shove a dagger through your chest before your markings alert you to their presence?"

"Well, then!" Beltran clapped his hands together. "Sarena, thank you very much for your hospitality. I assure you, it won't be long before we're on our way." He placed a hand on Rune's back and ushered her toward the cottage.

"Beltran?" The coin he'd tossed earlier sat on Sarena's extended palm.

He slowed, eying the key. "May I?"

Sarena's fingers curled back around the silver coin. "I don't think so."

"But darling—"

"Perhaps later. When I'm finished being angry with you."

"Of course." He dipped his head. "I trust you will let me know when that is."

Beltran followed Rune into the cottage and shut the door behind them. Losing that key was less than ideal. Had he thought about it for half a second, he'd have known better. Instead, he'd responded to Rune's situation. To *act* was one thing, and often admirable, but *responding* was simply a knee-jerk reaction in the face of panic. And it rarely came without consequences.

Bloody hell, what this Venator did to him was terrifying.

The key was gone, and there was nothing he could say or do that would change Sarena's mind. Their history had taught him that. Sarena would come to him when she'd calmed down. Hopefully that would be sometime within the next decade.

In the years he'd been away, Sarena's cottage had remained unchanged. It was small, simple, and contained only the necessities. A bed woven of vines hung from the ceiling—Sarena would never cut down a tree for something as simple as a bed. He knew for a fact that the timber used in the construction of the walls and ceiling had been collected from fallen trees the sprites could not save, as was their custom. The dishes were plain, handmade pottery, the chairs a combination of fallen timber and woven vines. Next to the bed were clay pots that were sprouting tiny seedlings and a canvas that Sarena was in the process of painting.

Rune moved about the cottage at an impossibly slow pace, looking at even the most mundane of items with intense scrutiny in what was obviously a futile attempt to avoid the looming conversation. She ran her finger over the rim of one of Sarena's handmade bowls. "You probably should've told her I was coming."

Beltran chuckled. He crossed his arms and leaned a hip against the small kitchen table. "Yes, I should've."

"Where are we, exactly?"

"The sprites' dimension resides in the same space as ours, but only the sprites—or those given permission—can cross between the two."

"Should I assume that was your permission she just walked away with?"

"Indeed, it was."

"She actually looked happy to see you . . . for about five seconds." Rune finally faced him. "But did you really have to bring me to an alternate dimension to talk? Surely there was somewhere closer."

"As you've already figured out, I brought you here to see if that agreement of yours could be undone."

"But we're still here."

The silence between them thrummed with its own energy.

Rune absently rubbed her thumb over the opposite wrist in what was becoming a nervous tic. He ached for her to speak, to explain what he wanted to know without him having to pull it out of her. Instead, she gave him her back and returned to studying Sarena's painting. Beltran suspected the move was motivated less by her appreciation of the art and more for an escape from his own unwavering focus.

Unbeknownst to Rune, Beltran was currently engaging in all-out internal war. The sides were split, the contenders formidable. On one end stood the coldhearted shifter he currently was; on the other, the shifter he'd been long, long ago. The two opposing sides could not occupy the same space, and they threatened to destroy everything he'd built. During the times he and Rune were apart, he'd make the decision to stay away from her, only to find himself running straight for her the moment the situation allowed. His life had become an excruciating exercise in self-torture.

Rune twisted her head to the side as she examined the far edge of the painting. Her profile revealed a soft smile of appreciation.

His knees weakened. A slew of emotions rose from depths Beltran had nearly forgotten he contained. Even as he stood there, staring at her back, his walls were crumbling. Unable and unwilling to fight his desires anymore, Beltran yielded another battle to this unexplainable and unexpected weakness dressed in Venator clothes.

"Rune, *why?*"

"You know why."

"No, I don't. Grey was injured. I could see that. But you heal. If you'd just given it some time, maybe—"

She whirled. "He wasn't wounded. He was *dying.* Feena shoved a poisoned tree branch through his gut."

"Maybe—"

"No! Listen to me. Even with Grey's advanced healing, those wounds were too substantial to recover from. And with the poison in his system, there was no hope." Rune's breathing increased at the recollection, and her hands fluttered out from her side, hovering and shaking the way Beltran imagined they'd done over Grey's lifeless body. "His wound was bubbling and foaming with poison. I tried to wash it out, but it just . . . There was nothing else to do! It was either this . . ." She held up her arm, motioning to the subtle bump under her skin—as if he possibly could've forgotten what they were talking about. "Or let Grey die!"

"So better you than him? Is that what you thought? That Grey's life was more valuable than yours?"

"Well, he sure as hell isn't *less* valuable."

"That isn't your choice to make!"

"*What?*"

Beltran cringed. He wanted to pull that statement back the moment it left his mouth. "Rune, that's not what I—"

"How dare you! If *anything* is my choice to make, it's this. I traded a promise to save Grey, and it wasn't the first one I had to make that night."

"Not the first . . . Rune, what did you do?"

She paled.

"Seven hells." He scrubbed his hands over his face. "Omri. I should've known, and instead I was the one who let you go off with him alone."

"At least Omri didn't bite my wrist and seal his promise with . . . with . . ." She shook her arm as if she could dislodge the nixie's mark. "This!"

Rune's panic bled out through her voice, and Beltran's heart sank. "You didn't know, did you?"

"That I was bartering with my life?" She wrapped her arms protectively around her middle. "No."

"Rune—"

"But I would've done it anyway. I'd already told the nixies to take me instead. And I meant it. If only one of us was going to make it, Grey was clearly the better choice."

"The better . . ." Beltran sputtered. "What if I disagree? What if I think that *you're* the better choice?"

"You weren't there. Were you?"

The blow from her accusation fell heavily. He stumbled toward the window, pressed down by the weight of his shame.

No, he hadn't been there. If he had, maybe Rune wouldn't have been forced to make a deal with Omri. Maybe her life wouldn't be at the mercy of the nixies. He'd chosen to stay at the council house that night because he'd had to—the risk was far too great.

And he'd do it again.

Because of this repeating paradox in his life, guilt had served little purpose. Why cripple himself with self-flagellation when he'd be forced to repeat his actions again anyway? Despite that, in this moment—knowing he'd do it all over again—he couldn't set the guilt down. It rose up like a separate entity, vicious and unrelenting.

Beltran sagged against the window frame. His head drooped, falling against the thick glass. "Leaving you and Grey to go in by yourselves"—he squeezed his eyes shut—"was one of the hardest things I've ever done."

"Then why did you do it?"

"I can't tell you."

"You said you couldn't set foot on Feena's lands."

"I can't. Not without consequences."

"Consequences? Worse than Grey dying? Worse than *me* dying?"

The horrible truth slipped out on a whisper. "Yes."

It was a miracle it came out at all.

"Well, then." Rune's voice shook. "If that's your choice, you don't get to have an opinion about what I do or do not promise. Or who I choose to save."

He groaned. "I want to tell you . . . so much. And it's making me crazy."

"Did you want to tell Verida?"

He flinched and rolled his head against the pane to look at her. "Low blow, love."

"Are you going to answer me?"

There was a fragility to her in this moment that he didn't see very often. Her spine was too straight, her eyes too wide. The tremble that had been in her voice was now barely visible in her lips.

Something snapped inside Beltran. He pushed away from the window, strode across the room, not knowing what he was going to do when he reached Rune, only that this woman completely unhinged him.

She retreated until she bumped up against the wall.

Still, he didn't stop. Beltran stalked forward, placing his palms flat against the wooden planks on either side of her head.

"Beltran," she whispered, her chest hitching. "What are you doing?"

They were so close that the puffs of air from her question caressed his lips. The sensation triggered everything he'd been trying not to think about, and his own breath came faster. He leaned in, taking a moment to bathe in her rich brown eyes . . . to appreciate the pattern of her freckles. By every god and demon that may or not exist, he wanted to run his fingers over each and every damn one.

He closed his eyes for just a moment, centering himself before he dared speak. "If you really want to know what I did and did not want to tell Verida, you'll have to answer my question first."

Rune's scowl was immediate. "I already did. I made the choice to save Grey's life."

He shook his head slowly. "No. Not that. I want to know . . . Why did you kiss him?"

A myriad of emotions flooded her face: surprise, confusion . . . and then anger.

"You jackass!" She shoved him away, following the momentum to step toward him. "You sat up in that tree, listening to every word we said, waiting until you got what you were looking for before you let us know you were there. You already heard everything!"

"But was it the truth?"

"Why does it matter?"

Jealously flowed through him like a disease. He seized a clay pot from the table and threw it against the wall. "Because it does!"

The pottery rained down in broken shards, scattering across the floor with pings and crashes. As the noise dropped off, Beltran and Rune stood unmoving. Encased in fearful silence.

Rune's mouth hung open. She was staring at him as if she'd never seen him before.

In truth, she hadn't.

He had just completely lost control.

The authenticity of these feelings was irrelevant, as was how hotly they burned. Beltran flashed Rune a smile that was as thin as the layer of skin it rested on. "I'm sorry. You're right. It's none of my business. We need to get you back to camp so you can get some rest; there's a long day ahead of us." He headed for the door as casually as he could and took hold of the latch.

"Yes."

The simplicity of the answer sent it over his head for half a second. Then he froze, emotionally backhanded by the implication. "Yes?"

"It was the truth. I kissed Grey because I was relieved he was alive. And now he wants something from me that I don't think I can give him."

Beltran turned on the balls of his feet and, painfully, made his way back to Rune. His steps were slow and stiff, and when he reached her, she wouldn't look at him.

"A bargain is a bargain," he began, certain it was a bad idea to continue. "No, I did not want to tell Verida why I can't go into Feena's lands. Occasionally, I felt a twinge of guilt for withholding it from her, but when I was with Verida, the words never threatened to crawl up my throat whether or not I wanted them to. When I was with her, the truth didn't come blurting out of my mouth at every inopportune moment. When I'm with you, it's a constant battle. My entire being is aching to show you who I am. I know, without a doubt, that I should run away from you as fast as I can. Instead, I'm standing here, with inches between us, feeling every bit of that space as if it were the miles it should be. And I don't know what to do with any of that."

"Then why?" The question came out in a desperate breath, driving it deeper into his heart. "Why would you eavesdrop on me as if my feelings didn't matter? You embarrassed me. You hurt and humiliated Grey." Her eyes were wet with tears. "It would've upset me no matter what, but after all the warnings I ignored about you, I came up that hill after the worst few hours of my life only to be treated like just another part of your game."

"I . . ." Beltran looked down at his trembling hands in confusion. What was happening? And why was it suddenly so hot in the damned sprite's cottage? "I . . ."

He couldn't talk. He was frozen, unable to negotiate the two sides of himself. One side screamed: *Stop talking immediately*. The other demanded: *Tell her the truth*. This was not him. He was not a lovesick adolescent, too nervous to speak and unsure of his actions. But here he stood, a bloody monument to the lot of it. Beltran growled in frustration and stormed for the door.

This time, Rune didn't call after him.

10

Beltran's dark leather wings exploded from his back as forcefully as the frustration coursing through his veins. He flew to the top of a nearby tree. The distance made him feel minutely better for all of a fleeting moment; then the unassignable irritation returned.

He didn't know where to go, how to think, or what he was feeling—besides a clear desire to stab a dagger through something. Using his wings as a counterbalance, Beltran dropped down to sit on an overhanging branch. He glared at the cottage door as if it were a point of personal offense, both wanting Rune to come storming out and hoping she wouldn't.

This constant paradox of feelings had left him drifting through an unfamiliar ocean, beaten down by waves and gasping for breath. The only thing he knew for sure was that the novelty had definitely worn off.

How bloody unfortunate the feelings hadn't.

He sighed. There was no way to know how close he was to his endgame. The right opportunity could present itself tomorrow morning or eighty-five years from now. It was why he kept everyone at a distance. Although some he held closer than others, none were allowed past the guarded doors to his internal vault. At times Beltran was sure the vault was located in his mind; other moments made him suspect it had been lodged in his heart. The answer was likely both. Twin doors. Twin locks.

Regardless, it was the place his secrets resided. And they were *heavy*.

It was one thing to lock up possessions, but when you locked up secrets, you imprisoned *yourself.* The shackles had been on for so long he'd forgotten their weight until Rune brought them to the forefront of his mind. Now the ache to release the burden was growing every day.

But . . .

If he told Rune bits and pieces, would he be strong enough to hold back the tide? Or would it all come tumbling out in his need to not be so utterly alone anymore?

Alone.

Beltran smiled bitterly at *that* pleasant dose of reality. He'd come to believe that in a world where everyone wanted to use him, it was preferable to fly solo. Better lonely than a tool wielded against his will. That remained true. But as evidenced by the current ache in his heart, he wasn't nearly as all right as he'd thought.

Motion caught his attention. Beltran narrowed his eyes, scanning their surroundings. From his vantage point, he could make out what appeared to be an ambush. Sprites were coming through the trees from three directions, dressed in dark green pants, long-sleeved tunics, and masks that covered their faces from the nose down. Royal assassins.

Good news traveled fast, it seemed.

Beltran was on his feet and diving before he had time to fully formulate a plan. He landed on the roof just as the first assassin slipped into the clearing. The sprite looked up, startled. Female, he guessed, from her slight stature. The other two came into view, forcing Beltran to take a step back and twist his body to keep all three of them in some portion of his field of vision.

He shoved his hands in his pockets and smiled. "Greetings! Sarena didn't tell me you'd be coming."

Three bows rose, arrows nocked.

"I came with permission," he continued loudly, hoping his voice carried well enough for all three to hear. "Surely Sarena mentioned that."

"We didn't speak to Sarena," the sprite directly in front of him called back. "The spells we placed during the wars alerted us to the presence of a Venator."

That he had not known. Interesting. It explained several things, including the limited casualties the sprites had taken in the wars despite the Venators having secured enough coins to launch an attack on the dimension.

The furthest assassin was cutting ever closer to the back window. Rune's markings were off, and though he'd have thought his voice would carry to the inside of the cottage, she either hadn't heard him talking to someone or was ignoring him. He suspected the second.

"I'm coming down." He held up his hands. "I mean no harm." Beltran moved carefully to the roof's edge and stepped off. "Rune, love," he called loudly over his shoulder. "Could you come out here, please? Slowly."

The two sprites he could still see were as tense as their bowstrings. They were keeping their distance, probably unsure what to expect. Nobody wanted to go head to head with a Venator . . . though they didn't realize that this one, although dangerous, was not nearly as trained as the ones they'd fought in the past. Better to fire arrows than engage in hand-to-hand combat. He could use that to his advantage.

"Beltran!" Rune flung open the door. "Unless you're ready . . . oh."

"Yes, oh," Beltran said smoothly. "Please allow me to introduce you to the royal assassins. I'd give you their names, but they haven't offered them." He inched his fingers backward, reaching for her. When she took his hand, he breathed a sigh of relief.

He might be able to fly them clear of the cottage if he could avoid the sprites' arrows, but they needed to get out of the realm. And that required a door. Wasting time trying to find another would increase the chances they'd be found. He also had no idea what type of magic the sprites had employed. Would the spell that brought them here continue to track Rune if they ran? Or did it just alert them to where she'd entered?

There were too many unknowns. They had to leave this realm from here.

He jerked Rune closer, pressing her against the sensitive skin of his wings. "Do not pull a weapon," he muttered under his breath. "Unless I ask for it."

There was a rustle inside the cottage. It was so soft that he would've ignored it had he not already seen the third sprite heading for the back window. He stepped away from the door, pulling Rune with him. Inside, glass shattered. "We mean no harm, as you can see."

"Our quarrel is not with you. Hand over the Venator."

Beltran edged Rune closer to the portal. The assassins knew full well where he was heading. The sprites changed course as one, cutting to the side and pursuing in a slow, methodical fashion—backs straight, knees partially bent, crossing one foot in front of the other. The tactic allowed them to keep their bows steady during the hunt, their arrows always on target.

"Shifter . . ." the one closest to them warned.

Sarena had always kept his identity a secret, and by the assassins' own admission, they hadn't spoken with her. He hesitated.

"Yes, we know who you are."

Beltran knew he needed to keep moving, but . . . "How, may I ask?"

One of the assassins cut right, spurring Beltran to counter. He sidestepped and pushed Rune further behind him.

"Beltran isn't a very common name, and neither are those wings sprouting from your back. Our king has eyes and ears all over your realm. He is most interested in you."

The revelation echoed around the clearing. *New realm, same story.*

A fourth sprite emerged from behind a tree and stepped directly in front of the portal.

"Beltran?" Rune said at his shoulder.

"I see him." He held up both hands in surrender. "Wait, please. If your king is so interested in me, perhaps I can speak with him. That is, of course, if we can send the Venator back to the other side."

"Our orders are very clear."

The sprites pulled back the final few inches of their bowstrings in unison.

"New plan!" Beltran spun and wrapped his arms around Rune, pressing her to his chest. His wings flared, and he thickened the sections of leathery flesh over his midsection as rapidly as he could. They wouldn't fly—but that's not what he needed right now. He heard the twang and tensed. One arrow ripped through his right wing, another through his left, and one hit the hardened areas he'd formed to protect his heart. He sagged forward.

"Beltran!" Rune slid her arms under his, trying to take his weight.

"Get to the house. There's another sprite in there. I need you to restrain him. Can you do that?"

"I . . . I think."

"Do not kill him, Rune. It's the only way."

She nodded.

"We go together. Now." Beltran kept Rune in front of him and his wings between him and the assassins as they ran toward the cottage.

She ripped the door open, coming face to face with the sharp end of an arrow. The sprite hadn't expected her, and he was too close. Rune grabbed the arrow, wrenching it down, and shoved him backward with her forearm.

Beltran slammed the door a second before a volley of arrows cracked against the outside of the cottage.

Finding the sprite so immediately upon entering had thrown Rune off guard as well. When she leapt forward to grab him, it was sloppy. The sprite easily flung her away. Beltran prepared to defend against an attack, but in the sprites' history, Venators had proved dangerous even on their worst days. With Rune on the ground and vulnerable, the assassin's focus shifted entirely to her.

Beltran waited a few feet away, hand wrapped around the back of a wooden dining chair, watching the scene unfold. *Come on, come on! I need to hear that voice.*

Rune rolled and pulled her feet back beneath herself, reaching for a dagger.

The sprite stalked forward. He readjusted his grip on the hilt of his assassin's blade. "I've dreamed of a moment like this."

Gotcha. Beltran surged forward and smashed the chair over the sprite's head. The assassin collapsed. Outside, the sprites were yelling to one another, coordinating their next move.

They were running out of time.

Beltran ripped the assassin's mask off and tied it over his own mouth. "Drag him over there." He pointed Rune to the opposite side of the hinged door—the only place that might keep them out of view. "Secure him with something. Quickly."

He started to shift—his wings shrinking, his still-healing wounds screaming. His clothes took on the look he imagined, as they'd been spelled to do. He snatched the bow the sprite had dropped and threw the door open.

"They went out the back window," he yelled with the fallen sprite's voice. "The shifter has her."

To sell the scene before they could question anything, he took off running around the house, praying the rest of the assassins would follow. If any of them stopped to look inside . . . it would be over. But if he'd taken the time to close the door, the illusion would've been shattered.

Beltran cleared the edge of the cottage and glanced behind. The thrill of seeing all three sprites following numbed the pain of his wounds. He pumped his arms faster and cut into the tree line.

"Is he on foot or in the air?" one shouted.

"On foot. His wings weren't healed yet. But they might be by now."

"Split up," another yelled. "Malcan! Call in the Yipsinger."

Splitting up was a wonderful idea. The Yipsinger was not. Sarena had told him stories of that creature and the part it played in the Venator wars of old. It was not something he wanted to meet.

Once the other three sprites had peeled off, Beltran skidded to a stop and crouched down. He quickly scanned his surroundings, ripped off the mask, and shifted into a tiny, inconspicuous bird. His body didn't feel right; he twisted his head and saw three bleeding, featherless wounds.

He should've healed by now—partially, if nothing else. Those lesions appeared fresh.

Beltran took off toward the cottage. Under the pressure of flight, the wounds sent searing streams of fire up and down his spine. He squawked in pain, but it didn't matter—there was no time to lose. He had to get back to Rune.

He stepped back into the cottage as a man. Rune sprung from around the side of the door, blade up.

"Woah!" he said. "It's me."

She dropped her arm, sagging in relief. "You're OK."

"I always am. Some find it annoying. Where is he?"

Rune pushed the door halfway shut and pointed. The sprite was tied up with vines that Rune had hacked from Sarena's bed. He was awake, though, and bent to the side at an awkward angle. Beltran immediately noticed what Rune had not: all five of the sprite's fingertips were pressed against the floorboards. Worse, his lips were moving.

Upon seeing Beltran, the assassin's mouth twisted slightly upward with glee as he continued whispering.

He was using his connection to the soil of the earth to call the others back.

"Time to go!" Beltran grabbed Rune's arm and practically threw her out the door.

They ran.

"Look for the shimmer!" An arrow whizzed by Beltran's shoulder. "It'll show itself as we get close."

"Why are they back?" Rune shouted.

"Because our little friend called them."

"What? How?"

"How do you think?" Beltran twisted, cutting right and then left as another arrow barely missed him. "Magic."

There was a rumbling under their feet. Rune stumbled. Beltran swore.

The Yipsinger.

The shimmer of the door appeared immediately to their right. The next rumble was louder, and the ground shook.

"What is *that*?" she yelled.

The door was too close. He'd have to turn around to make it. There wasn't time for that. Beltran threw himself to the side and slammed into Rune. They tumbled through the exit and landed in the eerie in-between space, where everything was and wasn't at the same time.

A shadowy arrow passed through with them, burying itself in the ground inches from Rune's elbow. She looked at it and then at him.

He grabbed under her arm and pulled her halfway to her feet, dragging her forward until the realm of Eon solidified.

There, she fell to her knees again, breathing hard.

Beltran dropped to the ground beside her. He rolled onto his back and groaned. "Those arrows had a little special something on them, I think."

"Aren't they going to follow us?"

"No. They're too fragile on this side. Vulnerable to attack." He chuckled to himself. "Place a splinter properly, and it might do the job. The last thing they want is to follow a Venator through that door." His three arrow wounds were burning; he closed his eyes. "When a sprite crosses into our world, they lose part of their form. It was the cost of creating their own realm."

"That's a nice thought . . . Wait." Rune stilled, and her eyes narrowed. "What do you mean, 'a little special something'?"

"Mmm." Beltran moaned and stretched his arms up, linking his fingers beneath his head. "I mean, I think they were a tad bit poisoned."

"A tad bit?" The tone and volume were impressively understated for Rune. Beltran would've given her credit for that, but . . . she shouted the next one. *"A tad bit!* What does that even mean?"

"Keep your voice down, love. It's still after dark, and I, for one, would really rather not fight with anything for at least a few hours."

"Are you going to be OK?"

"Should be. It doesn't feel like one of the more serious poisons. I suspect pirantian—its effects are more severe on sprites than on me. But I'm going to be sore for a bit."

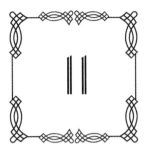

Zio stepped off the last stair. Using two fingers, she reached into a small, thin pocket sewn into her pants. "I need to show you something."

Ryker watched curiously as she withdrew a smooth brown vial that was corked at the top. As far as he could tell, it was neither glass nor metal. Although he still hadn't recovered from his and Zio's little "encounter" in the stairwell, the promise of seeing a vampire had helped put it to the back of his mind . . . for the moment.

"This is voctorium." She raised it above eye level and twisted it, as if she could see the contents swirling inside. "It's made from—"

A bellow rushed around them, sounding part predator and part machine, the volume earsplitting. Ryker jumped and ducked, spinning to face the threat. The hall was empty, but the blast went on. Vibrations shuddered through the walls. Mortar dust crumbled out from between the stones and scattered over the toes of their boots. He fumbled for the dagger on his belt while trying to protect his ear with the other elbow. The blade was only half out of its sheath when the roar faded and was gone.

Ryker straightened, breathing hard. "Wha . . . what was that!"

"That's Maegon. Don't worry. He's quite secure."

He twisted at the waist, ready to demand further explanation, but Zio was already walking away. In order to follow, he would have to turn his back to the source of the sound. Doing so made the hairs on his neck stand on end. He ran to catch up.

Zio continued as if nothing out of the ordinary had happened. "Voctorium is made from an innocuous-looking plant called voctoris that grows only in the Sumhim Valley. This potion, as I'm about to demonstrate, is original, unexpected, and holds unlimited possibilities."

As they walked, he noticed that each door they passed in this tunnellike hallway appeared to be reinforced. They were wider than other doors he'd seen, constructed from heavier wood, and braced with iron crossbars. Ryker's Venator markings started to flicker bright red.

Zio glanced at them and smiled. "Almost there."

She led on, stopping in front of a door without a handle. Zio placed her palm against the wood, bowed her head, and whispered. The seal on the door cracked. Shouts and snarls flooded out. She pushed the door wide open with one hand. "After you."

The room was the length of a gymnasium. Rows and rows of human-sized cages were lined up from one side to the other. The curved tops were too low for many of the prisoners; those snarling at Ryker and Zio did so either hunched over on their knees or while leaning against the bars and stretching their arms through, as if they could reach them.

"These are vampires?"

Zio whispered at his shoulder. "Every last one."

Ryker couldn't believe what he was seeing. Those red eyes were unnerving, and their thin, sharp canines made something dark twist in his gut.

"Do you remember what I've taught you?"

He repeated the lesson back "That they shouldn't exist."

"Exactly. Look at them. They're hungry. Do you see how badly they want to rip your throat out? How desperate they are to drink your blood? Can you imagine what a group like this could do if I freed them from those cages?"

He could. And what if these . . . these *things* were to cross through a gate and roam earth? They would prey on his friends, on his family! If Ryker ever had any doubt about the things Zio had been teaching him, it evaporated in that moment.

Zio brushed past him. Holding out one arm, she ran the underside of her pale wrist across the cages as she strolled between the rows. "Who's hungry?"

The vampires hissed and retreated, pressing themselves against the bars at the back of their cages as if their lives depended on it.

"Vampires pride themselves on their power and cunning." Zio's back was to him, but he could hear the amusement in her voice. "If you lock them up with bars thick enough to withstand their strength and then restrict their access to blood, they quickly become as helpless as a human. I keep these on the edge of starvation, leaving them too weak to fight their bloodlust. Which is why"—she looked coyly over her shoulder at Ryker—"although all of them know what I'm about to do, none of them will be able to resist." She took several more steps, scanning the cages before turning back to him. "Would you like to choose?"

A heavy thud of excitement triggered a grin he couldn't have stopped if he'd tried. Had Rune been there, he would've exerted the effort to attempt to hold it back. But with Zio, there was never a need. She offered him the freedom to feel what he felt without any of the shame that everyone else in his life had always thrown on him.

Ryker walked down the first row, evaluating the occupants. The red glow of his markings reflected off the metal cages. The vampires knew what he was looking for, even if he didn't, and they whimpered as he walked by. He loved the sound of it. He thrived on the way they looked up, down, around—anywhere but at him. This was power! A kind he'd always wanted for himself but had never been able to fully take. At least not without getting his ass thrown in jail.

He'd nearly lost himself to the high, breathing in the fear that surrounded him, when a male—tall enough that he had to bend at the waist in order to stand—dared catch his eye. Ryker squared up to the cage, expecting the male to back down. Instead, he saw his own disgust mirrored back to him in those unblinking red eyes.

Ryker pointed. "This one."

"Dracula will stop you!" The male threw himself forward. "When he discovers what you're doing, we will come for you. We will rip you from limb to limb. Wipe you and this Venator from the face of the—" He groaned, wrapping his arms around his middle.

"What's wrong with him?" Ryker asked.

Zio advanced on their chosen victim. "Right now, his body is literally eating itself to stay alive. He's in the beginning stages of transforming from a being of some intelligence to the monster he is." She held the vial in her teeth to free her hands, pulled a blade, and ran it over her wrist. Blood welled, spilling over the sides.

At the first scent of blood, there was a shift within the vampire. Ryker couldn't have identified what was different, but it was exactly like Zio had said: something changed. The vampire appeared nearly human one moment and animal the next. The male threw himself forward, cracking his own head on the cage. He stretched both arms through the bars, straining to reach Zio.

"Patience, pet." She sheathed the dagger and pulled the vial from her mouth, uncorking it in the process. "I can't give you *clean* blood, now can I?"

The two vampires on either side caught the scent of blood. They joined the first, slamming themselves against the bars of their cages over and over again.

"Clean blood?" Ryker's mouth dropped. "You're letting him *feed* on you?"

"Abhorrent, I know," she said around the cork. "But in this instance, worth it."

The smell of fresh blood continued to spread through the room until Ryker was surrounded by snarling, mindless leeches.

Zio took her time. She carefully dripped three drops of clear liquid onto her bloody wrist, pushed the cork back into the vial and returned it to her pocket. She then stepped closer to Ryker, angling her body so that her wrist pressed against the cage in a way that prevented the vampire from grabbing hold of her arm and pulling it through.

The male dropped to his knees and rammed the bars. Twisting his head to the side, he slid his mouth between the metal, opening his jaw as wide as the cage allowed. Then he jerked his head down and punctured Zio's perfect skin with those repulsive fangs.

Ryker gagged. He didn't remember going for a weapon, but he felt cold metal as his hand curled around the hilt of his dagger. The male sucked and slurped until Ryker thought he really would be sick.

Finally, Zio's imperialistic voice rang through the room. "Enough!"

The scent of blood had reached every corner, and the place was a madhouse. Zio's demand was ignored by everyone except the one who should've been the least able to stop. For the vampire on his knees, the effect was instantaneous. His mouth went still at her wrist. Blood leaked around his lips, dripping uselessly to the slate floor.

"Release," she commanded.

The vampire withdrew and got to his feet. He hunched in the center of his cage, staring at Zio with bright-red eyes and blood running down his chin as if there weren't another soul in the room.

She casually wiped the blood and spit off her wrist onto the leg of her pants. "Now, Ryker." She nodded to the male. "Watch."

The sound of frenzied animals continued all around them, but Ryker obeyed, looking only at the vampire Zio had just fed. It wasn't more than a few more seconds before the blood vessels in the corners of his eyes began to swell and darken. After that, thick, protruding black lines wiggled inward until they entirely crisscrossed the whites of his eyes.

Ryker frowned, tilting his head to one side as if seeing it from another angle would change the situation. "Uhh . . . what just happened?"

"The voctorium has now taken full effect." Zio handed him a key. "Open the door."

He had a million objections to opening that door—and half as many questions—but he shoved the key in the lock anyway. When he swung the door open, Ryker stepped back with it, ready for a fight.

The vampire didn't so much as blink.

Zio plucked the key from Ryker's fingers and vanished it back into one of her many pockets. She addressed the vampire. "What's your name?"

"Kiril."

Zio's gaze slid to a female one cage over who was still pawing for Zio's blood-smeared wrist. "Kiril, break her arm."

The vampire rushed out of the cage, blowing by Ryker, grabbed the female's arm, and wrenched it to the side, using the bar as a fulcrum. The female shrieked a millisecond before her arm shattered. It happened so fast Ryker could barely process it. Thick, jagged bone ripped through her skin as if it were paper.

Like a trained soldier, Kiril released his hold and snapped back to face Zio.

The female reached her good arm through the bars. She hesitated, staring at the mutilated bone, then rammed her hand down, shoving the bone back against the skin. Her scream was intense enough that it made even Ryker squirm. Still shrieking, she worked her arm back inside and then slid down the back of the cage, gasping and wheezing.

Kiril's focus was absolute. He looked to Zio alone, his gaze cold and indifferent.

"When voctorium is fed to a vampire, it strips them of their will, turning them into this." Zio motioned over Kiril. "Completely mindless, but extremely lethal, slaves."

"Is he . . ." Ryker inched closer. "Waiting for another order?"

"Yes. Go ahead. Tell him to do something."

Ryker knew exactly what he wanted to command Kiril to do. The day he'd stuck his dagger through that werewolf, something had woken up inside him, and though he wouldn't have readily admitted it, he'd been dying to do it again. He pulled his blade and held it up, silently asking for Zio's permission.

She waved the go-ahead.

The three steps to the vampire were spring loaded with solid adrenaline, and when Ryker pressed the tip of his dagger over Kiril's heart, he could barely get the words out without laughing. "Lean. Forward."

Kiril didn't move.

Ryker frowned. "I said, *lean forward!*"

Nothing.

Ryker resituated, ready to punch the blade into this monster's heart himself.

Zio started laughing. "We can't have a murderous slave taking orders from whoever is nearest him, now can we?"

It was immediately obvious how useless Kiril would be if just anyone were able to give him an order, and Ryker's arm slid back to his side. But understanding that did nothing to soothe his fury at having been denied this opportunity.

"He will obey only the one whose blood he's ingested," Zio said. "Kiril, I think it's time to pay a visit to Maegon. You know where to go."

Under his master's command, Kiril took one clean step back, pivoted, and walked from the room.

Ryker was exasperated. "*Who* is Maegon?"

"I'm not going to spoil the surprise." Zio slid her arm through his.

They walked arm in arm down the shadowy hall, following the mindless vampire at a leisurely pace.

Ryker was quiet, thinking through the things she'd taught him about this world and about adding voctorium into the mix. The possibilities were just as spectacular as she'd promised. "Are the effects permanent?"

A shadow passed over her face. "No. I thought I'd found a permanent formula weeks ago, but it wasn't successful."

"What happened?"

"When the gate between worlds opened, I sent my goblins through after the council's Venshii, Tate. The werewolves and several dosed vampires didn't arrive in time. Surprisingly, the gate opened again that evening. It was brief—barely a blip. Had they not already been there, we would've missed it. Once they were through, the vampires were the ones that were able to track Tate. I'm told they were minutes away from securing my victory when their minds shattered. Simultaneously." She tsked. "The voctorium proved too much for them. It boiled their brains in their abominable heads."

Ahead, Kiril plodded on mindlessly.

"How long do the effects last?"

Zio readjusted her grip. She slid her elbow further through his and pulled him tighter to her side. "It varies. I modified the formula. It's stable now and circumvents the brain-boiling side effects, but it's being metabolized at different rates. The fastest I've seen a vampire burn off the drug was around an hour. The slowest was just over three."

"And while they're under its influence, they'll do anything?"

"Anything." She looked up at him, eyes bright. "Imagine the possibilities."

"Oh, I am." Mindless vampire slaves to help take out their own kind? To attack the council? It was brilliant. "Does it work on other species?"

"I adore that you always ask all the right questions. Unfortunately, not at this time. What I don't know yet is whether the voctorium is only compatible with vampire genetics or whether I've yet to find the proper combinations. Time will tell."

The floor angled as they descended deeper into a castle that never seemed to end. The walls changed from laid brick to natural rough stone, as if this section had been carved from the mountain instead of built on top of it. Ahead, there was an archway with two torches burning on either side, illuminating carved symbols that ran up and around its length. Kiril crossed beneath it and turned, disappearing from view.

Two steps later, a wave of stench overwhelmed Ryker. He grunted and covered his nose with his forearm. The odor was both acrid and sharp, singeing his nose hairs and burning his eyes. The further they walked, the stronger it became, until Ryker identified the smell as decay, overlaid with the stench of a reptile enclosure at the zoo.

Zio and Ryker passed under the arch, but with the only source of light now behind them, the path ahead was pitch black. Zio whispered a series of words—he never could make out what she was saying. Ahead of them, bright balls of light flared, hovering above metal sconces that had been hammered into the stone.

Kiril waited, his back rigid. On the other side of him was open air.

Zio released Ryker's arm and strode to the lip of a stone overhang. When Ryker approached the edge, he took the last foot an inch at a time, craning his neck to look out at the cavernous opening.

In the center of the cave, three stalagmite pillars—large enough that he'd expect to see them gracing the front of a Roman temple—glistened with greens, yellows, and browns. Above, moisture shone across the uneven surface of the soaring, curved ceiling. Water slowly dripped from jagged points that looked like they had once been stalactites but had been broken off. How that would've happened, though, Ryker couldn't figure out.

He was looking down again at the three awe-inspiring stalagmites when he noticed that something was wrapped around the bases. It was so large that he'd written it off as an uneven part of the cave floor. But whatever was down there, it was alive. Its sides flexed in and out with heavy breaths, and green scales threw back the reflection of Zio's summoned lights. Large, leathery wings lay flat across its back, and its feet were so large that Ryker would easily fit beneath one. His brain supplied the name—*dragon*—but he dismissed it as soon as he thought it. There simply had to be limits to what could exist.

The monstrous thing raised its head, and Ryker's knees went weak.

When Zio said she'd sent a dragon after Rune and Grey, it hadn't been a code name. No matter how badly he wanted to, he could no longer deny that he was most definitely looking at a dragon. His anxiety peaked as he imagined his sister standing in front of *that*.

"Kiril." The name dripped like honey from Zio's lips. "Maegon is hungry. Get close to him, and stay within his range, but do try to survive."

The vampire crouched and leapt off the ledge. Ryker jolted forward, fell on one knee for stability, and leaned forward to watch as Kiril fell. The size of the drop left his mouth dry. The vampire, however, landed easily.

Ryker looked over his shoulder to Zio. "'Try to survive'?"

"Maegon likes a good hunt." The corners of her lips twitched. "And frankly, so do I."

The dragon lifted his head and sniffed the air. Then, with a roar, Maegon lunged out from between the stalagmites, spreading his wings wide. With the dragon now facing Kiril, Ryker saw the jagged scar over its missing eye. An uncomfortable lump slugged him in the throat.

Grey did *that?* Grey Malteer? The little punk ass who used to cower as Ryker and his boys threw him in garbage cans and stuffed him in lockers? For a brief moment, as he looked at the size difference between Kiril and Maegon, a measure of respect sparked within him.

Ryker scowled and snuffed it out.

He *hated* Grey.

He would *always* hate Grey.

There was no doubt that Grey was responsible for those damned council goblins showing up in his room and ripping him from his bed. And Grey was also the reason why, when Ryker was pulled from that bed, drunk off his ass and half out of his mind, Rune wasn't there.

Rune was *always* there.

Always.

Except for the night she had—for reasons he could not fathom—been with *Grey.*

Ryker's fists balled. That little bastard had his sister, and Ryker didn't care what damage Grey had inflicted on a dragon—he would be *damned* if he was going to let that stand.

Maegon's chest glowed, and he spread his jaws, spewing fire across the cave. The vampire leapt straight up, avoiding not only the main attack but the highest whispers of heat too.

Ryker startled at his own ignorance—at both the vampire's capabilities and the dragon's. He needed to let go of Grey Malteer for now and focus his attention on the battle. He needed to learn exactly what these two could do, and what better opportunity to do so than watching a fight to the death?

Kiril ran. Maegon swung his tail around, trying to swipe his prey's feet out from under him. The vampire moved fast enough that Ryker didn't actually see him jump until he was on the other side of the tail and still moving.

Maegon changed tactics.

The dragon lazily stalked around the stalagmites, smoke pouring from his nostrils. For the next few minutes, although he looked to be generally following Kiril, he shot blasts of fire in random directions. It wasn't until he'd launched six or seven fireballs that Ryker finally realized that Maegon was herding the vampire.

Taking the direction available to him, Kiril ran toward the edge of a canyon that sliced across the cave floor like a fractured fault line. The distance from one side to the other varied, and although it was further than any man could jump, it would've been doable both for a vampire and for a dragon. But the opening in the floor lined up with where the ceiling of the cave dipped low, making it impossible for Maegon to fly.

Kiril picked up speed, but when he reached the edge, he jerked to a stop. Wavering on his feet, he seesawed forward and back again. Maegon closed in, cutting off his escape route.

"Why is he stopping?" Ryker asked.

"Because jumping the canyon would put him out of Maegon's range, and I forbade him to do that."

Kiril turned around, slowly. Maegon rose on his hind legs and flared his wings wide, boxing the vampire in. Zio sighed in utter bliss. Maegon tipped forward. His head crashed over the vampire, teeth slicing through Kiril's waist even before his front feet smashed down.

The ledge they were standing on trembled.

The dragon shook Kiril's limp body back and forth, then tossed his head, throwing the vampire down his throat.

12

Despite Beltran's insistence that he was all right, Rune stood over him and watched as his eyes fluttered closed and his breathing changed. It was obvious he was only sleeping, but the fact that he'd fallen asleep on the forest floor, right outside the entrance to the sprites' realm, at night, with her there . . . All of it was proof that he was absolutely *not* all right.

But what was she going to do about it? Drag him across Eon on her back?

She didn't even know where they were.

Rune huffed, giving up on returning to the warmth and comfort of Arwin's tents tonight, and lay down next to him. The forest floor was as uncomfortable as it looked—which was fantastic when combined with the cold night air.

Shivering, she tucked her hands in her armpits and closed her eyes, but her mind was running a thousand miles a minute, and it wasn't long before she rolled her head to the side to stare at Beltran as he slept. Her gaze trailed over his dark lashes, across his cheekbones, and down to the pale-pink bow of his lips. With his face relaxed, the mischievousness had vanished, leaving only the handsome face of a man she was feeling more and more drawn to—whether she wanted to admit it or not.

Her breath caught—tangled up in an overwhelming ache to reach out and touch him.

She forced herself to look away, staring instead at the dirt-covered tips of her boots. Rune took several deep, cleansing breaths, studiously examining the pattern of the mud splatters. Oh, hell! Who was she kidding? This was doing nothing to squash the desire that was tingling through her.

She closed her eyes. *It doesn't matter what I want.*

The possibility of a relationship between the two of them was a disaster waiting to happen. How many warning signs did she need before she got that through her head? Half the time, she couldn't figure out whether he was lying to her or genuinely confused by his own complexity. The things Beltran had confessed to her in that cottage had been so thick with emotion she had to believe they were true. But in everything he'd both said and implied, there had also been agony. She didn't understand, and he always refused to explain. He never told her the full truth; at least he would admit when he was holding back, but still . . . He was making her crazy!

Sometime during Rune's mental recitation of what a mess she'd found herself in and how disaster and heartbreak were the only possible conclusions, she realized that she'd turned her head back to stare at his stupid, *stupid* . . . beautiful face.

Beltran took a deep breath in, startling Rune so badly she jerked to the side. He arched his back and stretched his arms over his head with a groan. Trying to cover her sudden movement and the fact that she'd been staring at him, Rune cleared her throat. "Oh, you're awake."

He kept his eyes closed, crossing his arms over his chest. "In a manner of speaking."

"Think we should head back?" She staged a loud yawn. "Maybe we can get a few hours of sleep before the sun comes up."

"That depends. Would you like to walk or fly?"

"We can walk? I assumed we'd traveled too far." She propped up on an elbow. "How long would that take?"

"We'd probably arrive past sunrise, and sleep would be out of the question. There would also be the matter of dealing with a very angry Verida who's found two empty tents at sunup."

"Then *why* are you asking?"

Beltran's green eyes flicked open. "Because, love. I know you don't understand how a shifter's body works, but I have to reform tissue in order to produce wings, and I'd really rather not tear open my still-healing, poison-infected wounds at the moment. If you'd like to fly, I'm going to need some time. But if you're incredibly anxious to be on your way, I'll happily drag my partially numb leg behind me." He raised his right heel up, peeked at it, then let it drop. "Not sure I understand why that's happening." He shrugged.

"I'm sorry. Of course." Rune lay back down, looking up at the tiny bits of sky visible through the tree branches. The insects chirped and hummed, and a bird gave a hooting call that was not quite owl and not quite whip-poor-will. "Are we safe here?"

"As safe as anywhere, I suppose."

Beltran's breathing grew heavier as he started to drift off again. Rune tuned in to the gentle in-and-out rhythm. She silently counted one, two, three on the inhalation and one, two, three on the exhale. Her own breathing became shallow as the rhythm pulled her back to the ball and the council house, where she'd danced in his arms.

There had been so many eyes on them, she'd been self-conscious and nervous, but it hadn't mattered. His breath had skittered across her skin in hot gasps that matched her own thudding heart. The world had fallen away with the feel of his hands on her bare back and the whisper of him at her throat. She'd wanted him closer then. In the cottage, she'd felt the caress of his breath again, and she'd thought he was going to . . . Rune clenched her fists. It didn't matter what she thought. He hadn't, and he wasn't going to.

Irritated at the entire situation and her continued response to it, she rolled onto her side. The uneven forest floor pressed into her hip and shoulder. The discomfort should've been enough to keep her awake, but her eyes dipped closed . . . once . . . twice . . .

Rune jerked up to sitting.

"Something wrong?"

"No." She rubbed her eyes. "But I'm going to fall asleep."

"That's fine. Get some rest. I'll keep watch."

"You're the one who was just poisoned. Besides, I obviously wasn't prepared for a battle in there. I can't be half-asleep if something else comes at us."

"That was my fault. I shouldn't have put us in the situation to start with. I wasn't thinking clearly."

Rune turned on her markings, just in case, and leaned back on her hands. All the thoughts she'd been rolling around were starting to nudge at the back of her lips. She knew she shouldn't let them out, but they were right there, and . . . "Beltran, about what you said—"

"No need to worry about that, love. It shouldn't happen again for a good long while." He glanced over and winked. "Emotions are pesky little things. Bury them enough, and they spring up at the most inopportune times."

Rune stared at him, incredulous, then snorted and shook her head. "*Oh, good*, you're back."

"What does that mean?"

"You know exactly what that means. I'm beyond tired of being held at arm's length by your witty sarcasm."

"I thought you found it charming."

"You said you wanted to show me who you were. So do it, Beltran." She leaned forward in challenge. "Who are you?"

The demand rolled easily off his back. "Nothing more than exactly who I appear to be."

"Fine," she snapped. "Then answer my other question. Why didn't you tell me and Grey you were there?"

Beltran's smile was flat and thin, and he held it a second too long. "Will you look at that? The poison seems to have dulled my truth-blurting issue. How fortuitous." He stretched and resituated, linking his hands behind his head and adjusting his posture like a preening peacock. "I think I'll keep that to myself."

"It involves me too. You don't get to just 'keep it to yourself.'"

"On the contrary. Simply because you're involved in a matter does not mean I'm bound to disclose every thought I have or everything you wish to know."

"Why are you acting like this? A minute ago, you were pressed against me, begging me to—"

"You know what? I'm suddenly feeling much better. Let's fly." Beltran jumped to his feet. As the shadow of wings unfurling rose above his shoulder blades, pain rippled across his face. He turned away—no doubt to hide the truth of what this transformation was costing him. But giving Rune his back left his growing wings exposed. Three angry red circles were visibly thinner than the rest of the dark, leathery skin. Blood dribbled from the largest one.

Rune hurriedly wiped away a frustrated tear. He would rather go through that than talk to her.

When his wings had grown to full size, Beltran faced her. His skin was pale, and his pupils had constricted to pinpricks.

"You're in pain," she said.

"There are different kinds of pain." Beltran offered his hand. "Tonight, I choose to endure this one."

Grey *slept*.

The plague of nightmares that perpetually stalked him hadn't made an appearance tonight. He was oddly aware of their absence; it would've alarmed him if he hadn't been so utterly exhausted. Instead, he gratefully leaned into the bliss, floating through a dream of silky black nothingness. Grey ran a mental finger through the substance that surrounded him, marveling as everything and nothing at all dripped from the tranquilized strands of his consciousness.

The shift came slowly.

He didn't notice the syrupy darkness seeping around the edges of his awareness until the blackness was so thick that he finally felt the change of depth in his colorless surroundings.

Something was wrong.

A tingling burst of anticipation jerked him awake—or so he thought. But when his eyes snapped open, Grey could see nothing—not the hand in front of his face or his feet beneath him.

The darkness now felt like a living, breathing thing, and it reached for more.

He recoiled, but the unnamable force flooded around him like the first wave of a tsunami. When the bleak waters receded, they sucked all physical sensation with them. Hearing, sight, smell, touch—everything that had anchored him to reality was gone. Without sensation, Grey was abandoned in a state of nothingness.

Completely disembodied.

Alive, but not.

There was no way for him to know how much time had passed when a light appeared in the distance. Having his sight back grounded him. Hearing returned next, a roar of sound materializing from nothing. Grey was surrounded by hundreds of voices whispering. They urged him forward, promising that if he could just get to the light, he'd be safe.

He'd been so lost in the experience that he hadn't seen what was happening, but the lie triggered his remembrance. *This* was how they started—the things Feena called visions. He knew what that light would bring, and he wasn't going to stand here and wait for it.

Grey ran.

The light rushed forward, growing exponentially larger as it did. It swept over him, turning his vision yellow and throwing him through the air. He tried not to flail, but it went against every instinct he had.

Grey landed facedown on a mossy floor. His palms were flat on the ground, and he pulled in a breath, only to taste that all-too-familiar combination of must, dirt, and decay. He gagged and squeezed his eyes shut, pleading to anything or anyone that might be listening to not let him be where he thought he was. He lifted his head. Air burst from his lungs, filled with grief.

Dead and dying plants hung from the walls of the underground cavern. Wilted flowers had crumbled and scattered dried petals across the floor. Bodies of long-dead victims once held tightly to the walls by healthy green vines now hung forward as the weight of their mummified bodies tore the vines out by their withered roots.

He was back in Feena's lair.

Grey was scrambling to his feet, preparing to run, when three fae marched in from three separate entrances to the throne room. They were dressed for battle and wore matching leather vests that covered their fronts and backs and were tied together with cords on the sides.

He recognized two of the faces immediately—he'd seen them leering at him through the half-drugged state he'd been in from the prolonged exposure to faery music. His chest grew tighter as he struggled to breathe over the memories of this place.

Behind the first three, row upon row of fae marched into the throne room in perfect formation. Their breastplates had been formed to fit the contours of their bodies and were studded around the neck with small stone rivets. The only variation in their armor was the weapon each had chosen: either a staff, a blade made of thin, clear material, or the long tubes they used for blowing their poisoned darts.

When Grey turned to face the throne, he found that the seat was now occupied by a male fae who had the same jet-black eyes as Feena and was wearing a crown made of gold-dipped vines. Unlike the former queen, who had lounged over the sides of her throne, this fae sat straight and tall. The exception was his right arm, which hung loosely over the side, holding a whip—the tail of which was moving from one side to the other of its own accord, like the lazy tail flicks of a satisfied cat.

Grey stared, confused. During his escape from the court, he'd been almost to the border when that fae had dropped from a tree. He remembered noticing those dark eyes and how strangely the whip had been moving. Grey had fought him. He'd shoved an adilat through the enemy's neck and killed him.

Apparently not.

The past was quickly forgotten, because kneeling now at the new king's feet was Tate. He was missing his trench coat, and the back of his shirt was ripped and bloody. The long, thin tears looked to be the work of the very same whip.

"Tate!" Grey lurched forward, not paying attention to the dangers around him.

A warrior walked straight through him, and just as before, his insides *stuck* to the fae. His lungs smashed against his ribcage. His optic muscles pulled so tight that Grey thought his eyes would pop from their sockets. He looked for an escape but was surrounded by row upon row of armored fae, nearly guaranteeing another collision. With only one choice, Grey gritted his teeth and pushed forward, running through the same guard again. He yelled out as his organs were now yanked against his spine.

Free, he stumbled toward the throne, searching for a safe place to stand, but the army had packed the room to overflowing. There was only one place to go. Grey backed up along the side of the throne, pressing himself against the wall in nearly the exact spot he'd been imprisoned the first time. Dead vines crackled behind him.

The male sitting on the throne rose, and the room went silent. "As you all know, the reign of our queen has passed, and I have taken up the mantle. But she has not left us alone. Feena waits, encased at the edge of our borders for her own survival."

Nausea washed over Grey. Feena wasn't dead, not completely.

"She has told me of her plans, and they are glorious! Tonight will be the first of many announcements to those who have supported Ambrose that we will no longer be ignored. With our champion fighting for us, we will finally show our fellow fae what we are capable of." He motioned toward the ranks. "Turrin. Secure the Venshii."

The sea of fae parted, and Turrin emerged. His tentacles had regenerated since their last battle, and they crisscrossed over his chest in front of the leather breastplate. He grabbed Tate's wrists and wrenched them behind his back, jerking him to his feet.

"Tonight," the new king bellowed, "we march to claim the respect that the council has so long denied us!"

The room erupted with cheers to their new leader.

"*King Keir, King Keir, King Keir!*"

Verida woke to shouting. She bolted straight up, scouring the area through the translucent sides of her tent. Listening for heartbeats, she found only one. Beltran and Rune hadn't returned.

The cry came again.

Outside, the spell work prevented her from seeing the other tents, but the smell of Grey's fear and sweat had seeped into the outside air, and the trail led her toward him as efficiently as an arrow drawn to a target. Once nearly on top of the scent, she reached out, blindly sweeping an arm from one side to the other until her fingers brushed the silken fabric. She hurriedly pulled her way around until she located the flap and stuck her head through.

Although Grey was technically inside, parts of him were . . . fading. Verida froze with her body half-in and half-out, trying to make sense of what she was seeing. He moaned and rolled his head. Two lines of blood were running in a steady stream from his nose and staining his front teeth.

"Grey?" Verida pushed her way in and dropped to her knees at his side.

She gripped his upper arm, trying to shake him, but though four of her fingers felt flesh, her thumb felt nothing. Startled, she looked down. Her thumb had passed *through* Grey's arm and was occupying the space where his humerus should be.

She swore and jerked away.

Verida knew more about Venators than she admitted, for reasons she kept tight to her heart, but she'd never heard about anything like this. And *this* looked very, very bad.

"No!" Grey thrashed out with both arms.

He hit her in the face with enough strength to knock her onto her elbows.

"Rana!" Verida pushed up, but when she looked back to him, Grey's hand had vanished, followed by his entire left side.

What is this?

"Grey . . ." She leaned forward, trying to keep her voice low. They had no way of knowing what was in these woods tonight. "Can you hear me?"

His back arched off the mat, and through the thin material of his shirt, Grey's ribcage flexed outward—as if something were pushing on it from behind. His bones popped and crackled as multiple hairline fractures raced through them.

His body was not meant to withstand this!

Verida did the only thing she could do. She threw herself across his midsection, forcing him flat to the ground and adding counterpressure.

Lost and desperate, she took a risk and yelled for the only person who might be able to help. "*Beltran!*"

Turrin wrenched Tate's hands behind his back and secured them with chains. While Turrin worked, Tate's face was stoic, his expression steady—no matter how hard the fae yanked on his arms—and he stared down King Keir with a look that Grey decided he never wanted to be on the receiving end of.

Turrin finished and stepped back.

"Your Majesty." Tate's use of Keir's proper title was flat. "I expect the deal I had with your mother will be honored."

The end of Keir's whip began ticking with sharp, rapid movements.

When he stepped down from the throne, he was exaggeratedly straight legged and flat footed, reminding Grey of an irritated child. Keir bellied up to Tate and pressed a long, thin finger under the Venshii's chin, pushing his head up—not because Keir was taller and needed to direct Tate's attention but because he could.

"What an asinine question. You know we fae keep our promises. Although . . ." Keir pushed Tate's head just a little higher. "There's a rancid taste in my mouth at the thought that you're soon to be reunited with your family after playing a significant role in the destruction of mine."

Tate's eyes were on the back wall. "*Your* family."

Keir's whip lashed out to the side.

The edges of Tate's lips quivered in the beginning of a smile.

"Make no mistake, *Venshii*. Once I have what I want, your contract will be renegotiated."

"I expected no less." Tate pulled his chin down, forcing Keir's finger deeper into the underside of his jaw until Tate could look him in the eye. "Do I get to keep my sword during negotiations?"

Kier scoffed. He dropped his hand and turned away toward Grey and the throne, smiling. But instead of taking the throne, as it appeared he would do, he used the distance to add momentum as he spun, flinging his arm out and backhanding Tate. The crack sounded through the room.

Tate's head snapped to the side, and he remained there, half-bent, his mouth working. When he deliberately swung his head back, Tate lifted his eyes and spat a mouthful of blood at Keir's feet.

Spittle and blood painted Keir's boots and pants. "Bastard," he muttered.

Tate pulled up his chin. His gaze was sharper, the set of his jaw firmer, and defiance rippled through every muscle.

"Letting you fight for us is chafing at my heritage."

"*Letting* me? What an honor."

Keir's wrist flicked to the front, and the end of his whip rushed up at a gravity-defying angle to wrap around Tate's neck. "There is nothing I'd like more than to watch you die."

"Will it chafe to watch your people die? When Dracula hears I'm fighting beneath a different banner, there will be many—" The whip tightened, inching over itself like a snake choking oxygen from its prey. Although it did strangle the end of his sentence, it did nothing to cut off Tate's growing smile.

Keir snarled and released the whip, yanking it back to rest by his feet. "You're enjoying this."

"Only a portion."

"Turrin."

No other instructions were needed. Turrin grabbed the chains that bound Tate's arms and kicked the backs of his knees. As Tate crumbled, Turrin pulled, forcing his arms up and his shoulders to overrotate. Tate finally grunted in pain.

Looking partially mollified, Keir ascended the throne. He stepped up onto the seat, raising himself above the room and ensuring every member of his army could see him. "We march," he called. "To the tunnels!"

Grey expected a cheer or . . . something. Instead, the rows of fae turned in silence, one after the other, faces solemn, and marched beneath the southeastern arch. Keir's whip hung to the floor, undulating in an S formation. He put one foot on the arm of his throne, watching his people with a spark in his eye, then stepped off the side.

Directly on top of Grey.

The king's foot passed through his windpipe, his heart, his liver. He fell to his knees. Keir stepped forward, dragging his stomach and lungs to the front of his body. Grey gasped for air and fell face first into a pile of dead vines.

Rune hadn't wanted to be this close to Beltran at the moment, but unless she was planning on walking back to camp, flying required her to be cradled in his arms. She was cold and tired, and it wasn't long before the steady beat of his heart and the warmth of his arms and chest had lulled her to sleep.

"Rune." Beltran jostled her. "Rune."

"Hmmm?" she mumbled. "Is everything all right?"

"We're going to land for a second. I thought I heard something."

Beltran chose an ancient oak whose leafy top stretched above the canopy. He lowered her to the thickest of the upper branches and kept his hands on her back until she'd braced one boot in the vee between the trunk and branch to keep her balance. "What are we—?"

"Shhhh." Beltran landed next to her, then stepped out along the branch like a seasoned tightrope walker, one foot directly in front of the other and wings pulled to his back. He scanned the black sky and shadowed canopy around them, swiveling his head as he listened.

Rune's markings flickered a faint pink—the same color they'd turned at the rock pools on her first night here. Fae.

"Beltran!"

Beltran's head snapped to Rune. "Did you hear that?"

"Yes." The call was soft and had been carried on the wind. "Is that . . . Verida?"

"Something's wrong. She would only be calling for me if it were her last resort." He hurried back, wincing as he scraped his wing against a nearby branch. "And you and I both know I mean *last*."

Beltran and Rune swooped into the clearing. He dropped her to the ground a little more roughly than he'd intended, and she had to stumble forward to catch her balance.

"Verida?" He couldn't see anyone, but he could hear the sounds of a struggle. "Verida!"

"Grey's tent—hurry!"

Rune was a step ahead of him. Using his earlier trick, she grabbed a handful of pine needles and threw it in the direction of Verida's voice. They scattered across the surface, barely outlining the tent. She sprinted for it.

Reaching the opening before Beltran did, Rune ducked inside. She screamed. "Grey!"

There wasn't enough room in that tent for all four of them. Beltran grabbed the top and ripped it up and away, freeing the magical ties that held it in place.

Rune straightened, her hands clapped over her mouth, and Beltran followed her gaze.

On top of the sleeping pad, Verida was stretched flat over a wildly bucking Grey. The entire lower half of his face was covered in blood, but there was so much that with only the limited light of the stars, it was hard to tell where it was all coming from. His skin was too pale, and both his eyes were enveloped in large, dark bruises.

Beltran didn't know what to think. By the color of Grey's skin and the closeness of Verida's face to his neck, his first thought was that Verida was feeding from him. Which would make very little sense. Realizing the blood was likely coming from his nose, Beltran next assumed that they were fighting. He surged forward, ready to grab Verida by the back of the shirt and attempt to yank her off, but at that exact moment he saw her hand slide *through* Grey's shoulder.

Verida cursed, grabbing hold of his bicep instead.

Beltran couldn't stop fast enough; he stumbled into Rune's back. "What in the hell is going on?"

"I don't know! Things are . . . *moving* inside him." Verida tried to look up, but Grey tossed his head so violently to the side that she had to readjust her hold. "I'm trying to prevent his ribs from popping out of his chest cavity. His heart is beating so fast it's going to burst if we can't slow it. And his muscles—"

Grey bucked up, his spine flexing into a complete arch.

Verida gasped and dug into the ground with the tips of her toes to keep from being thrown off. "—are ripping. We have to do something!"

Beltran grabbed Rune's wrist and jerked her tight against his side. "Has anything like this happened before?"

"No." Rune's skin was pale, and she shook her head. "He's never said anything."

"Beltran, do something!" Verida shouted. "I can't wake him up. I've tried everything."

"You've . . . what? He's sleeping?"

"Yes! Look at his eyes!"

Sure enough, beneath Grey's lids, his eyes were rapidly flicking back and forth.

"Off," Beltran demanded. He shoved Verida to the side and dropped to one knee, sliding his arms under Grey's back and legs. "Meet me at the lake." The pressure against his right arm vanished as it sunk into Grey's side. "Bloody hell! What is happening?"

He didn't wait for an answer, because there wasn't one.

"Back up!" he shouted.

Verida and Rune stepped away as Beltran stretched his incredibly sore wings wide. Grey was heavier than Rune, but the shifter didn't dare make his wings larger in their current state. The extra strain of takeoff tore two of his three wounds wide open. They were barely airborne before Grey threw himself backward, tipping them to one side and making Beltran nearly lose his hold. He frantically flapped to right them again, snarling a lengthy list of swear words at both the unconscious Venator and those damned sprites' poisoned arrows.

The lake wasn't far, but every second saw Grey's condition worsening. Blood was dripping from the corner of his mouth, and if he lost any more of his form, he was going to slip right through Beltran's arms.

Beltran gritted his teeth and bore down, pushing his wings as hard as he could. While the wind fought against him, he caught a whiff of a scent he'd know anywhere. Earth and moss and decay with an undertone that, although not definable, was identifiable. Feena's court. Impossible. He sniffed again, trying to make sense of it, but the smell was gone.

The lake came into view, and Beltran dipped closer to the ground, skimming over the shore. Praying he didn't drown the boy, he dropped Grey in the shallows and maneuvered to land just on the other side. In his haste, the bottom tips of his wings caught the water's surface. He jerked backward and crashed into the ice-cold water. When his feet finally found the sandy bottom, Beltran splashed forward, searching for Grey while fighting the drag of his wings.

He was never going to find him like this.

The pain in his wings was already searing, but they had to go. He began reabsorbing the appendages. It would've been painful regardless, given the poisoned arrow holes, but he'd already shifted once to get Rune back, then ripped the wounds wide open again taking off with Grey. The agony of the third time was blinding. Beltran wobbled to the side, kept on his feet only by the water that splashed around his chest.

The world tinted white.

14

Grey surged to the surface. His hands slapped at the water, looking for purchase. He arched his neck, gasping for air. Blood ran down his throat, forcing him forward. He coughed and sputtered, trying to focus. He had to figure out where he was—whether he was still in danger. But his head was throbbing, and when he looked to the right, his vision twisted and blurred as if someone had hit him upside the head with a sledgehammer.

The panic of having Keir step through him, of not being able to breathe, was still gripping him, and despite the pain and dizziness, he tried to run. But every breath was a knife in his lungs, and the resistance of the water was too much. His knees gave out. Grey dropped like a rock, submerging his jaw and nose once more. With no other options, he yielded, relaxing onto his back and using the water to buoy him up.

"Grey!" It was Beltran.

A profound sense of relief washed over him. He wasn't alone. There was splashing as Beltran moved closer, but Grey couldn't find the energy to open his eyes. His body rode the gentle waves the shifter created.

"All right, I've got you."

Needing to make sure he wasn't still wrapped in the nightmare, Grey muttered, "Beltran?"

"Who else?"

Arms hooked beneath his and started to pull him through the water. Grey lay there and allowed it. He didn't have the strength to do much else. Why was this happening to him? Every time he thought things might get better, they got worse. Water splashed into his mouth, and he coughed. Spasms followed, rocking through his chest and ribs. He cried out, pulling in on himself. His butt sunk to the sand.

"Up!" Beltran straightened his arms to brace them behind Grey's shoulders. "Come on. I'm not in the best shape. You've got to at least float."

He obeyed, stretching his limbs out and tipping his head back. "*Why?*" he cried.

"Why what?"

"*Why* is it so much worse this time?"

Water splashed in and out of his ears, creating a wash of sound, but there was no reply in it. Not from God. Not from the universe. And not even from the shifter who always had all the answers. Sand rubbed against the heels of Grey's feet. They were nearing the shore. Beltran pulled him out of the water, grunting, and beached him like an old, broken canoe.

He didn't know what it felt like to be trampled by a team of horses, but as he lay there struggling for air and musing about the idea, he decided it had to feel something like this. From a distance, he heard shouts calling his name, and he peeled his eyes open. Never had those tiny muscles required such effort to move.

Overhead, the stars were still out. He would usually describe them as twinkling. But tonight, all he could see was a host of malevolent creatures looking down on him, winking and laughing, as if his life were some great cosmic joke, the ramifications of which he'd never be free from.

Rune's face cut into his field of vision. "Grey?" He must've looked a hell of a lot better than he felt, because she heaved a deep sigh of relief. "You're all right."

He licked his lips, trying to loosen the film that coated his mouth. "I don't feel all right."

"Grey said, and I quote, 'It hurt more *this* time.'" Beltran sounded both exhausted and annoyed.

Grey tried to twist his neck to locate the shifter, but a sharp pain split through his skull. He moaned and squeezed his eyes shut.

"This has happened before?" Verida's voice came from close enough that it startled him. "Grey! Has this happened before? Answer me!"

"Give him a moment," Rune said. "Look at him. He's in pain."

"Of course he's in pain! I'm surprised he's *alive*." Verida sighed. "Fine. It looks like we're camping here for the rest of the night. Beltran, go get the tents and horses."

"Beltran's hurt too," Rune said. "He needs to rest."

The gentle caress of fingers trailed across Grey's cheek. He leaned into it.

"I had a little run in with some sprites." Beltran tried to laugh, but it was pained and cut off in a wheeze. "The poison is taking longer to get out of my system than I anticipated."

What was a sprite? Grey was sure he'd read about them somewhere, but the world was slipping away again.

"Beltran," Verida seethed. "You and I are having a very, very long conversation."

"Absolutely, darling. Just . . . tomorrow."

Tomorrow. Grey jackknifed up. His arms flailed as he reached for Rune. "I can't sleep. Don't let me sleep!" He wrapped his fingers around her wrists. With her acting as an anchor, the panic ebbed a degree. He focused on her face, trying to make her understand. "*Please*, please don't let me sleep."

"Grey." Her voice was shaking, and he could see the effort it was taking for her to be calm. "It's all right. You need rest."

"No. *No!* It could happen again. Please. You don't understand—"

"If it happens again, I'll have Beltran throw you back in the lake." Rune's smile was soft and crooked. She leaned forward, gently pressing him back to the sand. "I'll keep an eye on you. At the first signs of whatever just happened, I'll wake you."

The exhaustion of what he'd been through combined with his body trying to heal was thicker than the pain, and it dripped through his veins like anesthesia. His mind resisted, but it couldn't bypass the needs of his physical form. Grey's eyelids drooped against his will, and he was gone.

"Looks like I'll be getting the horses."

Rune traced Grey's dark eyebrows with her finger, overwhelmed with gratitude that he was alive. She glanced at Verida. "Do you want me to go back?"

"No. Stay with Grey. Make sure he's all right." She jerked her head toward Beltran. "Him too."

A few feet away, Beltran lay stretched out on the beach with one arm thrown over his face. Rune couldn't see if the wounds on his back were healing, but his chest rose and fell with full, steady breaths. Grey, on the other hand, looked terrible. Noting how tight the skin was over his jawbone, she frowned and pulled back, looking him up and down. His cheeks were sunken. He'd lost weight—a *lot* of weight.

How had she not noticed?

She'd been completely self-occupied—that's how. Rune sighed and swung her legs forward. Resting her chin on her sandy knees, she stared out at the darkness. The lake Beltran had brought them to was still as glass, giving no evidence of recent events. The longer she sat there, the more the smooth surface of the water irked her.

No matter what happened, the world always moved on. Grey could've died! It seemed only right that truly horrific things should leave a mark, something equal to the scars that those involved had to carry. She let her eyes flutter close, a rueful smile growing as she imagined what the world would look like if every tragedy were scrawled across its surface.

She opened her eyes and snorted. How had this become her life? She was sitting on a beach after almost losing Grey *again* and still carrying proof in her veins of her choice to save him the first time. She felt crisscrossed with scars inside and out. She wasn't even sure if she recognized herself anymore.

Up until the night she'd decided to step through that first stupid magic hole in the wall with Tate, every one of her life choices had felt so incredibly monumental. The grades, the games, the practices, trying to keep track of Ryker—they'd made her heart race as if everything were life or death. Obsessing over the stress was why she'd wished part of her life away, why she hadn't spent more time doing things that really mattered. And now, *true* life-and-death choices were her everyday reality. The wrong words got her thrown in the dungeon. Misjudging a situation could get her killed.

Rune tried to imagine herself returning to basketball practice, sitting through her college classes, following Ryker around on his drunken benders. It felt so . . . wrong. After being here and living through what she had, remembering what her life had been a month ago was like looking back on a childhood of lollipops and cartoons and then making the conscious choice to abandon all adult maturity and return to it.

For what?

To chase meaningless pursuits? Trivial goals?

The realization that she might actually *want* to stay in Eon was so uncomfortable that Rune hopped up, brushing the sand off her hands and backside. Verida wasn't back yet, and with nothing else to do, she went to check on Beltran—for no reason other than that he was the farthest away from the still water at her feet that had opened the door to this thoughtfulness in the first place.

"Breakfast!" Verida shouted. "Everybody up."

Grey's eyes weren't even open yet, and already his body was flagging an unnecessarily painful reminder of the night he'd had. His limbs were heavy, the thought of moving impossible.

"Now!" she added.

He moaned. The tent overhead was no longer one of Arwin's, but Grey didn't need to be able to see through it to tell that the sun was well into the sky. He pulled his chin down, expending the least amount of effort possible to look at the cloak that had been draped over him. By the size, it had to be Rune's.

He wrapped the edge around his fingers and slowly inched the cloak off, becoming more and more aware of how sore he was with every movement. Beneath the heavy wool, his clothes were still damp, and he was coated in sand. He tentatively crossed one arm over his chest to brush the grains from his neck and chest. He was almost there when the feel of a red-hot poker stabbed through his scapula. The surrounding muscles seized.

Grey opened his mouth in a silent scream.

"Hello? I *said*, breakfast!"

He was starving—more-hungry-than-he'd-ever-been-in-his-entire-life starving.

But also . . . terrified to roll over.

Grey steeled himself, taking several slow breaths through his nose— as if breathing would somehow make him feel like he had *not* been in four bar fights last night. He gingerly inched up to his hands and knees and, after a short recovery break, crawled toward the door. Every movement sent his own odor wafting around the tent. He reeked of sweat and fish.

Parting the flap, he looked out.

Three of the four tents had been repitched in a semicircle near the lake. The horses grazed nearby. Between the beach and the forest grasses, Beltran was crouching next to a firepit and intently digging through a large woven basket. His clothes and hair were rumpled and coated with as much sand as Grey's.

Verida stood over Beltran, already scowling. "Feeling better?"

"Much." Beltran tossed up a bright-red apple and nabbed it back again with a snappy flourish. "Thank you ever so much for checking."

"Hmph." She grunted, crossing her arms, and called to Grey, "How about you?"

"Uh . . . yeah, better." There was a little truth in that. He was in less pain than last night.

When he didn't move, Verida twisted at the waist, her lips pursed. "Well? Are you planning on joining us?"

Grey gave up on trying to hide his condition. He crawled out into the open with the grace of a geriatric, arthritic horse, dragging Rune's cloak across the ground in his fist.

Beltran chuckled. "He's definitely looking better. See how smoothly he moves?"

Once clear of the tent flaps, Grey now had to stand. Despite his best efforts, several squeaks, grunts, and whimpers passed his lips before he was upright. His face was scrunched so tight, he could barely see.

Verida swore. "Why aren't you healed?"

"I don't"—Grey pulled a slow breath in through his teeth and took the first step toward breakfast—"know."

"Darling, I know you're in a hurry," Beltran said. "But he does *not* look ready for a mission."

Verida's head snapped to the side before he'd finished speaking. "If I wanted your opinion, I would've asked for it."

Grey was far too miserable to navigate this drama *and* make his feet move. "I agree with Verida."

"I'm sure you do." Beltran lifted the apple in a mock toast, grinned, and took a bite.

The basket was loaded with fruit, dark brown bread, and hard cheese. Grey eased himself down. "Where did you get all this?"

"As I mentioned, the council requested that you and Rune play ambassador to a village that Beorn's pack had taken their retribution on. It's not far from here. Whilst all of you slept half the day away, I paid them a visit to announce we were coming and collected food."

Grey chose a small loaf of bread to start. "How was it?"

"The village? Beorn's pack was not merciful. Where is . . . ?" Verida looked around. "Mother of Rana. Rune! *Let's go!*"

"I'm coming, I'm coming!" Rune threw the flap of her tent to the side. Her eyes were red and puffy. The tight braid she'd worn yesterday had been ruined; little hairs stood out from her head in a halo of fuzz.

"Glad to see you're awake," Verida said.

"It's not like I had a choice, what with the crazed vampire shouting outside of my tent and all."

"Here." Verida picked up the basket. "A peace offering."

When Rune looked inside, she sagged. "You stole food?"

"No, I didn't *steal* it! Why would you even—?" Verida snatched up a loaf of bread and threw it at Rune. "Forget it. Eat."

Rune fumbled the bread against her chest. "I'm sorry. I just—"

"And next time"—Verida held the basket straight out and let it drop, splaying her fingers wide—"you can find your own breakfast!"

The basket hit the ground next to Grey and tipped. He lunged, trying to keep it from spilling, and immediately wished he hadn't. He leaned over the handle and wrapped his arm around the side, trying to catch his breath as he waited for the stabbing pains to subside.

"What's wrong?" Rune asked.

"Oh, him?" Beltran pointed. "He's *'better.'* Can't you tell?"

Verida rubbed the bridge of her nose as a string of curse words flowed. "We don't have time for this. It's a few hours to the village, and we have to arrive before nightfall. The humans are nervous enough without us arriving after dark."

"You know, I could've gone in for you." Beltran tossed the apple core over his shoulder and stretched to the basket for more, reaching around Grey. "They probably would've handled the warning better coming from a human rather than a vampire."

"You were otherwise engaged, sleeping off the effects of sprite poison."

"Did any of them figure out who you were?" Beltran asked.

"No. I chose not to wear my Dracula coat of arms."

"Hmm . . ." Beltran moved a loaf of bread, reaching for the cheese beneath. "I was under the impression that House Dracula once owned this land."

Verida went eerily still. "Shut your mouth, Beltran."

Grey pushed himself up. He might not have thought anything of what land Dracula did or did not own if it weren't for Verida's response. Her expression was what he imagined he might look like if someone had blurted out his darkest secrets.

Ignoring Verida completely, as Beltran often did when purposefully baiting her, he leaned back with his hunk of cheese and casually popped a piece in his mouth. "Rune, love, there's no need to hover." He patted the ground next to him. "Come, sit. There's more than enough room for two."

Rune had been watching the exchange carefully. At Beltran's flirtatious invitation, she huffed and stepped neatly around the basket to sit by Grey instead. She tore off pieces of her loaf and started to eat but kept glancing between Verida and the bread.

"What?" Verida snapped.

"Nothing. I just . . . No lectures about last night? Only breakfast?"

Verida snorted. "Don't be naive. We have plenty of time for that while we travel."

"Trust me, Rune, there will be no escaping her." Beltran winked. "Would anyone like to fly?"

Rune groaned. Grey flinched. Verida cut sideways to loom over Beltran, her glare boring a hole through the top of his head. When he couldn't ignore the fuming vampire anymore, he looked up.

The moment Verida had his full attention, she lowered into a crouch in the most controlled, excruciatingly slow transition Grey had ever seen. The more precise her movements became, the more power emanated from her. Perhaps it was the fact that Dracula had just been mentioned, but her current show of dominance announced her lineage. Even the way she moved her hands to rest on her knees screamed danger.

Verida and Beltran were eye to eye. To his credit, the shifter didn't blink. His face had been schooled into a mask of impassiveness that Grey couldn't fathom he was actually feeling. She raised her chin. "You're right, you conniving little bastard. There will be no escape, in the air or otherwise. You're stuck with me for the foreseeable future. But you knew that." Verida pressed a finger into Beltran's sternum. "I hope she's worth it."

Rune looked away.

"*She?* Verida, I'm only here under Dimitri's request." Beltran held out his food, hovering it just beneath Verida's nose. "Cheese?"

Positive there was about to be a murder, Grey hurriedly interjected. "Will somebody please tell me what happened last night and how I ended up in the lake?"

15

The cheese maneuver was not his finest moment, but Beltran wasn't one to back down. He kept his gaze locked with Verida's. "Do *you* want to tell Grey why I threw him in a lake last night? Or should I?"

The tiny muscles around her eyes tightened, followed by a warning shake of her head that was so slight her hair barely moved against her shoulders.

Because Verida's vampire senses were capable of perceiving so much, the further she stepped into her nature, the smaller her movements became. Beltran had discovered it years ago. The angrier a vampire got, the more vampire-like they behaved—a tell he used to judge how far he'd pushed things. Verida's foul mood at the moment had nothing to do with who was going to explain to Grey what had happened and everything to do with his mention of her former hunting grounds, which he'd chosen to bring up because he was in a rotten mood himself . . . and because he'd been aiming to hurt her. Neither were terribly good reasons. And given how little she was moving, he'd clearly taken it too far.

Reluctantly, he decided on a new course of action.

Beltran murmured under his breath, quiet enough to ensure that Verida was the only one who could hear. "I'm sorry. That was out of line."

She blinked, startled.

He always enjoyed taking her off guard, but the apology was burning the inside of his mouth and preventing him from reveling in her surprise.

Verida searched for any indication of sarcasm. Finding none, she leaned further forward on the balls of her feet, balancing in a way that defied human musculature. "I don't know what you're playing at, but one of these days, you're going to push me too far."

Before Beltran could respond, she was upright and facing Grey.

Crisis averted and the dreadful apology over with, Beltran leaned back on the palms of his hands and listened as the stories progressed from Verida finding Grey to every detail of Grey's dreams. Only, they weren't dreams at all—Beltran knew enough to know that for certain. These were visions. He brushed his hands off and was about to interrupt when Grey began relaying last night's vision: Tate, Keir, an army of fae, and the gladiator games.

Saints.

Beltran turned his mind inward. The voices of the other three diminished, becoming a hum of background noise. He leaned over his knees, staring at nothing in particular, as he worked to put the pieces into place.

The entirety of Grey's vision was illuminating, filling in multiple holes among the information he'd already collected separately and meticulously filed away. Beltran twisted and flipped each salacious tidbit against the others. When he couldn't find a seamless connection, he backed up and dug through his memory again, searching for something else that might fit the hole.

It was a game he'd learned to play as a boy, meant to teach both observation and deductive reasoning. Often, the practice would yield a partially constructed picture. Today, with Grey's help, a nearly complete story unfolded. There was one detail he couldn't figure out, but there was enough to determine that an immediate course of action was necessary.

He blinked back to the present and found himself sitting alone next to the campfire. Verida and Rune were heading for the horses, and Grey was carefully hobbling toward his tent.

"There's probably something you all should know," Beltran called.

They all turned, waiting, each face more annoyed than the last.

Beltran motioned. "You might want to sit down for this."

Rune groaned. "Of course there's something else. And of course it's horrible enough that I need to sit down." She slouched as she walked back, flopping cross legged to the ground. "What is it this time? Killer fae? Dragons?"

Verida smirked at Rune, placing a hand over her heart. "Why, Beltran, are you offering this information to us freely? I feel *so* incredibly honored."

"If you'd like me to charge, I certainly can." His usual witty charm fell flat, and his mouth twisted in thought as he worked out how best to lay everything out.

"Mother of Rana," Verida swore. She stomped back to the firepit. "He's serious."

"Deadly." Beltran lifted his head. "Let's start with what happened while Rune was in the dungeons—"

"Wait, what?" Grey was in the middle of easing himself down when he froze. "Dungeons?"

Beltran cocked a brow in Rune's direction. "What's this, love? Haven't told him that, either?"

"'Either'?" Grey's muscles weren't recovered enough to hold his half-bent position. "Rune, what is—?" He half collapsed, half sat, finishing his question with his eyes squeezed shut in pain. "What is going on?"

"Beltran, you are without a doubt the biggest ass I have ever met! Why can't you just keep your mouth—?"

"Enough!" Verida's voice broke over Rune's. She pointed. "Grey, stop trying to move. Rune, be quiet. And Beltran, spit it out. Now."

"Very well. But do try to keep up." He stood—the organization of the story was still fuzzy, and he needed to walk to keep things in order. "Based on Grey's vision, the first thing you need to understand about Keir is that he's his mother's son in the absolute worst way possible. The same goals and ambitions, none of the patience." Beltran paced in front of the small firepit. "If Feena were here, she would be marching into the games with three others—Tate, Morean, and Turrin."

"Morean's dead," Rune said.

"Did Tate kill him?" When no one said otherwise, he continued. "Hmm, impressive. Keir has just been named king and has already chosen a different path. Although he's held to his mother's instructions and is taking Tate to fight in the games, he's chosen to march not with a few but with all of his people, dressed and armed for battle. For us, that means we'll likely have an entire fae clan to deal with while trying to free Tate from a gladiatorial arena. Our real problem is that we don't know *why*. What would possess Keir to leave his lands unprotected from the council?" He paused, looking at each one in turn and waiting for an answer.

"Without Feena, there's no one there to keep the plants functioning," Grey pointed out. "I never saw any signs that anyone else was involved."

"You're right. The magic down there had been twisted, and she did that alone. But Keir's motivations are deeper than resurrecting his mother's dead flowers." He rubbed his hands together. "While Rune was in the dungeons, I spent some time flying over Feena's lands, looking for Grey. Instead, I stumbled upon Ambrose talking with her twin emissaries, Baird and Bashti. I discovered that Ambrose owns one of the top gladiators and that she'll be attending the next match. Which, from what I can gather, appears to be taking place during the same game we are now en route to. This is another problem for us. Having a council member in attendance while we try to rescue the Venshii we claimed to have in our possession won't go well."

"Slow down," Verida said. "Ambrose has a fighter. So what? The council members might not enforce the laws against the games, but they certainly can't be seen there. If Ambrose does own a gladiator, she'll send the twins in her place."

Beltran made a sharp turn and headed back the other direction. "I disagree. First of all, Ambrose told her emissaries she would be there. Beyond that, I know why she *has* to be there. You see, Ambrose has done something unique. She wagered her undefeated champion against an unnamed fighter for an unnamed prize. A bet like this has to be finalized in person. If she's not there, the match won't be allowed to happen."

Verida snorted. "I don't know what you thought you overheard, but Ambrose would never take a risk like that."

"Oh, but she would. Anyone will do anything if the payoff is something they can't ignore."

"What could possibly be worth the risk?" Verida's question wasn't so much a question as it was a commentary on her opinion of Beltran's intelligence at the moment. "If Ambrose loses, the other gladiator's owner could request anything. Anything! I saw one werewolf decline the lands and gold that were offered and instead demand that the losing owner move to the arena floor and run a silver blade though his own heart."

Rune gasped.

Grey was equally shocked. "If those are the stakes, what's the payoff?"

"The key to Kastaley."

"Kastaley?" Rune frowned. "Oh! Omri's lands."

"Exactly."

Verida shook her head. "Not possible."

"Why not?" Beltran asked.

"You know why not! Even if, and I don't believe it—"

"Of course you don't," Beltran interrupted. "Because I'm the one who said it."

"*But*," Verida enunciated, continuing her thought, "even if someone got their hands on the key—"

"I'm telling you someone did!"

Grey shouted over them. "What is so special about Kastaley?"

Beltran gave Verida a sharp look and, rolling out his shoulders, turned his attention to Grey. He hated when he allowed Verida to get under his skin like that. "Kastaley is one of the most well-protected strongholds in all of Eon. It was fought over for centuries. When the elves took control, they erected a pair of magical gates, securing Kastaley's last known weakness. As far as anyone knows, the magic is unbreakable, leaving the city accessible solely through the gate, which can only be opened by one of two keys. One is held by Omri, the other by the head of his guard."

"It's a bluff," Verida said. "It has to be. Who claimed they had it?"

"He referred to himself as Qualtar and was carefully disguised, but he did have the key in hand. I wondered at first if it was a ruse, especially when no cry of alarm went up at its absence. But then, during the meeting with Rune and Grey, the proceedings were interrupted by an elven fulgorian message. Omri broke protocol not only by listening to it immediately but by then rushing from the room without so much as asking permission to be excused from the proceedings, stating only that there was an emergency he needed to tend to. Coincidence?"

Verida looked to Rune and Grey. "Is that true?"

"Yes," Rune said. "He did . . . Wait, how did *you* know that?"

Beltran shrugged. "Use your imagination. In the message that the twins delivered to Ambrose, Qualtar's body was completely covered. But when he held out the key, it exposed his arm. A distinctly gray arm."

"So?" Verida said. "There are a million creatures who have gray arms."

"There's more than one species that presents with skin that color, but the predominant one is fae. The fact that Feena would lay down a plan to kidnap Tate after obtaining the only two things she knew would make him agree to return to the games as a fighter—Ayla and Brandt—all while a heavily weighted bet is being agreed to by Ambrose is highly suspicious timing. Which brings us to now. The entirety of Feena's people are marching for the games with their champion in tow, leaving their own lands unprotected. What possible reason could they have to do that? Unless"—he held up a finger—"they weren't planning on coming back."

Grey frowned and picked up a half-rotted leaf. He spun it by the stem, watching it twist back and forth. "You think Keir has the key to Kastaley?"

"I think it's likely."

"Then why not just use it?" Verida asked.

"To what? Storm the gates? Think about it. Feena didn't have the numbers to take over Kastaley, even if the gate were wide open. The elves would decimate them. No, I don't think that key was ever going to be used to attack. I think it's a pawn." The more he talked, the more Beltran was sure he was on the right path.

He ticked off points on his fingers. "They use the key to lure out Ambrose, knowing she would be desperate for it because she *does* have the numbers to take Kastaley and has wanted it back under fae control since the elves won it. Then they beat her at her own game, presenting Tate as their champion—the one gladiator who is almost sure to win against any opponent, and one she would never suspect were an available option."

"But why?" Verida asked. "You still haven't answered the most important question. What does Keir want?"

"That's the one thing I don't know. Nothing makes sense. They could be after Salandria—Ambrose's lands."

Verida nodded. "Salandria *is* in prime proximity to launch an attack on Kastaley. And if Keir wins, he maintains possession of the key."

"Yes, but I don't think Keir could gain the support needed to hold Salandria, let alone proceed to attack Kastaley."

"I don't understand," Rune cut in. "If Keir wins and takes Ambrose's lands, wouldn't he have Ambrose's people too?"

Beltran shook his head. "All Ambrose would be required to do is exit the city and hand over her title. Nothing says she couldn't turn around and win it back by force." He took a deep breath. They were spinning in circles. "The only thing I know for sure is that if Feena went through the trouble and time to set this up, she has a plan to follow through after the games. And no matter what it is, it has the potential to cause major disruption. We need to get to the Underground early, spend a couple days there listening for rumors and seeing what we can track down before we walk into those games blind."

"A couple of days!" Verida rubbed at the bridge of her nose. "I was planning on sneaking the Venators through. If we're spending any amount of time there, we need to start training them hard."

"Agreed. We should begin as soon as Grey's healed."

"I'm fine," he argued.

"No, you're not," Verida and Beltran said in unison.

Grey looked to Rune for backup.

She shrugged. "Come on. You can barely walk."

Beltran spent the rest of the afternoon and early evening alone. Grey was in his tent, under strict instructions to sleep and heal. Verida was hunting. The moment she'd left the clearing, Rune had abruptly stood, returned to her tent without a word, and not emerged since. With nothing else to do, Beltran walked around the lakeshore to think. He couldn't decide whether he was grateful that Rune was obviously avoiding him or whether that was the cause of the small ache in the corner of his heart.

He tipped his head back and breathed in deeply. The air was crisp and cool and faintly edged with a familiar floral scent. There were childer bushes somewhere close. The green bushes with their tiny, chalice-shaped yellow flowers had lined the shoreline near his childhood home. That lake had been his favorite place in all of Eon. Saints, it felt like an eternity since he'd been there.

The smell brought back pleasant memories at first but also rapidly pulled up the reasons why he'd left in the first place. He thought about that day more often than was probably healthy, but having the water and the flowers nearby created a recollection more tangible and intense than he was in the mood to handle at the moment. He finished the loop and set to work collecting wood and dried grasses for that night.

Beltran was lying back, propped up on his elbows and staring at the slowly crackling fire, when Verida returned. She walked right up and sat next to him, as if it were the most normal thing in the world and she hadn't been choosing the farthest seat from him for . . . well, a while. He looked at her quizzically.

Verida's eyes were on the tents. She pushed her blonde hair over her shoulder. "I'm worried about taking Rune and Grey into the Underground."

"I know." He sat up and pulled one leg up, throwing an elbow over his knee and leaning toward the heat of the fire. "The training you want to do will help them in the arena. What I'm most concerned about is whether or not they'll be able to stay in character while seeing what they might see down there."

"Who do you think the bigger problem is? Rune? Or Grey?"

"Both. Given what Grey went through at Feena's, I think he may have actually learned his lesson the hard way. But his heart is soft. And while Rune's performance at the council house was impressive, I think it was less of a show than she'd like to admit. Acting is easy when it's not acting."

"Hmph." Verida grunted. "Which part did she not fake? Convincing the council members she could behave like a noble or that last dance with you?"

"Hopefully both."

Her eyes cut to him. "I can't decide if I want to punch you or thank you for actually telling me the truth."

"I'd give you my preference, but if I've learned anything about you, it's that you do what you want."

Verida picked up a stick and tossed it into the fire, quietly watching it burn. "We didn't have a day to lose."

"I know, but we lost it. There isn't anything we can do about it now."

Grey's tent flaps parted, and he walked easily toward them—posture upright and holding himself like a Venator. His markings were flickering red. Beltran scanned them for any other variations in color.

"He's healed," Verida said under her breath. "Thank Rana and her saints." She called out, "It looks like some rest did you good."

"Well, I don't feel like I'm dying." He stretched out his arms and neck as he walked. "But I'm starving."

Beltran pointed to the basket, which was still two-thirds full of food. "Go ahead. Just leave some for the rest of us. I hear Rune gets cranky when she's hungry."

"You heard right." Grey grinned, plopped down next to the basket, and tore into it.

"You're in a good mood," Beltran said.

Grey shrugged, tore off a chunk of bread with his teeth, and reached for the cheese with his other hand. "I'm not in pain. That makes me happy."

Rune emerged—likely because she'd heard Grey's voice and knew she wouldn't have to be alone with Beltran. Her hair was even more tousled than it had been that afternoon, and she tried to smooth her braid as she walked, as if patting the hairs down would somehow convince them to return to the plait they'd escaped from.

Grey held out an apple, talking around a mouthful of cheese. "Hungry?"

"Yeah, thanks." She sat down and polished the fruit with the underside of her shirt before taking a bite.

"You know," Verida said, "maybe these dreams of Grey's are a good thing. Without the last one, we wouldn't have had any idea what we were walking into."

Grey's enthusiastic chewing slowed, and he worked hard to swallow.

"Mmm." Beltran perused the food choices. "We probably don't want him to have any more of those. If you want him to live, that is." He chose a small roll, plucked off a piece, tossed it in his mouth, and sat back to wait.

Rune cracked first. "Beltran!" Her voice was trembling. "Tell us what you know before I come over there and shake it out of you."

He took his time, looking Rune up and down as he slowly chewed. "I think I'd *very much* like to see you try." Beltran couldn't help himself—he winked.

Rune's fist clenched, and her nails tore into the skin of her apple.

"Would you like to see *me* try?" Verida twisted to look at him, her eyes a light shade of red. "Talk. Now. Or I'll do it for her."

"All right, all right. No need for violence." Beltran shoved the rest of the roll in his mouth and brushed the crumbs from his hands. "Grey isn't having dreams; they're visions, and there aren't many species capable of them. Even for those with the proper genetics, it's so dangerous that only certain individuals are chosen to practice the skill. Although a well-trained seer can see the future without danger, that's not what Grey's doing." He pulled up one knee and rested his arm across it. "When I was carrying him last night, there was a moment when I *smelled* Feena's court. I didn't understand it until earlier this afternoon. Grey isn't watching in a dreamlike state as things unfold—he's actually attending the event. Now, a true traveler has the ability to visit the past or the present. So far, it appears Grey has been limited to present events only. It's probably what's saved him. A traveler's spirit, soul, incorporeal form—whatever you want to call it—actually separates from their body and travels. Part of Grey stays at his origin point, and part of him visits . . . elsewhere. If you have the right genetics—a body that can endure this—it's a skill set that can be honed over decades until the users can actually control what they want to see. Human bodies, well—"

"Weren't meant for it," Grey finished. "Yeah, Feena mentioned that too."

"What's happening to Grey shouldn't be possible, and his human body is being torn apart. The only reason he survived his first vision was because his Venator blood saved him. I suspect that's why it's taking so long to heal this time—not because his body isn't repairing the damage but because there's so much."

"But why?" Rune asked. "Why is it happening?"

"From somewhere in Grey's lineage, he's picked up the ability from a species that can safely do it."

Rune shook her head. "But if that were true, it would mean that Venators can crossbreed and make something other than a Venshii. Tate told us that was impossible."

"Wherever this entered Grey's line, it didn't happen naturally. This was long before we realized Venshii were being created. Back when—"

"When your scientists and wizards were mixing DNA to create super Venators, killing half of them in the process?" At Beltran's surprised look, Grey's mouth twisted. "Read all about it in your library."

"Wait. Waiiiit." Rune dropped her partially eaten apple in the dirt and scrambled to her knees. "Are you telling me that I could be part . . . werewolf or vampire or—"

"Or something else that's causing me to have visions while ripping my body apart in the process? Yeah. That's exactly what I'm saying." Grey held one hand up, looking intently at the skin and bone as he twisted it one way and then the other. "You know, I think I'd rather be part vampire."

"Well, thank you, Grey. I'm glad to see your preference for my species falls just above being torn to shreds in your sleep." Grey started to apologize, but Verida cut him off. "I've heard enough problems for one day. What we need are solutions. Grey could die during one of these visions, so what are we going to do?"

Though the question was directed toward the group as a whole, the reality was that if Verida didn't know, there was only one of them who might. Three heads turned in unison to look at Beltran.

"You know how much I loathe to admit this, but I don't know. I'm going to need some time."

"We don't have time. What if it happens again?" Rune demanded. "What if Grey doesn't wake up the next time?"

"What exactly would you like me to do? I can't solve a problem without information. I'm not all-knowing."

"Argh!" Rune scrubbed her hands over her face and head, her fingertips pulling more hair from the messy braid. "Is there anything else we need to know?" Her hands slapped down on her legs with an exasperation that said there couldn't possibly be more.

But there was.

"There is one other thing." Beltran waited until Rune looked at him before continuing. "But that's yours to share, love." The daggers that flew from Rune's eyes were as sharp as the blades at her hip. "Don't look at me like that. This isn't about just you. Or me. This is about *us*." Beltran motioned around to the four of them. "What's going to happen when we're in that arena fighting who knows what and suddenly you have to go?"

Judging by the fury still in her eyes, his explanation hadn't done a bit of good. Rune put her hands behind her and pushed herself up on shaking arms. She slowly straightened to standing, bent at the waist as if the weight of the world were determined to keep her pressed down.

"Rune?" Grey asked.

Her head hung. With the exception of the subtle fluttering of her fingers against her thighs, she stood stone still.

"Rune?" Grey repeated. "What is he talking about?"

When she didn't answer, Beltran knew what had to be done, regardless of how guilty he felt about it. "Rune has a nixie bubble lodged in her wrist."

Verida moved so fast Rune didn't realize she was coming until the vampire grabbed hold of her wrist and turned it over. "Mother of Rana!" she shouted, shoving Rune's arm away. "Why?"

"Why do you think!" Rune yelled back. "You saw what Grey looked like when you left. You didn't wonder how he was still breathing? How we both made it back in one piece? You never even asked me what happened after you left us there!" Rune pushed Verida to the side, stepped over Grey's legs, and stormed toward Beltran. He scrambled to his feet. She shoved a finger into his sternum. "I don't know if I will ever forgive you for that, so I hope it was damn well . . ." Her voice jerked. She swallowed. "I hope it was worth it."

He could handle her anger. He could endure the way it opened the doors and showed him pieces of her Venator. But this was different. A clear and evident sense of betrayal was wound through her brown eyes. It nearly pulled an apology from his throat. "Rune," he said as gently as he could. "You can't just withhold something like that. This is life and—"

"Oh!" She threw her head back, barking a laugh. "I don't think so. You are *not* going to lecture me about that!"

Rune was so focused on Beltran she wasn't aware of Grey coming up behind her.

He gently placed a hand on her shoulder. She gasped and whirled to face him.

Grey's brows were furrowed, his eyes heavy and sad. "What does it mean? Rune . . . what did you do?"

She shook her head frantically. A noise tore from her throat that sounded like the cry of a wounded animal. She twisted, trying to move past him, but he placed his hands on both her shoulders. Beltran was only inches behind Rune, and Grey's fingertips were light and loose against her shoulder blades. Still, Rune sagged as if he were pressing her into the ground.

"Let me go, Grey."

"That lump in your wrist wasn't there until after the nixie's saved me."

"I don't want to hurt you. Please, *please*, just let me go."

Rune's head was hanging, and her pleading tore at Beltran's heart. There was a part of him—the part that was quickly becoming *hers*— that needed to spare her the pain. He tried to explain, "It means—"

Rune twisted so fast the end of her braid slapped against her neck. She raised a finger. "Don't! Don't you dare."

144

He took a breath, trying to calm his building frustration, and leveled her with a long, hard look. "Fine, love. Then you do it."

She deflated. Her hand fell back to her side, and she bit her lip, looking at neither Grey nor Beltran.

"This is ridiculous," Verida said. "*I'll* do it."

"No!" Rune shoved Grey's hands off her shoulders. "Enough! This is *my* story. My choice. And I will be the one to tell it."

Beltran expected her to run, to storm back to the tent. But she didn't move from the caged position between himself and Grey, her back and shoulders heaving with angry gasps.

Nobody moved. No one spoke.

In the silence, Rune's breaths slowed, and the tension in her body dripped away. She lifted a hand and placed her palm flat against Grey's chest. "Later," she whispered. "Please, I promise, I'll tell you later."

Grey looked down at her with such pain and tenderness that Beltran had to look away. The boy loved her—that much was clear. It was an old love that had been hedged up as to not let it out. But love nonetheless.

"When?" Grey asked.

"Soon. I just . . . I need some time."

16

Keir pushed his people all day and halfway into the night. Tate's muscles were large, his frame heavy—unlike the lean bodies of the fae—and marching for hours was not something he'd been designed for. Turrin's build was the only one similar to his own, and he appeared to be holding up well, but Tate had blood in his boot, and his legs felt like they were made of stone.

Tate had expected Keir to cut through the forest. Instead, they traveled through an extensive network of underground tunnels. He had no idea where they were or how far they'd traveled until they emerged topside. Although the night was lowly lit, Tate recognized the area immediately. They were just outside the western edge of the Dark Forest and within eyeshot of the same hill that he, Rune, and Grey had landed on when they'd exited the gate into Eon.

The sound of a horse snorting broke the silence that had infused the air. Turrin whirled, pulling the clear blade from his sheath as he stepped in front of the new king. Tate scanned the area and quickly located a horse and rider tucked between the trees, well within the shadows of the Dark Forest. The hiding spot was sound, and the spy would've gone unnoticed had the sudden appearance of the fae army not startled his mount.

The spy yanked the reins to the side, turning so tightly the horse was forced onto its hindquarters. He dug his heels into the horse's flanks, and the pair cut out across the open grass, choosing the terrain that would offer no disguise but afford the horse the extra speed that might allow them to outrun a fae. The spy's long hair was secured at the base of his neck, and moonlight flashed against a silver adilat that had been stuck through the leather ties. Adilats were not a common choice of weapon, and they were never disguised as hair accessories. But Tate had seen the look before. It was one of Dimitri's favorite spies—a human male.

Tate didn't know what story Verida had told Dimitri in regard to his absence, but he was sure it wasn't the truth, and a report of him traveling with Keir's people would be devastating. Luckily, he'd been placed deep within a group of warriors, three of whom also had blue skin. With this light, his company, and how tightly he was surrounded, it was extremely unlikely he'd been spotted. Still, Tate stepped further behind the tallest fae.

Unfortunately for the spy, Turrin had recognized the plan to outpace them. He'd resheathed his blade and was already running before the horse had finished its turn, tentacles unfurling as he went. As the horse worked up speed, Turrin's legs ate up the distance between the two.

The moment the fae warrior realized the horse would certainly outpace him, he lunged and shot two tentacles forward, wrapping them around the man's waist. Turrin planted his feet and braced his hands on his thighs. The muscles in his back bulged beneath his leather battle vest, and he leaned backward, yanking the tentacles home and ripping the man from his saddle. The horse continued on at full gallop, disappearing over the hill.

Turrin pulled the human through the air and smashed him to the ground at his feet. The man gasped, trying to reinflate his lungs.

He gripped at the long grasses around them and attempted to get up. Turrin's tentacles crisscrossed back over his vest as he took one large step and straddled the human. He leaned over, grabbed the man by his head, and snapped his neck. The body thumped lifelessly to the ground.

Tate felt remorse for the man's loved ones but simultaneously breathed a sigh of relief. No message would be returning to Dimitri about his whereabouts.

Turrin stepped to one side and bent over, pulling the dead man up and across his shoulders. He carried the corpse to his king, and they marched on, taking the evidence with them into the Dark Forest, where they could dispose of it away from the eyes of the council.

As they broke through the tree line and continued deeper into fae territory, the branches intertwined and the canopy closed above them, blocking out stars and moon, sky and sun. Blackened trees and blood-red leaves went on and on without end, eventually growing so thick that the ground below and the branches above merged into one monochromatic backdrop.

When Keir ordered the caravan to stop for the night, the clan went to work, preparing for camp and the evening's festivities. Tate was left restrained and alone. With his hands secured behind his back, he picked a tree and leaned against it, using his shoulders to take some of the weight as he carefully lowered himself to sitting.

Ever true to its name, the Dark Forest restricted all natural light, leeching it away as soon as it appeared. Even the bonfire's growing flames were not immune to whatever magic had infected this place. The orange glow that surrounded the flickering tendrils vanished long before it should've, leaving the bonfire's light limited and inadequate.

Keir didn't need to explain his choice to move through the Dark Forest. Tate saw it for what it was: stealth. It would've been faster to cut straight across to the north, traversing the river before Sarahna

Falls and then cutting due west to the Blues. By taking the tunnels and entering the Dark Forest from its far western border, they would be marching through much thicker terrain.

In addition, in order to remain within fae territories, they would have to take the long way, marching in a wide loop until they emerged at the tail end of the Blue mountain range and then cutting east. Though the fae's loyalties to each other were strange and tenuous, one of the few universal laws was the right of safe passage . . . up until that right was abused.

The first strings of music rose, and the fae began shedding their hardened leather vests in preparation for what would be the first of many dances. How they had the energy they did was unfathomable, but Tate had learned that lesson well in the arena. When fighting fae, he moved hard, and he moved fast. The longer the bout went on, the higher his odds of losing as his energy waned while the enemy's did not.

The music grated at Tate's ears. Although Venshii were said to retain none of their parental genetics, he seemed to be more resistant to fae music than most—a fact he didn't make public. Even so, it was a battle not to succumb.

While the other fae danced, Turrin kept himself aloof, his head held high as he patrolled the perimeter. Tate waited until he was close enough before calling, "Are you going to remove these restraints?"

Turrin adjusted his course. He stopped at Tate's feet and raked him with a loathing gaze. "Why would I do that?"

"When you tripped me earlier, the cuffs thought I was trying to escape and tightened."

He grinned. "I was aware."

"Were you also aware that my right fingers have been numb for hours? If blood flow isn't restored soon, you'll be explaining to your king why his champion had to have all of his fingers amputated on his sword hand."

Turrin's glee bled into a scowl. He leaned in and grabbed Tate's shoulder, twisting him at the waist and forcing his nose against the opposite leg. When the restraints released, Turrin gave Tate an extra shove, smashing his face against his own kneecap.

Tate stayed in that position for a moment, checking his anger as pins and needles exploded through his wrists and fingers. When he sat up, he calmly rolled out his shoulders.

"Don't try anything." Turrin's hand hovered over his sword. "I am aching to take revenge for Morean."

Tate's gaze slowly traveled past Turrin's blade and to the fae's face. "And I am aching for the opportunity to send you to join him." He gave the slightest shrug. "We'll see which one of us gets what they want."

Tate had no doubt that Verida would come for him—her neck was on the line for this too. But he'd trusted her implicitly with the safety of his family once before, and it was a mistake he would not be making again.

He could not—*would not*—go back to the arena empty handed.

Which was why, although his body was begging him to sleep, he couldn't. Not yet. The gold coin he'd smuggled out of the council house days ago was now partially embedded in the skin of his heel. If he didn't get it out and into the other boot, he'd be limping tomorrow. Although risky, the switch had to be done tonight, while the fae were distracted.

Across the blazing fire, Keir looked down on his dancing subjects from atop a ridiculous throne that he'd ordered constructed from branches and vines for this evening's festivities. Because . . . how utterly unacceptable to sit at the same level as your people while on a battle march.

The absurdity of it all set Tate's nerves on end. *Gods*, he hated the fae.

Their dancing grew more riotous, the music faster. Tate went to work. He loosened his laces and pulled the right boot off, knocking his heel against the side to dislodge the coin. He removed the sweat-and-blood-soaked sock next, hissing as the fabric ripped free from the oozing blister.

While he waited for Turrin to patrol the opposite side of camp, Tate took off the other boot and laid the socks out to dry. When the moment was right, he turned the left boot over, tapping it on the ground as if he were removing dirt. When he repeated the action with the right, he slid one hand over the opening, catching the coin as it fell and smoothly depositing it into the left. With the switch made, he tipped the boot forward, and the coin rolled to the toe and out of view.

He could not believe this was happening. After all this time, he would finally see Ayla and Brandt—but would be holding nothing more than two minuscule advantages. The underpinnings of a plan that revolved around a single gold coin, and a tenuous thread of hope that it would yield the desired outcome.

17

Tashara pressed her fingers against her temples, rubbing at the throbbing headache that wrapped from the base of her skull to the insides of her eyeballs. It did little to dull the pain. She was still ravenous and shaky, but her skin was no longer hot to the touch. The withdrawal symptoms were lessening. Ready to face the reflection in the mirror, she took a deep breath and dropped her hands.

Demon's breath! She looked like hell.

Tashara ran her fingers over the dark circles beneath her eyes, turning her head from one side to the other. They were worse today. The purple half moons were so large they lined the tops of her cheekbones, and her lips had lost their natural red pout, appearing nearly translucent.

In order to attend the last council meeting, she'd been forced to make up her face with paints and gels. Shax, of course, had known immediately. Not that she'd used paint—that much was obvious to everyone—but what it meant. What she'd *done*. Succubi were blessed with beauty that needed no assistance . . . unless they were starving themselves.

And there was only one reason she would be doing that.

Taking out a pot of red stain, Tashara swiped a brush through the center and carefully tapped at her lips, layering the color until it resembled its normal seductive intensity.

If a succubus ate in moderation, she could go days without needing more. But in helping Rune gain entrance to Feena's court, Tashara had feasted. Overindulgence was the curse of her species, one the incubi were immune to. It had taken less than an hour for her internal scale to tip out of balance. Tashara had emerged from fae territory an addict, and by the next morning, she'd progressed into a full-fledged succubain. A sexual predator and an instrument of death.

Unfortunately, the only cure for a succubain was enduring the agony of withdrawal. In other words: forced, precise, torturous starvation. When the symptoms began, Tashara had thought she would come undone, and through the days and hours of suffering, she'd cursed Rune's name. But it was no more Rune's fault than it was her own. She'd known what the price would be when she'd offered to save Grey, and she'd paid it willingly.

Tashara dusted her face with pale powder but found it useless against the bags and dark circles. Sighing in defeat, she reached for the jar of thicker face paint and began working it into the skin beneath her eyes. She patted, rubbed, and dabbed until she was satisfied that her complexion appeared as normal as possible.

Pushing back from the vanity, she headed for the wardrobe. Her legs shook as she stepped over the dress that she'd tossed to the floor after the council meeting. Her room was usually pristine, but she'd been hanging on by a thread and had given the servants the week off to prevent any accidents. Without the extra hands, it took some doing to wiggle her favorite dress over her hips.

When she next stepped to the mirror, she was pleased to find that, though she was sweating and out of breath, the reflection staring back otherwise looked almost normal. The dress she'd chosen was ruby red, and the neckline flowed from the outside of her collarbones to the bottom of her sternum. Her cleavage was amply exposed, and the scalloped curves hugged her breasts in all the right places, creating her preferred silhouette. The skirt was slit to the top of her hip, which made moving easier, and the weighted hemline ensured that anything she chose to cover remained covered.

Abstinence from her drug of choice was not possible forever, and if she intended to keep her heart beating, she was going to have to eat.

Tonight.

"There will be only one," she whispered to her reflection. "*Just one.* No matter how hungry you are, no matter how badly you want more. One."

Any more and she would be right back where she started.

The thought of living through the first two days of withdrawal symptoms again was almost more than she could bear.

Tashara picked up a gold coin she'd laid out on the dresser and tucked it between the tight swoop of the dress and her breast. The headache redoubled, and she staggered, catching her balance on the corner of the dresser. She had to go. Now. Before she was forced to feed on a servant.

The first portion of her trip through the council house was without real danger, and she moved with as much grace as she could fake. But as she grew closer to the dungeons, she had to pass through the servants' hall. It was late, and most were sleeping—as she'd planned—but there was an additional risk associated with evening. It wasn't long before the musty smell of sex hijacked her weakened willpower.

Tashara turned without thinking, following the scent. She identified the door and knew that behind the simple barrier were two servants. Two answers to her desperate need. Her body was aching for sustenance. She was starving, but the succubain desired more than eating to live. It wanted bliss. It demanded pleasure. She was craving *euphoria*.

Her hands slammed against the doorframe, stopping her forward motion. "No," she grunted between clenched teeth. "*No.*" She stumbled away, her hand pressed to the wall to keep from falling.

Tashara descended into the bowels of the council house, passing by the dungeons where Rune had been housed. The stone-block walls here were unadorned, uncovered, and wet from groundwater that trickled in through the porous rock. As she grew closer to the cells where the worst offenders were kept, the smell of mildew filled her senses until it finally gave way to the overwhelming stench of prisoners forced to bathe in their own filth.

As a succubus, she always struggled with a certain inner disdain at where she chose to feed. The needs of her succubain were even more decadent, and revulsion at her surroundings crawled up her throat, nearly turning her back.

When she rounded the final corner, the guard at the main door stumbled to his feet. He squinted down the darkened hallway, one hand on the sword at his waist. The thick, curving ram's horns on the side of his head made his appearance more menacing than Tashara knew him to be. Upon realizing who was approaching, he turned his gaze away.

Giving a succubus too much attention was never wise. Especially tonight.

"Tashara." Pastian's voice had a pleasant timbre to it that she always appreciated. "I didn't expect you this evening."

"I didn't send notice." Tashara pulled out the gold coin and cautiously reached out to set it on his chair, avoiding even the slightest touch—a precaution she didn't usually need. "I'll send more later for the inconvenience. And for your continued discretion."

He bowed his head. "Our appreciations, my lady. My wife told me the last box of provisions you sent were fine indeed."

"You are very welcome. Now, if you please."

"Of course." Pastian pushed a large bronze key into the lock and snapped it to the right. He grabbed the bars and swung the door open. The hinges squealed. "I would've lit more torches if I'd known you were coming."

"It's fine. I've already made my choice."

Pastian nodded. The apple of his throat bobbed as he swallowed.

Perhaps it was her interactions with Grey that were feeding Tashara's need to be understood, or maybe she was growing fond of Pastian, but for whatever reason, she hesitated at the door. "Don't worry. I only take the worst ones."

"I know, my lady."

"Good."

Small, filthy cells lined both sides of the dank hall, inhabited by those already forgotten by the council members who'd tossed them down here. The door clanged shut behind her, and Tashara relaxed for the first time since she'd left her room. Powers of seduction, guile, and deceit billowed through the dungeon unseen . . . but not unnoticed.

The newer occupants fell under the influence of her magic without resistance. The prisoners who'd been here long enough to witness her comings and goings stood in the corners with their backs to her and their eyes squeezed shut. She had no doubt they'd fled as far from the front of their cells as possible the moment they'd heard her speaking to Pastian. But their efforts were useless. Today, she was a succubain. Stronger and more persuasive. It would be no more difficult than flexing a finger to coax them past their fear and force their biology to react to her magic.

Two cells in front of her, beefy fingers wrapped around the bars as a prisoner tried to get a look at Tashara's curves with small, beady eyes. Others followed, pressing against their cell doors and calling out for her attention, unaware that if she gave them what they wanted, her face would be the last thing they ever saw.

Her hips swayed heavily from side to side as she passed the cells, grasping at energy to take the edge off her pounding headache. As a succubus, she could limit her pull to another's energy alone—much like skimming cream from a bucket. It wasn't very nourishing, but in certain situations, it was helpful.

Tonight, her pull was too strong, her reach overly aggressive, and what she took was pure life essence. Prisoners slid to the ground, too weak from the loss to hold their own weight. As they looked up at her from their knees, her lethal intentions should've been clear to them, but their minds couldn't break free of her hold. The only thing they were aware of was their own pounding desire.

Tashara's chosen victim was just ahead: a large werewolf from Beorn's pack. She'd listened for hours as a human detailed this particular wolf's actions in her village. His rapes were done publicly, the slaughters the same. When Silen's scouts captured him, Tashara had decided immediately that if depraved sexual pleasure was what he wanted, then that was what he would get. And this time, it would be the death of him.

The male was attractive at first glance and younger than she thought he'd be. He was solidly built, and the dark scruff across his jaw emphasized his well-proportioned features. He wasn't wearing a shirt, and his pants were slung low on his hips, showing off the hard ridges of his abdomen.

The full moon would be here all too soon, so Silen had ordered the prisoner drugged to prevent a change. She could see the telltale glassy shine across his hazel eyes. This was to her advantage. The drug also acted as a daily preventative, denying the male access to both of the werewolves' permanent gifts: his claws and superior strength.

Tashara stopped in front of his cell, releasing her hold on the others.

Reading the need in another's eyes was an art form, one she'd perfected. Grey, for example, had need, but only in response to her magic. Beyond that, the things he'd felt for her had been almost . . . innocent.

Pure, in so much as raw desire could be. In this wolf, she could see attraction, lust, and—most tellingly—a desire to control. Tashara smiled wide and pushed out an equally intense wave of magic.

The wolf threw himself against the bars, rumbling filthy promises of what he wanted to do to her.

"Hands. Down." Her sultry, enchanted tone tamed the wild dog, and he obediently lowered his arms to his sides. Tashara slid her hands between the bars and roughly gripped his face.

He licked his lips. "I'm going to enjoy this."

"Yes, I think you will." She pulled him forward until his cheekbones were pressed against metal and his mouth was accessible. She smirked. "Until you don't."

Tashara pressed her lips against his and breathed in. His essence, his soul—she didn't know what it was, in truth—leapt from him in rivers of energy. Having passed through only the initial phases of her withdrawal, her addiction burgeoned under the wolf's life force, demanding more as her body greedily gobbled it up.

Feeding was always pleasurable.

Unfortunately.

Today, it was the euphoric hit she'd been craving.

This wolf lasted longer than most, but as they neared the end, his skin turned ashen, and his eyes lost their hard edges. She pulled more, stealing everything until his legs crumpled. She kept her hold and guided him down until she was kneeling in front of him on the cold, damp floor—so immersed in her own high that she didn't care about the dirt, the chill . . . anything.

The last dregs of a soul were the most pleasurable, and Tashara could taste them on the edge of her tongue, waiting, ready to come when called. She ached for the flavor, desperately wanting to finish him—a desire that always made her despise what she was. Except in moments like this.

Tonight, she would not be ashamed.

Here, in the filth and the dark, she would mete out justice for those who could not claim it themselves, and this bastard would know *exactly* what was happening.

Tashara reeled in her magic.

He blinked back to reality, too weak to fight. "Please," he gasped. "I don't want to die."

"Tell me. Those you slaughtered in Cashel's name, the women and children you abused and killed. Did they beg for their lives?"

"Ple—"

Tashara dug her nails into his cheeks. "*Did they?*"

He nodded, his chin barely moving. It was all he could manage with what she'd left him.

"And when they pleaded with you to spare them, did you?"

Tears cut paths into his dirt-covered cheeks. "N . . . No."

"Then neither shall I."

The male's jaw fell slack, and his eyes went blank as Tashara inhaled his life force, pulling until the final drops of sweet nectar passed over the back of her tongue.

With the wolf's life energy flowing through her, Tashara was sustained but far from satiated. She placed her hands flat on the floor, breathing deeply to calm the surging succubain inside. She needed to return to her room, *now*, and sleep it off for the next twelve hours. After that, the cravings would lessen.

She rose to her feet.

The werewolf's corpse was slumped against the cell door, his hair white, his skin the color of ash, clinging to his bones in leathery folds. Nothing aged a body like a succubus feeding. The victim always had its revenge, pointing a finger at its murderer even in death. That was why Tashara paid Pastian as well as she did: he disposed of the evidence, she ensured the witnesses kept silent.

She smoothed out the lines of her dress and pushed her hair over her shoulders. "If anyone utters one word, one *whisper* of what you saw here tonight, I will return for you." She stepped forward, her heels clacking across the stone. "And if, due to your current circumstances, you find the offer tempting, know this. When I am done with you, I will track down your families. I will not stop. There will be no mercy. One by one, I will suck out their souls until your family tree ceases to exist."

The few prisoners that still dared to look at her slowly backed away into their darkened corners.

Her part was done.

But then a single strain of laughter trickled into the hall behind her.

"Succubus." The voice was light, airy, and female. Her words were wrapped with humor. "I'd heard stories of your beauty, but they did not do you justice."

Tashara found the owner of the offending laughter in the last cell on the right. The occupant was a small thing who lay stretched out on the floor. Without the additional torches Pastian normally lit, the light barely illuminated the front edge of the cell.

"Who are you?"

The small figure dragged herself toward the door. As she moved closer, the limited light showed bright-red hair and green skin. Fae. Too weak to stand, the female wrapped a hand around one of the bars and used it to pull herself up, shoving her face between two of them. Her head was so much smaller than the werewolf's that the metal rods pressed against the middles of her ears instead of her cheekbones.

"Kill me," she whispered.

It wasn't the first time someone had begged her to play executioner.

Tashara snorted and turned away. "No."

"I have information you want."

She looked over her shoulder at the pitiful thing with bland disinterest. "How could you possibly know what I want?"

The fae slid to the floor, her smile sloppy and drunken. "Becaaause . . ." She flopped onto her back, and her arms splayed to the sides. "*Anyone* would want it."

The nearest torch was four cells down. Tashara grabbed it and moved closer to determine exactly whom she was talking to. She didn't recognize the face, but the whites of the fae's eyes were dark blue.

She sneered. "You've been drugged."

The fae rolled her eyes. "Of *course* I've been drugged. It's the only reason I'm still here." She waved her fingers weakly. "She cut off my magic."

There were many things that could drug a fae, but only a few were terribly effective. Whatever had been administered was probably rare—and expensive.

"Who put you down here?"

The fae giggled and arched off the floor. She braced herself with her head, looking at Tashara upside down. "Kill. Me."

When Tashara crouched down, her dress fell between her legs, leaving one exposed from ankle to hip bone. The fae ran her tongue over her bottom lip suggestively, her gaze traveling from Tashara's thigh to hover unabashedly on her breasts.

"Tell me, you foolish creature, why do you want to die so badly?"

"Hmmmmm." She rolled to her side. Her legs scissored, inching the tiny bit of fabric that still covered her green skin up over her hips. "Because I'm going to die anyway, and Ambrose will make sure it hurts. But with you"—she swung her arm up, rolling her wrist and flipping her finger through the air as though she were scooping the topping off a cake—"it will be ever so enjoyable."

"How much did Ambrose give you?"

"How much what? *Oh*, the drugs." She brought her hands beneath her chin "*A lot*." She tilted her head. "I've never witnessed your kind feed before. Your prey was in the throes of ecstasy. It was beautiful."

"Until the end, when I forced him to feel every tear as I ripped out his soul."

The fae laughed with the same high-pitched titter that had interrupted Tashara on her way out. "But you will offer me mercy."

"Why would I do that?"

"My information is worth it."

"There is a fatal flaw in this plan. I cannot retrieve information from a dead fae." She stood. "And I've already fed this evening. You'll have to face your fate."

Tashara left the informant sprawled across the floor. She carefully slid the torch back into its place on the wall and was nearing the jailer's door when the fae shouted.

"Ambrose hired me to provide a veneer."

Tashara pushed on.

The fae sang, "Oh, *succubus*. Don't you want to know why?"

She stopped, pressing her lips together. *Obviously* she wanted to know why!

Every member of the council had their hands in something they shouldn't. This universal culpability meant there were very few sins that were unforgivable. However, the fact that Ambrose was not only employing a disguise but eliminating the one she'd hired to work the magic would suggest exactly that: something so heinous that it would be the end of her, either literally or as a council member. And this female was not going to give up the information until Tashara started feeding.

But if she fed again, she was going to lose control.

Tashara's steps back down the hall and past the cells were controlled, both because she was on the verge of snapping and because her decision was, as of yet, unmade.

The green-skinned fae was kneeling with both hands wrapped around the bars in anticipation. She smiled. "I thought that might get your attention."

"Tell me what Ambrose would need with a veneer."

"Mmmm . . ." She smiled. "I would like to tell you, but I don't work without payment. Here's how our deal will proceed. You will start feeding. In return, I will share what I know, one piece at a time, until you know what I know. And then, succubus . . ." She sighed. "I will be forced to trust you. After I've told you the final juicy detail, you must promise to finish me."

Tashara stood stone still, racking her brain and running through hypothetical situations that the fae queen might be a part of. She could think of nothing viable. Ambrose was nearly untouchable.

The would-be victim at her feet panted in anticipation. She nibbled her lip and arched her back to press her breasts forward—as if the sight of them were something Tashara had never seen before.

Think! What could Ambrose possibly be doing that would . . . ? She inhaled sharply. *Of course.* Ambrose had been the most vocal in regard to her disapproval of the Venators. *If* she were involved in a plot to harm them, that would be enough to incur severe disciplinary action.

"Before I make a decision, you will answer one question. If you refuse, I will leave you here to writhe on the floor with your knowledge until Ambrose comes for you." Tashara gripped the bars of the cell door. "Does this information you hold concern the Venators?"

The female grinned, her drugged eyes bright with excitement. "Yes. In one way or another, Ambrose's actions will be felt by your new pets."

Tashara's ears burned and she released the bars, clenching her fists at her sides. Grey Malteer had snuck up on her when she'd least expected it and had become one of her biggest weaknesses overnight. When she'd gone into Feena's territory, she'd known what would happen. But the last time she'd crossed the line into succubain had been so long ago that the years had dulled the full reality of it. Tonight, the agony was horribly fresh. The thought of returning to those first few days of withdrawal made her knees weak. But her blinding need for Grey to survive overrode all consequences.

She agreed to the terms.

There was no need to push her magic out tonight. She simply released the power she'd been fighting to hold back. "What's your name?"

The fae moaned, giving herself fully to Tashara's call. "Kit."

As Kit's soul slid into her, Tashara shuddered. She wanted it all. Now. "Start talking."

"Bashti smuggled me into the council house this morning." Kit struggled to her feet, her eyes locked on Tashara as if she'd never seen anything more beautiful. "Ambrose demanded that I build her a veneer."

Any patience Tashara had left was tied up in trying to keep the succubain in control. Her arm whipped between the bars and grabbed Kit's face, digging her fingers roughly into the fae's cheeks. "I know that! *Why?*"

Kit was in no hurry. She fell against the bars and pursed her lips further forward. "Kiss me."

Tashara hesitated for a second, then crushed her lips against the fae's. There was no delicacy, no seduction. Kit didn't seem to mind. Her tongue flicked out, running along the ridge of Tashara's bottom lip as she fed.

The more she partook, the richer the high grew, and a delicious warmth spread throughout her body. Only on the outskirts of her awareness could she see that Kit was growing weaker—and so was Tashara's strength.

She yanked away.

Kit's head fell roughly forward, smashing into a bar and cutting her chin. After what Tashara had taken, she could no longer stand on her own. She remained there, propped up by the door, blood dribbling down her neck.

Tashara held Kit in the sex-induced state of euphoria she'd promised, but her mind was swimming in an addiction-fueled haze. "Why did Ambrose need a veneer?"

"Oh!" Kit sighed. "You are every bit as heavenly as they said."

"I will leave you for her to finish," Tashara hissed. "So help me, I will."

"She didn't need *a* veneer, she needed *my* veneer. Mine are immune to stripping spells, you see, and Ambrose has a gladiator whose match she plans on attending in person."

Rage ignited within her. She slapped her hands against the stone walls between the cells. "A gladiator? *A gladiator?* Why would I care what Ambrose is doing in the games?"

"I'll tell you. But I need more." Kit was so weak she was struggling to breathe. "More."

It was against Tashara's better judgement, but she'd already waded so deep that her control was shattered. She flexed her power, pulling more of Kit's essence from a distance.

The fae slid to the ground, arching against the floor. Her eyes rolled back as she cried out in pleasure.

Tashara released, and Kit collapsed.

"You are cruel master, succubus." She ran her hand down her stomach with splayed fingers. "Whatever Ambrose has wagered on this fight, it's large."

"But do you know *what. It. Is?*"

"I can't tell you yet."

"You useless little urchin!"

"Ambrose is sure she will win. But she . . ." Kit started laughing, her body shaking with glee. "She doesn't know . . . why . . . she should be concerned!" She pulled in a deep breath and let it out slowly, flushing out the remaining laughter. Once calm, she rolled her head to the side. "Take off your dress, succubus. Your body is exquisite."

"No."

"Denying a dying fae her last desire." She sighed. "You are an evil one."

Tashara crouched back down and reached through the bars, grabbing Kit's hand. The fae smiled at the contact.

"Why should Ambrose be concerned?"

"Because. She thinks Tate is meeting up with your Venators."

"Fool! That's because he is!" Tashara let go in disgust. "Ambrose will be pleased to find you alive tomorr—"

"Does it not feel as good for you as it does for me?"

Tashara scowled. "I've had enough of this game we're playing."

"Very well." Kit settled in on the floor as one would on a bed, gently wiggling her shoulders and hips. "Take me to the brink, succubus. I will tell you everything, and then you will understand."

Tashara was holding back the full-fledged monster inside herself with a thread of self-control. Every moment she'd stayed, every bite she'd taken, had sawed away at the thread's integrity. She could still leave. It wasn't too late . . .

Grey.

The thread broke. Her magic rushed out. Kit was the target, but the effects spread throughout the prison. Tashara ignored the shouts of the men and focused on the writhing fae.

Her red hair went white first, starting at the roots and trailing out to the ends. The green of her skin faded next until—like the wolf before her—she had turned a sickly gray. Tashara pulled everything she could.

Kit's soul was hanging on by the smallest of tethers, and she wanted it. By the *gods,* she wanted it.

Tashara collapsed onto her hands and knees. "That," she panted, "is as far as I go. Unless you have something of value."

The fae was barely recognizable; she pulled in rattling breaths. "Ambrose is sure she'll win because she . . . owns . . ." Kit coughed. It was small, but her body jerked from the effort. "Dalbor. He is . . . unstoppable. There's only one who could . . . defeat him."

Everyone knew the gladiator Dalbor. And everyone knew his mentor and predecessor. "Tate."

Kit swallowed with great effort. "She was foolish, because she thinks that Tate is with . . . the Venators." She tried to smile, but her lips cracked and started to bleed. She grimaced. "But Tate is with Keir."

"How would you know that?"

"I have many lovers, succubus, and they have the loosest lips." Her giggle translated into a pained wheeze. "Tate is in chains and will fight for Keir. I sent word to . . . the Underground. Ambrose made the wager without knowing Dalbor's opponent, and she's bet her . . . her . . ." Kit's eyes fluttered shut.

Tashara slapped the floor. "Kit! Her what? She bet her what?"

The fae jolted, descending into a series of racking coughs. When she was done, she licked the blood from her lips. "Her council seat."

Time slowed. "*What?*"

"She's sure she'll win. She doesn't know. About Tate. The council spies will bring word, but not before . . ."

Kit trailed off again as her breathing grew shallower. But Tashara knew what she was going to say: not before Ambrose left for the games. If any of this was true, she was probably already gone.

Kit's eyes flicked back open. "Your Venators left . . . to find your Venshii. They don't know what they are walking into. But I know . . .

I know what Ambrose looks like." The smile she gave was weak, lop-sided, but full of victory. "Do we have a deal?"

If Tate really was with Keir, it meant that Verida, Grey, and Rune had lied. In complete unison with each other. Which meant the odds were that Kit was telling the truth and that they were on their way to retrieve Tate from the gladiator games—and not one of them knew that Ambrose would be there.

"We do."

Kit explained in halting, exact detail the veneer she'd engineered for the fae queen, and as payment, Tashara breathed in, pulling the last bit of life from Kit.

The residue of the fae soul was sweet and potent, and the final hit rushed through Tashara's system. Two victims in one night was usually safe enough, but tonight was not an ordinary night. With the second life consumed, she lost all control. Her enchanted net fell wide and long. From the other end of the hall, she heard the key slide into the lock.

There was exactly enough clarity left within her to know that if Pastian opened the door right now, he would not survive the night. Not only had she developed a fondness for the man, she was going to be in desperate need of someone to clean up her mess when this was all over. Tashara threw her will against her own raging magic, recall-ing just enough control to return the guard to his senses.

"Pastian," she screamed. "*Run!*"

The keys crashed to the floor as Pastian obeyed. She waited, lis-tening. When the sound of his fleeing footsteps faded, Tashara relaxed and straightened. Her eyes roamed hungrily over her unplanned vic-tims, who were no longer hiding in shadows. Each and every one had abandoned the safety of their corners, deceived, enticed, and utterly overwhelmed into the open arms of their demise.

Between Beltran's speculation about what the future might hold, Rune's impending news—which was still hanging over Grey's head—and Verida's comment that the wolf pack had not been kind to the humans, the ride to the village was somber.

They'd lost a day and a half waiting for Grey to heal from his vision, as Rune had refused to let Verida wake him earlier, just in case he'd needed the time. Which he had—not because he was still healing but because he'd been too terrified to fall asleep for hours. Physically, he felt back to himself. Mentally, the visions added one more problem to what felt like a dark storm cloud perpetually hanging overhead.

They rode for hours before an oblong stretch of man-cleared land became visible. Grey ducked to avoid a thick, low-hanging branch as his horse stepped between the last two trees. When he sat up, what remained of the village was unveiled. His heart sank.

Behind him, Rune sucked in a tight breath.

Verida's casual assessment that the wolves "hadn't been kind" was an understatement. The small village was a war zone. The ground was strewn with pots and clothes and handmade children's toys. Doors hung half off their hinges. Wooden window shutters had been ripped off and lay in pieces on the ground. Black scorch marks cut deep scars along hand-hewn log walls. Most of the homes had fared even worse, nothing left of them besides piles of burnt timber to mark where they'd stood.

Along the western side of the clearing, rows and rows of recently mounded dirt stood out against the green of the forest. He averted his eyes to keep from counting, but not before he realized that many of those graves were far too short to fit a grown adult.

Following Verida's lead, the four cut straight through the middle of the village.

As they rode past the first surviving home, Grey stared. There was dried blood streaked down the doorframe and along the windowsill. Claw marks had splintered the wood. And below a window box that had somehow survived was a distinct paw print, too large for a dog.

What did I do?

He knew in his heart that he'd left the council house that first night with the best of intentions. He'd wanted to save Valerian and her son. He'd saved neither. But when he woke in a cold sweat from the nightmares, watching Valerian burn in his place, he had repeatedly told himself that he'd done everything he could to save her. He'd given his all.

And it was that—his *all*—that had triggered *this*.

Bile burned the back of Grey's throat. How many fathers, mothers, sons, and daughters had been lost? How many had been murdered because of his shortsighted quest to save the one? But even as he thought it—even with the proof right in front of his eyes—a lost and broken part of him cried out:

Doesn't the one matter?

Verida pointed to the back edge of the village, where one row of homes stood relatively unscathed. "That's where the survivors have gathered. They know we're coming."

Beltran twisted in his saddle, staring at another pile of logs and ash as his horse plodded by. "What makes you so sure they didn't flee as soon as you left?"

"Because I let them know the Venators were carrying funds from the council to help them rebuild. They'll be here."

"Hmm." Beltran clicked to his horse, increasing the pace. "You know, Verida, sometimes gold isn't enough."

The fires that had swept through ninety percent of the village had been extinguished within feet of the surviving structures. Blackened grass lay flattened, cutting an uneven divide between it and the green vegetation. Straddling the line was a large firepit surrounded by log seating. The grass on the northern side hadn't yet been worn to nothing, and the rough ends of the logs were the butterscotch color of freshly cut wood.

A door to their left opened, and three men stepped out, one after the other. They wore simple pants and linen shirts in plain colors. The size of their arms and chests suggested they were used to hard labor; their worn, mud-covered boots confirmed it. The oldest of the group looked to be in his forties and had a thick, dark beard. The others were younger and covered in heavy scruff. All had swords strapped to their hips.

Verida reined in her horse. "Where is the rest of the village?"

The looks that all three of the men were giving him and Rune weren't new—in fact, since he'd stepped through the gate, he'd yet to be met with anything different. He was almost used to it. But because the villagers were human, which Grey still considered himself, their revulsion stung.

The bearded one stepped in front of the others. He addressed Verida but kept his focus on Grey and Rune. "It doesn't matter. You requested an audience, and you've got one."

"When I said an audience—"

Grey startled at the rise in Verida's pitch. He was familiar enough with the sound. They were moments away from a red-eyed vampire meltdown.

"It's fine," Grey interrupted with enough vigor to stop Verida's forward momentum.

She clamped her jaw closed and turned in her saddle, raking him with a seething glare.

"After what they've been through, it's completely understandable. If I had a family, I'd have hidden them too." Grey moved to dismount but waited with his hand on the saddle horn. He addressed the man who appeared to be in charge. "May I?"

Verida huffed loudly and muttered her displeasure at Grey's approach. He didn't care. These people didn't need threats; they needed hope. And they needed to see that Rune and Grey weren't like the old Venators.

He couldn't offer any of those things while standing behind an angry vampire.

The bearded man narrowed his eyes, no doubt waiting for the other shoe to drop—for Grey to get off his horse without permission. When Grey held his position, the man looked to his companions, who didn't appear to be able to make sense of what was happening either.

The leader nodded his consent.

"Thank you." Grey dismounted and slowly came around his horse. When he was within range, he held out a hand. "My name is Grey."

"Samson. Excuse me if I'm not in a hurry to grab your hand."

Again, Verida scoffed.

"I understand." Grey smiled and dropped his arms. "It's nice to meet you, Samson. I know you've met Verida, and these are Rune and Beltran." He put his hands on his hips and leaned back, looking up and down the row of homes. "What can we do first?"

Samson frowned. "What?"

"We have payment from the council, as promised, but it looks like there's a lot to be done to help you rebuild. Where would you like us to start?"

Grey had hoped the offer would put them at ease. If anything, it strung them tighter.

The man with the lightest hair amongst them spoke. "The council told you to *help* us?"

Verida snorted. Grey shot her a sharp look.

"Sorry." She smirked and gave an airy wave. "I tried to imagine that happening and couldn't keep a straight face."

"You'll have to excuse Grey," Beltran said. "The council has been trying to control his desire to fix every injustice and right every wrong-doing he sees, but . . ." He grinned at Verida, who was now glaring at him. "It just isn't working."

Samson crossed his arms. "If you're really here to help, come with me. We could use some hands in the infirmary." He extended a finger at Verida. "But not you. Or—" He motioned to Beltran. "Are you human?"

"Not exactly."

"Are you going to tell me what you are, then?"

"No, I don't think I will."

"Then you stay as well."

Verida dismounted and spun to face them with vampire speed. The men stepped back as she squared up. "I'm undecided whether I'm amused or annoyed by the fact that any of you think you could keep me out of somewhere I wanted to be."

"Uh, Verida," Rune said. "I don't think that's helping."

"Do you honestly think I'm going to send the council's Venators off with you?" Verida took deliberate, unnerving steps forward.

It wasn't the size of the steps that was making Grey's skin crawl or the way Verida was tilting her head from one side to the other while talking, like a deranged lunatic. It was her complete lack of fear as she faced down the three armed men. They knew that she knew they were no match for her.

Verida raged on. "You expected that I would stand here, waiting to see if you'd bring the Venators back, as if I am somehow beholden to your authority? Do you have *any* idea who I am?"

"*Saints.*" Beltran looked to the sky. "Somebody please stop her."

Samson regained his courage and, to his credit, moved toward— rather than away from—the fuming vampire. "If the stories are true, your Venators have nothing to fear from us. But the near dead and bleeding in our infirmary certainly have something to fear from you."

"How *dare* you! I have enough control to—"

"All right, that's enough!" Grey danced between Samson and Verida and held out an arm to block Verida from moving closer. "You brought us here to help. So let us help."

"Well done, Grey." Beltran slowly clapped from the back of his horse. "You've got more guts than I gave you credit for. You as well, Samson." His hands dropped to his lap. "Verida, let them go. Rune and Grey survived both Cashel and Feena. They'll be fine."

"No." Verida said. "Before anyone goes anywhere, we need information on Beorn."

"Then there's no point in you staying. We don't know anything." Samson's words were smooth and well rehearsed. "The werewolves came in the middle of the night, killed half our village, maimed and kidnapped another quarter. They set fire to our homes, and then they were gone. What you can see is all we know."

It had taken longer than Grey thought it would, but Verida's eyes finally washed red. He heard the men shifting behind him, no doubt moving their hands to their swords. The situation was disintegrating quickly.

Rune moved to help, freeing her foot from the stirrup.

"Wait," Beltran said, half under his breath and just loud enough to be heard. "Grey's got things under control."

"Uh, Samson, can you give us a minute? Verida, walk with me?" Grey didn't wait; he just walked. His stomach was in his throat, and he was positive he would turn to find her still stubbornly planted where he'd left her—or with her hands around someone's neck.

"Grey," Verida said at his shoulder. "I'm regretting bringing you."

He sagged in relief. "I need you to trust me."

"Why?" She cut in front of him, stopping him with a hand on his chest. "Because you're so experienced in the field of negotiation? We need that information! The longer we leave Beorn alone, the faster he'll gather a new pack. And the faster he'll be returning for you and Rune."

"I know that, but you aren't going to get what you need by threatening them. Look at this place. They've already lost everything."

"We're here to deliver a very generous payment from the council. I do not need to—nor will I—beg, grovel, or tiptoe around feelings to get the information we need."

Grey snapped. "All right, look! You and I both know that what happened to this village is the result of my choices. I owe these people a debt, and I'll be damned if I'm going to hand over a bag of money and act as if that's enough to make up for what they've lost. Let me do this. If nothing else, let me do it for me."

Verida's eyes faded back to blue, and she sighed. "You really are incredibly sexy when you put your foot down. I'd almost forgotten."

The switch was so unexpected Grey didn't even have time to try to control his reaction. His cheeks heated.

"And I did forget how adorable you are when you blush. Regardless"—she tapped his chest with her pointer finger—"I'm still tempted to rip that bleeding heart out of your chest."

"They say you catch more flies with honey."

"Of course you do. What does that have to do with anything?"

Grey bit back a smile. "All I'm asking is that we show them a little kindness and see what happens before you try to beat the information out of them."

Verida stepped back and pursed her lips. Her thumb tapped out a rapid rhythm against her left thigh. "Fine."

"Thank you!" He jogged back toward the three men, motioning for Rune. "Are you coming?"

As the three armed men escorted Grey and Rune away, Beltran slid from his horse and started to undo the saddle cinch.

"Beltran," Verida snapped. "What are you doing?"

He spared a quick glance over his shoulder, then heaved the saddle and blanket off the horse's back. "I thought that was obvious."

"Don't waste your time. We probably aren't staying."

"Well"—he walked past her and draped the saddle over one of the logs near the firepit—"I'm fairly comfortable in making the assumption that we are."

The calming influence that Grey had brought to her ill mood quickly flitted away as Beltran started to unbuckle the cinch on Rune's saddle.

"Beltran! We're a day behind, and we have no idea where Beorn is. For all we know, he's hiding nearby, waiting for the council to send the Venators. Unless we get some legitimate information, this is the last place we should be staying. If the humans won't talk, we have to move on—*before* nightfall."

"Relax. Let the boy work."

"In the infirmary? The answers we need aren't going to be found counting graves or dealing with sick and broken humans."

Beltran's expression was one she was familiar with: a soft smile set atop relaxed shoulders. It was the one he always wore to announce that he knew something she didn't. He walked past her with Rune's saddle.

Verida growled. "Just say it."

"Say what?"

"I'm not in the mood to let you talk me in circles until we reach wherever it is you're aiming. Save us both the time and the headache, and spit it out."

Beltran chuckled to himself as he patted the muzzle of Grey's horse and began unbuckling the bridle. "Did you just see Grey? I mean, did you *really* see him?"

"Jumping headlong into something he knows nothing about? Again? Yes, I saw."

Beltran was quiet as he continued to remove the gear from Grey's horse. When he passed by Verida for the third time, he leaned over the saddle he was carrying and put his face inches from her own. His green eyes were bright, and he lowered his voice. "You didn't see *anything*."

Before she could respond, he moved on.

He dropped the saddle on the log next to his and Rune's, then turned to face her. "You were too focused on what you wanted to accomplish to see that Grey is taking you exactly where you want to go. The difference is that he's chosen to go around"—Beltran motioned in a circle with his pointer finger—"to the back door instead of trying to batter his way through the front."

Verida breathed in the longest, slowest breath she could, using it to hold back her desire to scream as Beltran calmly strolled over to pat the horses and send them off to graze. If he touched her mare, no amount of breathing in this world would save him.

He left her horse where it was and took his time meandering back to where he'd left the saddles, casually choosing a seat on the ground.

He leaned against one of the logs and looked up at the sky as if it were the most lovely day and he simply couldn't help but observe it.

Rana! It infuriated her when he did that, and he knew it. *Very* well.

Beltran laced his hands behind his head, taking a few more moments to enjoy the view, then turned and looked at her. "What?"

Her hands were shaking. But she would not give him the satisfaction of exploding. She. Would. Not. Verida crossed her arms, tucking her hands into her sides to hide the tremors. "Here's what I'm going to do. Instead of threatening to rip your throat out, I'm going to—"

"You've already done that," he interrupted. "Multiple times. This week."

Her lips pressed tightly together.

"Apologies." His grin was anything but apologetic. "Continue."

"I've decided to ask you nicely to enlighten me as to whatever magic Grey is working that I don't see. You are going to do so without riddles and without talking in circles. And then, when you've finished, you're going to tell me what the hell you were thinking, taking Rune into the sprites' realm, along with *every. Single. Thing* that happened there."

"Or . . . I could tell you everything that happened that is of any consequence to you and this mission."

"*Or* . . . we could revisit the throat ripping. After that comment about these lands once being controlled by Dracula, you deserve it."

"I said I was sorry."

"Which is the only reason I'm using my manners."

"I would be remiss if I didn't point out that this entire offer is very one sided."

"Beltran!"

He leaned forward and threw an arm over his knee. He always managed to look at ease, no matter what she was threatening him with, which made her want to threaten him all the more.

"Verida, darling, you've been so focused on turning Rune into someone who can move within the circle of the council that you've overlooked Grey's potential entirely."

"Have I? So sorry. I've been a little overly focused on keeping the idiot alive."

"Will you stop hovering and sit?" When she didn't move, he added, "I can't think with you glowering down at me."

"We both know that's not true." Verida acquiesced anyway, marching to one of the logs. Kicking a leg over, she straddled it, facing Beltran.

"I didn't always want to be what I am," he began.

"Oh, are we waxing poetic now? Wonderful."

He cleared his throat. "*I didn't always want to be* who *I am.* I fought against it. I saw a different future for myself. But I learned a long time ago that I could try to become someone I wasn't, *or* . . . I could be a spectacular version of who I was."

She cocked an eyebrow. "Considering you can become anyone you want, I'm failing to see the validity of this life lesson."

"I can *look* like anyone. You, of all people, should be able to provide a lengthy list of qualities I can't seem to actually possess."

"For starters, you're selfish. Manipulative, sneaky—"

"I didn't ask for the list, darling. Simply making a point."

Verida smirked.

"Rune has the ability to be who you want her to be. Her mind is beautiful and quite capable of keeping up with the ins and outs of the council. She has the tools to become a diplomat and emissary. Grey, on the other hand, will never be that. Not because he's not smart enough but because he thinks differently. We can teach him. He'll improve, but he'll always stand behind Rune in formal meetings. Grey offers something else—something new. He possesses qualities that no one in Eon has ever seen from a Venator."

"Stupidity? Impulsiveness?"

Beltran rolled his eyes. "I specified something that had never been seen. *Think*. Grey just stepped into an impossible situation and took all three of those men completely off guard. Why?"

"I *said* no questions and no games."

"Because he *cared*. Don't you see? Grey has a level of empathy that neither you nor I nor Rune possesses. He showed those men kindness and compassion for the same reason he's almost gotten himself killed twice since arriving: he feels too much for some situations but, as it turns out, just enough for others. Those are the traits that will get you your answers here. Not threats."

Verida stared at the ground, processing. "I forget, sometimes," she mumbled. "That his vulnerability could be anything other than a weakness."

"Grey will inspire a whole new kind of loyalty, the likes of which the council has never seen. Because of that, they will remain blind to his potential until it's too late to stop the revolution. Mark my words, Verida—the creatures whose lives Grey touches? They will die for him."

Grey and Rune walked side by side, following Samson to the infirmary. They were flanked by the two other men, whose names hadn't been volunteered. Each man rested one hand on the hilt of his sword and kept himself at a distance.

It was strange at first. On earth, if someone was being escorted, their guards stayed close by. It took Grey a few seconds before he realized that the humans were accounting for his and Rune's enhanced speed and strength. The extra space was to allow them time to pull their weapons.

When they reached the last home on the row, Samson stopped. He gave the Venators an appraising look that conveyed both his curiosity and his complete lack of trust. He pushed open the door and extended his arm through the threshold. "Welcome to the infirmary."

The interior was dark. The window shutters were closed tight, leaving a few flickering candles as the only sources of light. Those same shutters also trapped heat, body odor, and the scent of excrement and infection, wrapped in the sharp tang of medicinal herbs—all of which fled through the now open door.

Rune twisted her body to the side and bent over her knees. Her back heaved as she gagged. The pungent combination assaulted Grey's senses, too, but he braced himself, refusing to react no matter how hard his stomach rolled.

Samson crossed his arms. "Of course, if you'd rather not—"

"No. We're happy to help." Grey stepped through the door. Once inside the makeshift infirmary, his Venator eyesight adjusted rapidly.

The room had been cleared of furniture, and the plank floor was lined with patients draped with a mishmash of blankets and sheets. Some slept on pillows. Others had folded up clothing to rest their heads on. Several village women moved about the wounded, stepping on tiptoes in the spaces left between bodies.

A slim woman with a long face and a hooknose was the first to notice Grey. She squeaked and slapped her hands over her mouth. The tray she'd been holding clattered to the floor, barely missing a patient. The patient in question jackknifed up, then groaned from the sudden movement and collapsed to the floor, his arms wrapped protectively around his middle. The two other nurses stopped what they were doing. Heads turned against pillows, and every bit of movement and conversation ground to a halt.

"Grey," Rune whispered at his shoulder. "What are we supposed to do?"

He twisted to look at Samson, but the man offered no direction. He just stared with a challenge in his eyes.

"We help them," Grey said.

He walked up through the center of the room, aiming for the woman he'd frightened—only because she was the closest to him. Holding eye contact was impossible, though. Anytime he directed his attention toward her, she would take a step back, looking to the windows on either side of the room as if she were preparing to take a flying leap out of one of them.

Trying to ease her worry, Grey stared at his feet . . . and, thereby, at the victims laid out on the floor. To his right, a woman groaned and rolled her head to the side, exposing an oozing werewolf bite on her neck. The pattern and depth of the teeth marks, combined with their location, ripped Grey back to his first night in Eon. Valerian's words washed through his ears. *There is no hope. I will change on the first full moon.*

He stutter-stepped.

The woman Grey was approaching finally called out in a panicked squeak, "Samson!"

"It's all right." Samson's assurance was useless, as the suspicion in his voice completely overpowered it. "They say they want to help."

The poor thing was shaking so violently that Grey stopped with plenty of space between them. He held out his hands, palms up, trying to look nonthreatening. "What can I do?"

She opened her mouth, but the only sounds that came out were the breathy starts and stops of unattached syllables and consonants.

"There are several chamber pots that need emptying," Samson suggested from his position near the door. "Aren't there, Fern?"

Fern gasped. "The cha . . . the chamb . . . But these are the Ven . . ." She motioned to Grey and Rune with one hand while clutching her chest with the other. "Samson!"

It was a test. Grey knew it. But poor Fern looked like she was waiting for Grey to stick a sword through her gut at the offense.

"Chamber pots are no problem." He smiled warmly. "Just point me in the right direction."

"They're uh . . ." Fern was clawing at the fabric of her dress, pulling it into her fist with one hand while she pointed to the brass pots lined against the edge of the room with the other. "There and there and . . ."

"Of course. I see them now. Thank you." Grey motioned for Rune to follow.

The two of them worked quietly, taking the pots out back and dumping them. When they were done, Grey asked for the next chore. The first couple of hours were spent carrying out menial tasks—replacing blankets with clean ones, cutting new sections of muslin for dressings, crushing herbs for treatments. All while Samson hovered silently in the shadows, watching every move they made.

When Fern finally exhausted her list of hands-off chores, they were directed—with undisguised reservation—to assist the patients. Grey began by checking the bandages of the woman nearest to him, with plans to move out from there. But the patient was alert and so panicked by his presence that he had to ask Fern to take over. After that, he specifically chose those who were asleep or partially unconscious.

He worked quietly, changing bandages and irrigating wounds. He rubbed salve on burns and placed a purple herb with large, flat leaves over bruises. There was solace in all of it. His actions in the infirmary didn't *undo* anything—he knew that—but they did ease his guilt back a few steps from the ledge of being unbearable.

Grey finished securing the knot on a fresh wrapping and stood to find his next patient. On the next row over, Rune was kneeling next to a young man. She gently pulled back the muslin from a burn on his chest. Goo and puss strung from the wrappings to his blackened and blistered skin. She heaved and gagged—the sound obnoxiously loud in the quiet room.

A worried Fern looked up. She was in the middle of adding extra sutures to a young girl's cheek. Grey waved Fern away and hurried over, crouching next to Rune.

Air hissed through her teeth, and her hands were shaking as she jerked at the edges of the muslin.

"Hey," he whispered, placing a hand on her shoulder. "What's going on?"

She squeezed her eyes shut. "I'm trying . . . I . . . I just . . ."

"Do you know what? Here." He reached across and gently freed her fingers from the wrappings, then laid the muslin back over the man's wound. "I'll do it."

"No, it's fine, I—he needs help, and . . ." Rune used the crook of her arm to scrub away her tears. "What's wrong with me?"

"There is *nothing* wrong you. You came storming into a faery stronghold to save me. Remember?"

"But why are you . . . ? You're so calm. I thought if I just kept pushing, it would get better, but—"

Grey playfully nudged her with his shoulder. "Rune, I hate to be the one to tell you this, but we can't all be good at everything."

What started as a sob ended as a laugh, and she nodded through her tears.

"Go on," he said. "Get some rest. I'll find you later."

Rune got up, still wiping her face with her arm. Grey sat back on his heels and watched as she trudged to the door, her head hanging. It was the most dejected he'd ever seen her.

"That bad?"

He looked down to find their patient awake and studying him with interest. "What?"

"Do I really look that bad?" The young man flashed a grin that was all teeth. "I've chased women off in my day, but I don't think any vomited at the sight of me."

Grey chuckled. "I'm pretty sure she was reacting to my smell. I haven't bathed in a while."

The young man's wincing laugh was cut short as he cringed. "Ow."

"Hold still. I need to get some fresh bandages on you." He gathered the supplies closer from where Rune had set them. "What's your name?"

"Liam."

"It's nice to meet you. I'm Grey." He carefully began pulling back the section of bandage that Rune had already freed.

Liam winced.

"Sorry about that. Hold still."

"Maybe you should give me something to bite down on, and"—the wrapping snagged, and Liam jerked—"just rip it off!"

"I'm sorry, I'm sorry!" Grey leaned over to see what had happened. A section of the muslin was stuck inside the wound. He glanced to Liam's face. "This is going to hurt. If I rip it off, Fern will have my head. Some of your skin is still salvageable, but it's fragile. I have to take it slow."

Liam nodded, and his hands gripped at the fabric of his pants, steeling himself for the imminent pain. "You're different than I—"

Grey popped the first inch free.

Liam gasped, then finished his sentence though gritted teeth. *"Thought you'd be."*

"I really hope so. Almost there." Once he freed the section that was adhered, the rest of the bandage lifted easily. Grey set it aside. "Apparently my ancestors sucked."

"Sucked?" Liam looked down at the burn on his chest. Satisfied that the worst part was over, he let his head fall back and sighed in relief. "Sucked what?"

Grey burst out laughing. It was so loud that poor Fern jolted and surged to her feet, overturning the ground herbs she'd been applying.

"Sorry!" He sheepishly waved. "Sorry."

Fern shook her head, the expression on her face murderous. She huffed and returned to work, starting with the spilled herbs.

Grey leaned down, whispering. "I don't think she appreciated that."

"Fern's sense of humor only comes out after several ales."

186

"That is very good to know." He reached for the jar of salve. "*Sucked* is a saying from where I come from. It means that they were horrible people."

"The Venators were that. But . . ." Liam's eyelids fluttered in pain and exhaustion. Grey could tell he was fighting to stay awake. "It would be nice to be *something*. Even if it was a Venator." His head relaxed to the side.

Grey thought as he carefully dotted fresh salve across Liam's raw skin. "What would you rather be?"

"Anything, I think. Being human is the worst thing you can be."

"What do you mean?"

Liam's eyes closed. "Helpless," he murmured, drifting off to sleep. "I wish I wasn't . . . helpless."

Helpless.

Tears flooded Grey's eyes without warning. Liam's shape blurred, and Grey blinked furiously to clear his vision. He worked as fast as he could to salve and replace the old bandages, but every second he stayed felt like hours. There was a vice around his lungs, and it was getting tighter and harder to breath. His throat burned.

He had to get out of this room.

Grey smoothed the last piece of muslin over Liam's chest. Leaving the extra wrapping and jar of salve where he'd found it, he stepped into the thin aisleway and ducked his head, wishing again for the security blanket of his old hair.

"Venator." Samson had been standing in the corner so silently Grey had almost forgotten he was there. The large man pushed off the wall and stepped into the limited light of the main space. "Where are you going?"

"I just need some air." Grey quickly glanced at him from his half-bent position. He knew for certain that if he lifted his head or met anyone's eyes, he was going to fall apart. "I'll be right back."

His voice sounded as strangled as it felt. Luckily, Samson didn't say another word.

Grey walked past the man, his movements stiff and jerky and his boots feeling like blocks of cement. He burst through the door and pulled up short, rapidly scanning the village and sucking in mouthfuls of air like a fish out of water.

Liam's truth had forcibly shoved Grey back over the proverbial edge, and his pain had surged far past what he could bear. He needed seclusion, and he needed it now.

On the thin strip of grass between the infirmary and the home next to it, freshly cut firewood had been arranged in stacks of about five feet tall that leaned against the walls. Grey slid down next to one of the piles, using it to shield himself from view. He pulled his legs to his chest, dropped his head, and released, trying to mute the sound of his sobs the best he could.

The breakdown was twofold, triggered by his intimate recognition of Liam's desire.

I wish I wasn't helpless.

That sentiment summed up Grey's entire life on earth and had translated straight across into Eon. Since arriving here, he'd watched a woman burn to death in his stead, been tortured by a fae queen, and watched Tate step into his place so he could escape, and now his body was disintegrating while he slept.

He was exhausted, hurting, and helpless to save himself or anyone around him.

The inequalities of this world were so insurmountable that he didn't see an answer. How could he possibly hope to make anything here better? Because, like a fool, he *had hoped*.

And then he'd met the humans of Eon.

Could he have been any more naive? Humans were essentially at the bottom of the food chain. To even consider the possibility that the inhabitants of Eon would ever view them as anything besides disposable was laughable. Humans lacked magic, speed, and a host of other abilities that the rest of this world wielded—abilities those other species had done *nothing* to gain. They were gifts of genetics. That was it! But because they had been born into the right house, those species were blessed for all time, while creatures like humans and the Venshii suffered.

How would he ever be able to wield enough influence to change a problem like that?

I wish I wasn't helpless. The sentence was running through his head on repeat. He gasped for air with a wide mouth, trying to soften the hissing of his pain as he drowned in a sea of his own weakness.

The sound of someone clearing their throat startled him. He lifted his head to find Samson leaning against the corner of the infirmary. Grey jerked to his feet, swiping at his eyes and cheeks—as if he could deny what he'd been doing.

Samson's expression was cold and unreadable as he crossed his arms. "I'm surprised you're upset by human problems."

Of course he was.

Grey was too tired to be offended, and part of him realized that Samson could understand no more and no less than the truth he'd lived. However, if they were to get anywhere, he had to help Samson see a piece of *his* reality. He looked to his feet, wiggling his toes in his boots. "Are there stories of earth here?"

"A few."

He nodded. "Did you know that we don't have the same creatures you have here? No vampires, werewolves, none of them. I didn't even know what a Venator was." He held out his arms. "These markings didn't appear until we were attacked by goblins a few weeks ago. It was right before Tate brought us through the gate." The words were slow in coming as he worked through how to explain what his life had been like. "My family, as far as I knew, was human. My whole life has been nothing but 'human problems.'"

Grey finally dared to meet Samson's eyes. "I know I don't look human to you, and these markings mean something different to you than to me. But in here, where it matters"—he beat his fist against his chest—"I *am* human. I will *always* be human. Whether or not my skin marks me as something else."

The declaration fell heavily between them, and this time it was Samson who looked away. He kicked at a scruff of grass, his lips pursed in thought beneath his thick beard. "Beorn made an announcement before he ordered his pack to attack. He said we could thank the Venators for the deaths of our people."

"He's right." The words were out before he could even think of holding them back. "It *is* my fault."

Samson's head snapped up.

Grey didn't want to see the judgment in his eyes—the hatred that would surely be there once he finished explaining. But after what his actions had cost this village, he also couldn't disrespect Samson by looking away.

"The first night we arrived, a man—a human—came to the council house. He'd been attacked and nearly killed by a werewolf who'd taken his wife and son. He begged for our help on his knees. He was dying, right there in front of us. Blood was . . . *everywhere*, but the council refused to help them. So I . . . I snuck out, thinking I could save them."

Samson's brows had been pulling tighter and tighter together as Grey's story progressed. "You went against the council's orders . . . to rescue a human?"

"Yes."

"And did you save them?"

Grey knew the question was coming. It didn't make it hurt less. He wanted to run, punch something, pick up one of the logs behind him and throw it as hard as he could.

"No. The son was already dead by the time we found the pack. We were able to get the wife out, but Cashel had already bitten her. Her name was Valerian. Later that night . . . she . . ." He quickly looked up, trying to roll the tears back, then pulled himself taller, preparing to face the worst of the truth. "I couldn't save her. Instead she died saving me." He swallowed. "That night, we were able to kill Cashel, but we didn't understand pack law, so we left Beorn alive. Now he's taking out his revenge on every village he can find. Beorn wasn't lying. This *is* my fault." Grey's voice kept cracking, and he barely got the next sentence out. "I failed that whole family, Samson, and I failed your people too."

Grey waited for what he deserved. Instead Samson pushed off the corner and placed a hand on his shoulder.

"Get some rest," he said softly, "and get cleaned up."

"What? But . . . I can finish helping Fern. Please, let me help."

"I expect we'll eat within the hour." Samson motioned. "And you're a mess."

Grey looked down. He was covered in blood and fluids he didn't want to spend time identifying. "But—I can—"

"No." Samson squeezed his shoulder. "You've done plenty. Besides, I have someone I'd like to introduce you to at dinner. He'll be scared enough without you being covered in both Venator markings *and* blood."

20

The council meeting had been scheduled as a lunch event, but the food had come and gone, and they were still missing two members. Omri never did send word as to why he'd left in such a hurry. Nor had he returned. More interesting was the fact that Ambrose was also missing. Tashara's eyes kept cutting to the empty chair across the table—potential evidence that the information she would, in a few hours, be paying dearly for might have been worth its price.

With her body still on the high of the previous night, she looked and felt fabulous. Her eyes were bright, and her lips were red and plump. But she was on borrowed time. Once the excess left her system, the succubain would demand more, and the first signs of her withdrawal would begin. The cravings would be almost unbearable, and in order to leave her room she would be forced back to her paints and creams to hide her pale lips and sunken eyes.

As the rest of the council members waited for one or the other to arrive, Tashara attempted to strategize, but the sound of meat ripping at the end of the table was so distracting she could barely think. She rolled her eyes to Silen, whom she'd desperately been trying to ignore—a difficult feat, considering the spectacle he was making of himself.

After the meal had finished, he'd proceeded to request that the kitchen prepare him a plate of ribs to "pass the time." He was currently on his third serving and was tearing at the bones and sinew as if he were propped up at the dinner table—with its fine silver and sparkling goblets—in wolf form. He tore off another chunk of meat. It hung there, dangling half out of his mouth, until he loudly slurped it in.

Tashara's lip curled.

Arwin was sitting directly across from her and had wisely come prepared for the inevitable delays. He was busily bent over the table, scribbling notes on parchment. She couldn't help but notice that—as per usual—there was a smear of lemon sauce on the corner of his paper. The wizard was perpetually dripping food and drink—a phenomenon she'd found quite disgusting when she'd first arrived. But the consistency of the occurrences, combined with his jovial attitude, had made the spills and blunders endearing.

Arwin glanced up, catching her staring. He smiled. "Did you need something, Tashara?"

"Hmm? Oh, no. I was just noticing that you've spilled some sauce." She pointed. "Just there."

"Yes." He rubbed at the stain. "I suspect it was on my elbow before I began working. I considered calling for a linen to clean it with"—he looked over Tashara's shoulder to the back wall of the room—"but the server seems to be otherwise occupied."

When the server in question removed Arwin's plate earlier, he had immediately caught Shax's eye. Tashara didn't need to look to see what was happening. She could smell it.

"Ah, well." Arwin shrugged. "A little lemon sauce never did any permanent damage to anything I'm aware of." He returned to his work.

Tashara's lips quivered. He never failed to brighten her mood, and though less jovial today than normal, he was one of the few who treated her as if she were something other than an abomination.

"Where *are* they?" Dimitri snarled.

Arwin sighed and set down his quill. "I don't think anyone in attendance is more aware of that answer than we were before the meal started." He leaned back in his chair, twisting one way and then the other. His spine cracked and popped. "What I do know is that I've grown weary of these chairs. Why must they be so uncomfortable?"

Silen spoke around a mouthful of meat. "I don't find them bothersome." His red hair had fallen over his shoulder, and several strands were stuck to the glazed coating of the rib he was demolishing.

If Tashara had ever had an appetite for regular food, she would've lost it long ago.

"Hmph." Arwin grumbled. "When your bones start to ache with age, we can revisit this conversation."

"We might as well get started." Silen pushed his plate away, pulled the linen from his lap, and tossed it onto the table. "I went to check on my prisoner this morning. He was dead."

"Dead?" Tashara absently traced the scrollwork on the arm of her chair. "How?"

"Murdered."

Arwin looked up sharply. "Are you sure?"

"Quite. And he wasn't the only one. Pastian informed me that *seven* of our prisoners died last night. He suspects poison."

"Poison? Impossible." Although Dimitri was participating in the conversation, he was completely focused on Shax, who was nuzzling the server boy against the wall. "No one is allowed access to those cells."

"*Almost* no one," Silen said. "But they do have to eat. The food of all seven victims had been laced with arceena—I checked the bowls myself."

"Arceena?" Tashara couldn't breathe for a second. Although the poison did mimic the same graying of the skin that her kills induced, closer inspection would dispel that theory, as it did not age the skin. "Are we sure?"

"Have you seen the bodies?"

"No. The corpses were carted out and burned to prevent another rat infestation."

"How convenient," Dimitri said.

The edges of Silen's nostrils flared as he stared down the table. "What are you implying?"

"That even a human nose can make out the smell of arceena, yet you maintain that seven prisoners consumed it without noticing."

"The cells were full and have been for some weeks. The smell was completely masked by the stench of those dungeons," Silen said. "I couldn't detect it myself until I took the bowls out into the hall to examine them. I questioned the servant responsible at length, but she maintained her innocence, claiming to have no idea how it happened." He scoffed. "Foolish girl."

"Silen . . ." Tashara looked up from beneath long lashes, batting them for good measure. "Have you considered that the servant may be telling the truth? There are any number of places where the poison could've been added."

"Incorrect." Silen used his pinky nail to pick the leftover shreds of meat from his teeth. "It could not have been the cooks, or it would've been added to all the meals. The servant plated the food and chose her victims. She was the only one who could've done it."

"I'd like to speak with her," Tashara said. "See if she saw anything—"

"I had her executed this morning."

Tashara pushed herself upright in her chair, shocked. "Silen!"

"Don't look at me that way, temptress. I followed the law. She died for refusing to admit her crimes."

"When did we start executing people in the council house based on *wolf* law?"

"When the murder falls under wolf jurisdiction."

"And were all the victims wolves?" When Silen didn't respond, she crossed her legs, leaning back. "Exactly."

"Silen." Arwin patted one old, wrinkled hand against the table. "Just because you could not get the servant to talk doesn't mean that nobody could've. There are things we needed to know, such as if there might be another in our kitchen with plans to kill someone more valuable." He waved. "Like yourself."

Silen just stared, as if the wizard's comments were so asinine he could not comprehend them.

Arwin sighed deeply, massaging the bridge of his nose. "Perhaps next time you could inform us of your plans to execute someone *prior* to killing them."

Dimitri slammed his fist on the table. "Shax!"

Arwin jumped and swore a string of words under his breath that were so unfamiliar they could've been a spell, for all Tashara knew.

Shax had his palms flat against the wall, boxing in the glassy-eyed young man. The servant was Shax's taste, to be sure: fresh faced and inordinately pretty. The incubus lazily pulled his head up, looking half as drugged as his victim. "Oh, is my presence requested?"

Tashara turned and draped a wrist over the back of her chair. "It would be interesting to see what would happen if you fed when invited, instead of having to spell the poor lambs. I suspect you'd starve to death within a month."

"Although I'm honored that you're concerned about my health"— Shax gave the boy one chaste kiss and dropped his arms—"the use of magic only speeds up the inevitable."

Tashara rolled her eyes.

"How long has it been since *you've* eaten?" he asked.

"I'm fine, thank you."

He shoved his hands in his pockets, and his eyes shone with delight. "Oh, darling, I can see that."

"Enough!" Silen growled. "Can we get on with the meeting? If I'm forced to listen to these two anymore today, I'm going to feed them both to my pack."

Dimitri waved a dismissive hand. "Honestly, Silen, if you're going to threaten somebody, you have to actually follow through. I've lost count of how many times this scene has played out. It's grown tedious."

"How quickly we dissolve into madness. Are we endorsing the murders of council members now?" Arwin moved on to rubbing his temples. "I'm remembering why I busy myself outside of these walls."

Silen leaned back in his chair, staring at Shax as if he were solving a puzzle. "I could rid him of his ability to speak but leave him alive. If I was careful."

Shax sauntered over, uncharacteristically calm under Silen's assault. "You could try. *Maybe* you could stop me before I stopped you." He shrugged. "We'd have to see."

Tashara startled, looking first to Shax and then to Silen. What was happening? She swallowed Silen's insults and his ego because she was accustomed to such things—from nearly every member of this council—and because, frankly, *underestimated* was a position she didn't mind holding.

Shax never fought back because, at his core, he was a coward.

Silen stood slowly, unfolding his immense size in dramatic fashion. He placed his hands against the table, taking a moment to bend his elbows for a proper display of the width of his shoulders. His muscles flexed beneath the thin fabric of his white shirt.

Peacocks, the lot of them.

"I don't like what you're insinuating," Silen rumbled. "And I suspect you'd find it difficult to seduce me with your throat ripped open."

Dimitri, looking rather amused, settled back, interlacing his fingers, quite content to let the scene play out.

Arwin's bushy white brows furrowed. The motion caused the wrinkles to sag lower around his eyes. "Silen, sit down. You, too, Shax." He flicked a finger, and Shax's chair scooted out in anticipation of his arrival. "My bones are aching, my stomach is roiling, and had I known what I would be expected to endure this afternoon, I would've taken some soothing mint tea with lunch. As it is, I would request some now, but . . ." He looked to the servant, who was still leaning against the wall. "I fear the lad may not recover for some time."

Shax dropped smugly into his seat. Arwin looked decidedly less amused. He crooked the same finger, and the chair slid forward so fast that Shax had to scramble to grip the arms.

"Demons and glory, Arwin!"

"My apologies. But as you can see, I've grown rather cranky without my mint tea." The wizard placed his hands over his chest and atop his beard, one after the other. "Silen." He eyed the empty chair behind the still-posturing werewolf. "If you don't mind."

Silen's red hair had fallen in front of his shoulders, framing his square jaw and tight eyes. He struggled with anything that gave over the alpha position to another. He took a moment to assert his own dominance, looking at each member around the table in turn and daring them to say a word, before he reluctantly sat.

Tashara rolled her lips, trying to hide her humor at the ridiculousness of it.

"Very good." Arwin smiled tightly. "Now, my understanding was that the purpose of this meeting was to discuss an attack on Feena. If this is indeed the direction in which we are proceeding, there are things I must attend to. I can't spend the day negotiating petty arguments."

"Thank you, Arwin, for bringing us back around." Dimitri turned fully in his chair, facing the incubus alone. "Shax, I can't tell you how . . ." He pulled in a slow breath through his nose. ". . . *pleased* I was when you volunteered to be the first in at my side. Have you sent word to your people yet?"

Shax took his time, tugging at his vest and smoothing his hair. "I was planning to do that this evening."

Dimitri leaned his elbows on the table and tented his impossibly long fingers in an innate display of deviousness. "This evening? How fortuitous."

"It was my understanding we were set to move," Silen said dryly. "My people are already on their way."

"I've received some interesting news and have decided to push the timeline back by at least a week. This will give the incubi warriors plenty of time to arrive." Dimitri leaned just a little closer toward Shax. "You do have warriors, don't you?"

He paled. "Of course."

"*Good.*" The word slid out of the vampire's curled lips overpronounced and with profound emphasis.

"You understand, of course"—Shax straightened his vest . . . again—"that the incubi are spread across the land. Gathering them will take some time."

"And yet . . . you chose to *wait.*" Dimitri unfolded slowly, holding eye contact as he relaxed back into his seat, making it abundantly clear that he never expected Shax to follow through in the first place. He then faced forward to address the rest of the table. "I sent out the spies, as we discussed. We've received a report that there is a fae army marching west of us."

"Led by whom?" Tashara asked.

"They were spotted just before they entered the Dark Forest, which is making it difficult to procure information. One of my spies was killed. The other was watching from a distance. He was able to identify Turrin without question and is fairly certain the army itself is being led by Keir. I prefer to make battle plans based on certainty, but Turrin's presence does confirm that the army is Feena's."

A shock buzzed through Tashara. Ambrose *was* missing, and Keir *was* marching.

"If Keir has left the territory with an army, it means Feena is temporarily without her usual protection."

"She is never without protection," Arwin said. "The magic in that forest is formidable and played a large part in our last defeat."

"But this time, we know how she was powering the magic, which is where you come in," Dimitri reminded him. "As well as Ambrose— if she deigns to grace us with her presence before then."

"No." Silen shook his head. "It's a trap. Why would Feena send half her army away after our Venator lived to tell us what he'd witnessed in her court? She knows we'll come for her. If Feena has sent an army marching, it's because she's trying to draw us in."

"Dimitri," Tashara said, "have you considered the possibility that Feena isn't afraid of an invasion because she knows something we don't?"

"Of course I have. And then I thought of the obvious reason behind her sending her army out."

Arwin gave Dimitri a withering look. "My old friend, while I normally enjoy your brooding dramatics, can we please just get to the point?"

Tashara's lips twitched. She looked down, tilting her chin to one side and using her hair to block her face from Dimitri until she got a hold of herself. The things Arwin could get away with saying to him were her favorite part of these meetings.

"Desperation," Dimitri announced. "That is how Rune and Grey got out alive—Feena has grown weaker since the last time we tried to take the territory."

The table was quiet.

Arwin scooted to the edge of his chair. "Is *that* what knowledge you gained from their survival?" he asked. "That Feena has inexplicably grown weaker, not that perhaps the two Venators we've introduced are far more capable than we thought them to be?"

Dimitri's sneer was perfectly executed. He lifted his chin. "Are you suggesting that two Venators, Verida, and whatever little help Omri sent were a more powerful combination than the armies we attacked with last time?"

"I've found that the suggestions of an old man are generally ignored around this table and are, therefore, wastes of breath. I was simply asking a question."

Shax spoke up. "If Keir is marching and you believe this to be the opportunity to strike, why are we waiting?"

"Because we can. Let Keir march until he is out of range and unable to respond to Feena's distress call. We will pull in our people, take the time to prepare, and then . . . when the situation is ideal . . . we'll attack."

"If I might point out the obvious . . ." Tashara took a second to adjust, recrossing her legs in the opposite direction to ensure that the forward momentum of the conversation had stopped, decreasing the likelihood that her comment would be rolled over. Silen's head swung to watch, his eyes traveling up her calf. "Given this new information, I find Ambrose's absence suspicious. Being fae herself, isn't it possible that *she* is after Feena's lands? If she received the same information as Dimitri, she could be launching her own attack as we speak." When Tashara wasn't immediately shut down, she added, "Perhaps we should send Beltran to see what he can find."

"That is an excellent suggestion," Arwin said.

Silen crossed his arms. "I concur."

"Demons and glory!" Shax held a splayed hand to his chest and looked around the room in mock horror. "Do we have a unanimous decision? Wonders never cease." He dropped his arm, looking quite pleased with himself. "Where is the miscreant, anyway? I haven't seen him in a couple of days."

Dimitri was still as stone. "The 'miscreant' is already on a mission."

"Oh?" Arwin managed to look genuinely curious—which was a better expression than the one Silen was currently wearing. "I don't recall this conversation."

"That's because we didn't have one. I made the decision to send Beltran with the Venators."

Silen's hands gripped the arms of the chair so hard Tashara heard snapping as the wood started to give way. "You. *What*?"

"You think I would send our Venators out without someone I trust reporting back to me?"

"I thought that's what Verida was for," Tashara said.

Dimitri's lip curled at the vampire's name. "She has made me question her loyalty of late. Beltran is keeping an eye on her as well, for all our sakes."

Silen stood slowly, his barrel chest heaving with building fury and his chair screeching against the floor. "You're telling me that as we prepare to go to battle against an enemy who has prevailed against us before, you've sent out one of our most valuable assets to *babysit*?"

Dimitri stood as well, meeting the challenge. "I've sent one of our most valuable assets to ensure that what could potentially be our two *greatest* assets remain loyal to the council. Did you not stop to think about what would happen if we released the Venators into this world and they went rogue? If they were to gain a sufficient amount of training before we found them?"

Shax laced his fingers behind his head, grinning as he watched. "Well, this isn't good."

"Of course I did," Silen snarled. "We would kill them, just like we killed the stray Venators that hid across this world the last time."

"Except *this* time, we have gates opening and closing outside of our control. They know how to get into our world, Silen. What if a door opens and the Venators cross back to earth, only to return with more?

Or did you stop to consider that if we sent our two Venators wandering around with no more protection than Verida, it would be only a matter of time before Zio got her hands on them? Together, we have created the potential for a disaster that may well end us all, and I fully intend to mitigate the situation in order to ensure that doesn't happen."

Silen growled. His back arched, and claws exploded from his fingertips.

Dimitri exposed his fangs in response, his eyes flooding red.

Unlike Shax—who still looked delighted—Tashara did not want a front-row seat for this particular battle. "Arwin?"

The old wizard sighed. With Silen at one end of the table and Dimitri at the other, he was positioned almost perfectly between the two. Silen slammed his hands on the table, raking his claws across the fine wood and splintering the finish. Tashara jumped.

"Shax?" Arwin asked mildly—as if they weren't moments away from disaster. "Maybe you'd like to help?"

Shax snorted. "That would be ill advised."

"We are a council," Silen raged. "Decisions are to be made together. But you, *vampire*, consistently forget that. You dare to stand here and lecture me about the Venators when it was you who sent them after Beorn's pack. A move that ended in a disaster that is still unfolding. Perhaps the time of your leadership has passed."

Tashara rubbed at her head. The testosterone was flowing for different reasons than the one she preferred, but it was all she could smell. Given their distracted state, she could've easily redirected both of their attentions. But Shax was right. Interfering was a terrible idea. At some point, she would have to release her hold, and when Silen and Dimitri realized what she'd done . . . Well, keeping residence at the council house would be out of the question for years.

Dimitri placed just his fingertips on the table, leaning forward in a more sophisticated version of Silen's pose. "Don't threaten me."

Arwin rolled his eyes to the sky and shook his head. The threats continued to volley over the table between vampire and werewolf as the wizard put his hands down and pushed to his feet.

Tashara couldn't look away.

He whispered words under his breath, then flung his arms out to the side, wrists up and palms flat. Dimitri and Silen were picked up, thrown, and suspended in midair, hanging with their feet inches off the ground, pressed against a wall of shimmering power. "That. Is. *Enough!*"

The poor serving boy finally snapped out of the aftereffects of Shax's influence. Seeing the chaos, he yelped and ran from the room.

"Curses." Arwin's shoulders rolled forward as he visually tracked the boy's escape. "There goes my tea."

Tashara covered her mouth with her hand.

Arwin's glare snapped back to his two prisoners. "As for you both . . . Beltran is gone. So be it. Dimitri, Silen is right. You cannot continue to make decisions on your own. Silen, I agree with Dimitri. The Venators need to be watched. Now, I would very much like to release the pair of you and finish this meeting with a measure of civility. But a warning: if I am forced to pull you both from your childish squabbling again, it will be *far* less gentle." He dropped his arms.

Dimitri and Silen hit the floor.

Arwin brushed at his robes with quick, sharp strokes. "My knees are getting old, a concept that neither of you will ever understand, so I urge you both to take note when I say"—he eased himself back into his seat, picked up his beard, and flopped it to the center of his chest—"the aching in my bones is miserable, and if I have to stand again without warrant, I will be very, *very* crabby."

21

After Rune fled the infirmary, she discovered to her dismay that Beltran and Verida were nowhere to be found.

There were still no women or children in the village other than those she'd seen in the infirmary. Some of the men were hurrying to prepare dinner, while the rest steadily worked to clear debris from around the burned-out homes. But no matter what job they were performing, they were all actively pretending she didn't exist, avoiding both eye contact and proximity.

In order to offer help, she would've had to force someone's attention by either jumping at them or chasing them down—and she was pretty sure neither of *those* actions would go over well. The thought of returning to the infirmary sent her heart racing. Rune had never done well with sick people—or old people, for that matter. She didn't know what to say or do, and the sight of either made her inexplicably uncomfortable—as if being burned or blistered or turning eighty was catching.

Alone and completely useless, Rune found a small section of grass that had survived the blaze and plopped down to wait. Thankfully, it wasn't long before Grey, accompanied by Samson, emerged from between the infirmary and the house next to it. They were in the middle of a conversation and looked comfortable with each other, which was odd given how suspicious Samson had been only hours earlier.

Rune went to push herself up, intending to follow Grey, but then, deciding that maybe she shouldn't interrupt whatever was happening, lowered herself back down. Although . . . She rethought the second decision, wondering how bad it looked that she was out here doing nothing, and got one foot back beneath her. Then rethought *that* decision.

A shadow fell over her. Rune looked straight up into Beltran's lopsided grin.

He put his hands on his hips, giving her a once-over. "Were you planning on making a decision at some point?"

She stayed there for a moment, half-up and half-down, before begrudgingly surrendering to her lack of current options and dropping cross legged to the grass. "Go away."

Beltran sat next to her. "You think I'm so easily dissuaded? I'm offended."

She was still angry over what he'd done—dropping the bomb about her nixie bubble without even talking to her about it. She glared, trying to drill her current feelings through his stubborn, shape-shifting skull.

His smile only grew larger.

Irritated, Rune reached for a flat oval rock. She watched Grey and Samson, who were laughing as they walked like they'd known each other for years, while she flipped the stone over, around, and under her knuckles.

"I had no idea your fingers were so . . . nimble."

She would've been annoyed with anything he'd said, but there was an innuendo in his tone that particularly set her off. Rune adjusted her hold, twisted, aimed just over the top of Beltran's head, and threw it as hard as she could. He yelped and ducked. The rock snapped against the blackened wood of a cabin wall and fell. Charcoal and ash fluttered down behind it.

Beltran sat up like an ostrich withdrawing his head from a hole, quite surprised to find it still attached to its body. "Well, then." He cleared his throat. "Was that a statement to my presence? Or something else?"

She pointed a finger. "I'm *so* mad at you right now."

"I know."

It was absolutely the truth. She *was* furious at him, but . . . that wasn't what had her on edge at the moment. She dropped her arm and pulled her knees to her chest. "I had to leave the infirmary. I couldn't handle it."

"Ah, I see."

"Why am I so useless?"

"We're all useless from time to time, love."

She looked at him, incredulous. "*That's* your pep talk?" She snorted, shaking her head. "Fantastic. I feel so much better, thanks."

"Even I can't escape that truth today. It's almost sundown."

Rune blinked at the abrupt change in topic. "*And?*"

"And I'm sitting here as the light vanishes, utterly useless and counting on Grey to make this all work. The humans are going to have to make a choice: send us on our way, or bring the women and children back from wherever they've hidden them. It's not safe in the forest at night, especially after recent events."

"What do you think they'll do?"

"Well." Beltran shifted positions, groaning as he lifted his arms to stretch out his back. "I've moved in this close, and nobody has come at me with weapons yet. That's a good sign. And Grey is playing his part masterfully."

In the center of the gathering area, a fire was already burning. Samson had supplied Grey with a bucket and brush, and he was bent over, scrubbing at the back of his neck.

"Grey's not playing," Rune said. "This is just who he is."

"You're right." Beltran didn't take his eyes off him, intently watching every move he made. "As much as I hate to admit it, it's impressive."

Rune placed her palms on the ground and pushed up, twisting so that she faced Beltran. "Let me see if I'm following. After Grey killed Cashel, took out a dragon's eye—"

"I did help with that."

"—and survived Feena, *this* is what gets to you? Him being kind?"

"It impresses me a hell of a lot more than running off half-cocked into every disastrous situation he can find." Beltran finally tore his eyes from Grey, locking his gaze with hers instead. "Have you ever rescued prisoners of war?"

"Uh . . . no."

He leaned back on his hands and crossed his legs at the ankle. "When you rescue people who have been severely mistreated for long periods of time, you can almost always count on one thing. Although they'll be grateful for release, they aren't the same beings that they were when they went in. In order to survive, they develop both scars and coping mechanisms. Upon release, the things that helped them survive change them. Some become depressed or fearful. Others lose themselves to bitterness or the need for revenge. Many close themselves off and become lost in their resentment.

"But . . ." Beltran lifted his chin like one would raise a finger. "There's usually at least one in the group who's different. They live through the same atrocities as the rest, but they come out better. Sometimes kinder, more loving. Maybe more resilient." His intensity faded, and his voice dropped to a murmur as he wandered off into reminiscing. "For so many years, I noticed it, but I couldn't understand it." He jerked his head. "Look at him, Rune."

In front of the fire, Samson had brought several men over to introduce them to Grey, who smiled broadly and shook each of their hands. But Rune didn't think that's what Beltran wanted her to see. What was most noticeable was Grey's genuineness, which shone even brighter than his Venator marks.

"The answer to my question was so simple, I couldn't see it." Beltran's smile was carved in bitterness. "It's a choice. Simple as that. One I don't think I'm capable of making."

While Grey and Samson moved from person to person, the sun had dropped so low that the light was now filtering through the trees.

"What are they doing?" Beltran muttered. "We're out of time."

Rune glanced at him. The sun had moved since last she'd looked, and he was now backlit with so much brilliance that it had turned the individual strands of his hair into a golden halo.

He was a vision.

Anger forgotten, Rune was swept away with the desire to kiss him.

"Rune?"

She startled, realizing she'd been staring so obsessively that she hadn't even realized he'd been looking back at her. Embarrassed, she reached for the only thing she had.

"*Why?*" she demanded.

He leaned away, frowning in confusion. "Why . . . what?"

She jutted her wrist out, waving it in front of his nose.

"Oh, are we doing this now?" He placed a finger on the bones of her wrist and gently pushed it away. "I was truthful when you asked me the first time. You can't withhold something of that magnitude on a mission like this. Grey and Verida had to know."

"So you've withheld nothing that might make a difference on this mission?"

Beltran thought about it. "I don't know."

"You don't know?" She leaned over her knees, incredulous. "The man with *aaaall* the answers doesn't know if he's withheld information."

"I'm much older than you, Rune. Much, much, *much—*"

"I get it."

"I've held back a lot of things from a lot of people, for my protection and theirs. I can't possibly know what will or won't affect us until the situation presents itself. I know you don't understand, but—"

"No. I think I understand perfectly. It would be exactly like how I *might* get a nixie call while rescuing Tate." She tilted her head to one side. "Or I might not."

Beltran's grin was slow in coming. "I have nothing to say in argument. Masterfully done. Do tell. Did you walk me into that? Or did you get lucky?"

Rune shrugged. "You'll just have to guess."

From across the clearing, Grey and Samson were heading in their direction.

"Ahhh," Beltran said brightly. "Finally. The question about where we're staying tonight is about to be answered. On your feet." He got up, brushing the grass from his hands. "Let's not make a worse impression than the one Verida opened with."

"Not a high bar," she mumbled.

Rune's ears were burning at the prospect of facing Samson. She'd had to walk right by him on the way out of the infirmary. He'd watched her shame-filled steps and tracked her progress, turning as she went like a clock-wound toy soldier.

Samson stopped at Grey's side, several feet from Rune and Beltran. He crossed his arms. "Where's the vampire?"

"Not far, I'm sure." Beltran put a hand to the side of his mouth and shouted. "Verida!"

Rune rolled her eyes, but a moment later, her and Grey's markings lit red, and Verida stepped out from behind one of the charred homes near them.

"You called?" She strolled up between Beltran and Rune. "Loudly."

"We would be honored if the representatives from the council would stay with us this evening to rest before you continue on your journey," Samson said. "I'll retrieve the others, and then we'll eat. I'm afraid the food will not be befitting emissaries, but it's all we have left."

"We are grateful for whatever you have to offer," Grey said warmly. "Truly."

"He's been gone a while," Rune said.

Grey didn't think it'd been all that long since Samson had left to retrieve the rest of the villagers, but it did feel like forever. He'd requested that Grey and Rune wait near the forest to meet them while Verida and Beltran stayed out of view. Samson felt that a slow introduction would be better, and Grey agreed.

"Do you think something happened?" she asked.

The anxiety in her voice made him look away from the tree line. Rune's markings were red like his own, but her face had lost three shades of color, and she was wringing her hands. "Hey," he said. "It's going to be OK."

"What if I say something stupid and make it worse? Or what if I panic and run, and they tell us to leave, and Verida freaks out, and—"

"Rune." Grey placed a hand on her arm. "You can do this."

She didn't even look at him. "Maybe I should wait with Verida and Beltran. You're better at this stuff . . . Samson needs you, not me." As if that was that and the decision had been made, she started to turn, heading back toward the fire.

"Woah, woah, woah." He stepped in front of her. "What are you doing? We're a team."

"Exactly. We are. Do you know what teams do with players who suck? They *bench* them. Which is exactly what I intend to . . ."

Grey's lips were trembling.

"It's not funny!" Rune punched him in the arm and tried to cut around.

"Hey!" Grey took a giant step to the side, blocking her and holding out his hands. "Just listen. I'll make you a deal. You stay and do your best. If it gets to be too much and you need to walk away, you fake a stomach ache, and I'll . . . I'll bench you."

She cocked an eyebrow.

"Not enough? All right, how about a seizure?" Desperate to lighten the mood, he leaned closer and whispered, "Hemorrhoids?"

A single burst of laughter shot out of Rune's nose. "Hemorrhoids?"

He shrugged and winked.

"Please explain how you use *hemorrhoids* to get out of uncomfortable situations?"

"Well, there would have to be some awkward readjusting, maybe several reaches back . . . to, uh, you know."

"Mmmm, so you're an *experienced* hemorrhoid faker."

"Hasn't failed me yet."

The first sounds of children crying jerked Grey from the moment, and he stood taller. "They're here."

He faced the trees, standing side by side with Rune. There was a flash of movement.

Rune nudged his shoulder with hers. "Thank you," she whispered. "I needed that."

"Anytime."

Samson stepped into the clearing, leading a group of women, children, and the elderly. The youngest among them sobbed and clung to their mothers' skirts. When the group caught sight of the Venators, their walking slowed to a shuffle. Samson urged them forward, but every time someone picked up a foot, their legs lifted so slowly that it looked like they'd been fitted with weighted shoes.

Grey supposed that in a way, they had been—fear was a heavy thing.

Samson waved encouragingly, but his enthusiasm couldn't override what their eyes were seeing: danger. The closer they grew to Rune and Grey, the slower they walked. Samson's gestures lost energy and dropped into exasperation. Grey smiled, hoping to put the people at ease, but their terror showed in their flared nostrils and the lines between their brows, in the way their feet moved forward while their bodies angled back. They were far beyond soothing.

When the Venators and the villagers were twenty feet apart, the humans froze in place, refusing to take another step, while the wails of their children grew louder. There were grunts and grumbles as Samson pushed his way through the group, taking a little boy from a woman's hip as he did. She shouted his name in protest.

Samson whispered to the boy as they walked. The little boy's head snapped to the side, and he looked at Grey, his eyes growing wider than should've been possible. He then wrapped his thin arms around Samson's neck and buried his head.

When Samson stopped in front of Grey and Rune, he ran his hand over the little boy's sandy hair. "They're nervous."

"Understandably," Grey said. "They have no reason not to be."

"This is my son. Thomas." He angled his chin down, pressing it against the top of Thomas's head. "Can you say hello?"

The boy whimpered and pressed his face deeper into his father's neck.

"Come on." Samson peeled the boy away but had to hold him at arm's length to prevent him from leeching back on. "Thomas, it'll be all—" Samson set him on the ground, and the boy promptly threw himself against his father's leg. He sighed. "Son. Would I ever let anything hurt you?"

The boy shook his head.

"Well, then? Trust me." He patted his son's small back. "I told Grey that I knew someone who could give him information about the werewolves. I don't suppose you know who that could be?"

Thomas shook his head furiously this time, flinging his fine hair back and forth.

Samson's smile was slight but enough to alter the line of his beard across his upper lip. "Very well. Do you think you might remember after dinner? When your mother and I are both there?"

Thomas didn't agree, but he didn't shake his head no either.

Samson ruffled his son's hair. "That's my boy."

Hoping it might help Thomas relax, Grey crouched down to his level. "It's nice to meet you. I'm Grey."

Thomas twisted his head slowly, rubbing his face against his father's pants until one light blue eye was visible.

Grey smiled warmly and motioned. "This is Rune. She and I grew up together, somewhere very far away. Before we knew . . ." He looked down at his glowing arms. ". . . well, about these."

The boy opened his body outward, keeping one hand against his father's leg for security. "Why are they so bright?"

It wouldn't have mattered what the boy asked; just the fact that he had spoken made Grey's heart soar. "That is an excellent question, but

I have no idea. They're a little annoying. How am I supposed to fall asleep like this?"

Thomas didn't need to know that he could turn them off at will or that they turned off on their own when he fell asleep. The slight deception was worth the payoff. The corner of the boy's lips turned up in a smile.

And then, without warning, Grey was ripped from the moment.

He felt the same evening breeze on his skin, but the landscape had changed. Around him, a different village stood, wrapped in the downy white blankets of deep winter. He squinted. The reflection of sun off snow was too bright, but it was more than that. The entirety of the scene, from the wooden shingles to the emerald-green tree boughs, was too bright. Overexaggerated. Like a dream, or a memory.

But this wasn't his memory. It was Feena's.

A little boy ran for a well, his hair the same sandy blond as Thomas's, his pants made from the same black cloth. He may have been a year older—it was hard to tell. This little boy leaned over the stone lip of the well and, holding the rope in one hand, reached for the bucket that hung in the center with the other.

Grey squeezed his eyes closed, but her memory only focused, dragging him in tighter—like a close-up on a movie screen. Pale-yellow hands reached in from out of frame and grabbed the boy around the waist, jerking him away. Abandoned, the bucket fell. The rope snapped and whipped through the pulley, vanishing into the black depths below.

Still balanced on the balls of his feet, Grey wobbled. He slammed both hands to the ground to steady himself.

"Grey?" Rune said.

"I'm fine." He opened his eyes, grateful to see the he'd returned to the present, and turned on a brilliant smile. "I'm fine. I just didn't sleep well last night."

Thomas had edged back toward his father.

"Nights aren't my favorite. I've been having a lot of nightmares." He shrugged. "I bet you don't get nightmares, do you, Thomas? Not with your dad keeping watch."

Thomas bit his lip, then nodded his head.

Grey faked a gasp. "You *do* get nightmares?"

Thomas nodded again.

He plopped down to sitting as if it were the most shocking thing he'd heard all day. "What do *you* do after you have a nightmare?"

Thomas backed up again.

"You don't have to tell me. It's OK. I just"—he lowered his voice, speaking from one side of his mouth—"wasn't sure what to do about mine . . . and was kind of hoping you had some ideas."

Thomas looked back at his father, then inched closer, using a cautious side step and eyeballing Rune to make sure she hadn't gotten any closer.

A whimper sounded from the boy's mother, and she cried out, "Thomas!"

Samson held up his hand, trying to reassure her. "It's all right."

"When I have nightmares . . ." The little boy drew himself up, as if he were pulling courage from somewhere inside. "I get a hug."

Tears welled in Grey's eyes, and when he spoke, his voice cracked. "A hug?"

The boy looked unsure. He dug the toe of his shoe into the grass, then lunged forward, throwing his arms around Grey's neck.

Grey froze, scared any movement on his part would set off a panic. But when nobody screamed or ran to jerk the boy away from him, he slowly wrapped his arms around Thomas's tiny back. The innocence, the kindness—it was a breath of fresh air. He tucked his face into the boy's neck. "*Thank you.*"

Thomas pulled back and offered a toothy grin. He then ran straight past his father and leapt into his mother's outstretched arms.

Samson chuckled, rubbing at his beard. "That's my boy."

Grey got to his feet, brushing off his pants. "How old is he?"

"Six," Samson said. "Almost seven."

The world dropped out from beneath Grey's feet. *Six.* He stumbled backward, unable to remember how to breathe. *Six.* The trees were tilting sideways. *Six.* His legs wouldn't cooperate. He staggered to the side.

Rune rushed to brace him up. "Grey, are you all right?"

Her voice rung with a hollow distance.

Thomas was six. With his wide eyes and his innocence. His complete trust. *Six!*

Grey's mind reeled.

Current understanding collided with past misunderstandings, breaking something wide open inside of him. Enlightenment—maybe clarity—dashed in and out of focus as he thought of his own life at six, and at seven, and . . . Oh, God, he couldn't breathe.

Rune gripped his arm, squeezing hard. "Grey!"

"Yeah." He shook his head, trying to clear it. "I'm fine. I just . . . need some food. That's all."

"Sure." Rune's frown was deep, and her hand slid away. "Food."

22

Tashara's hand rested on the door as she fought what had to be done.

She'd already paced the floor of her room, thinking through the predicament from every angle, and could come up with nothing. She needed more time! But that was one thing she couldn't have. Every passing second whittled away another piece of her control.

It had become obvious that this obsession with the young Venator would lead nowhere good. In the course of just a few days, she'd stepped over her personal line—twice. But the possibility that Grey might get caught unaware in the middle of Ambrose's schemes was driving her mad.

A tremble shuddered through her. Tashara moaned. Her fingers curled into a fist against the door, and the edges of her nails scratched across the wood. It was the first wave of cravings, and it would only get worse from here. No matter how much she wanted to go to Grey, to protect him, to stand in front of him—as she'd done with the fae— she couldn't. Not this time.

She didn't know where he was to warn him, only where he would eventually be, and trying to meet Grey there would be disastrous. Her arrival at the gladiator games would coincide with the worst of the withdrawal symptoms, and the games weren't just a display of violence—they were a celebration of debauchery in all forms. She would not be strong enough to withstand the sexual energy of her surroundings, and she would be lost. Lost in desire, in her own power, her own need. If she saw Grey in that state, she would want him more than she'd ever wanted anyone.

And she would kill him.

On that matter, there was no doubt.

If Tashara wanted to ensure his safety and guarantee that her own sacrifices had not been in vain, there was only one conclusion: she needed help. And that was the problem, because help became favors, and favors became shackles that, before she knew it, would be pulled so tight that she wouldn't be able to step in any direction without being forced to do things that she'd sworn she never would.

Precious time had ticked away with her hesitation, but the answer remained the same. She slipped from her room, checking that the hallway was clear, and hurried for the stairs. The light green fabric of her dress fluttered out behind her, rippling with a movement that mimicked the roiling of her stomach.

The moment her feet hit the tiled floor of the foyer, her steps slowed. The succubain inside stirred, and her head turned of its own accord, away from where she was heading and down the hallway that led to the dungeons.

Just one, it whispered, *to take the edge off. It would be better for everybody.*

She knew all the prisoners' stories and had verified their offenses. She knew who was there because they'd upset the wrong council member . . . and who deserved to die. Even after the accident last night, there were many left in those cells who had earned the fate of having her as their executioner.

You're doing this world a favor. You're not an abomination—you're a savior.

She squeezed her eyes shut and grabbed the top scroll of the banister for strength.

Partake. Make yourself stronger.

It was the succubain talking, but merciful hell if the whispers didn't make sense. She willed her feet to move away from the detour. The tip of one soft-soled shoe slid forward.

"You look particularly lovely today."

Shax.

Tashara didn't know when he'd fallen in behind her—she'd been so consumed with the whispers of her own mind and the rumblings of the succubain that she hadn't heard a thing. But to let him know that he'd caught her unaware was to admit weakness.

She needed him distracted.

It had been years since Tashara had looked at Shax with anything besides disdain. So she took a moment to draw her hair over her shoulder—the way he liked it—before spinning to face him, oozing suggestion, from her heavily lidded gaze to the cock of her hip.

Shax, still a few stairs up, jerked to a stop, wobbling so far forward that she thought he was going to have to take another stair to regain his balance. He cleared his throat, reset, and descended the rest of the way with his usual debonair smoothness.

In order to hold on to the air she'd chosen, there was no option but to really look at him. She'd always been aware of how attractive he was—that bronzed skin, those wavy black locks, and those beautiful blue eyes; that had once been the *only* thing she'd seen. But it hadn't been long before his features became merely a velum overlay, shining and glorious while the dark reality of him lurked just beneath. Today, her vision was hopping back and forth between the surface and the depth—her need versus her disgust in a war between Tashara and the succubain.

She despised many things about Shax, but more than anything, she hated how much he enjoyed being what he was.

She slid a hand over her hip, pressing her dress tighter to her curves. "You surprised me today, standing up to Silen like that."

Shax chuckled and dropped off the last step with a flourish. "It surprised him too. Did you see his face?"

"I couldn't have missed it." She made a show of looking him up and down before murmuring, "What has gotten into you?"

"What's gotten into to me?" he mused. "I don't think you're expecting an answer to that question." He moved as close to her as he could. The toes of his shiny black shoes slipped under the hem of her dress. "But"—he ran a thumb over her bottom lip—"I think I'll tell you anyway."

No matter how much it made her skin crawl, he was testing her, and Tashara knew an opportunity when she saw one. She let her lips part, allowing him to run his thumb over the wet inside edge.

Shax huffed in appreciation and dropped his hand. "I've grown weary of being treated as if what we can do is of no consequence simply because we choose not to employ our considerable powers on the council members. Haven't you?"

She gave a delicate, noncommittal shrug. "Perhaps I like to be underestimated."

"I do not. And I've played small for too long. We both have." He smiled. "Those fools have no idea what you're capable of."

"My skills are well known."

"You succubi spend all your time downplaying your potential. Not a single member of council has ever felt the sting of succubus magic, and no one else could tell by looking at you that they were in danger of feeling it today."

There was no use denying it.

Shax's smile grew wider. "I didn't think you had it in you, Tashara. This changes a great many things."

"It changes nothing."

His gaze sparked through his thick black lashes. He wrapped his arm around her waist and pulled her up against him, stretching her limits to their breaking point. "I have more power than any of them know," he whispered. "More than you know. I am a king, Tashara."

It sounded like the raving of a mad man, but even an insane Shax would know better than to spread about his dreams of power and glory so freely.

"Why are you telling me this?"

"Because I can clearly see what *you've* been up to." He pulled her tighter, his voice dropping so low she could barely hear him despite the proximity. "After your feeding last night, I've started to wonder if you could be my queen."

"My feeding?"

"Come now." He slid his cheek against hers until his lips rested against her earlobe. "I can see what's happening. You're radiant today; I can *feel* the fullness rolling off you." He inhaled deeply. "You smell erotic. You smell like," he groaned, "a succubain."

How had she not known that an incubus could smell a succubain? How had she not known that her scent would change? Probably because succubains were not spoken of in proper circles, except to curse their weakness. Becoming a succubain was frowned upon at best and forbidden at worst. To think otherwise put the whole species at risk. Those who chose to live as succubains stayed well clear of other succubi, for their own safety, and worked hard to hide their tracks.

Shax pressed his cheek more firmly against hers. "Demons and glory, you are like the sweetest of honeys. My knees have gone weak, and that hasn't happened in a very, very long time."

Desperate to rid herself of his lips, she nestled her own against his neck. His fingers went loose in surprise, and she stepped clear of them, staying bent at the waist to let her lips linger long enough to disguise the intentions behind the action.

"Shax, if you're going to propose something, get on with it. I've been at the council house too long. The games have exhausted me."

"The games have taught me not to play my entire hand."

"Ugh!" She huffed and smoothed out her crumpled dress. "I have things to do."

"Patience. I will say this. I'm currently laying the groundwork for . . . *more*. As you know, the population of my people is small in comparison to most of our fellow council members. It has slowed preparations. But if our two species were to work together . . ." He reached out, trailing one finger lazily from the hollow of her throat toward her cleavage.

This time, her hand snapped up to catch his. "You wish to be king? And what did you have planned for me? Queen?"

"Not until today." His laugh was breathless. "Never until today, my succubain."

Tashara squeezed, rolling the knuckles of his fingers against each other. "A queen is not at the king's disposal, Shax, but by his side. You will touch me when I allow it."

The delight on his face was unexpected.

"I would have it no other way." He held her furious gaze without apology as he delicately untangled himself from her grip. Once free, he dipped his head. "Until next time, Tashara."

She felt the sting of his magic flowing out behind him as he walked across the grand entrance. For a moment, she was irritated that he'd even thought to try influencing her. But the trickle of magic wasn't for her. The double doors to the main ballroom opened, and a maid emerged, following Shax and his call down the hall.

Laying the groundwork for more . . .

She had no idea what his words meant and no time to think about it.

She hurried on toward Arwin's quarters. She'd visited the wizard there once before and hadn't had the desire to return since. Chaos and dust made her skin crawl.

Tashara knocked. Her hands twitched with deepening tremors, and she cursed Shax's name for the minutes he'd stolen. The door creaked opened, but the threshold was empty.

She poked her head through the doorframe. "Hello?"

"Come in, come in."

She stepped inside, closing the door behind her. Though she knew the voice had been Arwin's, the only visible signs of the wizard were the belongings scattered and piled around the room. Against the opposite wall, the bed was a disastrous, lumpy mound of blankets and coverlets. She couldn't help but imagine him crawling into it at night and burrowing around like an old, blind mole.

As she crossed the room, Tashara carefully placed her feet to avoid an open book, a still-wet robe, and some mushrooms that appeared to be growing between the floorboards near his bathing tub.

"Arwin, really, why won't you let the maids attend to you?"

Behind a waist-high stack of books, he slowly hinged his body up from bent over to standing. "Because I know where everything is."

"They could at least dust"—she motioned—"the . . . well, the surfaces, while leaving everything in its place."

"True, true. But I've decided that the dirt keeps me grounded, which keeps me healthy." He moved a book from one stack to another. "Which, by default, keeps me young."

"And the mushrooms?"

"Mushrooms?"

She pointed.

He squinted. "Those are new. I'll check whether they're of a useful variety. If not, perhaps I'll let the maids attend to them. Please, have a seat."

She eyed the armchairs. They were no exception to the pervasive dirt. "No, thank you. I value this dress far too much to subject it to that chair." They needed to get to the point of her visit, but she couldn't help herself. "Arwin . . . Are you implying that inhaling dirt keeps you young?"

"Not implying."

She grasped her hands in front of her and smiled. "And what of that arthritis you were complaining about?"

He chuckled as he moved to the old wingback chair nearest her. "I've always liked you, Tashara."

"I thank you for that. More than you know."

He braced his hands on the chair's arms and dropped himself into the seat. "To what do I owe the honor?"

"First, let me compliment you on your negotiation of our earlier situation. Perhaps I should arrange for Ambrose and Omri to be absent more frequently."

"I would thank you to not. Displays of power are incredibly bothersome."

"And then there's that arthritis."

"And that." He stretched his back out, groaning as he spoke. "It also irritates Dimitri."

"That's not terribly difficult." Her hands were now trembling to the point that simply holding them together wasn't going to be enough to disguise it. Gritting her teeth, she took the seat across from Arwin.

He raised a bushy white eyebrow. "Changed your mind about your dress?"

"Not at all." She brushed the dust from her hands and pressed them against the sides of her legs, hoping to hide the shaking from Arwin's view. "I simply rethought the amount of faith I hold in the staff. I'll be sending the dress for cleaning straight away."

Arwin laughed out loud. "I hear they're quite capable. Not that I would know." His eyes sharpened. "Are you here because of what happened in the dungeons?"

The wizard's directness was a frequent source of complaint, and she'd expected it. What she hadn't expected was his lack of judgment in regard to the . . . situation. He just sat there, with kind eyes, hunched in a ratty armchair and looking as if he might only be waiting for that cup of mint tea.

"Arwin, do you think I could prevent you from using magic to defend yourself?"

The old wizard jolted, which launched him into a coughing fit. "I'm sorry?" He wiped the back of his hand across his mouth. "Are you asking me if you could seduce me to the point that I wouldn't have the desire to magically defend myself?"

She swallowed. "I am."

"You came here to ask me that?"

"No."

"Ah, then I think I understand." He resituated, taking a moment to smooth out that ever-ragged beard of his. "You are a very stunning woman, Tashara, and I suppose if you chose the right moment and didn't give me a chance to get my wits about me, it would be possible."

She let the weight of the answer sink between them, knowing it wasn't necessary but feeling better in spite of it. "I didn't intend for the dungeons to happen as they did. I was coerced past my limits by a fae named Kit."

Arwin rubbed at his chin. "Kit . . . Kit. I know that name."

"From what she told me, she was quite well known for her skill with veneers."

"Ah, yes." He snapped. "That's it. Red hair. Very popular through the Underground."

That was the last remaining question Tashara had had in regard to Kit's story. "That's her. She shared some information with me last night in exchange for her death."

"Her death, you say?"

"She found my methods preferable to Ambrose's."

"Can't say I blame her. But if I may: Kit claimed that Ambrose imprisoned her?"

Trying to reveal as little information as possible, Tashara breezed over the request for clarification. "Because of several extenuating circumstances, I need to get a message to Grey. Can you help me?"

"Grey?" He shook his head. "No, I'm afraid not." Arwin laid his hands in his lap, one over the other.

He didn't have to say a word. Tashara understood. He was waiting to see whether there was any more information she was willing to share before he explored further options. She nibbled the inside of her lip, debating the wisdom of telling him exactly what she knew. If Arwin betrayed her, this all would be for nothing. On the other hand, if she couldn't get Grey the information she'd obtained, it left her in the same position.

Tashara proceeded reluctantly, telling Arwin everything Kit had shared—save the actual details of Ambrose's new face.

By the time she had finished, the old wizard was still as stone. "This is quite a predicament. You have trusted me, and I thank you." His eyes went blank—a look she rarely saw on him, regardless of the time of day or situation. When they refocused, he swung his hardened attention in her direction. "In order to move forward, I find myself needing to trust *you*."

She perked up, a smattering of hope rising over her increasing tremors. "You *can* get a message to Grey?"

"No."

The beat between the wizard's first word and his next seemed to stretch on endlessly. He was clearly still debating the wisdom of trusting her. She held her breath, aware of every tiny movement the wizard made. He pulled in a mouthful of air.

"But I can get one to Beltran."

23

Grey had been invited to sit with Samson and his family for dinner. Although Rune, Verida, and Beltran hadn't been told they weren't welcome, they hadn't been issued invitations either. Rune couldn't help but feel a little relieved.

The village had gathered around the fire, which was surrounded on four sides by freshly cut log seating, each side two logs deep. Samson and Grey sat in the center of the front row. Rune sat with Verida and Beltran on the back row, directly across the fire from Grey. Predictably, the three strangers were surrounded by empty spaces. With almost exactly enough room for those in attendance, this meant that the rest of the villagers sat snugly together, bumping elbows as they ate a dinner of roasted elk, sweet root vegetables, and coarse brown bread.

Eventually, the drums started, then the singing, followed by the dancing.

The dancers circled around the fire, in couples and alone, moving with the beat of the drum. They threw their heads back, stomped, and twirled with a freeness that Rune could only dream of. As if nothing in their world was wrong.

Beltran reached out for her plate. "Finished?"

"Hmm? Oh, yes. Thank you."

He set her plate on top of his and moved them both to the ground.

From across the fire, Grey had stood and started to make his way toward them, but he was repeatedly stopped by villagers. Between that and trying to avoid the dancers, he was making slow progress.

Beltran intently tracked him, his eyes pulled into thoughtful slits.

Rune elbowed him. "What? I know that face."

"The boy's walking straighter."

Grey's posture *was* different. It wasn't the rolled shoulders of his past, and it wasn't the stiffness of the Venator persona he'd been testing out. She'd hated that one immediately; it had been cold and hard and not at all him. Tonight, he walked with confidence and ease.

She searched her memory and couldn't come up with a single instance when she'd ever seen him look like that, even before his trench coat days. He'd always been the strange, sad kid. The one who hovered alone at the edges of the playground and wouldn't look up at you when you asked to borrow a red crayon. Since becoming a Venator, he'd had moments of confidence. But never, ever ease.

And she wasn't the only one watching.

As Grey passed, women's heads turned, and the looks they gave him were most certainly not fear. Rune covered her mouth with the back of her hand.

"What's so funny?" Beltran asked.

"He is completely oblivious to the way they're looking at him."

"Are you referring to the rapt attention? Or complete lust?"

"The lust, definitely." She giggled. "The best part is, he wouldn't believe me if I told him."

Beltran seemed genuinely puzzled. "Why not? He's attractive."

"Extremely attractive." Verida leaned back on her hands. "You should see him with his shirt off."

Rune nodded. "And he has nooo idea."

"Poor sap," Beltran said.

"Oh, I don't know," Verida purred. Her eyes undressed Grey from a distance. "It's part of what makes him so utterly delicious."

"Ew!" Rune recoiled. "Don't ever call him delicious again. Why . . . ? What . . . ?" She sputtered. "Seriously, I can't unhear that!"

Verida rolled her head to lean it on her shoulder, batting her eyes at Rune. "Jealous?"

"Not exactly. But hearing you refer to Grey as if he were a tasty snack is weird." She shuddered. "So, *so* weird."

When Grey finally arrived, Verida was still aggressively eying him. His weight shifted from one foot to the other. "*What?*"

Verida smirked and shrugged. "Nothing. Do you have some answers for me?"

He crouched down by Rune's feet, angling his upper half slightly away from Verida as though she might bite him at any second. Which . . . by the way she was looking at him . . . Rune wouldn't have been shocked if she did.

"Beorn's pack is splitting up." Grey's voice was just loud enough to be heard over the music. "Some are going on to the Blues like we thought, but the rest are headed to meet with Ransan."

Beltran put an elbow on a knee, addressing Verida over Rune's lap. "Beorn's looking to make alliances."

"Samson thought the same thing," Grey said.

Verida stared intently at the base of the log in front of them, drumming her fingers against her thigh. "I don't like this. We're too close to Ransan's territory. If Beorn gets word of where we are, we could easily end up caught with Beorn's pack in front of us and Ransan's behind."

A couple spun in front of them, almost stepping on Grey.

"Agreed." Beltran watched them until they were out of range. "We'll need to distance ourselves from this place first thing in the morning, but we also have to know where the packs' alliances lie. I can fly out on a reconnaissance mission tomorrow while you three move out of reach. Once you're far enough away and I've heard everything I need to, I'll deliver that damned summons the council sent with us."

"About leaving . . ." Grey cleared his throat. "There was one more thing."

"Only one?" Beltran clicked his tongue. "How disappointing."

"After the attack, Beorn shifted into a man and announced that the Venators were responsible for the attack on the village."

"*What?* But we . . ." Rune stopped, thinking back to how they'd been received. "That explains a lot."

"Beorn promised that the human who provides *any* werewolf with information about the Venators' whereabouts will be richly rewarded."

Verida started to rise from her seat, already searching the crowd for danger.

Grey hurried forward. "Verida! The members of this village are all accounted for." He waited for her to sit back down. "But—"

Rune groaned. "Why does there always have to be a *but*?"

"—they did catch a man trying to sneak off into the woods. They've already secured him for the night."

Beltran sighed. "And just like that, it's time to go."

"Maybe." Verida was drumming her fingers again. "Do you trust him?"

Grey frowned. "Who?"

"Samson. Do you believe everything he's told you?"

"Absolutely."

She leaned forward, resting one arm across her legs and pointing with the other hand like a general giving orders. "I need you to convince Samson to allow me to guard the prisoner."

They stared at each other, Grey in disbelief at the request and Verida in refusal to budge. He finally broke away and looked over his shoulder to where Samson was intently watching the exchange. "Umm . . . I don't think—"

"Listen: aside from the three of you, I have the best shot of making sure nobody gets in or out of wherever they're holding the traitor. If Samson won't agree to the terms, we have to go. *Now*. But if he does, I'll make sure the traitor stays put." She stretched a little farther to tap Grey on the shoulder. "While *you* spend the rest of the evening doing what you do best."

Grey was leaning farther away from her now, and he cut his eyes to Rune—as if she had the answer to what Verida wanted him to do.

She did. Rune grinned and took a second to mimic Verida's posture. "Make sure they *all* love you."

Verida rolled her eyes at Rune's mockery and sat back, leaning on her hands. "Exactly. I can make sure that the dissenter doesn't leave before we do, but Grey, I need you to ensure that the rest of the village doesn't *want* to."

Grey started to object, probably to deflect or downplay his ability to do what they'd asked, but then, to Rune's surprise, he closed his mouth. "All right. I'll see what I can do."

Grey had worked his magic, and Verida had left for guard duty. Which left Rune alone with Beltran again. Samson's wife—at least, Rune assumed she was his wife; they'd never been properly introduced— had cautiously approached and offered them both some tea. Though Beltran politely declined, the fire was shrinking, and the night's chill had edged farther and farther in. Rune readily accepted the offer and sat with her hands wrapped tightly around the hot tin mug, sipping at the faint taste of mint to keep warmth flowing through her.

At least half of the villagers had already turned in for the night. Grey was moving slowly and methodically through the rest—sitting with them, talking to them, holding their hands, offering his shoulder for their tears. More than once, Rune thought she should join in, but each time, her heart seized with panic, and she found herself frozen to the spot.

Beltran cleared his throat. "Are you going to tell me what's wrong?"

Rune rolled her neck, trying to loosen up her shoulders. "Who said anything was wrong?"

"Well," he drawled. "You."

She cocked an eyebrow.

"Every few minutes, your hands get tighter around that mug. You stop breathing. And then you sigh as if your heart is breaking." He put a hand over his chest to illustrate. "I mean, really, love, you aren't even requiring me to put in effort tonight."

"I'm still furious."

Beltran chuckled. "Not nearly as much as you're trying to be."

"I'm going to punch you in the face."

"I'm amenable to that suggestion . . . Wait, did Tate teach you to throw a proper punch? I can take the Venator strength, but if your form is correct, I might need to rethink—"

"Shut. Up."

"As my lady requests."

His eyes were twinkling in the way they always did when he found himself quite clever. Unfortunately, she'd come to realize it was also the look that guaranteed he would not stop pressing a point until he got what he wanted.

Frankly, she was exhausted and not in the mood for a full-court press. She rolled her eyes. "Fine, I'll talk."

"Only if you want to, love. I don't want to be accused of coercing you."

She smacked her mug of tea down next to her. It sloshed over the side, splashing across his hand and wrist and soaking into the wood. "I really am going to punch you in the face, and I'm not telling you whether or not Tate taught me how to break your nose."

He picked up his hand and shook most of the tea off, wiping the rest on his pants. "You're very attractive when annoyed. Have I told you that?"

"Is that your version of a compliment? Because it sucks."

"Apologies."

"You can't apologize while smirking!" She went for her tea but stopped. "Is *that* why you work so hard to piss me off? Cause I'm"—she made air quotes—"'attractive' when angry?"

"From time to time."

She scoffed. "You're like a ten-year-old boy."

"Not all the time! Occasionally, it just happens. But the real question is: Are you going to continue to sit here and banter with me all night while blaming the fact that we aren't talking on me, or do you want to just tell me what's wrong? By all means, I can continue if it's helping—"

"Fine!" She slouched forward, resting her chin on her fist. "Just stop talking."

Right in her sight line, Grey was helping an old man to his feet. Once steady, the man took a moment, smiled, and patted Grey's cheek like he was his long-lost grandson.

"Do you remember what happened at the council house? When the humans saw me?"

"Ooh, vaguely. No one could stand still because they all wanted to run screaming? Mothers hid their children from you? Flinched when you talked? That sort of thing?"

"Yes! And now look at this. They're literally crying on his shoulder."

"Rune." He paused long enough that she twisted her neck to look at him. "I've been watching you watch Grey all day. And I'm going to be honest, I'm confused as to why you're still surprised."

"I'm not surprised. I'm just . . ." Rune shivered and closed her eyes. "What is so different about him?"

The unspoken question, the one she couldn't verbalize, was, of course, *What's wrong with me?*

When the answer to her question didn't come, she opened her eyes. Beltran was still and watching Grey. Quietly, she studied Beltran's expression, his shoulders, everything about his demeanor. Her heart started to ache again—the way it had in the sprite's territory. Maybe it was her exhaustion, but she was having a harder and harder time remembering why she shouldn't feel any of the things she was feeling.

"An eternal truth that you would do well to learn is that hate and fear will always shine a light on differences rather than similarities. It's difficult to see redeeming qualities within those you fear or think of as your enemy." Beltran spared her a quick, sympathetic glance. "That's why they react the way they do to you. Because Grey offers them something you can't."

She couldn't decide whether she should be hurt. She was human . . . at least, she thought she still was. "I don't understand."

"Grey's past is a mystery to me—a fact that's gotten under my skin a bit, if I'm being honest." He winked. "But I'll tell you what I know. His hurt is . . . darker than what I see in you, and it oozes from him. They see it, and I know you've seen it."

Guilt rained down. "Yes, but I should've noticed it sooner."

"It's easier to trust someone who understands. I suspect that once the humans were able to look past Grey's Venator markings, they found something they didn't expect: themselves. You're still foreign to them. Not just your species, but your . . ." He struggled for the right word. "Innocence, maybe?"

Rune couldn't say exactly why that rubbed her the wrong way. Maybe because, in her mind, his word choice read the same as *naivety*, which made her feel twelve.

She snapped up straight and blurted, "Innocence!"

"Love, it's just us. Let's be honest for a moment." He waved an arm, indicating all those who still remained. "I want you to look at these people—really look. Think about where they live. This threat that destroyed their homes and killed their friends and family, it didn't come out of nowhere. It's hung over their heads for years. They've lived knowing that any day, the werewolves could storm in here and wipe them out. And if not the werewolves, the vampires, or a fae that someone had inadvertently wronged. They know fear, pain, and death. Before you came here, what did you know of any of that?"

Rune wanted to argue that she knew fear and pain, and that it had hurt! Things had been hard for her too. But the truth was that she knew more about guilt and shame, perfectionism and obligations than anything Beltran had listed off.

"The fear I lived with was different," she admitted. "And before I walked through that gate, I'd never feared for my life." She frowned. "Do you think . . . Grey?"

"I don't know. Maybe. All I know for certain is that the life he's lived was very different from yours."

"How?" she demanded. "How could you possibly know that?"

"Life leaves marks. They aren't visible at first, but they reveal themselves in situations." He nodded toward Grey. "Look at him. He's able to empathize with these people because he understands them. You feel sad. You recognize that they're in pain. But you don't understand.

"Rune." He reached over and tucked a piece of hair behind her ear. The feel of his fingers against the thin skin on her neck sent a tremor down her spine. "You're fearful and stuck on this log because you have no idea what to say."

Her vision blurred with unexpected tears.

"You don't need to feel bad for not suffering enough. You and Grey are a team, one I suspect was carefully chosen. You will do what you do best, and Grey will do the same."

She turned away, wiping at her face with her arm. "Sometimes I hate your mind-reading skills."

He reached around and put a finger under her chin, gently urging her to look at him. She yielded easily. Their eyes met, and with his finger still under her jaw, he leaned forward, whispering, "Sometimes I hate that I don't actually *have* mind-reading skills."

Electricity crackled between them.

Rune's breath audibly caught, and Beltran's hand dropped like a rock, breaking the moment—just like so many that he'd broken before.

"No," he said brightly, crossing one leg over the other. "I take it back. Where's the fun in mind reading? No challenge at all. Although, I would very much like to see your world. I'm growing desperately curious."

Rune swallowed down the bite of rejection, made palatable only by the clear signs that her feelings were reciprocated. "You would hate earth."

"Why?"

She picked up her tea and took a sip, smiling over her mug. "It would be no challenge at all. You'd be bored out of your mind. There aren't even any weird creatures. Just humans everywhere."

"Weird creatures? I'm certain I should be offended."

"You'd have to get a job as an accountant or something."

"What is that?" He pressed his shoulder against hers, nudging her. "Would I get to participate in clandestine missions?"

"Close, but better. You would sit at a desk all day and painstakingly add numbers together."

"Numbers!" Beltran recoiled. "At a desk? That sounds horrible."

She laughed.

"Is that what you would've done if you'd stayed on your side?"

"No, I'm terrible with math. To be honest . . ." The answer was personal and something she'd only really hinted at to Grey. She held the truth about her family close out of shame and familial responsibility.

"I probably would've done whatever my mother pushed me to do. And hated it."

"*Your mother.*" Beltran repeated the words with reverence. "Saints, I didn't even think about your parents. Do you miss them?"

"Sometimes. Our relationship was . . ." Strained? Horrible? Guilt inducing? ". . . difficult at times. I do worry about what they must be going through. Ryker and I just vanished. They don't even know whether we're dead or alive."

"I'm sorry."

"Yeah." She took another sip of her lukewarm tea. "Me too."

"Thomas!"

Grey had just finished telling two women goodnight when he heard the shout. His head popped up in worry that something had happened. Thomas was running toward him, a huge grin plastered on his face, hauling another little boy by the hand.

"Thomas!" His mother, Lily, gave up chasing him and put her hands on her hips. "It's time for bed!"

"I just have to say goodnight to Grey," Thomas yelled without looking back, too focused on dragging his friend around the edge of the campfire.

"The Venator needs his rest, too, young man."

"I know, Mama, but I promised!" Thomas skidded breathlessly to a stop in front of Grey. The other little boy, suddenly finding himself out in the open and face to face with a Venator, edged behind Thomas, nervously peeking around his shoulder.

"This is Nicholas," Thomas said, puffing out his chest. "He wanted to see your arms."

Grey smirked. "He did, did he?"

Nicolas shrunk further behind Thomas.

"He's still nervous." Thomas rolled his eyes, as if the other boy were being absurd. Which was funny, given that it had been only hours since Samson had had to peel him off his shoulder to get him to even look at Grey. "I *told* him there was nothing to be afraid of."

Grey stifled a laugh. "Nicholas. That's a good, strong name. I like it. Way better than mine." He angled his body so he could address Nicholas around Thomas's shoulder. "Mine's a color. What if your mother had named you Green? Or Pink?"

Nicholas's face brightened.

"Come on." Grey jerked his head and held out his arms. "Your mothers are going to start panicking if you don't get to bed soon."

Nicholas inched out from behind his friend, staring at the Venator markings in wonder.

"How old are you?" Grey asked.

"Uh, um . . . uh—"

"He's six," Thomas answered. "Same as me. Go on, Nicholas." He put his hand behind the boy's shoulder and pushed. "Just touch his arm. It doesn't hurt."

Nicholas bit his lip, and his face scrunched up in apprehension. The boy inched forward, looking like he was psyching himself up to put a fist into the fire. His pointer finger connected with the thickest section of a bright-red swirl on Grey's forearm. When nothing happened, he relaxed and smiled, first at Thomas, then at the markings, and finally up at Grey.

All he could see were the boy's fingers. They were so small. *He* was so small. Innocent and almost incapable of fending for himself. When Grey smiled back, it was forced, and the joy that had been present in the interaction shattered painfully against his skin.

He watched the two boys giggle about his Venator markings through foggy lenses tinted a lifetime ago. Grey had been six once too.

That was the year his mother remarried. Six had been the beginning for him—and the end.

As he stared at these two little boys living amongst the horrors of Eon, he couldn't imagine hurting them. And if anyone else hurt them in *any* way, he couldn't comprehend setting one ounce of blame on their tiny little shoulders. But that was where he'd placed his. His blame, his guilt, all heaped on shoulders that size, buried inside eyes that had once been open and full of wonder, shaken down to fit into a child's understanding of how life worked.

It was that placement that had etched a very specific belief across Grey's mental landscape for years: *It was all my fault.*

The declaration made sense. It had always made sense, and he'd never thought to question it. In the years that followed their creation, the words had become solid and real and completely engrained. But now, looking at these two innocent faces, watching them giggle mere days after their lives had been contaminated by the evil around them, his belief began to erode. Like a line in the sand trying to stand against the tide.

In that moment, six-year-old Grey's sense of responsibility imploded.

Thomas and Nicholas were standing firmly in the way of his flawed logic, and it *didn't* make sense anymore. Thirteen—almost fourteen—years ago, Grey's maturity and experiences had been so limited that his own culpability in those acts could not possibly stand.

The sudden clarity should've been beautiful.

It wasn't.

Grey was confused. Even as he considered the possibility of setting aside years of guilt, parts of him resisted, poking back with sharp jabs. His mouth went bone dry as this new realization ripped apart the core truth that he'd stacked the rest of his belief system on.

And he was lost.

He wanted to run and sink. Scream and cry. Punch his fist through a wall and curl up in a ball. Panic and contradictions seized him, eddies of emotions swirling and breaking against the one thing he'd always held as an irrefutable fact:

It was all my fault.

"Thomas!" Lily shouted again. "That's enough. It's time for bed. Right now."

Grey startled.

The movement scared Nicholas, who yanked his hand away.

He forced another smile to cover his current systematic collapse. "You better go. I'll see you in the morning, OK?"

As the two ran off, Grey kept his head down, worried his reignited darkness would leak out like acid tears and burn everything and everybody they touched.

"Such sweet boys," an older woman nearby said.

"Yes." The syllable came out on a croak.

"Are you all right?"

"Yes."

"Are you sure?"

He nodded, still looking at the ground. "I'm fine. Nicholas reminds me of someone I knew. A long time ago."

It wasn't until the last member of the village had retired for bed that Grey finally wandered over to where Beltran and Rune had been waiting. Despite his successes today, the boy looked despondent.

"What's the matter?" Rune asked.

Grey tried to lift his head but only made it as far as staring at her boots. "You told me to give you time," he mumbled. "And I have."

It took longer than it should've for her to understand what Grey was asking, but Beltran knew the moment she did, because she shriveled in on herself.

"Yeah, you're, uh . . ." She swallowed, then inched her way up to standing as if she'd just been asked to appear before an execution committee. "You're right. We, uh . . . I guess we should probably talk."

Although they were facing each other, Grey was twisted a little to the right while Rune had positioned herself a bit to the left. The picture was pitiful; they both looked as if they were waiting for death itself to make the final approach. He would've laughed if the mood hadn't been so somber.

Out of mercy alone, Beltran slapped his hands on his thighs and stood. "As fun as this is, I think I'll leave you two alone to discuss recent events." On his way by, he patted Grey on the shoulder. "Great job today."

"Thanks."

Beltran was dying to know how this conversation was going to go, and every step he moved away from it made him question his commitment to the choice. He shoved his hands in his pockets, whistling pleasantly and pondering the conundrum as he strolled away.

"Wait. Beltran!"

He smiled but kept walking, forcing Rune to grab his arm and pull him to a stop.

"Wait!"

He looked down at her. "Yes, love?"

She licked her lips, backed up a step, rested her hands on her hips—her nervousness was adorably comical—then dropped her arms straight. "I wanted to ask you to promise me something."

"Go ahead."

"Don't . . . I mean . . . Could you not . . . ?" She huffed and started again. "Please promise me you won't follow us."

That was the exact request he'd been expecting from the moment she called his name. But seeing how uncomfortable she was in asking it sent immediate irritation spearing straight through his gut. "Why? Up to nefarious activities?"

Her eyes went wide. "Are you serious?"

He shrugged.

"I can't believe that you would . . . You know what?" She took a deep breath in. "That's none of your business."

"I hate that saying—it's antiquated and rarely applicable."

"All I'm asking is that you have a little respect for Grey and me and give us the privacy to have a conversation"—she pointed a finger—"that *you* initiated, by the way."

"I hadn't forgotten."

"Without worrying whether or not you're listening from a tree."

"There's something you should know about me, love. I'm not great with promises." He smirked. "I thought Verida would've made that abundantly clear."

The last jab had the desired effect, but as Rune's face twisted in anger, he wasn't exactly sure why he'd wanted to land it in the first place.

"Fine." She turned sharply and stormed away, adding a final flippant remark with the exit: "Do what you want."

He usually did, and he was a second away from saying so when she stopped. She'd only made it three angry steps, but even with her back to him, he could see the internal struggle. Her body swayed a little, forward and back again, as if making the decision a second time. Stay? Or Go?

Beltran waited, posturing for a fight.

When she looked back, her anger had given way to something softer. "I changed my mind. I'm not going to ask you to promise. I'm just letting you know that Grey and I would really prefer to have this conversation in private."

He waited. For more. For the *catch*. When nothing came except the sharp crack of a dying firepit log, he was spurred into action and closed the distance between them. Beltran was hesitant, and wary, and when he circled around to face her, he took the turn a hairsbreadth from her shoulder. "You aren't going to ask me to promise?"

"No."

"Why not?"

"Because I think you regret the promises you've broken in the past, and I'm choosing not to put you in that position. And because you asked." Her head moved from side to side, wavering on the accuracy of that statement. "Kind of."

Her gesture was so unexpected it melted through his walls and suspended the ever-present need to push her away. Again.

"*Seven hells.*" He brushed his fingers along the edge of her jaw, marveling at the feel of her skin against his. "You, Rune Jenkins, are quite the conundrum."

Her breath caught, as it had earlier, but it was she who broke the moment this time. Her eyes cut quickly to the side, checking on Grey. Beltran was surprisingly unbothered by the boy's silent intrusion.

"I will give you your privacy tonight," he said. "I can't promise anything beyond that."

"I know."

Her reach extended further into his heart. Rune had respected his needs, and in doing so had acknowledged that Beltran was the way he was, without asking him to change. He closed his eyes for a moment, feeling the depth of the emotion. "Thank you."

Her eyebrows twitched in a frown that was there one moment, gone the next. "For what?"

"No one"—he took a reluctant step backward, letting his hand fall away—"has *ever* offered me what you just did."

24

Grey wasn't sure what had possessed him to demand an answer from Rune now, but here they were, alone, facing down the moment, with countless unspoken words stacked between them. Desperate to break the spell of silence that held them captive, he cleared his throat.

"Do you, um—" His voice was rough and gravely. He had to clear it again. "Do you want to go somewhere else?"

"Not really."

It felt like his pimply twelve-year-old self had asked Rune if she'd like to go make out and had been shot down. "Oh."

"It's warmer here by the fire."

"Are you cold? Do you want me to go find your cloak?"

Rune sat down on the log nearest the barely burning fire and patted the seat next to her. The cold of the wood cut through Grey's pants and chilled the back of his thighs. The empty space between him and Rune was a void that both repelled and attracted the two beings on either side.

Rune picked nervously at her nails, and Grey stared at his feet, leaving the burden of the conversation to their surroundings. Words and accusations sprung in and out of existence, whispered not by two young Venators but by the pops and crackles of the blackened wood in the fire as it slowly marched toward its own collapse.

Grey breathed in. When he exhaled, the words of his whisper cut through the air like a whip. *"What did I do?"*

"Do? What are you talking about?"

He braced his hands—working up his nerve—and then spun to face her, bending one leg in front of him across the log. "Ever since we left Feena's land, things have been different. And I know everything was my fault. If I had just listened, nothing would've . . ." He trailed off. He didn't need to run the list by her. She'd been there. "I understand that you're angry, but—"

"I'm not angry."

The rest of the air he'd gathered to get through his question rushed out in an irritated huff. "You don't have to lie to protect me. I'm not a kid."

She shook her head, her lips twisting in a wry smirk as she silently chuckled. "Eeeeverybody wants me to talk. You, Beltran, Verida. But when I ask any questions, I get shut down, ignored, or yelled at. Where does that leave me? Standing there like an idiot, completely confused, with no idea as to why the other person is falling apart and shutting me out."

It took Grey a moment to catch up to the abrupt change in mood and direction, but yes: falling apart and shutting her out was what he had done. For good reason. He scowled. "Oh, I get it. You're angry because I won't tell you what you want to know."

"I'm not angry, Grey! Damn it!" She slapped her hands down and twisted to face him. "Don't you know a *thing* about women? I'm hurt. *Hurt.* And a little pissed off that I'm having to spell it out."

His eyebrows furrowed deeper. He was a little "pissed off" himself—and growing more so as she stared at him expectantly. Obviously, she thought that because he'd "hurt her feelings," that should be enough to motivate him to divulge the one thing that he'd never told anyone.

"Grey?"

"No." He surged to his feet, glaring down at her, and repeating the only word left available to him. "*No!*"

Without a thought as to his destination, he stepped on and over the log and stormed back through the burned-out village.

"Grey!"

Six. That was the answer to Rune's delicately dropped question. It was the word he'd been wanting to scream into that unbroken swath of stars above him for hours. He wanted to shout the number into the ether. Cry it out for the universe to hear.

The answer to all the whys.

The truth in every question.

God damn it!

He had been *six years old!*

Behind him, Rune tromped across the burnt and crunchy grass. Not trying to catch up, just following. Her calm, continual steps were infuriating, and her presence acted as a catalyst, shoving reality against his already weakening barriers. Grey's mind had become a building storm cloud, and as the fronts battered against his restraints, he had no doubt that if Rune continued, he was going to break.

He was going to tell her.

The angry part of him wanted to turn and throw a rock, to deter her like a stray dog. The other part—always at odds with himself and never quiet about it—silently pleaded with her not to give up on him just yet.

Ahead, on his right side, a half-burnt door hung at an angle. Grey reached out and slammed it shut. The force ripped it from the damaged hinges, and the door crashed to the ground, breaking into three pieces.

He cringed and hunched his shoulders.

When he reached the trees, the hum of insect chatter filled the air, along with a sharp, biting call that sounded like the teeth of a saw blade across a metal sheet. Grey ached to run, but after the two nearly fatal choices he'd made since arriving in Eon, he'd finally learned his damn lesson: vanishing alone into an unknown section of forest was not a great idea.

Still, he stepped through the tree line, resisting the adrenaline pumping through his body and intending to walk in just far enough to escape. From Rune, from Thomas, and from everything crashing down around him. But the sound of Rune's feet followed at a constant pace. When he was as deep in as he dared go, he growled and stopped, looking left, then right. With nowhere to go but in circles, he gave up.

He leaned his back against a tree trunk, crossed his arms, and waited. She walked like she might pass by him but then, at the last second, made a sharp turn and faced him head on. In the dark, her features were muted, but he could make out the thin, impassive shape of her lips. If *stubborn* were a statue, Rune would've been the sculptor's muse.

Maybe it was because he was tired—mentally, physically, and emotionally—but whatever the cause, as time ticked on, Grey's remaining defensiveness slowly melted away. His arms fell to his side in surrender.

"Rune." Her name lodged in his throat like burning tar. "You've known me forever. How could you not know?"

"Know what?"

"Tashara knew . . . almost immediately."

"Knew *what*?"

When Grey's confession began—as he'd known it would—all the thoughts, fears, and suspicions that had run on repeat through his head for years spilled out in random order.

"Tashara confirmed my worst fear the day I got here—that it really didn't matter how hard I tried to hide my demons or how many people I kept at arm's length, because everyone had seen the truth. I wasn't surprised, just gutted. I could feel it, you know?" He stared, unseeing, at the tree branch that hung over Rune's head as he rubbed his hand over his abdomen, scrunching up his shirt, trying for the millionth time to wipe off the stain. "I was marked. Tainted with some sort of black ink I couldn't wash off. At school, I used to walk down the halls and try not to be seen. But people would look at me, and then at each other, and I knew they were having one of those silent conversations. The ones made of glances where nobody actually says anything but somehow says everything."

"You don't know that—"

"I would tell myself that I was being crazy." His voice rose over the top of hers. He couldn't stop, not now. "That nobody actually knew what I was hiding. But I never fully believed it. How could they not know? And now, here we are, and I'm starting to think that you really *don't* know what you're asking me to tell you. And I want to be relieved, but instead I'm just really angry."

He finally met her eyes. "How?" he demanded. "*How* could you look at me, talk to me, all those years, and not see it?"

The expression on Rune's face about broke him. She legitimately had no idea what he was talking about.

He shook his head bitterly. "Wow."

"Grey." She reached out but withdrew when he flinched. "You spent so much time pushing me away. How can you expect I would know any—"

He lunged forward, pounding at his chest. "Because I would've known! If it were *you*, I would've known!"

Rune rocked back, staring at him like she'd never seen him before.

Which . . . he supposed . . . she really never had.

He had always worried about what secrets she might unravel when looking into his eyes. It was why he kept them lowered, hidden beneath a wall of hair. But the reality was worse than any scenario he'd imagined. Because when Rune Jenkins looked at him, she saw *nothing*.

He was suffocating in a sea full of air.

Grey filled his lungs with it, but it wasn't capable of easing the binding pain across his chest. He turned and walked away.

"I'm sorry!" she called. "Is that what you want me to . . ." Her words trailed off, and he could hear her jogging to catch up. "I was a terrible friend. I should've tried more. But *Grey*, I'm here *now*. I'm just not a mind reader—"

"Have you ever done something horrible?" His eyes were glued to the dark in front of them. "And it was so bad that you were sure that all anyone would need to do was look at you and they would know what you'd done?"

"Not really."

"*Seriously?* You've never stolen a piece of candy or . . . or . . . *anything?*"

"I mean, I—"

"You've got to be kidding me!" He picked up his pace. He couldn't do this. Not now, not to her, not ever. It could die where it had started: in his heart. He could hold it. Right there.

"Grey! Just stop for a second." She grabbed his elbow and jerked him back. "I don't do confessions well at a sprint."

"And I don't do confessions at a standstill," he shot back.

"That's fine. You asked me a question, too, so I'll go first." She took hold of his hand.

Startled, he looked down as she gently pulled his fingers over and placed them against the strange lump under the skin of her wrist. "After Feena attacked you, your wounds were substantial. Verida said you probably couldn't have healed anyway, but the poison Feena used took away any chance you might have had. I tried to rinse the poison out. I don't know if you remember, but nothing was helping, and you . . ." She looked up at him. "Grey. You died."

He heard the words, even felt the muscles on his face tighten into a frown, but the sensations were slow and distant, as if the action were being performed by an alternate version of himself.

"In the last moments, the woman you saved, Alyssa, she called the nixies and pleaded for your life. Told them how brave you'd been and how you sacrificed yourself for her. But it wasn't enough." Rune's voice was starting to shake. "They wouldn't help you because you were a Venator. So I . . ."

He had a bad feeling creeping up the back of his neck, and he could've sworn the lump beneath her wrist was getting colder. "You what?"

"I . . . I mean, they wouldn't . . ."

"Rune—"

"I just need you to understand that—"

"Just tell me what you did!"

Her chest jerked forward as she threw the words out, pushing the truth as far away from herself as possible. "I told them that if they would save you, they could take me instead!"

"What!"

It felt like someone had dumped a bucket of ice water over his head. Grey ripped his hand free of her wrist. He searched her face, trying to understand and realizing as he did that he was here *and* so was she. "Wait . . . But we're both alive. Why?"

She sighed. "They didn't want my life in exchange for yours. They wanted a promise instead."

The statement fell between them like a rock. Grey had known before entering Eon that you didn't make promises with the fae. And that lesson had been very clearly rearticulated in Feena's court.

"*Rune*," he keened. "Tell me you didn't."

Her fury contorted her face, pushing her eyes into squints and thinning her lips. "Of course I did! This bump is a nixie promise, and—stop shaking your head at me! What was I supposed to do? Just let you die?"

"Why?"

"Why? *Why!*" Her hands went to her hips, and she stomped in an angry circle, her lips moving with words he couldn't make out. She jerked to a stop, glaring at him. "Listen, I know this is hard for you to believe, *Grey*, but I care about you."

He barely heard her. He stumbled to the side and leaned a forearm against a trunk, resting his pounding head. Although he didn't think he could bear knowing, he *had* to know. "What did you promise?"

"They didn't say."

He squeezed his eyes shut. "Even better."

"When they call, I have to come. If I don't, the bubble will keep moving until it hits my heart."

He groaned from a place so deep that his core truth just slipped out right behind. "I'm not worth it."

"Damn it, Grey!" She seized his shoulder and pulled him away from the tree, squaring up. "What is it going to take for you to hear me? Huh?" She slammed her palms against his chest. "You *are* worth it. And I'd do it again! I swear to God, if you say one more word about not being worth it or so much as *imply* I made a mistake, I will do whatever I have to—just short of murdering you myself—to make sure you regret even thinking it."

The anger in her brow softened just a little. "*Anytime* there's a choice between saving your life and not, I'm going to pick you. Every. Single. Time. So stop moping around, pull yourself together, and open your eyes. The only person who can't see how incredible you are is you."

When Rune's words dropped off, Grey escaped in his usual way. He looked down, staring at the pine needles that poked up at strange angles like tiny booby traps. The hiss of his breath mixing with hers created a rhythm of push and pull that went on and on like a locomotive chugging its way down the track.

She was close enough that he'd seen the sincerity in all that she'd said, and it hurt. Her words were sharp and uncomfortable, and they pushed him to think in a way he'd forgotten how to. To believe she hadn't seen his trauma but *had* seen *him* required reframing his entire existence. Even considering it burned so hot it was turning him to ash.

Thinking that he wasn't worth it, that he was broken, unlovable, odd—that hurt in the usual way. It was comfortable pain, in a space he'd learned to call home. But . . . if she really cared, and if he was really worth caring for—that would catapult him into a new place with no rules. The feelings were too intense, the thoughts foreign and out of bounds, and they caused the connection between his mind and heart to feel like an overcharged circuit board that had just blown a fuse.

Rune's breathing began to slow, and the steady in-and-out motion of her breath slowly rocked his panic away. Grey settled into it, letting his emotions calm and his mind quiet. He didn't realize how long they'd been standing there until the hum of insects flared back to life.

He snorted and muttered, "Look at you. Finally learning patience."

She smiled. "Leave it to you to teach me something unteachable."

"It started when I was six."

The statement was abrupt, just like the confession had begun, and Grey waited, simmering in the first of many truths that were now floating free just inside his lips. He could feel Rune holding her breath, and he held his own in turn. When nothing happened, he sat down and scooted back to rest against the tree.

"My mom got remarried, and my stepdad seemed nice . . . at first. When mom got a new job working nights, my stepdad was in charge of making sure I had dinner and getting me to bed on time. He, uh, he—"

The tears came with a vengeance. Turned out he hadn't avoided them or beaten them—just buried them. The pine needles blurred, and his surroundings dripped and ran like watercolor. "At first, he took things really slow."

Grey's mind wound back, shining a brighter light on his trauma, and he shrunk with it, feeling like the small and helpless child he'd been.

"When he would t-touch me, he would apologize like it was an accident."

Rune exhaled. "Oh my God, *Grey*."

"Please, don't. Not yet. I . . . I'll never get through this. I—"

She knelt in front of him, placing her hand on his knee and frantically shaking her head. "You don't have to tell me. I'm so sorry for asking. I should've—"

"When he stopped pretending it was an accident, he would make me do things. My body would . . . respond, and . . ."

The whole world was pressing down on him. Grey scuttled out from under her touch and stood. He needed to feel taller—larger. His muscles were shaking, from his shoulders to his calves, and he felt like he was going to both fall over and throw up. He put his hands on his hips and leaned over his knees.

"He would tell me it was my fault. That I obviously liked it, so I shouldn't tell my mother. And I . . ." Grey didn't want to say it. It was a confession that he'd never even had the courage to *think* all the way through from the start to the end. It was just a subconscious understanding that always sucked him under. "And I . . . I didn't know whether I liked it or not."

The words hung in the air as if the sound itself had given them permanence.

He couldn't move. He could barely think.

There was a rustle as Rune got up. She approached him the way one would a wild animal, and when she touched his shoulder, he flinched.

"You were just a little boy," she whispered. "Of course your body responded. Just because it felt good doesn't mean you played any part in it."

He wasn't sure what gave him the courage to do it, but very slowly, he turned his head to look at her, and he saw his own tears reflected in her eyes.

She squeezed his shoulder. "It's just biology."

He sighed. "I never could make myself believe that. But today, talking to those little boys . . . They were six. That's exactly how old I was when it started. And I *looked* at them, Rune. I saw how small they were, how innocently they thought, the things that made them laugh. I was horrified. For the first time ever, my memory of the abuse faltered." His voice rose as the ultimate question clawed its way up his esophagus. "I don't understand. How could it have been my fault?"

"It couldn't."

"But . . ." He tilted his head back, blinking hard. "Even after seeing those boys, the rest of me is so damn broken that I still can't tell myself it's OK. Everything went on for so . . . *long*. I couldn't stop it. I wanted to stop it. But it just kept happening. I . . ."

The first full-fledged sob shuddered through his ribcage. They kept coming, one after another, and then Rune was there, wrapping her arms around him as he sunk to his knees. Her hands moved over his back, his arms, then cupped the back of his neck as he jerked soundlessly against her, crying into her shoulder.

When the sobs had tapered down to nothing and he'd wrung himself out completely, he stayed with his cheek pressed against her clavicle. His body was exhausted, numb, and inexplicably lighter. He poked and prodded, searching for what was missing and trying to understand the strange calmness that had overtaken him. And then he knew.

The behemoth of a thing that he could no longer sense . . . was shame.

The secret he'd worked so hard to withhold had multiplied over the years, growing until the shame became an unwelcome tenant. Though the remaining effects that stemmed from the atrocities he'd endured would be far more difficult to deal with than simply saying the words, the act of keeping the secret—with all its accompanying shame, worry, and assumptions—had been a far heavier burden to carry.

And he had carried that pile of shit like his life depended on it.

The damage was there, but it was time to move forward and see if he could heal. Grey had absolutely no idea how to even start that process, but for the first time in forever, he thought it might be possible.

He gently extricated himself from Rune's embrace. "Thank you."

"Thank you?" She searched his face, incredulous. "I made you tell me the biggest nightmare of your life. I'm ashamed of myself."

"Don't be. Thank you for being someone I trusted enough to tell."

"Well, I did save your life." She sniffled and placed a hand over her heart in a mockery of sainthood. "I guess that does deem me trustworthy."

Grey grinned. "Yes, it does."

"Can I ask you one more question?" She rushed ahead as if he would cut her off at any moment. "You don't have to answer if you don't want to, and I'll completely understand—"

"I'm not sure how much more personal it can get, Rune. Ask me whatever you want."

"That night . . ." She lifted her wrist in explanation of which night she meant. "You told me you didn't want to live."

Grey opened his mouth to explain, or at least to try to, then realized what had happened. He squeezed his eyes shut, cursing his own stupidity for not having seen it sooner. Rune had offered her life to the nixies in order to save his, *minutes* after he'd said he didn't want it.

"Was it because of the abuse?" she asked.

"Yes . . . I think." He scrubbed his hands over his face. "I can't believe you told them to take you . . . after I had just . . . Rune, I'm so sorry."

"It's OK. I just want to understand, and I don't."

He struggled to find appropriate words where no amount of explanation would ever truly make sense to her. "It's hard to sort out where one thing ends and another begins. When you feel as broken as I do, everything just hurts . . . all the time. And sometimes it makes me do dumb things. Like when that man showed up at the council house, begging for our help. I knew it was stupid and dangerous, but I . . ." Tears filled his eyes again, and her form blurred. "I spent so many nights wishing someone would save me, and nobody ever came."

They were interrupted by the crashing of branches. Both Grey's and Rune's markings simultaneously flared up. Red. A form that looked human and was moving at the speed of one tore through the forest to their left.

Rune whirled, pulling an adilat from the weapons pocket on her leg. "Who was that?"

"I don't know." Grey's hand hovered over his dagger with indecision. "But if it's a member of the village and we chase after them, everyone will be terrified of us by tomorrow afternoon."

"Oh, yes." Verida strolled into view. "By all means, let the human traitor run right by you. Not a problem."

"That was . . . ?" Rune pointed. "That's the guy you were guarding?"

"Yes."

"How'd he get out?"

"Rune." She tsked, cocking her hip to one side. "I'm offended you had to ask. Obviously, I let him out."

Grey wasn't following. "You what?"

"I need to see whether he heads for Ransan's territory or whether there are any other wolves in the vicinity I need to be worried about." She crouched, leapt, grabbed a branch, and pulled herself up. She then used it to leap to a higher one. "I'll have him back before anyone knows he's gone."

"Unharmed?" Grey called.

"Mostly. I *am* getting hungry."

"Verida!"

"I'm kidding, Grey. Relax." Verida jumped from one tree to the next until they lost sight of her.

"I . . ." Grey motioned in the direction she'd gone. "Do we follow?"

"If she'd wanted our help"—Rune flipped her pocket flap up and dropped the adilat back in—"I think she would've asked for it."

25

Amar had been ordered to the edge of Ransan's territory, waiting for the return of Beorn's first and the final approval of Ransan's demands in the alliance between the two alphas and their packs. Amar was then to escort Beorn's pack members back to camp, where the alliance would be finalized with a celebration.

He waited, leaning against a large boulder that poked up from the earth, his thoughts already on the move and following a familiar path. They trickled and hop-skipped through past and current offenses against him until he finally reached his dreams of glory—the power, the wealth, and, of course, the long-overdue recognition. Amar could taste it all. The flavors swirled together and sat on the back of his tongue, teasing his palate but never fully satisfying him.

Up until a few weeks ago, Amar had belonged to Cashel and Beorn's pack. When the Venators descended into camp, he had been, according to all reports, out hunting. In truth, his absence had been due to entirely different reasons.

When the sun went down that night, Cashel had stood with Beorn at his side and demanded an end to Silen's reign. That wasn't unusual—the pair had been ranting about a plan to overthrow Silen for years—but this was different. Cashel announced that Ransan had lost wolves to the Venators and that it had been enough to convince the other alpha to join his cause.

In order to prevent outing himself as Silen's spy, Amar rarely made trips to the council house. But this news had to be reported. He left to go "hunting" with the others, departing from the human boy's scent shortly after leaving camp and heading southeast. He was certain that Silen would commend him for his fine service. Instead, the wolf had half strangled him against a wall. The scratches he'd left down Amar's face went to the bone and took days to fully heal.

Silen. That wolf's ego had only grown since being named to the council.

There had been a brief, glistening moment in Amar's painful history when he'd thought his luck was looking up—that being chosen as Silen's spy was an honor that would one day lead to the path of glory he'd been dreaming about. Realizing that would not be the case had been a rude awakening.

Amar didn't appreciate being treated as if he were nothing more than a maggot who had mastered the art of speech. Angry and losing hope, he'd found another who appreciated his value, and no one was the wiser for it. As he left the council house that night, bleeding and sucking air through a bruised windpipe, he'd seen something extremely interesting. Venators. Scaling down the cliffs of the council house.

His report on *that* had been received with all the grace and appreciation Silen should've shown.

Amar was smart and capable, and under the direction of his new general, he leaned into the very thing he'd always hated. It was because of her advice that he would continue to bear the abuse and disdain of the packs. Let them treat him as though he wasn't worthy. Let them order him around like a servant. It only made it easier to move amongst them undetected.

To his right, Beorn's first strolled into view like the pompous ass he was, interrupting what was about to be a glorious mental recitation of Amar's own unappreciated assets. Amar set down his dreams of glory and picked up his subservience, dipping his head to his "superiors" and escorting six of his former pack members to Ransan's camp. He spoke only when necessary, letting his "betters" carry the conversation.

Let them talk. Soon they would discover who was the better among them.

Amar led the visitors straight to their meeting in Ransan's tent, staying poised in the back as a good boy did. Just in case anyone needed anything—of course. He listened and memorized the terms of negotiation as well as every argument and personal viewpoint voiced.

When the alliance was finalized, the celebration spilled into the main camp. Cider was poured, tongues were loosened, and Amar exercised his cleverness by pretending to drink while cataloguing information that spilled more frequently than ale. Eventually, the pack was so drunk he didn't even need to mime the act of drinking—carrying his mug and laughing loudly painted the illusion. However, there were a few members that could hold their alcohol, and it was far later than he would've preferred when the last man finally tipped over.

Amar set down his mug, brushed off his pants, and headed into the woods. He'd hidden the items required on the very outskirts of the territory. The full moon wasn't upon them yet, and he sprinted through the trees on two legs. The dark of night was already yielding to the deep blue of predawn, and it was imperative that he be back in camp before the pack woke. Too many absences became unexplainable, and he was at the threshold of that number.

The cave he'd chosen was small and set into a ravine that was only visible from a precise angle. He cut in from the east, looking for the telltale red berries that grew around the cave's opening. His vision was not nearly as sharp as it would've been with a full moon, but it was still heightened in comparison to his original days as a human.

It was that humanity that held him back.

Amar would never advance, not within any pack. He would never be anyone's first. Because he was not a full-blooded wolf, he would never be anything. He was simply a human who'd fallen in love with a wolf, and because they couldn't bear to part, she'd bitten him. It was sheer luck that at the time he'd been turned, her pack had been low in numbers. They'd brought him in as an extra body and a much-needed soldier. But he was never truly accepted. It hadn't bothered him . . . until his wife was killed.

Alone and grieving, his unrelenting pariah status had become excruciating. It was in the midst of that that he'd agreed to spy for Silen, hoping to find acceptance from the most powerful werewolf in Eon.

But no.

A flash of red caught his attention, and Amar focused in on the berries, following them to locate the overgrown lip of earth. He dropped into the ravine, branches snapping beneath his feet as he landed. He pushed his way past the thorny berry bush, paying no heed to the small cuts over his hands and arms, and stepped into the cave's modest opening.

The ceiling was low, and he ducked, stooping until he could walk no deeper. He dropped first to his hands and knees and then to his belly, having to wiggle in order to access the furthest tip. When he was as far as he could possibly go, Amar reached, fumbling for an edge on the smooth, rounded stone. He rolled it to the side, exposing the leather satchel he'd hidden in the small cavity beneath.

As he emerged from the cave, he held the satchel behind him, ready to drop it into a bush at the slightest hint that he might not be alone. He sniffed the air and listened for movement. Everything was as still as when he'd arrived.

He pulled open the drawstrings on the bag and retrieved a smaller leather pouch from within. He opened it and, as he'd been taught, sprinkled the white sand in a circle on the ground. The next item was a long, thin vial. He uncorked it and sniffed. Blood. Old, rancid blood. But blood. Careful not to break the line of sand, he drizzled the sticky substance into a puddle at the center. The final item was a small bone with black letters that he couldn't read etched across its surface. Amar tossed it into the blood and stepped back. A flash of light flared so brightly he had to look away, covering his eyes with his arm.

When he looked again, a glowing portal was waiting for him. This was his future. *This* was his destiny. Smiling, he stepped through.

Ryker and Zio were in the middle of breakfast. It wasn't even dawn yet. He'd complained about the required schedule, but she wouldn't budge, repeating that there were not enough hours in the day to prepare him. Which was just . . . great. Predawn was to be the start of his day for the foreseeable future. Not being hungover every morning made it easier—that and the view—but it still sucked ass.

Zio was in her usual seat—at the head of the table and to his left. Her hair was down today, and the platinum waves fell over the blue silk sleeves of her dress. She pulled her napkin from her lap and set it next to her plate. "Tell me about your sister."

Ryker paused with his fork halfway to his mouth. "Rune?"

"Do you have another one?"

Ryker laughed, trying to slough off his stupid question. "What do you want to know?"

Zio picked up a large red berry—similar to a strawberry, minus all the tiny seeds. "Anything you'd like to share. She's obviously important to you, and you're important to me." She glanced at his nearly empty plate. "Do you need more?"

"Yes, please."

The training had been nonstop and more draining than his football two-a-days. He was always ravenous. A human girl—a mouselike thing in a dress so big it hung off one shoulder—scurried from the room to get another plate for him.

"Rune is . . . loyal," he said. "To a fault."

"How so?"

"I wasn't . . . great to live with the last few years."

That was an understatement.

He cut a piece of sausage, dragging the knife loudly against the porcelain plate, using the delay to psych himself up. It was hard to talk honestly, but he wanted Zio's trust. And if he wanted to know her secrets, he would have to share some of his own.

"It never mattered what I'd done or how bad it got; Rune stood by my side. She defended me to everyone, whether or not I deserved it." Saying those words aloud put him face to face with the reality of his own behavior. "Actually, I never deserved it, but she did it anyway. Rune took my crap, my mother's crap, *and* my mother's crap that was directed at me. She was always there for me, even if she got hurt in the process."

"You feel guilty."

"Yeah," he admitted. "I love my sister. I would do anything for her. But . . . I didn't. All I really did was make her life miserable."

Zio picked up her porcelain cup of hot, steaming tea and leaned back in her chair. "Was it always like that?"

"No."

The servant girl scurried in with a new plate piled high with sausages, eggs, and biscuits, all slathered in a thick, meaty gravy. She sat it at Ryker's elbow, bowed, and darted away.

"Rune and I used to be really close. One year, for our birthday, she saved her money and bought me—" He'd already reached to his neck, ready to pull out the pendant they shared, before he remembered.

"Right," he mumbled. "She gave me a necklace, yin and yang, but the last time I remember having it was before I woke up here."

"I'm not familiar with that name. Does a yin and yang have powers?"

"Uhh, no." He explained the circle design with its opposing colors and its meaning—two sides of the same coin, different yet balancing. "And we really did balance each other, but Rune was always the good one." He laughed, remembering. "She'd always go along with what I wanted to do, because that's what twins did—at least, that's what she'd say, but then she'd confess everything to Mom two hours later."

"Rune received the dragon's share of humanity's guilt, I see."

"Yeah, I guess." He dug into his plate, shoveling large bites of biscuits and gravy into his mouth.

Zio was watching him intently over the rim of her cup.

He swallowed. "What?"

"I'm sure it's nothing, but I've found that if someone struggles with guilt, the trait tends to manifest itself somewhat universally. As you were talking, I wondered if that was the case with your sister?"

"Sure, I guess. Rune felt guilty about a ton of stuff." He grinned. "This one time, she decided to ignore something Mom asked us to do. It was stupid—I can't even remember—but she didn't do it. Then she felt guilty about *not* feeling guilty." He launched into laughter but quickly trailed off when Zio didn't join in.

She gently set her cup down. "I worry, Ryker, that you should prepare yourself."

"For what?"

"With as much time as Rune has spent with the council, the situation could be precarious. The council members may be vile, but they are persuasive. And clever. No doubt they've already deduced this weakness in your sister and are actively finding ways to use it against her. Without you or me to teach her the true nature of the beasts she's dealing with . . ."

Ryker could feel his blood pressure rising. He clenched his fork, his arm shaking so hard that the biscuit was in danger of sliding into his lap.

"I've upset you," Zio said, as if they were disagreeing about his taste in jeans. "That wasn't my intent."

"Then why do you keep doing this?" Ryker realized he was yelling, and he pulled back. But he was furious, and his words continued to come out clipped. "Every time we talk about Rune, you act as if she's too stupid to see the truth. All you do is tell me that I'm never getting her back. I refuse to accept that. She's my sister, she's walked through hell for me, and I'm not just going to give up on her because she landed in a worse place than I did!"

"Ryker." The sound of his name on her tongue softened the edge of his anger. "I've come to care for you, and I worry about your heart if things don't go the way you've planned. I do want Rune by your side, and I want you to be happy. The things I say are only because I don't want to see you hurt."

Ryker's shoulders started to relax. "You don't need to worry. The only thing my sister doesn't understand is how to give up on me."

"Loyalty is a lovely trait, to be sure."

Zio didn't say it, but Ryker knew it was there. He shook his head and shoveled in another mouthful of biscuit, speaking around the buttery bread. "*But?*"

"But, out of concern for you, I feel obliged to point out that loyalty is not always tied to a single individual."

He frowned. "What do you mean?"

"Surely your sister also feels something for Grey. They've fought side by side in Eon. It's difficult to keep from developing a deep connection when the circumstances are life and death."

Grey. Ryker stabbed the last sausage with more force than necessary. "She was always defending that loser."

"You honestly feel no kindness or camaraderie toward the young Venator? Didn't you grow up with him as well?"

He slammed the fork onto the table. The sausage rolled. "I *hate* him. I want to rip his heart out with my bare hands."

Zio tilted her head to one side, evaluating his outburst. "Perhaps you will get an opportunity, but I suspect it might upset your sister."

"She doesn't have to know. Does she?"

"No, she doesn't."

Zio smiled, and malice danced back and forth between them. This was why he loved being here. Never once had Zio made him feel bad for voicing his desires. No matter what they were.

"Tell me something. Why do you hate Grey?"

Rune had been asking him that for years, and she wasn't the only one. He'd never been able to be honest . . . until now. "Because Grey knew about this, *all of this*, and he never told anyone."

"I don't think I understand."

"Remember how I told you that I saw those goblins the council sent, and the . . ." He paused as he struggled to remember the name Zio had used. "The blue guy—Tate. I was just a kid when it happened, and I didn't know any of this existed, so I legitimately thought I was insane."

"Of course."

"So there I am. It's the middle of the school day, and I can't stop thinking about what I saw. I'm feeling batshit crazy. And then Grey walks in late, wearing this oversized black trench coat."

"I'm not familiar with that term. Trench coat?"

"Oh, uh . . ." How did you explain that to someone who wasn't from earth? "It's the coat Tate wore when I saw him. Does he still wear it? Long, black, with, uhh—?"

"Ahhh, yes. He does. Continue."

"So Grey is wearing this stupid coat, and I start having flash-backs. My hands start sweating. I can't breathe. I'm gasping for air. My buddy is looking at me like I've grown a second head. And do you know what Grey did? That little bastard wore that coat day after day, year after year. And then he would bring these damn books of his to stack on his desk about vampires and werewolves. He would set them down and straighten them and then look right at me. I don't know how he knew, but *he knew*, and he made it his quest to personally mock me."

Ryker snorted. "Rune thought I was nuts for hating him like I did, and she would've thought I was even more crazy if I'd told her the truth. But it looks like I was right, wasn't I? This whole time, Grey knew everything, and now we're here, and Grey has exactly what he's always wanted."

"Which is?"

His lip pulled up in a sneer. "Rune."

The dining room doors opened, and Elyria stepped in. She raised her chin, speaking to the back wall. "A portal has opened outside the main gates. It's one of your wolves."

Zio pushed her hair over her shoulders. "Ryker, markings on. As I taught you."

He fumbled for a bit, searching for the mental switch to throw. When he found it, his markings flickered maroon and green. He'd had several lessons yesterday, and if he remembered correctly, maroon meant werewolf, and green meant that there were goblins within range.

"Very good. Elyria, show him in."

The wolf must've been waiting outside the doors, because he walked in seconds later. He was a plain, middle-aged man—brown hair, brown eyes, thin lips, and no defining facial features to make note of. He wasn't particularly tall, maybe around five foot five, with a lean, muscular frame, and he carried a leather satchel over his shoulder. The definition of average.

It wasn't right, how normal they all looked.

"Ahhh, Amar." Zio greeted him with a plastic smile. "You have news for me?"

"I would never risk exposing you otherwise." Amar was facing Zio, but his eyes had trailed to the side and were fixated on Ryker.

Ryker scowled, rolling a dinner knife between his thumb and forefinger.

"Amar, if you wish to rise in my ranks, you'll need to learn some manners."

The wolf's eyes snapped forward. "My apologies. I just . . . I hadn't seen one of the Venators up close. I didn't realize there was a third."

"And now you know." She pointed to the chair at her left. "Sit."

He straightened to his full height and walked with stiff, military-style steps, pulling out the seat with unnecessary flourish. When he sat, a wave of body odor, edged with the scents of dog and wood, smacked Ryker upside the head. He didn't try to hide his disgust.

"I'll refill that while you're here." Zio held out her hand and took the dust-covered leather satchel he passed over. She pushed her plate away and set the satchel in front of her. "Well? What do you have that was important enough to make the trip?"

"Beorn's men arrived in camp tonight."

She loosened the drawstrings and pulled out a vial. "Cashel's son. The one who survived the Venator attack?"

"Yes. Beorn met with Ransan earlier and asked him to honor a deal he'd made with Cashel."

Zio held out a hand. "Ryker, may I borrow a blade?"

He handed over his dagger, hilt first.

"The purpose of the original alliance," Amar said, "was for the two packs to bind together to allow them to challenge Silen for his council seat. But Beorn has bigger plans now. He's making multiple alliances, aiming to form one large pack and positioning himself as alpha. He plans to unseat Silen first, then launch a wave of attacks to claim everything from the coastline to the base of the Blues."

"That would include Silen's homelands. Interesting. And ambitious." Zio cut the pad of her finger from beneath her nail to the first knuckle without flinching. The blood ran in a thin line from the tip of her nail into the vial. "Those lands have been held by Silen's family's line for hundreds of years. The last time a pack dared to challenge their hold was when Venators still roamed." She glanced up. "What does the illustrious alpha have planned after that?"

"There hasn't been any talk of specific moves, but with your permission, I could offer an educated guess."

She gave a curt nod.

"Once Beorn has a united territory of that size and Silen's pack members have joined his ranks, he'll turn his sights to unseating the rest of the council members. It's possible that he'll start by clearing out the inhabitants of the Dark Forest to weaken the fae's hold near the council house and prevent himself from being boxed in on all sides by fae and elf."

"This plan of his will be problematic when Silen finds out."

"Beorn is securing his alliances while actively putting distance between Silen's pack and himself. He's hoping his numbers will be strong enough to fight back by the time the scouts find him."

Zio corked up the vial, then pressed a linen napkin against her finger. "And I'm sure if Beorn succeeds in usurping Silen's seat on the council, he will take full advantage of his newfound access to the Venators."

Amar swallowed. "I would imagine."

She handed Amar back the satchel. "Come now. You've been such a valuable asset, don't withhold from me simply because there's a Venator sitting at my table."

"Beorn has a blood debt to repay, and he intends to honor his father."

"Of course. How much did you tell Silen about the attack on Cashel's pack?"

"Only that it was the Venators. Since I was here, delivering you the news of the two Venator's exit from the council house, I didn't have many details. Silen was not pleased."

"I imagine not. Is he to thank for that new baby-pink skin of yours?"

Ryker focused on Amar, trying to see what Zio was talking about. It was faint, so faint he hadn't noticed it all. But there, across Amar's cheek, were four long lines slightly lighter than the rest of his face. Claw marks.

"Cut me to the bone this time."

"Is he becoming suspicious of your activities?"

"Not yet. That night, many were out, hunting a human boy they'd nabbed for sport. I told Silen I was participating in the fun and got distracted with a female, and by the time I heard the howls and returned to camp, the Venators were gone." Amar resituated in his chair. "Although, it's strange—Beorn has been telling the packs that Silen and Dimitri were both there that night and that they ordered the Venator attack."

Zio tossed the bloody napkin to the side and leaned forward on the table. "Now *that* is interesting."

"But they weren't. The Venators and Tate left the council house alone. When I returned to report the attack, all the council members were in meetings. I talked to some of the guards and servants, and near as I can prove, neither Silen nor Dimitri left the council house that night."

"Thank you, Amar." Her smile reached all the way to her eyes. "You've been most helpful."

"Of course." The wolf handled his dismissal with grace. He stood, bowed, and was nearly to the doors when Zio called.

"Did the pack agree to Beorn's request for an alliance?"

He turned at the waist. "The most important players have. Ransan has called for a complete pack vote, but it's expected to be unanimous."

"Cast your vote, but make sure you aren't in camp tonight."

His eyes widened. "But it's the full moon."

"So it is."

"I will do as you say, always. However, I would be remiss if I didn't point out that I have been absent from camp for a number of recent activities. With the full moon and a vote, there will no doubt be another celebration. Between leaving to report to both you and Silen, it's getting difficult not to raise suspicions."

Zio drummed her fingers against the table, her brows pulling together. "It's time I send a message. When my soldiers arrive, you'll climb a tree. Do that, and I guarantee you'll not be harmed. From there, you'll watch the attack, ensuring Silen gets a mostly accurate report of the perpetrators. Our only remaining problem is explaining how you were both in camp and the sole survivor."

"The s . . . s . . . sole survivor?" Amar stammered.

Zio dictated the rest of her plan, and with each additional detail, the color faded a little more from Amar's face. She motioned him back. "I'm going to need some of your blood this time."

Ryker waited until the stunned-looking wolf had left the room. "You're attacking?"

"I'm sending Ransan a few unwelcome guests, yes. I think it's time I see how well my mindless soldiers can carry out orders in the field."

Ryker was constantly grasping at every word, name, and political rule that Zio dropped, trying to fit everything into the undefined map in his head. Currently, it looked less like a map and more like a pile of random information. "So . . . we don't want the packs to combine?"

"Oh, we do."

"Then why aren't you waiting until Silen figures out what they're doing and attacks?"

"Because he won't, at least not openly. He knows that doing so will only seal his fate faster."

"But . . ." Ryker was trying to understand, but the pile of useless information he'd stored was living up to its name.

"What you don't know is that there are no vampire strongholds between the council house and the Blues. Which means that if vampires were to suddenly decimate Ransan's pack, it would be assumed that the attack was issued by the one place a merger of that magnitude would threaten."

She waited for him to fill in the blank.

"The council?" Ryker ventured.

"Correct. This will incite an all-out war between the packs and the council. Even the stronger alphas who would normally resist Beorn as their leader will have no choice but to align with the less-experienced wolf to avenge the attack." She placed her hands flat on the table and pushed up, the silk of her skirt rippling like water. "Let me ask you this—how do you destroy an enemy that has more resources than you? An enemy you can't possibly defeat in battle."

He stared, his mouth hanging open, so far out of his depth he didn't even know where to begin.

"You help them destroy themselves." She leaned across the table, her voice smooth as velvet. "And when all that's left standing are the smoking remains of what used to be, you walk in and seize what belongs to you."

"Teach me." Ryker shoved his chair back. The legs squealed against the floor. "I want to know *everything*."

27

Verida worked to saddle the horses while Rune and Grey said goodbye to the villagers. At least, that was what Grey was doing. Rune was hovering at his shoulder like a nervous child. Verida rolled her eyes. She threw the dual bags behind the saddle and adjusted the leather strap that connected the two, balancing the weight across the horse's hips.

The villager she'd tracked last night had run straight for Ransan's pack, suggesting that Beorn had, in fact, left the area. Once she had that bit of information, Verida had dropped from the tree and knocked the man out before he knew she was there.

It never ceased to amaze her how stupid someone could be.

It was *possible* Ransan would've handed the man his reward as promised, but it was more likely that he would've held the human until tonight. A full-moon hunt of someone who'd *willingly* walked into camp was legal and not something many alphas would be able to resist. Lucky for this idiotic human, she was kind enough to carry his limp body back to the village in one piece.

Beltran strolled up, whistling. "Good morning."

"I'm not getting your horse ready."

"I slept well. Thank you for asking." He ran a hand over the soft velvet of his horse's muzzle, talking to it instead of to her. "I never asked her to saddle you, did I? No. But she's all in a huff about it. Completely unnecessary, if you ask me."

"Nobody did."

The horse blew its lips, spraying Beltran with a mix of air and spittle.

Chagrin wound through his expression, from the raise of his brows to the way he lifted a heavy arm with a limp wrist to wipe his face. "Be honest with me, my four-legged friend. How did Verida bribe you to do that?"

The humor of the situation tickled her, but she couldn't crack a smile. Her capacity for joy was weighed down, buried beneath the heaviness of what she knew this day would hold for her.

Although Beorn did appear to be out of the picture for now, she'd still been up half the night trying to figure out how they were going to get around Ransan. All she'd been able to come up with was a pile of useless ifs. *If* they hadn't lost a day and a half to Grey's vision, they would've been past the territory before the full moon. *If* Beorn hadn't already been talking to Ransan about the Venators, the four of them might've crossed by the outside edge of werewolf territory unnoticed—even with the full moon. *If* they could abandon the horses. *If* they could have Beltran fly both them and the horses over the top of Ransan's territory without anyone or anything seeing. And the most ridiculous . . . *If* they'd only been in this situation in a different area, there might've been someone to reach out to—the council, supporters of her father, resistance members.

Ifs. Utterly useless.

The reality was that from now until they reached the Blues, they were on their own. It was only then, when she'd discarded all the ifs and was left with only what was, that the long-term safety of the group had boiled down to a single reprehensible option.

She'd desperately tried to talk herself out of the realization, substituting the ifs for a string of rationalizations. Grey, Rune, and Beltran had survived wolves before. With the four of them, they could do it again. But the problem wasn't just surviving the night against Beorn's pack. The real issue was twofold. It would almost certainly incite a political nightmare for Silen and Dimitri, who would demand either the Venators' return or their heads. And a battle of nearly any size would be another announcement to Zio of where the Venators were. If the sorceress sent out that dragon again, someone—or everyone—was going to die.

Verida could rationalize all she wanted, but the bottom line was that a battle with Ransan's pack had to be avoided. Which meant spending the night in the old Venator ruins was the only option. Before she'd fallen asleep, one last thought had crossed her mind: *I lost Tate's family. I deserve this.*

She picked up her saddle and looked out at the rising sun. Whether she deserved it or not, the day had barely started, and her dread was so thick it tasted of tar and pain.

"We can have Grey lead with my horse," Beltran was saying. "I'll fly ahead to see where Ransan is camping within his territory. Then we can choose the safest place to pitch our tents tonight."

"No." She pulled the cinch tight. The horse snorted and stamped a back leg in displeasure. "It doesn't matter where we pitch those tents, and you know it."

"So what? We do nothing?"

"I have a plan." Verida put one foot in the stirrup and swung up into the saddle. Her blonde hair caught in the wind and fluttered across her face. "If we hurry, we should be out of danger before sunset."

Beltran peered up at her. "How?"

She wrapped the reins around her left hand and pulled the horse around. "Mount up!" she called to Grey and Rune. "It's time to go."

She tapped the horse's side with her heels and clicked, taking off at a canter for the western side of Ransan's borders. As she broke through the tree line, she waited for the sounds of hooves approaching, posturing for a fight.

They must've sensed her desire to be alone, because there were no shouts from Rune asking her to slow down and no sarcastic digs from Beltran. For the rest of the day, the three of them rode together, keeping a steady distance of several lengths between them and her.

Verida pushed the horses hard, stopping to let them rest only as often as was absolutely necessary. The deeper they cut toward the Blues, the more the landscape around them began to change. The water-heavy ferns and more delicate plants around the council house were yielding territory to heartier trees and thick, compact bushes with smaller leaves and thin spines to keep the birds and rodents from stripping the branches bare. The fae preferred the wetter climates as well, and both by day and by night, signs of their touch were becoming fewer and farther between as they approached the mountainous desert.

The sun was worryingly low in the sky when her horse's gait changed. The ground here was softer. It was the sign she'd been waiting for, and she began actively looking for the head of the small stream they would follow all the way to their destination. She found it in a deep divot between two ancient trees.

The pool was no bigger than a bathtub. Water ran out one side and down the incline, cutting through the dirt and exposing both rock and sediment. The original riverbed had once run straight through this area but had moved underground long ago.

This was the moment when her plan would become abundantly clear to Beltran. She took a tight breath and turned her horse west. As she'd expected, it wasn't more than a few seconds before she heard one set of hoofbeats approaching fast.

"Are you taking us where I think you're taking us?" Beltran asked.

"Probably."

"There's nothing left, no wards, nothing. You know that."

When she continued to ignore him, he moved up, keeping his horse at a pace with hers so they rode side by side.

He lowered his voice. "Why would you want to show the ruins to Rune and Grey? It's no safer than any number of places we could sleep tonight. I could fly us somewhere. We could sleep in the trees." He reached out and set a hand on her elbow. "*Verida*, listen to me. It's not even defensible."

"Not from the outside, no." She snapped her reins and pulled ahead. The stream was shallow, and she maneuvered into the center. It wasn't a perfect cover of their tracks, but it was better than nothing.

The sound of the horse's hooves splashing through water and cracking against smooth stones was so reminiscent of the last time she'd been here that her mind filled in the rest of the narrative. She could hear laughing, hers intertwined with his. She could feel his arms around her, his lips on her neck. *Rana!* Verida was trapped—lost in the streams and lakes of her past. And she was drowning.

Beltran was there again. "Are you all right?"

"Fine."

"Verida, I've tried not to question you since we left. Truly, I have—"

"But you're going to now."

"This is madness," he hissed. "There is no getting into that fortress. Arwin and I spent three days here while he tried to force his way through without setting off an explosion. Even if I set that aside, which"—he shook his head—"is a lot to ask, and if I assume that after we can't get in, we can still find somewhere safe to stay for tonight . . . Rune and Grey, they're . . ."

"They're what?"

"Are you *sure* it's wise to show them this?"

She set her posture before twisting her chin to look at him. "The longer Rune and Grey are here, the more they'll learn about their ancestors and ours. Better we walk them into the past than into a battle that could announce our location. I think we can both agree that the last thing we need is the reappearance of Zio's pet."

Beltran rubbed at the back of his neck. "I'd really rather not go through another battle with a dragon. Still . . ." He looked over his shoulder at Grey and Rune. "We're asking them to risk their lives for the same people who did that." He pointed forward to what he knew was coming. "The ruins aren't going to be motivating, and we can't lose them now by adding to their fears and suspicions."

She snorted. "I'm sure they aren't going to like it, but where are they going to go?"

The line of Beltran's mouth thinned, and he sat back, no longer bothering to keep his voice low. "Don't get too comfortable in that line of thinking, darling. There are always escape options available to the miserable."

"Misery is life," she snapped. "And escape is bought and paid for."

"I disagree. Escape is something you choose. It's free and always there. Those who stay, trying to buy their escape, are doing nothing more than demanding payment for their wrongs. Don't think that because this is the path both you and I have chosen, it's the only one."

Beltran knew where they were headed now, and he clicked, pulling his horse to the front of the line. Verida glared at his back, her eyes going red at his words.

28

Zio walked briskly toward the weapons room, Ryker just behind. "If you truly want me to teach you all I know, it will require more than learning how to fight. There are hundreds of years of politics and histories to understand. You must learn how to outwit, as well outfight, your opponents."

"I know that."

"You haven't the slightest idea."

Ryker sighed. "Where are we going?"

"Does it matter?" His impatience rubbed on her nerves almost as much as the incessantly loud clomping of his boots.

"No."

"Then do not ask. Instead, pay attention to your surroundings. Ensure that you know where you are and how to get back. Look for possible threats and defensible locations." She motioned to a cove in the stone wall they were passing. "Such as that. Listen and watch at all times. Once a moment has passed, there will never be a second chance to observe what was. You can rescout a location, but the smaller things, the more important things—conversations, shared glances, items on a table—will have disappeared on the winds of time, never to be gleaned again."

She looked over her shoulder, first at him and then at his feet. "And for demon's sake, soften your steps. You walk as if requesting a knife in the back."

Ryker was silent for the rest of the journey.

The weapons room was just past her own quarters and behind an unassuming wooden door. She angled herself sideways, signaling for Ryker to face the entrance head on. Once he was in place, she reached, brushing across his chest in the process, and pushed the door open, revealing the interior.

This was one of only a handful of rooms that ran along the outer eastern wall of the fortress—and thus one of the few with useful windows. Rays of morning light were cutting through the thick glass, and Ryker's eyes grew wide, his gaze hopping from one glittering piece of weaponry to the next.

"*Woah.*" He started to move forward but stopped himself, looking first for permission.

"Go on."

He grinned and stepped in, turning slowly as he walked to look up and down the walls. "You have everything!"

Zio centered herself in the doorframe but stayed out of the room. "A Venator must be a master of all weapons. Knowing how to use what is accessible will be the difference between life and death. However, in addition to general prowess in battle, Venators also possess individual gifts or abilities that manifest as they age. Your ancestors recognized this, and they trained their children one on one, teaching each child how to maximize their specific mental and physical gifts. When Venator training begins, the individual chooses the weapons they will carry and what fighting styles they will specialize in. Today, we choose yours."

Ryker dragged one hand across the edge of a long table, looking at the carefully organized lines of daggers, throwing stars, adilats, and more. "Which ones can I have?"

"That is not up to me."

"But . . ." He frowned. "I don't know what to do with any of these. How am I supposed to choose?"

"Instinct. Pick up anything that calls to you. Feel it in your hands. You'll know."

He moved methodically through her cache, picking up blades of varying lengths and styles. He passed by the bows and arrows with hardly a glance. Zio appreciated the usefulness of a bow, but it didn't surprise her that he wasn't attracted to them. Ryker Jenkins had proven himself to be the kind of man who would not enjoy watching his kill drop from a distance. The next weapon he picked up was large—the length of her forearm. The blade extended straight for a few inches before angling sixty degrees. He hefted it, checking its weight and showing the first signs of any real interest in a specific piece.

"That's called a halvnor," she said. "Use it properly, and you can take a man's arm off in one swing. Do you like it?"

"I do. Will it work?"

"With your strength? It's a fine choice."

His focus was pulled to a set of small, handleless throwing knives next. He pinched one end between his thumb and pointer finger, tilted back so the blade rested against the fleshy part of his hand, and searched for a target, finding one in an old wooden shield hanging on the wall. He bent his arm at the elbow and flicked his wrist. The blade thudded into the bottom edge of the shield, sinking deep.

His form wasn't perfect, but it was more accurate than she'd expected from his first attempt.

Ryker marched to retrieve the knife, his smile becoming a crooked, dangerous thing. "Just like throwing the paper stars we would make in calculus. Sort of." He jerked the knife free of the wood and held it up, twisting it from one side to the other. "I like these."

"Good. Take the set. There's a thigh pocket on your left leg with loops and thick leather lining. It will keep them accessible and prevent them from clanging together or stabbing you in the leg." As he loaded up the pocket sheaths, she continued, "If you want them to be lethal, aim for the eyes of your victim. If that's not possible, any exposed flesh will do. The wound will buy time for you to choose a more substantial weapon."

Ryker hefted a fine longsword from the wall, checking its balance the way she'd taught him. It was clear from his expression that he had no questions about this blade. He'd already chosen it. She pointed him to the extra belt he would need to carry the sword at his hip. Next, he chose and sheathed a dagger—a fine, twelve-inch, double-sided piece with a leather-wrapped handle—and quickly reached to add another.

"No," she said. "Vary your lengths and styles. What about those?" She pointed him toward a large variety of handheld battle-axes.

Ryker's grin evened out, now stretching from ear to ear. He hefted the handle of his chosen weapon up until the base of the ax head rested against his hand, then lowered it again, gripping it midhandle to swing across his body. He chuckled darkly. "Oh, I like these."

"I thought you might. They work in close quarters and are extremely lethal when thrown properly. I'll find a larger one for you to practice with as well, but to keep on your person, I would suggest choosing three handhelds. They sit in those loops at your waist, opposite the sword. Having multiple will give you the freedom to throw one and still have more in hand."

The axes varied in size and design, and he worked his way through the options, choosing the ones that best fit his hand size and physical strength. When he'd slid all three handles through the loops of the reinforced fabric, something caught his eye on a table of smaller weapons. He crossed the room, reaching for one in the middle of the table—a punch dagger. This weapon was smaller, more obscure, and had never been a popular choice among the older Venators. The blade was no more than four or five inches, and the handle was turned sideways so the blade and handle together formed what looked like the letter *T.*

It was the first of his choices she hadn't anticipated him being attracted to. "Interesting."

"It's small, but . . ." He trailed off as he wrapped his fingers around the grip and wound up, punching into an uppercut. "Under the chin." He pulled back and swung in an arc. "Side of the neck. In the ear." He nodded to himself as he continued to look it over, adjusting his grip.

She couldn't help her smile. "Leave that one."

"What? But you said—"

"And I also said . . . *leave it.*" She stared him down until he returned the punch dagger to its resting place. "Very good. This way."

Her room was a few steps down the hall, and she moved quickly, taking hold of both latches on the double doors and pushing them wide open. Zio was lowering herself into the chair on the side of the room opposite two large wardrobes when Ryker stepped over the threshold.

He stopped, looking around. "Where are we?"

"My quarters. There is something for you in the wardrobe on the right, left panel door."

His stride was slow, obeying while trying to take in as much of her personal space as possible. His eyes jumped from the oversized bed, with its blue and maroon silken bedding, to the couches and chairs, whose backs and seats had been embroidered with ornate needlework. The furniture bore the tales of men and monsters—images stitched in thread of glorious battles from a time so traumatic that Eon would never forget it. The art on the walls consisted exclusively of landscapes and had been painted by various artists throughout the years.

The landscapes were her way of surreptitiously holding on to important memories. Each image was a mental trigger to a moment in her past that was growing further away from the present than she'd ever expected. Had she realized how long traversing her chosen path would take—and the lines she would cross to stay on it—she likely would've never set the first foot down.

When Ryker reached the wardrobe, he opened both sides, looking behind the left panel as instructed. Though there were at least twenty different weapons hanging there, he reached for the one she'd intended: a punch dagger of much finer workmanship. The ends of the *T* had been set with large green jewels. The blade itself was made of silver, and the handle had been wrapped with fine eel skin from the Ronadian Sea.

"It's amazing."

"In the past, not many Venators chose that particular weapon."

"Is this yours?"

"It was, a long time ago. Now it's yours. A symbol of my belief in you. Use the angled sheath. It will set your grip before you pull it and will keep it clear of those axes."

Zio rose from her chair and headed for the balcony. She'd left the doors open to let in the morning air. It was a path she'd taken many times—past the giant braziers and over the weathered slate floor to the black iron railing. The sun was well over the mountain peaks now and had turned the tops of the trees that carpeted the world beneath them a brilliant green. Ryker came up next to her.

She rested her hands on the rail. "That is the Black Forest below us. The line of mountains you can see in the distance is the highest peaks of the Blues."

"It's incredible. Hey—" Ryker grabbed her hand and turned it over. "You're healed."

She'd wondered how long it would take him to notice. The expansive length of time had been a disappointment. "I heal same as you."

"Does everyone here?"

"No." She withdrew from his touch and leaned to one side. The chill of the metal railing easily cut through the thin, silken material of her skirt. "Though many have advanced abilities in that area."

Zio watched Ryker carefully. He was thinking, and his face pulled tighter as he slouched forward to brace his forearms on the black iron. His markings were some of the stronger ones she'd seen, wide and thick with harsh, jagged angles. They fit his personality well.

"The Venators of old always had a master. One master to one student. If you wish for me to train you, you have to be open and willing. Parts of you will need to change, and your ego will have to stand aside."

"I can do that."

She pursed her lips at the naive self-assurance he always flung about so casually.

"Ryker." Needing him focused, Zio waited for him to turn his head and look at her. "This world has taken everything from me. Perhaps it was my destiny, but when I look back, what I see is suffering created from my own resistance to change."

Memories of the past surged to life, wrapping their fists around her throat and trying to strangle tears from forgotten wells. Zio stopped, letting her mouth settle closed and breathing through her nose, mentally demanding the return of her control.

As for Ryker, the boy waited patiently, unable to see the storm beneath her surface.

When she was sure her voice wouldn't shake, she continued, "I used to be direct, concise, and was frequently accused of rashness. In my darkest moment, I realized my tactics had to change. I've learned to work patiently, to operate in the background and the underpinnings. I have spent decades setting single pieces of my plan into place, and I emerge from the silence of this fortress only long enough to keep the fear of me alive. To remind them of my presence."

"But you have magic. Why don't you just use it to get what you want?"

"My magic is unique. It's unexpected and misunderstood. Because of this, I've been able to accomplish things that no one else in Eon has been able to manage for hundreds of years—such as the portal the wolf Amar just used to report to me. They are less limited than the portals known to the wizards, and though I can't portal through proper protections spells, they're easier to create and work in two directions. It has increased my effectiveness, and often I receive messages far faster than the council. But . . ." Her mouth twisted, loath to admit specific chinks in her armor. However, if she were to open Ryker's eyes, she had to illustrate the angle required for him to see. "There are a great many things I cannot do. For example, I wouldn't dream of facing Arwin in a duel."

"The wizard on the council?"

"Yes. He's phenomenally powerful. His magic is far and above what I currently possess. Yet despite his skill and the nuisance I make of myself, the old man has never tried to attack me head on."

"Why not?"

"Because Arwin has never seen anything like me. He doesn't understand how I can do what I do. My advantage is not in my power but in the fact that I understand him perfectly while he has been left unsure about me. I know my enemy. I can predict when to move forward and when to retreat. Arwin knows only that I appear powerful at times but have also failed to challenge things he would've expected me to—such as the wards he's placed around the council house. It's the unknown that makes him wary. It forces him to question whether I'm holding back or incapable. Keeping my enemies on unstable ground is a tactic I exploit. Instability leads to insecurity, which makes an individual choose things they otherwise might not. I long for the power to swoop in and wipe out all those who deserve it, but I don't possess it. Which leads us full circle. What do you do when you have an enemy you can't defeat?"

He repeated back her earlier lesson. "You help them destroy themselves."

"I've launched many attacks with armies I've bought, but purchased armies lack devotion to a cause. They're weak. They win battles, but I know that in the end, they will lose the war. Still, I continue to send them out."

He frowned, puzzling through what she was giving him. "Why would you do that?"

"I'll show you."

Zio placed a hand on Ryker's shoulder and applied gentle pressure. As he straightened, she moved closer, sliding her other hand over the top of his hip and pressing her breasts against his chest. She lifted her chin, and her lips parted in invitation.

Ryker's surprise passed in a fraction of a second. His lids drooped with desire, and without stopping to consider what lesson she might be showing him, his eyes searched her face with the desperation of a dying man in a desert. He lowered his head. But it was not her lips that stopped him but the kiss of a blade against his back.

He exhaled. "What did I do?"

Zio twisted the blade and smiled. "It didn't occur to you that I had a blade on me, did it?"

"No, I . . . but . . . *Why?*" He frowned, mumbling to himself. "You're always armed. Why didn't I think you had a dagger?"

"Because I asked for yours at breakfast."

"So?"

"I never said I hadn't brought one, but asking for yours was enough to solidify the assumption in your mind. Why would I ask for your blade if I had one of my own? To make sure that message was not interrupted by any doubt, I stayed in the doorway when you entered the weapons room. And when you opened my wardrobe, I ensured I was nowhere near it, making it clear that I had no opportunity to replace the assumed-to-be-missing blade. Which leads us to now, where you are stuck in both an embarrassing gaffe and a deadly situation. One push, Ryker. That's all it would take for me to shove this dagger through your back and into your kidneys."

"I made a mistake."

"No, you made two. You see, you've been with me long enough to understand what I'm capable of. I've made no attempt to hide my skill level or my inclination for killing. And yet never once have you stopped to think that having me this close to you would be dangerous. Why not?"

Zio added pressure. Ryker winced. "Because you've never hurt me before."

"That's half the truth, and a foolish trail of logic. The most deadly enemies are the ones that flit under your nose, that live in your house, are your friends and family. Your observations should never be colored by personal feelings. It leads to . . ." She stretched up on her toes, wrapping her lips around the word. "Assumptions."

He grunted.

"Now let's speak of the other half. What is it, Ryker? Why are you not concerned I would harm you? Have you not seen how dangerous I can be? Do you not realize what I am capable of?"

"I . . . Yes, I have, but I didn't . . . I mean . . ."

Zio applied more pressure, certain she'd just drawn blood.

Ryker drew a sharp breath through his teeth. "I don't know."

"I do. You're obsessed. Too distracted with what you *want* to see anything else." She finally released him and stepped back, eying the blood on the tip of her blade. "Obsession has destroyed me four times over. And it will no doubt do it again. But until then, I will meticulously employ it against my enemies." She smoothed out her dress. "The council will expect me to attack with an army because it's what I've usually done. The longer I sit up here in this stronghold, the harder they look for signs of the next attack. And while they guess what I will do and which things I am and am not in possession of . . ." She raised an eyebrow.

"They don't see the knife coming for their back."

"*Exactly.* One of the many blades I've placed is primed and ready to fall. Which means you and I will be heading for the gladiator games to assess the damage and collect what is mine."

29

The tree marked the way. It had filled Verida's dreams and nightmares for years. Dreading the moment it would occupy her vision again, she intentionally kept her head down, refusing to see. Still, she knew the moment it came into view because, behind her, Grey's and Rune's horses slowed as they pulled back on the reins.

"Gawk while you ride," she ordered. "We need to be secure before that sun sets."

Everything in her was screaming to keep her eyes on the saddle horn. Everything, that is, except a smoldering desperation to experience one last piece of *him*.

She looked up.

The river that had once run through here had been a mighty tributary of the Sarahna, and its inescapable power had cleaved straight through one of the many plateaus that squatted across the landscape. The two walls of the canyon now towered on either side of what was left: a delicate, trickling stream. Hanging in the middle, with the bulk suspended in midair, was a gnarled and ancient oak. The entirety of the root system holding it in place was exposed. The oldest roots were now the diameter of dragon tails and bridged from one side to the other. They gripped the surface of the cliff across the upper face and down the sides. Smaller root sections hung straight down and drilled deep into the streambed to tap into the underground water system.

The tree was one of only two things that had survived the cleansing Eon and its inhabitants had exacted from this place.

The setting sun filtered through the root system in rays, laying out the path they would take. Nobody spoke a word as they passed beneath the tree, each choosing slightly varied paths to avoid roots that now looked more like pillars standing before a great hall. The light reflected off the stream and turned it from blue to bright gold.

Verida squeezed her eyes shut.

"I love this time of day," he'd said. "The tree is telling me, 'Welcome home.'" When she laughed at him, he'd pointed and said. "Look, it even rolls out a golden carpet for my lady."

She'd told him he was an idiot. Her heart had swelled anyway. Now her throat was closing, and all she could taste was the tar-like dread she'd awoken with.

Beltran stopped in the clearing ahead. She refused to look at him as she rode past.

"Are you sure?" he asked. "There's still time to go right instead of straight. They don't need to know."

But the Venators were close enough to hear.

"Don't need to know what?" Rune asked.

"I'm sure." Verida snapped the reins.

"If this goes badly," he called, "it's on your head."

That was certain. But there was only one who would be suffering tonight, and this pain was all her own.

Beltran resigned in the face of her silence. "So be it."

On the other side of the clearing, an opaque mist obscured the ruins of the Venator outpost. In the beginning, it had been protection. The council and their resources had eventually broken through enough layers of the magic to penetrate it, but they never could figure out how to dissolve it entirely. Now it just hovered here, impervious to wind and rain and obscuring proof of things this world wanted to forget.

Behind her, Beltran was trying to prep Rune and Grey for what they were about to see. Words like *battle*, *last stand*, and *no survivors* pattered against Verida's ears until she stopped listening and rode her horse straight through. The world turned to a white haze for one brilliantly calm moment, and Verida wanted to stop and sit, to hide somewhere that was not the past and not the present. Somewhere that was absolutely nowhere at all. But when the full moon rose and Ransan's pack went out hunting, this nowhere would rapidly become somewhere once again. Verida didn't rein in her horse. She cleared the wall of mist, and the devastation spread wide before her.

In the beginning, the Venators had worked side by side with the leaders of Eon to ensure peace, and Verida had visited this place often. She'd been a young vampire then, still learning how to help police her father's jurisdiction, long before everything went so horribly wrong. Before the revolution was born. Before the plan to exterminate her kind had been preached amongst the Venators like a religion. Before the wars. And a great many years before the Venators—in the name of righteousness, moral responsibility, and justice—had become the very monsters they'd feared.

Before *him*.

Looking at the outpost now was like staring at two drawings simultaneously. The first had been painted in full color, teeming with life; then it had been set under a layer of muslin, and the same space had been etched over it again in charcoal and ash.

There'd once been beam-constructed homes, market stalls, animal pens, and a bakery. Little carts that sold trinkets and mementoes collected on earth and brought back for those families who'd stopped crossing between worlds. Now there was nothing but rubble, filth, rotted wooden beams, and sun-parched bones. The bones should've been dust by now and long returned to the earth, but the magical barrier seemed to be offering a protection Verida didn't understand from the elements. The Venators still lay where they'd fallen, weapons resting on or near articulated fingers. But their markings had been only skin deep, so the skeletons presented as human.

She turned her attention to the only surviving structure of the outpost—the reason she'd come. A seamless and solitary pillar of impenetrable basalt rock roughly the same size as the largest tower of the council house. Beltran had been right in his concern: without access to the Venators' tower, this location was utterly defenseless.

The first time Verida returned to this place had been after the wars, and she'd been with *him*. The bodies had not been skeletal yet, the scene gruesome, but they'd needed somewhere to hide. He'd shown her inside, and then it was just him and her: a Venator and a vampire all alone in an outpost that had been the ground of this region's final stand. If you could call it that. What Rune and Grey were about to walk into was the site of a massacre—a handful of Venator stragglers who hadn't crossed through the gates with the rest and had tried to hide here.

But at the end of everything, the irony of the tower's final two occupants had never been lost on her. Or on him. Their time together had driven his belief in the old ways deeper, and he had made those ways her own.

As the other three emerged through the mist, not a word was spoken. Neither Rune nor Grey asked where they were or what had happened—Beltran must've done a thorough job of explaining, and she supposed she was grateful for that. As there was no straight path to where she was headed, Verida dismounted and walked the rest of the way on foot, stepping over and around everything from broken carts to swords and bones.

Despite their obvious efforts to remain calm, both Rune's and Grey's hearts started to race as they observed the details within this graveyard that had been so cruelly and accurately frozen in time. Rune stood over the full skeleton of a Venator whose clothes hadn't fully finished crumbling away. No doubt she saw herself in it, because her breathing jolted into a series of rapid, skittering exhalations.

Beltran gently patted her shoulder as he made his way to Verida. "We're losing light. You really know how to get in?"

She looked him straight in the eye, knowing what he would put together. "Yes."

"You're telling me you've been inside?" Beltran leaned closer in that way he did, staring into her eyes while his own rapidly flicked back and forth, searching for truth or deception. When the steady rhythm of his heart added two extra beats, she knew that he knew.

His pupils dilated, and he jerked back. "Saints, Verida. I . . . I di-didn't realize."

He was stuttering. Beltran never stuttered.

She drew herself taller. "Yes, well, I'm afraid my father did."

"I'm so sorry," he whispered. He could barely hold her gaze, looking as unsettled as she'd ever seen him. "When I told Dimitri why your father was upset with you, I didn't know how serious the relationship . . . Oh, bloody hell. Verida, *I swear*, there was no other way."

She gripped him by the shirtfront and yanked him forward. "That's what you keep telling me, but you haven't once told me what the hell that's supposed to mean." She shoved him away. "Stay here."

The tower rose nearly a hundred feet and at first glance looked untouched—as if nature had dropped it there, decided it was as good a place as any, and moved on to work with something less difficult to maneuver. But Verida knew what she was looking at. This hunk of rock had been manipulated to just short of crumbling to a pile of dust. With the exception of the spell work holding the door, the Venators had done the construction themselves, determined that no outsiders would know its secrets—especially not the council.

This tower had been built to hide something beyond its people, and though one naive Venator had been in love with one equally naive vampire and brought her inside, he never had shown her whatever secrets the tower had been built to protect.

It didn't matter. Tonight, she would make sure it protected these Venators in his memory, and she would ensure that his ways were also their ways. It was the least she could do for him.

Verida walked around the tower, looking for the first piece of the puzzle. There, fifteen feet up, she saw the natural dip in the rock that looked like a claw mark. She jumped straight up and swiped her finger from the tip to the end. It lit yellow from within. She reached to the right as she fell, gripping the knob-shaped stone just long enough to activate it. The next steps followed in a natural, flowing sequence, and she closed her eyes, working from muscle memory. When she'd touched the last section of rough and pockmarked stone, she stepped back as the multiple points flashed with one final pulse.

Rune, Grey, and Beltran all inched closer around Verida, staring at the unyielding basalt and holding their breath. She never could remember how long it took from the time she completed the sequence to the time the door opened.

"Verida?" Beltran said.

"Almost."

He looked to the dwindling rays of the sun. "When?"

There was a pop, a hiss, and then the perfectly camouflaged tower door hinged open. Simultaneously, the wizard mist that surrounded them vanished. It didn't blow away or fade—it was just gone.

"Hey." Rune's head swiveled like she was a groundhog looking for predators. "Where'd it go?"

"It doesn't matter. Inside. Beltran and I will get the horses taken care of." Verida put a hand on Rune's back and pushed, repeating the motion with Grey.

"Verida! Come take a look at this." Beltran had slipped off and was now fifty feet away, looking over a crumbling wagon. "Hurry."

She pointed at Grey and Rune in turn. "Stay. There." But when she came up next to Beltran and looked over the wagon's edge, there was nothing more than the skeletal remains that had been there minutes ago.

Beltran took a hard, deliberate step to one side, positioning himself between her and the tower. His green eyes shone. "What did you do?"

"You stood there and watched. I opened the door."

"The spell work in that mist is one of the greatest unknowns surrounding the Venators' secrets, and you weren't the least bit surprised when the barrier vanished. Do you know how many wizards have tried to eliminate it? Arwin and I spent three days here while he muddled through every spell he could think of."

"We need to get inside before the sun drops below the horizon. I'll explain later."

"No, you won't. The minute we're inside, you'll dodge, evade, and threaten until I leave you alone. And if that doesn't work, you'll use the fact that Rune and Grey are there as an excuse to keep from talking. Right now, their markings are indicating only your presence. You'll tell me now."

"*Or what*, Beltran? You'll refuse to go inside? I could leave you out here, lock that door, and not worry for a second that you were in any danger."

"Are you guys coming?" Rune's voice pinged off the stone of the tower's interior, raising her pitch. "What is this place, anyway?"

Verida glanced around Beltran. The base of the fortress had been used for storing weapons, many of which still hung along the walls. Grey was reverently running his fingers across the hilt of a broadsword. A set of stairs had been carved straight out of the rock and occupied the bulk of the base level. Rune stepped onto the first stair, craning her neck to see the top.

"Don't go up there." Verida shoved past Beltran. "I need to find us some light."

Beltran's hand snapped out, grabbed her elbow, and pulled her against him, shoulder to shoulder—Verida facing one way, he the other.

"I don't ask you for a lot of things." His voice was deep and earnest, grinding roughly as he worked to keep his words just above a whisper. In every moment between her and Beltran that had been of any significance, he'd always sounded a lot like this. It sent a shiver up her spine. "After everything that's happened between us, I've tried to allow you to keep your secrets as your own. But I have to know what you did. It could be very important to the both of us."

"How could you possibly know what's important to me?"

"I don't think I do." Beltran lifted his chin, the skin on his neck pulled taut. "You surprised me today."

Verida wasn't nearly as skilled at reading body language as Beltran was. It was a game to him. To her, it was often a form of expression that she couldn't fully decipher. But his tone had already pulled her into hyperawareness, and in that space, she saw the change in him and knew what was happening. His walls were down.

"You know I was the one who told Dimitri that Dracula had caught you in a tryst with a Venator."

She wanted to scream at him, to seize the word *tryst* and shove it down his throat.

But his posture.

The sweat dripping from his hand to her elbow.

There was more.

"Dimitri said you'd been acting odd. He'd gone looking for you more than once and discovered you missing. He suspected something, something serious, so I told him one secret to protect another."

"What did Dimitri suspect?" Verida could feel Beltran wavering against her, weighing cost against consequence.

"Your involvement with the resistance."

The air caught in her lungs. Her free hand inched toward the dagger at her hip. If she were fast enough, she could have it through his eye and into his brain before he could shift.

"Please don't," he murmured. "Rune and Grey won't react well to that. I've known for years. When Dimitri started to suspect your involvement with the resistance, he told me that he planned to speak to Dracula about it. He thought Dracula already knew and that he'd sent his wayward, traitorous daughter straight into the heart of the beast, hoping that service to the council would reform you."

"That's the most ridiculous thing I've ever heard. My father would've removed my head."

The sun flashed and was gone. The world remained silent. No howls. Not one. The lack was unsettling. Verida grew even more alert, listening, smelling, carefully watching Rune's and Grey's markings for the first sign of maroon.

"I know. But one word from Dimitri was all it would've taken to make your father suspect. And we both know that in your father's eyes, suspicion is only a hairsbreadth away from guilt. He wouldn't have stopped until you'd proved your lack of involvement."

Beltran let the implication hang like breath on a cold winter's night. Given her past crimes, there would've been only one way for Verida to prove her innocence. Dracula would've insisted that she infiltrate and destroy the entire resistance from the inside out, bringing him proof of her deeds one head at a time.

"I had to stop Dimitri before he triggered a sequence of events I couldn't control, and there was only one secret I could think to divulge that might subvert what was coming. The real reason Dracula sent you away. The first—and last—truly personal thing you confided in me."

Verida's breath was coming faster. The day Dimitri had called Verida in, gloating of the things he knew, had been horrific. One of the worst days of her life.

"I knew Dimitri would be so disgusted by the revelation of you being with a Venator that he would stop looking for the resistance around every corner. He would blame future mistakes on your per-ceived weakness or on an inherent character flaw—as he does with anything he finds beneath him."

Her father had sent Dimitri back to the council house with a sou-venir. She would never forget the flash of white as Dimitri pulled her father's "gift" out of his breast pocket.

"In order to hide your involvement, the truth was the *only* thing that would stand. I couldn't embellish or manipulate, because I knew Dimitri would take his report to Dracula to verify the information. When your father confirmed the real reason for your exile, then and only then would Dimitri stop looking for a connection between you and the resistance."

Inside the tower, Rune plucked a dagger from the wall and held it up to the limited light. She was pretending to look at it but had clearly angled herself to witness Beltran and Verida's exchange over the blade.

Beltran's confession marched on as he stared out into the mist. "I knew what I had done was unforgivable, but I didn't fully compre-hend until today—when I realized what type of relationship you and this Venator must've had. You would not believe the pain I feel at my betrayal of your trust if I tried to explain it to you, so I will not. But even now, even wishing I could take it back, I can still see no other way."

"Why didn't you tell me any of this before?"

"The way your hand is still hanging over that dagger was taken into consideration."

She flexed her fingers. Although forgiveness remained a far-off glimmer, her perspective had shifted. She relaxed her arm to her side. "Then why are you telling me now?"

"I'm begging. I'm offering you the truth in hopes that you'll trust me enough to tell me how you dissolved the barrier."

Verida took her eyes off the Venators' markings just long enough to look up at him. "I don't know how it works."

His head dropped in defeat.

"I just know *why*. In the last days, they employed a wizard to strengthen the spells on the door—to tie the magic with Venator blood so that the entrance couldn't be breached by enemies. Instead, the wizard betrayed them and tied the magic to the perimeter. To open the door was to bring down the wards for a few minutes. Once the door was shut, the perimeter would reset, but not before it allowed their enemies through. When the outer barrier was finally breached by the council, it was the remaining haze that kept the armies at bay, obscuring how many Venators and what weapons were waiting on the other side of it. The Venators knew they were severely outnumbered. They couldn't risk clearing it."

"Which is why—"

"—why there was no one inside the tower when the siege took place, yes." The moment was over, and she jerked her arm free, wiping his sweat off her skin. "Now help me get these horses unsaddled and the tack inside. I haven't heard a single wolf. Something is wrong."

30

With the tower door pulled shut, they were plunged into darkness. The red glow of Venator markings tinted the edges of the stairs and splashed across the floor. It was a color Verida would rather not have seen painted over the inside of this particular structure; how ironic that she was the cause.

"Cozy." Beltran craned backward. "Somehow I imagined this place with a little more flare."

"It was a military outpost. Were you hoping for chandeliers?"

"That seems a bit ostentatious. But some furs would've been nice."

He didn't see the glare Verida cut in his direction. "We'll stay here tonight. There are beds upstairs. Food will have to wait until breakfast. Anything that was here is long gone."

"Did the beds belong to . . ." Rune's gaze trailed up the stairs. "Them?"

Her eyes went as red as those blasted markings shining back at her. *Them, tryst, fling.* The words both Beltran and Rune had chosen continued to imply casualness and a lack of value. "Them?" she repeated. "*Them?*"

"Verida. Rune didn't mean anything."

"Oh?" She swung her head in Grey's direction. "Thank you for the clarification on her behalf. Please let *Rune* know that if she would rather sleep on the floor, she's more than welcome."

"What did I—?"

"Excuse me, I have a fire to light." Verida took the stairs two at a time, relieved when the others didn't follow.

Her vampire hearing easily picked up Rune whispering to Beltran. "What was that all about?"

"She's just tired . . . and worried about Tate."

"Not that—*that*. Whatever you two were talking about outside."

"We were discussing the plan for this evening. Nothing you need to worry about."

Grey grunted. "Sure. Remind me not to make plans with the two of you if that's what that looks like."

Verida smiled. She really was fond of Grey—when she didn't want to twist his tender heart from both ends to toughen it up. She stepped onto the second floor, and the smile faded as quickly as it had come. Her eyes fluttered closed, and she cautiously sniffed the air, preparing herself for the flood of emotions that would no doubt follow.

There was nothing.

The old Venators had carefully cut ventilation shafts through the walls during construction, matching them up with cavities and blemishes in the exterior stone to hide them from view. Over the years, the air had been naturally exchanged, and the old smells had been replaced with those of the forest. She relaxed. There was a chance she might be able to get through this.

The second floor was pitch black, but her vampire eyesight could discern the shadows of furniture, fixtures, and the boat-sized fire bowl in the center of the room, stacked with wood and tinder. There was an odd shape, however—something lying over the back of one of the chairs. She approached slowly and picked it up. The leather vest was soft as butter and well worn. Her knees grew weak. She remembered now; he'd laid his weapons vest there because they'd been in a hurry. The feel of it in her hand pounded at her brain with the force of a giant's fist, churning up all the thoughts and feelings she'd refused to think on since the night her father had found them.

Memories rose like specters, and the darkness coalesced in front of her, taking the form of a broad-shouldered, dark-haired Venator. She ducked her head and shoved straight through. Imaginary wisps of the past trailed over her exposed skin, clinging like spiderwebs. She clutched the vest to her chest with one hand and brushed at her arm with the other, but there was nothing to dislodge, and the sensation remained, sticking with a stubborn refusal to be pushed aside.

You will not forget, it said.

Not in this place.

Not tonight.

Verida fell against the wooden door of a bedroom—his room—and fumbled at the latch with heavy fingers. The leather vest had set the stage, and the clicking of metal threw her back in time.

They had been surrounded by tendrils of herb-rich smoke in the main room.

"Stop fumbling with the latch," she'd giggled. "You look like a nervous child."

He'd wrapped an arm around her waist, pulled her to his side, and kissed her neck. "Maybe I am."

The door in front of her yielded. The memory vanished, and Verida was alone again.

She stumbled inside the room—cold and dead without his presence. She threw the vest onto the bed, desperate to have it out of her hands, and pulled her chin up as she walked. She stared at the ceiling, refusing to look at the single bed, with its down-filled mattress, its blue coverlet, and the leather weapons vest she'd just added. Verida groped for the side table, missing the knob to the drawer twice. When her fingers finally found it, she roughly pulled it open and grabbed the only two things he'd ever kept inside—a sparking grip and a small piece of rock that had been mined near the Ranquin volcano. The stone was called salenium. It had a silvery shine and contained tiny flecks of gold. The sparking grip was shaped like a horseshoe with the ends hammered in.

Tools in hand, Verida rushed back out the door and approached the bowl, eying it like the viper it was. Those logs had been collected by her and placed by him. They'd been stacked in the way he always did, carefully layered to create air space so the flames would catch. The bundles of tinder had been tied by his hands. He'd prepared the fire bowl that morning under the expectation that they would be back. Instead, this wood had been waiting years for a spark. She ground her teeth, determined to be stronger than a pile of logs, and struck the sparking grip against the rock once, twice. Both wood and tinder were extraordinarily dry, so the fire transitioned with ease from embers to flames.

Light washed across the room. It was exactly how she'd remembered it: a perfect circle with doors around the perimeter that led to bedrooms. The chairs and couches were all simply constructed of wood. No frills, no upholstery, and easy to clean. The room's most prominent feature was the fire bowl. It dominated the floor, its size perpetually out of balance with the space's needs. It was long, wide, and shallow and rested on a pillar that had been carved with symbols Verida recognized only enough to associate with magic.

As the fire bowl obscured her view of the hole in the floor that led to the staircase, Beltran appeared to rise from nothing. His eyes were bright as he methodically surveyed the tower, taking in every detail. Rune and Grey emerged next. Verida hadn't expected their presence to amplify what she'd been feeling. But seeing them in this space, wearing battle clothes, their markings announcing them as the rightful owners of the tower . . . It was as if no time had passed at all.

Grey didn't look like *him*—the boy's skin was lighter, his eyes the wrong color. But he had a gentleness that was reminiscent of him. Verida had recognized it the first time she'd seen Grey in that inn, but she hadn't allowed herself to dwell on it. His inability with weapons and his penchant for always leaping before he looked had made it easier to pretend there was no familiarity to him. But in this space, it was unavoidable. The connection between Grey and *him* was forged.

Rune crouched next to the pile of lumber and baskets of tinder and picked up a bundle of herbs, twisting it back and forth between her fingers. The ancient stems crumbled to dust, flaking over her black pants.

She stood, brushing off her hands. "If this was a Venator stronghold, how'd you know how to get in?"

Grey turned his head, and all Verida could see was his dark hair and the line of his shoulders. The red glow of Venator markings. Her heart was galloping out of control, and her lips started to form another name.

"Verida?"

She jolted. "You aren't the first Venators I've met. I, um, need to put these away." She held up the rock and sparking grip. "I'll be right back." She nodded. "Right back."

Rune's brow furrowed. "Are you all right?"

"Fine. Get comfortable. Choose a room, if you'd like. I'll be back."

She'd already said that.

Verida tried to walk calmly, but every step was faster than the last. When she reached his room, she carefully closed the door behind her. The light from outside slipped in around her feet and lit up everything she'd tried not to see. The bed, the blue cover, the simple wooden nightstand. And, in the corner of the room, the longsword that had belonged to his father.

She fell back against the door, clutching her arms around her middle as her mouth stretched in a silent wail. It was too much; her unheard cries would not stop. Years of feelings redoubled, one against the other, until she was writhing against the door.

Her back arched, and she clenched her fist around the salenium. As its rough surface tore through her skin, a sharp bite of physical pain bloomed. It was there she found escape. She seized the distraction, wrenching herself closer to the only answer she'd ever found.

Vengeance. For what had been taken from her.

Imagining the price she would exact from her father, Verida forgot his father's sword in the corner; the nightstand, where he always had a dagger within reach; and the bed, where they had shared so very many things. Revenge unraveled in her head, step by step, leading her out of the darkness.

Verida's breaths slowed. She pushed off the door, rolling her shoulders and loosening up her neck muscles, thinking only of ripping her father's heart out. When she felt calm enough to rejoin the others, she crossed the room, opened the drawer to the nightstand, and dropped the rock and grip inside. There were two hard clunks, and then something else rattled. She frowned and pulled the drawer to its edge, exposing a small velvet bag tucked into a shadowed corner.

The bag easily fit in the palm of her hand, and when she closed her fist, the shape of the item within became apparent. Verida's knees went weak. She reached back blindly, feeling for the down mattress, and slowly lowered herself to the dusty bed. Trembling, she uncurled her hand and pulled the drawstrings apart. Nestled inside the velvet were two wooden rings. She brushed her fingers across the tops and inhaled sharply.

He'd been lying on his back, shoved against the wall so the bed would accommodate them both. Their fingers intertwined, his thumb running over hers.

"Those rings Vega wears are—"

"Ridiculous," she'd finished for him.

"I was going to ask if they were from your family's vault."

"Of course. She always chooses the largest ones, as if she needs to announce her status to all of Eon." Verida scoffed. "Why in Rana's name do I need to prove I have a fortune by dripping it from my fingers?"

He stared at the ceiling. "What kind of ring would *you* wear? If you had one."

"None."

"But if you did."

"*None.*"

"*But if you did!*"

"Why do you want to know so bad?"

"I'm just trying to understand you better."

"Why?"

He'd rolled onto his side and propped up on an elbow so he could grin down at her. "Because, Verida of House Dracula, you perplex me. And occasionally annoy me. Look." He leaned across her and grabbed his dagger from the side table. "I chose this blade because I liked the feel of it in my hand but also because the rest of the daggers had filigree work, jewels, or both. I like my things simple. I didn't want anyone to look at my weapons and think, *There goes someone of status.*"

"You wished to be invisible?"

He evaluated the dagger. "Sometimes."

"Hard to do with Venator markings."

He grunted and stretched across her again, returning the weapon to the side table. He then flopped flat on his back and went silent. Her refusal to answer the question was bothering him, though she didn't understand why.

"If you insist on defining me with a ring, I would choose a band."

"A plain band?"

"No. I would want it to mean something." She held up her hand, turning it as if she were already wearing a ring. "I would have it engraved."

"With what?" The question was whispered almost reverently.

She'd had to think about it, and he had waited. "Something that marked where I came from and where I was going."

With the same amount of reverence she'd felt in his question that night, Verida pulled out the smaller of the two bands. The engraving was a little rough and had obviously been done by hand, but it ran around the center of the ring in a pattern she was intimately familiar with. She gasped.

He had been lying on his stomach, and she had been stretched half over him, tracing a finger down his spine—as she often did. "Your markings are less angular than most I've seen."

"I think that means I'm a good lover."

She laughed out loud. "Does it?"

"Is that skepticism I hear?" He rolled onto his back and grabbed her, pulling her against his chest. "Do you doubt the conclusion?"

"Hmmm. I can't remember. It's been so long."

He cocked a brow and smirked. "I think I'll remind you."

And he had.

The ring was engraved not only with his Venator markings but with a second layer carved over the top. Letters. Verida twisted the ring between her fingers, putting the words together.

Until The End.

A sob ripped free, and she slapped a hand across her mouth.

His heart rate had been slowly increasing, and perspiration had beaded across his forward. She'd wondered what he'd been working up to, but she'd waited.

"Come home with me," he blurted.

"I'm already in your bed."

"No, Verida. Not the outpost. Let's make a home somewhere safe. Where it can just be us."

She sat up. "Go into hiding?"

He nodded. "We could pretend to be human."

"How am I going to pretend to be human with these?" She pointed to her teeth.

"Well," he pretended to think, pursing his lips. "I suppose we could file them down."

She slugged him.

"I was joking." He chuckled, rubbing at his arm. "I love your fangs. You know that."

"It's not you I'm worried about."

He pushed up, careful not to knock her off the bed, and gathered her hands in his. "I don't care what anyone else thinks. I want to be with you. Forever."

The moment, however beautiful it was, could not survive, for his desire was already her biggest fear. She jerked her hands free of his. "Don't say that!"

"Why not?"

"Where are we supposed to go? You were already in hiding, and I found you. There is nowhere for your kind to go."

"There has to be somewh—"

"Even if we found some desolate cave at the top of the Blues, froze our asses off, and never left, you don't have forever! You have *years*."

He took her face in his hands, his touch calming her in a way that nothing else did. "I love you."

Verida hadn't thought it possible. Yet the words cracked something open between them—a door that had, until now, been closed.

"I love your fangs. I love your temper, even if I am worried that someday you're going to break my arm." He grinned. "I love every single thing about you."

She could do nothing but stare at him in wonder. "I . . . I love you too."

He grabbed her hands and pulled them to his chest, pressing his own over the top. "Forever doesn't mean *forever*. It means . . . It just means . . ." His dark eyes snapped up. "Until the end. What more could we ask for than that?"

He had kissed her then, long and slow. And when he was done, he pulled away and slid one hand under her jaw. "I love you, Verida, until the end."

The words echoed through the years, and she moaned, clutching the ring to her chest as she tipped to the side, laying her head against the same blue coverlet they'd whispered their hopes and dreams on. She wanted to feel his skin, to rest her head against his chest, to hear his heartbeat. Verida reached out for the other ring, dragging the velvet bag across the covers and clutching it as she curled in on herself.

Until the end.

He must've started working on the bands the next day, while she was out pretending to be the dutiful daughter her father had still thought she was. He would've been here, carving, not knowing they had only weeks until the last day of their forever.

Verida turned her face into the mattress, breathing in the dust and dirt, muffling the sounds of her sobs as she said his name over and over again.

"Dominick."

Amar was stretched flat across the tree branch—his legs locked at the ankles beneath it, his arms over the top—staring at the field of bodies and blood that had been a bustling camp not even an hour earlier. There would be no wolf run tonight, because as the sun set and the full moon rose, he was the only one left to feel its power. Sole survivor— that's what Zio had said. He'd doubted her. He would never make that mistake again.

He'd been instructed to wait in the tree for the next player in Zio's plan to come to him, but Amar almost hadn't made it onto the branch at all. For reasons he still couldn't comprehend, he'd been sure that the portal would open in the middle of the meadow; it had made sense at the time. Instead, it had opened less than an hour before sunset in the southwest corner of camp, where he'd been collecting firewood. It had opened, in fact, five feet behind him. Which made sense now, considering it had been his blood that had allowed her to open a portal in the first place.

An exceptionally tall female had emerged, her feet on the ground before Amar even finished turning. Raised black veins had run through the vampire's eyes. She'd seized him by the throat and lifted, looking straight though him as if he wasn't there at all. More vampires rushed from the portal opening, parting around them as they descended on the pack. Amar's feet had churned through empty air, and he'd clawed at the female's hand. As shouts of warning rose up behind him, he'd croaked out the only word he thought might help.

"*Zio.*"

There had been no recognition on her face, but it had worked. She'd tossed Amar to the side like an old, gnawed bone. He'd bounced once, and when he landed the second time, two ribs broke. He couldn't wait for them to heal, so he'd gritted his teeth and scurried up the nearest tree to watch Zio's plan unfold.

Because the portal had opened before sunset, no one had been able to shift into wolf form, giving the vampires an edge despite their smaller numbers. The real advantage came in the tirelessness of Zio's warriors. Regardless of injury, they'd kept coming, as if they didn't feel pain. And their speed never wavered, attacking at full force—sometimes while spurting blood from their jugulars—until they literally dropped dead. The battle was short lived, and wolf and vampire alike had succumbed until there were only three survivors left—two vampires and Ransan. The alpha fought hard, but it wasn't enough. The moment he fell, the two victors had frozen midstep, a hush washing over the field.

Amar had looked from one vampire to the other, trying to understand what was happening. There was a sudden flurry of movement as the female twisted at the waist, seized the male by the head, and broke his neck. Amar startled, almost falling from the branch. She hadn't even looked at her victim before she was walking again, stepping on and over bodies. The vampire was clear of the massacre and almost out of the meadow when she stopped in front of a tree with an ax embedded in the trunk. She'd wrenched the weapon free, turned to face her dead kin, and smashed the blade into her own skull.

Amar's jaw dropped.

Blood poured down her face, but as death started to take hold, something had changed. Her eyes opened wider, as if she'd just realized what she'd done. Her arms started to fall, growing weak, but in a last act of will, she'd reset her grip on the ax's handle, squeezing so tight that Amar could see the bulge of tendons and muscles down her forearms. Then she'd dropped to her knees, tipped to the side, and lain still.

"Don't make me come up there," a male voice called from below. "You didn't pay me enough for that."

He looked down. He'd been so lost in replaying the scene in his head that he hadn't heard or smelled the incoming vampire. Zio had told him to hire one and had left him little time to do it. Originally, he'd thought he'd choose a female, but this particular male had been inordinately attractive and extremely vocal in his hatred of Dimitri. His skin was golden, his jaw delightfully square, and his fingers long and elegant.

If Amar was going to willingly allow himself to be bitten, he intended to enjoy it.

The male pursed his lips and crossed his arms. "Are you coming down? Or upping your advance?"

It wouldn't matter how much he paid him; this vampire wouldn't be enjoying any of it. Amar dropped from the tree. "Don't forget what I've bought."

The male looked over Amar's shoulder at the meadow behind him. "I've already forgotten, and only a fool would be near wolf territory on a full moon."

Before Amar could say anything else, the vampire grabbed him by the shoulders and pulled him forward, roughly sinking his teeth into his neck and pulling blood in long, painful jerks. He'd heard vampires could make this process enjoyable. This one didn't bother.

The instructions had been to leave him on the verge of death, with just enough blood to keep his heart pumping. He hadn't stopped to think of one thing: What would stop the vampire from finishing him off?

The world was spinning, and the vampire dug deeper, jerking his head and tearing the skin on Amar's neck wide open. He'd felt bad paying the male for his services while knowing that Zio would have him eliminated before the night was out. He felt that no longer. This one deserved everything that was coming to him.

The tower was quiet as Beltran paced the floor. Rune and Grey had finally gone to bed, and Verida never had emerged from that room she'd disappeared into. He needed to lie down himself—sleep had become a scarcity since they'd left the council—but something was off.

He looked first for the most logical explanation, wondering if perhaps he'd underestimated the tower's ability to insulate sound. Beltran peered at the ceiling, located a ventilation shaft, and positioned himself beneath it. The opening to the outside did allow him to hear a little more, and he picked up the faint cry of an owl. But there were no howls, not one. No sign of the monthly hunts or celebrations. It was as if the pack had vanished from the area entirely. Verida was right. Something was wrong. But what?

He took a quick minute, passing by the fire bowl with its intriguing inscriptions, to check on Grey—ensuring the boy was asleep and not trapped in one of his visions. He then grabbed a chair and pulled it beneath the shaft, dropping wearily onto it. Beltran had intended to listen, but the exhaustion pressed down relentlessly.

Resting his head on his fist, he dozed in spurts, constantly reawakened by the silence. He must've finally fallen into a deeper sleep, because when he woke, his wrist was throbbing, and his eyelids no longer felt like they were full of sand. He looked up. The light outside had turned the inside of the shaft from black to dark gray. Beltran got to his feet and headed for the stairs.

"Where are you going?" Verida was leaning against the doorframe, her hair mussed with sleep.

"How long have you been there?"

"Not long. I was about to wake you."

"There's nothing out there. Not one sound. I don't care what alliances they did or did not form—nothing stops a wolf pack from running on the full moon."

She nodded, wrapping her arms around her ribs. She was clutching a red bag in her fist. He didn't ask.

"I'm going to find the pack and see what's happened. I'll give you a day's head start before I deliver the summons the council sent. Push the horses as much as you can. I'll meet up with you late tomorrow night."

"Beltran?" She looked down, her thumb making circles over the top of the red bag. "Why did you work so hard to hide my membership in the resistance?"

He'd already opened the door to that topic and saw no point in lying to try and close it. "I always protect my own interests. You know that."

The vampire had dropped Amar to the ground like a sack of potatoes and vanished. He'd been flitting in and out of consciousness since. Sometimes, he thought he saw a full moon. Other times, he was sure he felt the heat of the sun baking his skin. But regardless of the time, he was lost in nightmares of black-veined eyes and his long-dead wife, all while feeling the tightness in his chest as his heart strained to pump what little blood he had left.

The vampire had been told to remove enough blood to ensure that Amar was still near-dead when Silen found him. But he couldn't wake up. Was he near-dead? Or dead-dead? As his subconscious pondered what dead-dead would feel like, he detected the first scent of decomposing bodies mingling with the smell of meadow grass. That implied near-dead, didn't it? The ability to smell? In a brief moment of lucidity, he found himself wondering if Zio would care one way or the other.

A bird chirped. Something poked into his side.

"Hey! What yous wants me to say?"

Amar startled, his eyes flying open. The light was searing, and he moaned, squeezing them closed again.

"Wakes up!" Something, or someone, kicked him. "You has to tells me what yous wants me to be telling Silen?"

Silen . . . Silen . . . Amar blinked several times. Above him, the sun was high in the sky, and the leaves flitted in a soft breeze. Following the source of the sound, he rolled his head, grimacing. Without blood, he couldn't heal, and the dual wounds on his neck were still raw and throbbing.

Standing at his side and wringing its hands was the gray-skinned, bat-eared creature that Amar had met once before at the council house. Danchee.

"What—?" Amar's voice sounded like a bullfrog had taken up residence in his throat. He licked his lips. "What do you want?"

"It's lates. Yous sleep too long. What's the messages?"

"I'm alive?"

"Yes, yes." Danchee rolled his hands one over the other, as if trying to clean something off. "Messages. Hurries!"

Hurry? He could barely think. What was he supposed to say? What was the plan?

"Tell Silen . . . the pack was murdered."

"All rights." Danchee turned away.

There was more. He knew there was more. But what? "Wait! Tell Silen I barely survived. Tell him I suffered blood loss but that you found me . . . uhh, you found me . . . looking for survivors." Yes. That was good. Noble. "Tell him . . ."

Amar didn't remember drifting off, but he woke to dirt pelting him as Danchee tunneled off to deliver the message. He spat, too tired to wipe his face, and stared at the tree leaves, running through the conversation. He'd done well. The story was perfect. Except . . . His already slow heart rate dropped.

Except for one thing.

Looking for survivors had sounded like a brilliant idea, but it meant that when Silen or his scouts arrived, Amar would need to be out *there*, among the dead. Groaning in anticipation of what this would cost him, he heaved himself to the side and began to drag himself toward the meadow. Every inch of land he conquered lit up a new pain center in his body. He was nearly out of the trees when a shadow passed overhead. The wingspan was too large to be a bird, the angles too harsh for feathers. Amar's first thought was *dragon*. But it was no beast. Instead, a human-bodied, leather-winged creature landed in the clearing.

Amar lay still, squinting through the strands of grass as the creature's wings shrunk to nothing and disappeared within the man's back. A shifter! He could barely believe his eyes. He'd only ever heard rumors. Flattening himself further, he watched as the shifter moved around the clearing to take stock of the carnage. The man knelt by several bodies, turning them over so he could see their faces and taking time to intently study each.

A wave of dizziness yanked at him. He fought against it, but it was no use. He passed out again. When he came to, the sun was farther along its axis. The shifter had moved all of the bodies into a pile and had stacked the precut firewood in camp around them. A funeral pyre. As a precaution, the meadow grasses had been cleared to the dirt for several feet around. The shifter pulled a rolled-up piece of parchment from his pocket and tucked it under Ransan's dangling arm, then touched a burning stick to the tinder. Flames caught hold, grabbing onto clothing and hair alike as they climbed to the top of the pyre.

No, no, no, no!

This shifter was destroying every piece of evidence. Even disregarding the fact that Zio had clearly wanted Silen to find what had been done, the more immediate problem was Danchee—who was about to report that Amar had been alert enough to give him a message. Alert enough, even, to "check for survivors." But somehow incapable of stopping someone from wiping out every piece of evidence of a vampire attack on a werewolf pack. All while surviving . . . again.

Amar pushed away from the scene, trying to return to the forest without being seen. He turned his body and dragged himself along, pulling one forearm over the other. He could not be here. He couldn't be anywhere Silen or his scouts could find him.

Silen would kill him this time.

Without a doubt.

32

Beltran waited at the lip of land that stood between the last lingering dregs of the forest behind him and the haphazard drop of loose dirt and rocks that fanned out below. He stepped forward, letting his toes hang over the edge. This new desert landscape would usher them all the way to the Blues and deep into the Underground. He scowled at the clear line of trees and bushes that followed the river into the distance. The barren landscape they were about to enter harbored very little shelter and only one route that would keep the horses fed and watered.

He'd worked against some dismal odds, but this trip was stacking up nicely to be one of the worst. Already unhappy with how many open-ended problems they were facing, he now had to add the implications of the nightmare he'd discovered at Ransan's camp—the evidence of which he'd burned to the ground. Although a lack of evidence would slow the progression of the fallout, it identified neither the culprit nor the motivation behind the act. A repeat performance was likely imminent.

Beltran ground his boot against the edge of the ridge, dislodging clods of dirt and watching as they pitter-pattered down the slope.

This was not the first time he'd found himself in a scenario of this magnitude, and he'd walked away from all of them—bravery never served anyone from the grave. But doing that now would mean toppling everything he'd been building. As such, he'd spent the last few nights trying to work out a plan, but every blasted thought started with *if* or *maybe*. Two words he loved while speculating, because he was damn good at that and was always fairly certain of the direction things would tip. But now he was running scenarios with giant black holes peppered through the middle and was forced to use the *ifs* and *maybes* bloody properly!

Behind him, he heard the first snort of a horse, followed by the clop of hooves. Finally. He shook off the tension running across his shoulders and faced the forest, lifting his head to smile at the three approaching horses.

Verida's expression was murderous. "Where in Rana's name have you been?"

"I had a few problems to deal with."

"Problems that took you *three* days?" Rune shouted, leaning over her saddle. Her horse's ears lay flat. "I thought you were dead!"

Beltran's smile grew. She'd been worried. He winked at the incoming freckled ball of fire. "So little faith in me. I'm genuinely offended."

"I told her you were fine," Verida said. "And probably at the council house reporting to Dimitri."

"No, didn't do that." Beltran stuck his hands in his pockets and looked up at the sun. "Though maybe I should have."

Verida snapped the reins. Her horse picked up its pace, reaching him before the others. She pulled to a stop at his shoulder and glared down. "What is that supposed to mean?"

"I have a lot to share with you." He jerked his chin toward Grey. "Have you been training them?"

"It infuriates me when you ask questions that insult my intelligence."

"Good. I'll join you this evening. Give them some new creatures to fight. Any plans for dinner? Or should I track something down?"

Verida swung off her horse. "I'll find food. You get those two as deep in as we can and set up camp."

"Not planning on returning soon?"

"It might take some time for me to run off all of my fury so I can actually listen to what you have to say instead of having to sit there and test my self-control." She smiled tightly and slapped her reins into his hand.

"We're heading that way?" Grey's feet hit the ground, and he walked to the same lip Beltran was standing at, looking out over the valley.

Verida strolled away, calling back over her shoulder, "If anyone has any requests for dinner, speak now, or don't speak at all."

"No frogs, please," Grey said. "Too little meat, too much work."

"Can't argue with the boy's logic." Beltran tracked Grey's line of sight, following it out across the desert they were about to cross. "Homey, isn't it?"

"Actually, yeah. Hey, Rune." Grey motioned for her to come. "You have to see this."

Rune had been hanging back. She dismounted and stepped between the two men. "Woah."

"Right?" Grey pointed a finger, pulling it across the line of the horizon. "Even the spacing is almost identical. Look at the break between those two hills."

"It's exactly like the foothills behind campus."

"I know. I never thought I'd miss that place, but this is making me a little homesick."

Rune gave a half smile. "Me too."

Beltran thought they were kidding, but the nostalgia on their faces said they were not. He took in the barren landscape again, searching for value in the location. "This is what earth is like? I expected more."

"There *is* more," Grey said. "But this looks like part of earth, just like it's part of Eon."

"But . . ." Of course he hadn't expected all of earth to look the same. That wasn't what had confused him. "But why would you live in something like this? Almost nothing makes its home down there. It's too inhospitable."

Rune and Grey shared a look and a chuckle.

"What?"

"On earth," Rune said, "we lowly humans make *everything* hospitable. We can bring in water, light . . . and even adjust the temperature."

"But there's no magic on earth." Beltran waited for an explanation Rune's smirk said wasn't coming. "All right, you have my attention. How?"

The smirk unfurled into a full grin as she cocked her head to the side, looking up at him from beneath thick lashes. "We use our evolved brains." She tapped her temple. "Maybe you Eon inhabitants should give that a try sometime."

Grey snorted, choking on his own spit as he launched into laughter.

33

Grey held his breath as long as he could, peering through the murky water. He waited until his lungs were burning, then planted his feet and pushed off the riverbed. Rocketing up, he broke the surface. His momentum pushed him higher, and he stretched his spine, reaching for more—for blue sky and freedom. But gravity in Eon was equally as cruel as on earth, and it reeled him back. The river caught his descent, and he bobbed to a gentle stop with his feet resting on the bottom. When goose bumps erupted over his exposed skin, he sloshed toward the bank.

Once on land, he grabbed his pants, but without a towel, pulling on the skin-tight Venator clothes was a challenge. It took a ridiculous amount of dancing, jerking, and swearing before he finally got them up and around his waist. The other pair of pants and the shirt he'd washed were still sopping wet. He threw them over his shoulder and trudged up the small hill to camp.

When he cleared the main apex of the incline, their camp came into view. Four tents were pitched and waiting, clothes were drying over a low-hanging tree branch, and a meager fire was crackling away. Beltran was still bathing downriver, but Verida had returned and was sitting near the fire next to Rune, skinning a long, thin snake.

Well, at least it wasn't frogs.

As Grey approached, Verida stopped working. She lifted her head and pierced him with those blue eyes. He was surprised to find them empty of anger for the first time in days but was acutely aware of the way her heated gaze moved over his chest and stomach in unabashed appreciation . . . and the way Rune's did not. He was uncomfortable, pleased, and disappointed all at the same time, but he wasn't feeling the need to duck his head, roll his shoulders, or cross his arms over his chest to hide his shirtless body.

That was new.

The closer he came to the fire, the more Verida's lips pursed. He did his best to ignore it, focusing instead on the subtle changes happening inside himself. He felt . . . *lighter*. The crushing shame that caused him to curl in on himself under any sexual look or comment—or attention of any kind, really—lacked the weight it had had before.

As he hung his pants and shirt over a tree branch to dry, he contemplated what might've brought about the change. The answer struck him like a bolt of lightning, and he froze, still gripping the wet pant legs. He would've laughed if the answer hadn't been so bitter. Instead, he rolled his eyes at the irony.

To find control over his trauma, and to start acting instead of reacting, Grey had shuffled the cards he'd been dealt in every way he could think of, always trying to gain the upper hand. The one thing he'd never thought to try. . . was releasing the deck.

He pulled on a clean shirt and his cloak, then sat next to Rune in the grass. She was wearing her cloak as well but had left off her boots and was digging her toes through the soft green strands of grass.

"No pine needles." She grinned. "It's amazing."

"Enjoy it while it lasts." Verida added the last snake to the fire and pulled off two of the three that were cooking. "Another day, and we'll be sitting in dirt and rocks." She passed two skewered snakes to Rune and Grey in turn.

Beltran appeared over the ridge, carrying his wet clothes. Grey couldn't help but notice his ridiculously perfect body. The abs, the pecs, the biceps. What would it be like to simply shift your body into proper form? No diet or exercise, just . . . perfection. The concept annoyed him immensely, but it didn't seem to be bothering Rune.

Grey leaned to the side and muttered at Rune's shoulder, "You're drooling."

Rune jumped. "I am not."

"You are." Verida pulled Beltran's dinner from the fire.

Rune grumbled something unintelligible as she peeled off a strip of meat and popped it into her mouth.

"Hurry up!" Verida called to a casually strolling Beltran. "Yours is done and getting cold."

"We can't have that, now can we?" He reached out for his portion as he passed, continuing on to hang his wet clothes on the tree.

The snake wasn't bad at first taste. But then Grey chewed . . . and chewed and chewed. Rune's throat bobbed as she struggled to swallow her first bite. Verida didn't seem to notice. Sitting cross legged on the ground, she watched Beltran like a hawk.

"Three days," she said once he'd hung up his clothes and sat down with the group. "Where did you go for *three days?*"

Beltran gripped the skewer with both hands and took the snake meat between his teeth. He pulled back, wrenching a piece free, then frowned. "I'll make you a deal," he said around his chewing. "If I tell you, you will promise to never, *ever* be in charge of cooking snake again." He swallowed and held up the skewer, peering at it suspiciously. "Saints, it's like trying to eat a belt. This was alive earlier today, wasn't it? Or did you just find it lying dead?"

Verida crossed her arms. "Grey? What do you think of the meal?"

He was trying to chew with less of a show than Beltran was putting on, but the only way to get enough force to grind through it was to partially open his mouth. "A belt might be harsh. But it's a little . . ."

"You should never lie to Verida." Beltran grabbed the snake with his teeth and ripped off another piece, grunting as he did. "She hates it."

Verida jerked her head toward Beltran. "He would know."

Grey deflected. "What do *you* think, Rune?"

"I'm not asking her," Verida said. "I'm asking you."

He sagged. "It might be a *little* like trying to eat a belt."

"Critics. The lot of you." Verida yanked the last snake off the fire— the one she'd just added, the one that was likely *not* overcooked—and threw it over her shoulder. "Beltran, you've won the right to cook tomorrow. Now talk. If you didn't go to the council, where have you been?"

"I went to deliver the summons as we agreed," he said, still chewing. "But when I got there, Ransan's pack had been decimated."

Verida leaned forward, bracing her elbows on her knees. "What do you mean *decimated?*"

"The only thing decimated can mean. Every single pack member had been killed." He swallowed and looked to Verida. "It occurred to me that this might be to our benefit, until I realized that the massacre had been carried out by vampires."

"*What?*" Verida hissed. She searched his face as if she were waiting for him to start laughing and then tell them what had really happened. But Beltran's expression was stone.

"That's not possible," she said. "No. It had to have been someone else."

"The proof was there. The battle took place in Ransan's camp, and vampires were scattered among the dead."

"Isn't this a good thing?" Rune looked from Beltran to Verida and back again. "It's like you said—we don't have to look over our shoulders for Ransan's pack anymore."

Verida huffed and shook her head, then bolted to her feet, pacing rapidly.

Grey swallowed another bite of rubbery snake meat. "Why am I getting the feeling that this is worse than Rune and I are realizing?"

"Because it's *far* worse," Beltran said. "There are no vampires in this area, at least not any clans. If there were a clan nearby, it could be suggested that an altercation had taken place, blows became a battle, and the end result was the massacre I found. But without any local clans, we're left without a single explanation as to why the vampires would've been there in the first place. Thus, it can only be assumed that the attack was ordered either by the vampire leader closest to the pack or by a council member. In this case, that would be Dimitri."

Verida dropped into a sudden crouch next to Beltran. "Did you recognize any of them?"

"I didn't. But I studied their faces to see if you would." Beltran dropped his chin, looking at Grey and Rune from beneath his brow. "Face shifting is unnerving, I'm told. You can look away if you need."

He closed his eyes, and his face started to morph. Most of the changes were hidden by the position of his head, but the effect was still eerie. His forehead grew larger, his ears moved outward, and his hairline shifted back. When he looked up, he'd become a wide-nosed man with a thick chin and deep-set eyes. Verida shook her head no. He tried again. A woman this time. Still no. On the third try, the face was much closer to Dimitri's—thin nose, sharp chin, but with a wider jawline and larger eyes.

Verida's hand flew to her mouth.

"You know this one?"

Grey and Rune both winced at the same time. Hearing Beltran's voice come out of a completely different face was bizarre.

"That's not possible." Verida leaned in, closely examining the features. "This is one of my father's top counselors. Kasove. House Pietrala."

"Saints." Still Beltran's voice. "Would Kasove have struck out on his own? Started an uprising among the vampires like Beorn and Cashel were trying to do within the werewolf ranks?"

"No, never. He was kinder than most, which led some of the others to push him around in the councils, but he is . . . *was* unquestionably loyal to Dracula." She dropped back to sitting.

"There is one other thing," Beltran said. "Watch."

The blood vessels in his eyes started to swell, undulating unevenly. It looked like tiny bugs were crawling through his veins and pushing at the surface as they forced their way through with rounded backs. Grey shuddered. Then, like a balloon giving way to breath, the veins suddenly bulged outward and turned from red to black, cutting dark cracks through the whites of his eyes.

Beltran pointed. "Every single one of the dead vampires looked like this."

"But not the werewolves?" Rune inched closer, peering through the incoming twilight. "What in the hell *is* that?"

"It took me a while to get the look right. The blood vessels are engorged and swollen. From what, though, I don't know." The black veins dissipated until they were flat again. "The pressure it adds to the eye is painful. I can only hold it for so long. And no, Rune—only the vampires."

"Could it be a disease?" Grey asked.

"Not one that I've ever seen," Verida said.

"Is it bothering anyone else that he's still wearing a dead vampire's face?" Rune ran her fingers down her cheeks as if she wanted to rip the death mask off Beltran herself.

"Right, sorry." Beltran dipped his head, then looked up as himself. "There *is* one more thing."

Verida growled. "No! You already said 'one more thing' one more thing ago!"

"The victor of the battle was a vampire. I found her dead on the outskirts of camp."

Rune frowned. "The survivor was dead?"

"I probably wouldn't have noticed her if it weren't for the fact that she was lying outside the battle zone. Her hands were still wrapped around the handle of the blade that was embedded in her skull. It was strange, but when I looked closer, I realized that given the angle of the ax, the wound could only have been self-inflicted."

Grey lost his appetite for what was left of his snake leather. He set it to the side. "You're saying she survived the massacre, walked away, and then committed suicide. With an ax?"

"We have to go back." Verida was already starting to rise. "If anyone else finds them—"

"Stop." Beltran grabbed hold of her arm and pulled her back down. "Already taken care of. I burned it all. No matter how grateful Silen will be to have Ransan out of the picture, he can't let a vampire attack stand and maintain the support of his people. As to the length of time I was gone . . ." He grimaced.

"Aaand there's more." Grey tossed a hand in the air—it was the only thing he could think of to express his frustration.

Rune elbowed him in the side.

"After I burned the evidence to the ground—messy, disgusting work, by the way." He shuddered. "You're welcome. I haven't had to deal with that amount of carnage firsthand in years."

"Get on with it!" Verida snapped.

"I found tracks. Someone else survived, and judging by the distinctive trail of dirt, whoever it was had already relayed the events to Danchee, who likely headed for Silen."

The effect of the name on Grey was immediate, and for a second he was back on the edge of Feena's forest with Morean and Turrin approaching as Danchee wrung his ears, yelling that he was "sorries."

"It was too late to catch Danchee," Beltran continued. "So I followed the tracks instead. I found a werewolf, drained of blood and half-dead, dragging himself across the forest. I followed him for a day and a half. When he finally reached his destination . . ." He shook his head. "I've never seen magic like that. The wolf retrieved a bag from a cave and used the contents to create a portal in seconds, without the help of a wizard's orb. He stepped in, the portal closed, and he was gone."

"A portal!" Verida said. "To where?"

"I can think of only one person who is known to have new magic."

Rune sat up straighter. "Zio."

Beltran nodded. "By the time I returned to the clearing, Silen's scouts were moving in. I don't know what Danchee reported, but without any other witnesses and nothing but ash and bone to go on, they won't have enough to retaliate. But they'll be on high alert."

"They have the bones!" Verida shouted. "A vampire skull looks distinctly different from a werewolf one! And I don't care how long you let that bonfire burn, those skulls are still going to be recognizable."

"I was smart enough to remove the vampire heads and dispose of them elsewhere. Saints, Verida, I'm not an infant."

Another day, another cover story with fifteen subpoints Grey would never have thought twice about. Having supernatural skills was fantastic until you started a war because you didn't think to remove the vampires' skulls from the scene of the crime.

Verida lashed out, picking up a piece of a branch from the ground and throwing it toward the hill. "Nothing makes any sense!"

"I know, and it doesn't matter. For now, we're locked into our course. When we get to the Underground, we can ask around and see how much of . . . *everything* we can unravel. But unless something miraculous happens, we'll be walking into that arena half-blind, and *if* we walk out, we'll be in the same situation. Such is the reality. We're just going to have to work with it."

"Then we better make sure we're as ready as we can be." Rune got up, brushing her hands off on her pants. "What are we training on tonight?"

Beltran grinned. "I'm so glad you asked. I've got a lot of nervous energy to work off and a host of exciting ideas of how to do it."

34

As the fae army broke camp for the final time, Keir chose twenty of his people to accompany him and ordered Tate bound and hooded. They left the forest's outskirts and turned northwest for the final leg of the journey. Tate knew if they marched at full speed, as they had been marching, it would take nearly three-quarters of the day to reach the gates of the arena.

Even without his sight, he tracked their path with near exactness. As one of the few gladiators who consistently survived the games, Tate had spent his life being passed first from arena to arena and then—as his skills and reputation grew—from one owner to the next. It wouldn't have mattered what direction they'd come from or if Keir had blindfolded him the moment they'd entered the Dark Forest; he would've always known exactly where they were.

By moving through the Dark Forest, Keir had avoided traveling openly, hiding from the eyes of the council and circumventing what would've been a final crossing through the desolate stretch of land between the forests and the even more inhospitable plateaus that followed. Unless travelers were aiming to stop by the Underground, most avoided that path when possible. Tate had once preferred it. It was faster, and it had been of no consequence to him who or what spotted him. He was already a prisoner, bought and sold to fight to the death. What did he care where he fought his battles?

Before Ayla, dying outside of the arena walls had been the most he could hope for.

Hours passed, and fae stamped tirelessly on around him. He was blind, stumbling on any piece of earth, rock, or vegetation that wasn't flat, and his head spun from being forced to recirculate his own hot, stale breath.

The ground inclined sharply, and though the pain in his heels was so severe that he could feel every step jarring clear through his teeth, Tate felt relief. They would be within sight of the arena now. The sun was beating on his west-facing side, the light continually interrupted in predictable breaks by the jagged peaks of the Blues. Ahead, the first foot crunched against pebbles, grinding the tiny stones against one another. They'd arrived.

He was in the middle of the group, so it was another few steps before he felt the sensation of his own feet sinking into the soft bed of gravel. He thought he'd been prepared for this moment, but the emotions it brought back were stronger than he'd anticipated, and his heart raced. The ground beneath them rumbled as the guard giants stepped aside from the main gates to allow Keir access to register his fighter with the arena master.

Tate had returned.

"Venshii." A hand grabbed the back of his hood and jerked him to a stop, pulling the damp fabric tight against his nose and mouth.

When the pressure released, Tate hung his head, pressing the folds of his hood against his chest and tenting the fabric outward. Though the opening was less than an inch, it was enough. Fresh air flowed in, sweeter than honey, and he arched his back, inhaling deeply.

If he were to breathe quieter and listen harder, he'd be able to hear Keir speaking with the arena master. But it wasn't necessary. He knew every word by heart. The questions regarding him had been uttered more times in his life than his actual name.

Gladiator owner? Name for the records? Any predetermined opponents? Any predetermined wagers? Are there any monikers associated with this match for either party? Will you be holding the purse for the betting, or will you be paying the house for their services? Any additional terms to be set down by the master? What services and commodities will you be paying for?

The questions had always inspired fear and apprehension within him, because they were always the first step to the next battle. He'd learned years ago that forcing himself to be calm in the face of fear was impossible. Fighting fear and trying to seize a different state of mind by force served only to put him into a state of battle, creating the opposite effect. Distraction had been the key to his success and survival. It was imperative that he think on anything *besides* the singular need to stay alive. When he was distracted, he was good at what he did. When he was distracted . . . he *liked* what he did.

Tate used his own rapid breathing to muffle Keir as he thought about the pain in his boot instead of the immense gate he was facing. Since he'd alternated which boot the coin was in every night, it had ripped open first the blisters and then the scabs so many times that there were now two deep red wounds that would not heal. Once inside the arena, the first course of action would be to ensure his feet were salved and well wrapped. Keir would no doubt pay for whatever medical attention Tate asked for . . . and more he did not.

A hand wrapped around his bicep and jerked him forward, hauling him closer to the gates.

"He is not to be unhooded until he's below." Keir's voice came at Tate's shoulder. "Any practice bouts are to be shielded from view by the wizards. I do not care how much the privacy costs. Are all my requirements clear?"

"Quite." The answer came in the voice Tate had been praying to hear. Sarley. "A single cell away from the others, one guard I trust. The gladiator's name is Samwell. His owner will be listed as Qualtar, who will, at the time of victory, be listed as a moniker for you. King Keir, I assure you, we work with many matches of this level and always function with the utmost care and concern for the owners' interests."

"Somehow I doubt you've ever worked with anything of *this* level." Tate could hear the tilt of Keir's head as he looked down his nose at Sarley, saying more than he should have in the name of his own pride. "Keep to the terms, and you'll be rightly rewarded after his match."

"Your Majesty, it is an honor to serve you." Sarley had always been the picture of formality . . . until she got below decks. "Is there anything else?"

Tate smiled beneath his hood.

"Make sure he's well fed. I don't want him sick before the match. And keep the harlots clear of him. He is not for sale, not for any reason, time period, or amount."

"Admirable. It will be done. One last piece of business I'm required to cover. For the match between Samwell and Dalbor, both you and Dalbor's owner, Abosa—"

Keir snorted. *"Abosa.* Not very clever, is she?"

Several fae snickered.

Dalbor. He'd known that was who it would be. But hearing it wasn't any less painful.

Sarley continued without recognition of the interruption. "—have been assigned to view the outcome from the wizard's box. Terms will be set, agreed upon, and bound by both magic and blood prior to the match.

I am not privy to the terms of this arrangement, so I will only ask: Have you come prepared with whatever it is you're expected to have?"

"Of course."

"Good. I will let our head wizard know that everything is in order. Please arrive one hour prior to the commencement of the games. You and Abosa will be escorted to the box, and the rites of agreement will be carried out prior to the opening of the main doors to the arena. As per arena terms, no other guests, escorts, or guards are allowed with you as you're led to the box or after you've entered it. The doors to the box will close once the agreement has been made and will not open until the final match—which will be the battle between Samwell and Dalbor—is over. Please be prepared to enjoy the entirety of the events."

"And . . . *Abosa* will be abiding by the same rules?"

"Of course. Equality reigns at the arena. Sign here, please. Very good. We are finished." Sarley's hand slapped her chest as she bowed in the particular way that was hers alone. "Welcome to the arena, King Keir. Congratulations on your rule, and long may you reign."

Tate heard the jingle of her key chain and felt her tiny hands wrap around his wrists. "I assume these restraints will remove themselves once he's secured?"

"Of course."

"Very good." She turned Tate's wrists as far as they would go to the right and then to the left. It was customary to examine the product before taking possession of it. "For future reference, if you wish your gladiator to be able to hold a weapon, you should never bind him with such tight restraints. You're lucky he didn't lose a finger."

"It wasn't luck." Keir's voice was thin. "It was precision."

"Understood, Your Majesty." Sarley shoved Tate forward. "Move, Samwell."

She kept a tight hold on his wrists, applying pressure to direct him one way or the other. Tate knew the path. They walked in silence past the giants, through the gates, to the left, under the supports for the highest rows of the arena's seats, around the perimeter, down the ramp, and into the maze of cells for competitors, slaves, and beasts.

"That's far enough."

Tate stopped, and Sarley ripped off his hood.

She stood at chest height to him and was as beautiful as she'd always been. Her skin was the ebony black of the elves, her delicate frame a nod to her fae heritage but with the curves of a succubus. Her hair was braided in hundreds of tiny plaits that looked black down there but shone deep blue in the sun.

"Shit." She placed her hand on her hip and pursed her lips. "I knew it was you."

"Hello, Sarley."

"What in the hell are you doing back?"

He gave her a withering look. "It was necessary."

She'd stopped them in the center of the wagon wheel—a circular room with a low ceiling and dirt floors. From here, multiple tunnels branched off, leading up to the arena, across to the outdoor stables, and down to the gladiator cells and medical facilities.

Sarley looked around Tate's hulking girth, checking the multiple halls for movement. The guards were easily bought, despite her constant attempts to recruit ones she could trust.

"I should've known I'd be seeing you the minute they hauled Ayla back down here."

"And Brandt."

She sighed. "Your boy has gotten big. The resemblance to his father is clear, and there are a lot of eyes on him. I held things off as long as I could, but I was forced to send him out to the practice bouts this week. I expect the offers will start as soon as the games conclude."

Tate's teeth ground together, the enamel screeching.

"I did the best I could to keep him out of sight, but someone announced his and Ayla's arrival to the entire Underground before I could squash it."

"I know. I'm grateful for any effort on my behalf." He rechecked the halls himself, looking each way, then lowered his voice. "I need to speak to you. Alone."

"Are you cooking up trouble already?"

"When have you ever known me to cause trouble?"

She threw her head back and laughed. "Not you. You're as innocent as a lamb, *Samwell*." She scoffed. "Samwell. Honestly. How Keir thinks that giving you a fake name and putting you in a separate cell is enough to keep word from spreading about your return is beyond me."

"If I'm in my own cell, do you think . . . ?"

She put a hand on his arm and squeezed. "Of course. You didn't have to ask."

"Thank you."

"I'll bring them both immediately. But first, those fae bindings have to come off before you lose a finger to Keir's *precision*." She stepped back and motioned wide, adding a half bow. "You know the way."

"You trust me to walk without guidance," he said dryly. "Sarley, truly, the honor is too much."

She chuckled. "I don't need to trust you. I trust myself. But let's say it's me honoring you."

He laughed his first real laugh in some time. "You always leave me my pride."

Tate led the way down a hall he was all too familiar with. Despite Sarley's astounding beauty, there would not be a single innuendo shouted as they moved deeper into the bowels of the arena. No one would dare. Sarley was the child of a rare union between an elf and a nixie. Her abilities had never been seen before, and the council had named her new species sirens. She'd grown powerful and feared—until the day she sung her siren song to the wrong enemy and the council demanded action. One very potent nixie bubble from her mother later, and she was bound to this place as punishment, the length of her term unset. Which was unfortunate for her, because Sarley was the perfect jailer in an environment such as this. All she had to do was open her mouth to subdue threats from any side of a cell door. No one was in a hurry to replace her.

"It smells the same in here," Tate said.

"Like shit?"

"If that was all it was, I wouldn't have bothered to mention it."

It *was* shit, but also sweat. And blood. Moldy bedding and decaying rat corpses caught in the walls. All mixed with the acrid tang of despair. At least, that's what he'd decided it was. A feeling so thick it took on a life and odor of its own. As they passed the first barred cell, he heard an exclamation and the sound of feet hitting the ground.

"Tate?"

The sound of his name being uttered again in this space brought the rest of the gladiators to the fronts of their cells. Hands and arms extended through the bars; cheeks and hips pressed against them. He knew every face. Some he'd trained. Others he'd fought in show matches. All of them had lived and loved and lost together.

Near the end of the hall, pale-green forearms slid between the bars, their muscles so thick they barely fit. The occupant leaned the first curve of his ram's horns on the cross support, staring at Tate with soft yellow eyes. "I'll be honest, my friend. I'd hoped to never see your ugly face again."

Tate stopped in front of the cell, giving the male the respect he'd earned. "Hello, Dalbor. Your reputation has grown. The stories get more incredible every time I hear your name mentioned."

"Once I got you out of the way, it was a lot easier to look incredible." He stared at the ground, tapping his fingers against the outside of the bars. "It's you, then? This mysterious gladiator I'm to fight."

"It is."

"I wondered who they were bringing in." He glanced up with a weak smile. "I don't want to kill you."

"That's good. I don't want to die."

"I toasted your escape, you know? I even added a line." He stepped back and lifted an arm, miming as if he were holding a glass. "To Tate. Let us never see him again."

"Ah, my friend. I always hoped to see you again, just not in here."

"What is this?" Dalbor grinned widely. "Your time away has made you soft as overripe fruit. Maybe there's hope for me after all."

Tate chuckled. "Maybe."

"Sorry to break up this reunion, but we have to get Samwell here into his cell," Sarley said. "You have several training sessions before the main event. I'll let you two decide if you'd rather train together or apart."

Tate looked hard at his friend and future opponent, speaking slowly and deliberately. "I think *together* would be preferred."

Dalbor's brows furrowed, but he agreed. "Together, then."

The first of his many bricks laid, Tate turned and walked backward toward his cell, calling down the hall, "If any one of you chooses to shout at, whistle at, or proposition my wife, I will personally ensure you are incapable of making sound ever again."

Laughter erupted.

Beside him, Sarley's tiny frame moved through the hallway with presence equal to any gladiator's. She nudged him with her shoulder. "Good to have you back, Tate."

The little humor he'd managed to summon dropped. "I wish I could return the sentiment."

344

"Yeah, yeah." She purposefully left several open cells between Tate and any others. "This should meet Keir's requirements while giving you and your family as much privacy as I can offer."

"Thank you."

The lock in the door clicked, and the fae bonds unraveled. Tate hissed as blood rushed into his fingers. He called to Sarley's back, "I'll need a healer as well. As soon as you can."

She turned, scanning him from head to toe. "For what?"

"My feet. They'll need salve, bandages, and these boots will probably need to be replaced."

"Understood."

Finally alone, Tate slid his eyes up the wall to the tiny barred window. This hall was the only one that stood partially aboveground. It was situated between the outer walls of the property owned by the arena—where they kept animals both for food and for show in the games—and the inner wall, the taller one that wrapped around the sand-covered floor and pinned both the gladiators and the audience within one space for their spectacle of sport.

The cell itself was simple. A wooden-framed bed that would barely accommodate his shoulders and a chamber pot that would be permanently removed the first time he tried to use it as a weapon. It wasn't much, but it was clean and private. Tate sat on the floor in the back corner to ensure he was out of sight from the others and unlaced his boots. In order for his fingernail to catch the rough edges of the gold coin, he had to shove his finger into the hole in his heel. His breath hissed between his teeth as he pried the coin free and hid the blood-crusted token in his pocket. The muscles in his legs were trembling as he jammed his foot back into his boot, but if his plan worked, he would gladly suffer ten times the amount of pain.

He leaned his head against the wall, staring out the miniature window at a thin piece of sky. It felt like an eternity before he heard the familiar jingle of Sarley's keys. He scrambled up to standing . . . and was lost. He didn't know what to do with his hands, his feet . . . his face. Should he apologize first? Hug her first? Did he smile? Or cry? He was desperate to see them and yet frozen to the ground. What would they look like? How would they react to seeing him?

"Tate?" Ayla's voice was hesitant at first, but redoubled. "Tate!"

He sprung to the door, pressing his face against the bars. She was walking just behind Sarley, more beautiful than he remembered even in the filthy shift they'd given her to wear. No amount of dirt could hide the brilliance of her mocha skin. He met her eyes, those beautiful feline eyes that had unnerved him when they'd first met. He wanted to take her and hold her, smooth his hands over the long line of her back and kiss her full lips.

As his mind was unraveling at the marvels of his wife, he became aware of the towering shape behind her. Sarley was right; his boy was not a boy any longer. He was already taller than Tate but had a face he remembered wearing as a teen, only with two differences: the brown skin and slit eyes of his mother. Tate saw what Sarley had meant about the buyers. His son's shoulders were still growing, and though his muscles were not as thick as they would become, with his heritage taken into account it was enough to show what would be.

His lips formed the letters of his son's name, but he found he could not speak the sounds. Sarley pulled the door wide open and stepped to the opposite side.

The tiniest of cries escaped as Ayla threw herself at him. He wrapped his arms around her, dipping his head against her neck, smelling her hair, feeling it against his face. He squeezed, pressing the shape of her against him until they molded into one.

"Ayla," he murmured. "I'm so sorry. I'm so, so sorry."

She arched her back in order to grab his face between her hands. "Stop apologizing, you enormous blue lout. I love you."

"I love you too." He yanked her back against him. "Saints have mercy, I love you. I didn't think I'd ever see you again." Over Ayla's shoulder, he stared at his son. "Either of you."

Ayla gently separated herself from his embrace and stepped to one side, leaving a path between father and son. The distance was nothing and felt like everything. Brandt's first step was stiff. The next came faster, and then he was rushing for his father. The feel of his grown son in his arms left Tate choking on air and his eyes burning with tears.

Sarley's soft voice broke into the moment. "I will leave you three alone for as long as I can. Had Keir not specified otherwise, I would house you all together permanently. I'm sorry." The door clanged shut.

"Wait." Tate kept his face pressed against his son's for several more wonderful seconds before pulling away. "I need to speak with you. All of you."

Sarley looked down the hall, where Tate was sure every gladiator within earshot was hanging through the bars. "Here?"

"Unless you have a better idea. We don't have much time."

35

The training had begun. Circling Grey was a wolf whose shoulders were even with his own, while Rune was left to fight a vicious blonde. She blocked with her forearms—right, left, right. She moved—step, step, spin, right, duck, left. But Verida was dropping attacks from every angle at dizzying speeds, and nearly every third attempt broke through Rune's defenses.

A fist caught Rune's shoulder blade. She gasped and dropped her arms a fraction of an inch, leaving her face vulnerable.

"This is life or death!" Verida shouted, swinging an arm around.

"I know"—she ducked—"that!"

"I have no idea how you're still alive."

"I guess"—she twisted under Verida's raised arm and elbowed her in the stomach, finally enjoying the sweet taste of satisfaction as she connected with softer flesh—"I'm just really lucky."

Rune made the mistake of savoring the momentary win, and Verida's forearm caught her in the throat. She bent backward under the impact, but Verida was waiting there too. A hand pressed against her spine, bracing her for a millisecond, then pushing up and out. Rune was lifted off her feet and went flying across the clearing, legs and arms flailing.

The ground was coming up fast. In a last-minute decision, Rune twisted, angling herself to take the fall on her right shoulder and hip. She smashed down. The impact rattled through her elbow. The dagger in her hand was knocked free, and it spun out of reach. She growled and pushed up on her forearms, turning her head to locate the threat behind her.

Verida leapt through the air at a height and speed Rune hadn't witnessed since the council house tower, when she'd been half-crazed with blood loss. The vampire landed at Rune's feet, teeth bared. Rune yelped and rolled over, scurrying backward on her palms and heels like a crab.

Verida lunged, seizing her ankle. "I could've already eliminated you if I'd wanted to."

She kicked out, breaking the connection, and scrambled toward the blade. Her fingers wrapped around the hilt, and she whirled, half-crouched with dagger extended.

Verida's head was lowered, her blonde hair framing red eyes. She transitioned into a stalk, her steps as even as silk unfurling. "I've seen you in battle. You don't think. You just *do*. That's the reason you're alive. You have to practice the same way."

"In *what* way? With the inner Venator you keep telling me to hold back? I don't know what you want!"

"You have been *lucky*, and luck runs out. In that arena, one mistake is all it will take. And this time there will be no mercy . . . and no nixies to save you."

A roar of pain stopped Verida in her tracks. Her head snapped up. Across the grassy expanse, the wolf was leaning to one side and whimpering.

Grey reached out. "Beltran, I'm sorry!"

The wolf snarled at him and limped away, crossing behind the tree they were using to dry their clothes.

"What happened?" Verida demanded.

"I . . ." Grey looked at Rune and Verida in turn, holding a hand out in a plea of understanding. "We were just practicing."

Beltran roared, the sound changing from wolf to human midyell. He hobbled into view, one arm wrapped around his middle. "You broke my damn rib!"

"I'm sorr—"

"No. Please explain to me, *Grey*, what it was about not going a hundred percent during training that you did not understand?"

He wasn't the only one struggling with that concept. Rune rubbed at her throbbing elbow and threw a glance to Verida.

"I was trying to go easy," Grey said, "but you took me by surprise. I just reacted."

"*I'm supposed to*—" Beltran's lips thinned, and he took a heavy step forward, one hand reaching out, ready to throttle Grey where he stood. But the movement was too much, and he grimaced, wrapping his arm back around his ribcage. "I'm *supposed* to surprise you, you idiot. That's the point! And *you're* supposed to not accidentally kill me."

Grey's mouth moved with the beginnings of words, but he stopped and dropped his head, weakly repeating his earlier sentiment. "I'm sorry."

"I know. Now drop that blade." Beltran pointed with his forehead. "No more practicing with daggers."

"How long before you're healed?" Verida asked.

Beltran rolled his head to the side, swinging it around to look at Verida as if it were suddenly three times its normal weight and could no longer be properly turned with his neck muscles. "Heal? Who needs to heal?" He smiled so brilliantly that the sarcasm didn't require words to hit its mark. His lips then dropped as if pulled by puppet strings. "The break will heal soon enough, but the next creature we were planning to train with was a giant. I have to ensure the bone is completely restored before I start adding that kind of mass. I'll need time."

"Can we keep working with something else?" Grey asked, an edge of desperation in his tone. "Something smaller?"

"Hmm . . ." Beltran walked straight up to Grey with a subtle sideways limp. "Let's imagine for a moment, shall we, that I broke your rib, then reached through your chest to wiggle it around a bit." He cocked an eyebrow. "Sound like fun?"

"Not really."

"Because it's not. Until this is healed, I'm not shifting again. Verida will have to take over. Besides, from the looks of it, Rune could use your help anyway."

Rune scowled.

Beltran didn't even look at her before adding, "Don't look at me like that. It's true, love."

36

Everyone had gone to bed, but Rune couldn't sleep. There were too many things on her mind, only one of which was the Venator graveyard they'd spent the night in. She'd tried to ignore the fact that it bothered her, but every night since, when she lay down to sleep, her fears scattered through her mind like cockroaches.

Outside, the fire was still crackling, which was surprising but sounded much better than the thoughts running through her head. She crawled from her bedroll and stepped out to find Beltran fully dressed and feeding the flames from a pile of small twigs.

Startled, she blurted, "Why aren't you sleeping?"

He put a finger to his lips and motioned toward Grey's tent.

"Sorry," she mumbled. Padding across the soft grass, she sat next to him. "I thought you'd already gone to sleep."

"And I you." He grabbed another twig and stuck it in the fire, pulling it out once the flame caught and watching it burn. "Verida and I have been taking turns at night, making sure one of us is alert in case Grey has another vision. With me having been gone for three days, she needed to rest."

Rune winced at her obliviousness. She hadn't even noticed that Verida had been staying up. "Has Grey had another one?"

"No. Lucky for him. And if he can hold out until we reach the Underground, maybe we can find some answers."

"We're pinning a lot of hope on this Underground." Rune pulled her knees to her chest and wrapped her arms around them.

"Hope is usually not associated with that place. But it *is* well connected and well informed, which is what we need." He glanced at Rune's arms and then did a visual scan of their surroundings.

"What?"

"That early warning system of yours is always glowing red because of Verida's presence. It makes us vulnerable to vampire attacks. And after what I saw in that camp, that's exactly who I'm worried about. It would be nice if your markings could tell us how *many* vampires were nearby."

"It would be nice if they did a whole lot of things." She held out her arms, then wrapped them back around her legs. "Like turn invisible."

He glanced up, bemused. "You don't like them?"

"I haven't really had time to decide if I like them or not, but they annoy me." At his confusion, she clarified, "I never got a choice. They just showed up."

"Ahhh, I see. It might help if you focused instead on how useful they are in keeping you alive." The burning stick began dropping ash onto Beltran's hand. He used it to poke at one of the larger logs, which collapsed, throwing up a cloud of bright ashes. "May I ask you a question?"

"Probably."

"How can you tell if your makings are activated when they aren't alerting to anything?"

"You mean when they're just black?" She shrugged. "When they're off, I feel almost human again. When they're on, it's a current—like a constant flow of energy. But it's subtle. I didn't even notice it was there until I learned how to shut them off."

"Fascinating."

"Why? Can't you recreate Venator markings?"

Beltran turned his head away, but not before she noticed how the corners of his mouth tightened.

"What?" she asked. "It's a simple question."

"Not really."

"Yes, it is. Can you or can you not recreate Venator markings? It is literally yes or no."

"What it is, is a breadcrumb. A loose piece of thread." He pinched his fingers together in front of his chest and pulled outward. "I hand you the answer, and then you pull, tugging until I either lie to you or allow more answers to unravel"—he dropped his hand back to his lap—"trusting that you won't use them against me."

His eyes were bright, and his shoulders had squared up with hers, daring her to push him further. To ask just one more thing. It was a look she'd seen several times now since leaving the council house. Rune weighed her next words carefully.

"Thank you for being honest with me. I know that's hard for you."

Beltran swore under his breath. "And there you go again. Saying the only thing that wouldn't send me running to patrol the perimeter on foot." He sighed and looked skyward. "If I could hate you for it, I would."

"Oookay—"

"Instead . . . I'm grateful. Which is frustrating me further." With his chin still up, his eyes cut to her. "You were worried about me, weren't you?"

"When you didn't come back for three days? Of course I was."

"Do you shout at everyone you're worried about?"

"Usually. It's my thing."

Beltran smiled and picked up another stick. He took his time stirring and poking at the embers while the wood popped and cracked.

"Just so you know, I didn't follow you and Grey. You never asked me. One way or the other."

"That's because I decided to trust that you didn't. But thank you for telling me. It means a lot."

"Well, love . . ." He discarded the twig and leaned back on his elbows, shifting and rolling his hips to get comfortable. "I'm still a touch annoyed about whatever knowledge I passed up. I probably needed to know—given what we're about to walk into."

Rune couldn't argue his point. She'd run through her conversation with Grey a hundred times, and every time, she'd remembered something new from their past that finally made sense. How he would respond to certain things, the choices he made, his loner tendencies. And all the times he'd clammed up or shut down and exactly what she'd said or done to cause it. The horrors that Grey had shared *were* directly connected to the choices he'd made here, and they would continue to influence him. But, even knowing Beltran was right, she would not betray Grey's confidence by sharing the details of his past.

"I can't tell you what we talked about. But I do have a question for you." She set her chin on her knees. "About how to help him."

"I would be happy to assist."

He sounded overly eager. "Because you want to help, or because you're hoping that in the process I might accidently spill something pertinent?"

Beltran sat up and scooted closer, pressing his hip against hers. He leaned over and whispered in her ear, "Maybe a little of both."

She grinned. "That's what I thought."

"Besides, love, I've taught you better than to use that word with me. Where I'm concerned, *everything's* pertinent. But go ahead. What can I do?"

The warmth of his body against hers was heady, and she knew she was toeing a dangerous line. Not a lot would have to slip out to accidently tell Beltran everything. But Grey needed her, and Rune hadn't the slightest idea how to be there for him. She hadn't been to a lot of funerals, but the current situation felt a lot like one. Everyone would offer condolences, then stand there awkwardly, and because there was nothing else to say—because what do you say to that—they would all walk away. But she didn't want to walk away from Grey. Not again. That was all she'd ever done his entire life.

"Grey went through a lot, just like you said, and he was always alone. He always felt helpless, and I think he's stuck in that place. But I . . . I have no idea what to say or do to help him get out."

"Are you sure that's all it is? Grey has made a lot of dangerous choices since arriving. Trying to save a human from a werewolf pack, running into Feena's territory to help find Tate's family. Helpless people don't usually leap off ledges unless it's to end their own pain."

Rune twisted her toes back and forth against the grass. "I think he does feel that way, but I think he's also determined not to feel that way anymore."

Beltran's brows furrowed. "That's a dangerous combination."

"Why?"

"Because if you evaluate his past behavior, you'll see that his determination to not be helpless is manifesting in rash, impulsive decisions. You have a similar problem, and just like Grey, you don't see it."

She let go of her knees and twisted just enough to look at him while remaining in contact with his shoulder and hip. "What do you mean?"

His spine was rigid, his gaze aimed straight forward. "Can you not think of a single scenario that may present itself sooner rather than later that will likely trigger you to respond from a place of emotion rather than logic, possibly resulting in a rash decision?"

She knew. Of course she knew. "Ryker."

"Why? It's not helplessness. For you, it's something else."

She was so sick of people implying that caring about her own flesh and blood was a weakness. "It's not anything else! Ryker was my responsibility, and getting him back is not rash or stupid. I was supposed to take care of him, and I failed. It's my fault he's here and that he's been kidnapped by Zio, and I have to . . ."

"To what?" Beltran asked. "Get him home? Love, you can't even get yourself home."

Her fists clenched, tearing up pieces of grass between her fingers. "I don't know what I'm going to do, but I have to make sure he's safe."

"The irony of this conversation hasn't yet occurred to you, has it? That you're sitting here analyzing Grey while ignorant of your own issues?"

If he was trying to piss her off, it was working. "And what exactly are my iss—you know what? No. Never mind. This was a mistake. I should've just gone to bed." She put her hands flat against the grass to push up.

Beltran grabbed her wrist.

"Let. Go."

"Please, wait. I'm sorry." His fingers slid free. "I knew exactly what to say to make you upset, and I used it to deflect the conversation away from myself. Old habits."

Rune relaxed and, to her annoyance, found that regardless of the motivation behind his tactics, she now needed to know what he'd been referring to. "What's my issue?"

She'd expected to see smugness, but Beltran's eyes were wide open. They were clear and lacking in judgment, superiority, or any of the other forms of amusement that so often blocked the way. He was revealed from the fronts of his eyes to the back of his heart.

"Your helplessness translates into guilt, and you can't let it go. You continually take responsibility for and insist on shouldering things that are not yours to carry. It hurts me to watch, because I don't know how to help you see it."

It was so blunt, so harsh, that it wiped her defenses, and for a second, she couldn't deny the truthfulness of the statement. But then again, they weren't talking in generalizations. This wasn't just about her. It was about her *and* Ryker, and that was different.

Nobody understood what was really going on, and how could they? They didn't know him like she did. If someone could prove that Ryker's acting out *hadn't* been a result of his Venator blood clashing with his circumstances on earth, maybe she could let it go. But until then, this—he—was her responsibility. Hers. Once she got Ryker back and helped put him on the right path, *then* she could let go of her guilt over his choices. He deserved a fighting chance.

No; where Ryker was concerned, her guilt was not misplaced.

Rune didn't realize how hard she was scowling until Beltran spoke. "And I've lost you. I wish I could say I'm surprised."

"You tell me how I'm supposed to set down guilt that *is* mine to carry, and I'll gladly do it!"

Beltran took a long, slow breath. "Fine. I can't help you understand something that's based on falsehoods if you're not willing to see them for what they are." Punctuating his surrender, he laid straight back, weaving his fingers together behind his head. "In answer to your question that I so deftly avoided . . ."

His words trailed off, and Rune rolled her eyes. "Changed your mind already?"

"I seem to be stuck somewhere in the middle."

She grunted, too annoyed about him bringing up Ryker to be amused and too tired to coddle him. "I don't even remember what we were talking about. What question are you almost answering?"

"Whether I can create Venator markings. Although I could increase the melanin in my skin to make something that looked like them, I couldn't make them function. It's the same principle as if I shifted to look like Arwin. Taking his form won't allow me to do magic. Supernatural capabilities are not something that can be acquired by shifting."

She pondered that for bit, then lay down next to him. "Why was that so horrible that you tried to avoid sharing it?"

"It wasn't. It's a natural assumption. If I could do magic by shifting into a wizard, I obviously would. I'm not a simpleton. But that was the first thread. I've admitted a weakness, and now you'll want to know them all."

He was right.

Rune's mind revved. Before he'd even finished the sentence, it was off and running, working through what he had and hadn't chosen to do in different circumstances and questioning the whys and hows of it all. "I, uh—I should get to bed."

"What's the matter?" He chuckled. "Don't think you can stop yourself from proving me right if you stay?"

"I don't know how many times I have to tell you—mind reading is annoying."

"Again, I'm just highly attuned to body language. I knew the second you thought of your first question; your muscles tensed."

"I need to learn that."

"You know more than you think you do. You sense my discomfort better than most. When you asked me to promise not to follow you, you knew how much it upset me, even while I was actively baiting you to lose your temper. It's why you changed your mind and didn't ask me to promise." He rolled over and rested on an elbow. "Still need to go to bed?"

Rune's breath caught in her throat. He was beautiful. Heart-wrenchingly beautiful. "I probably should."

"You know . . ." His gaze trailed to her throat. "The Underground and the arena will both be dangerous. An argument could be made that you might need to know some of my limitations. Given the circumstances."

"It could." Rune swallowed around the lump in her throat.

He closed his eyes, dark lashes brushing the tops of his cheeks. "There are many people who would very much like to know some of the things I'm about to tell you."

"But why—?" Her voice cracked. "Why are you telling me?"

"I need to." He reached one hand out and brushed it over her cheek so briefly that it was gone before Rune's heart had finished accelerating. "Despite how it may look to you, I am forever hunted. Part of my protection lies in what people do and do not know about me. I hide in plain sight, but no matter how clever a camouflage is, once others know what they're looking for, it's always easier to spot."

"I understand."

"Then ask your question." He motioned to his ear, and his lips quirked up on one side. "But very, very quietly. I'm not sure Verida's asleep."

Rune lifted herself higher, arching her back and bracing on her forearms as she whispered in his ear. "When we were running from the dragon, I asked whether you could shift into one. Do you remember what you said?"

He pulled back and smiled gently, shaking his head no.

"We were running down the fire line, and you shouted at me, 'Not a good idea.'"

"And I stand by it. Not a good idea at all. It's on my list, though."

"Your list? You're just torturing me now."

He ran a finger along the inside of her arm. "Yes, I am. Which is only fair. You torture me every damn day."

Rune shivered.

He leaned closer, putting his body within inches of hers and urging her to lie back. When she was completely flat on her back, he whispered so softly into her ear that she had to strain to hear him over the gentle puffs of air that tickled her eardrum.

"The shifting ability is genetic. But like anything, it has to be learned. I can't just see something and decide to shift into it. It's more complicated than that. Have you ever looked at the inside of something?"

"Like a person?"

"Sure. Or an insect?"

"I dissected a frog in middle school."

"Forms, bodies—whatever you want to call them—are all dependent on precision of design to function. Muscles must pull and support the body correctly. Blood vessels have to run through the correct locations and maintain the proper diameter to keep limbs alive. A heart cannot be too big or too small to support the system it's running. Teeth must be the right size to allow the jaw to hinge and produce the proper bite force so as to not overstress the muscles and bone. All of these things must be understood . . . and understood *exactly*. It is not enough to estimate. The difference between a human's body and a giant's, for example, is staggering. You would think that you would just enlarge the body, but you can't. A giant's joints are actually shaped differently in order to support the weight. If I were to try to simply enlarge a human body, it would end badly for me in innumerable ways."

"Wait, wait, wait." She pushed past him to sit up. "You're telling me that—"

He put his finger over her lips. "Shhhh."

Rune got to her knees and pressed her lips against his ear. "Everything I've seen you shift into . . . You're telling me that you know *all* the blood vessels in them, every single tiny one?"

"Yes."

"What about that rat? When you were puffing up like a hideous undulating fish?"

He laughed and sat back on his heels, returning to an appropriate volume for conversation. "That hurt. But I knew my limits. I just started shifting into something else and then back to a rat again."

"If it hurt, why do it?"

"Because it was funny and absolutely worth it to see the look on your face."

"Does it always hurt?"

"Depends. My preferred forms I'm used to, so it's a mild, accustomed discomfort. Less familiar forms can hurt, depending on what I'm doing."

"So, you don't know—"

He snapped a finger as a reminder, and she leaned forward again.

"You don't know the inside of dragon well enough to shift into one?" she whispered.

He rolled his cheek against hers to trade whose lips were pressed against whose ear. "I don't know the inside of a dragon at all. They're rare. To get my hands on one—"

"Your *hands* on one?" It clicked. Everything fell into place. "Oh my God. You've got to dissect something you want to shift into."

"And now you see."

"You . . . *wow.*"

"It's the only way to make sure I know everything about the form."

So many more questions. Her eyes moved rapidly from Beltran's face to the ground as thought after thought competed for her attention.

"See?" He pinched his fingers as he had earlier and pulled out that invisible thread. "I wasn't exaggerating. One answer always leads to more questions."

"But, I mean . . . Where do you get the bodies?"

He pulled away, took her by the shoulders, and looked her dead in the eye. His answer was in the silence. Beltran got the bodies in whatever way he needed to.

"Oh," Rune said weakly.

His head dropped, and he shook it bitterly. "My risk in sharing was twofold. Giving you the knowledge to hurt me was the first, but the second was that you would never look at me the same." His hands slid free from her shoulders and onto his thighs.

"Beltran . . ." She rethought what she intended to say, not wanting to reassure him with something that she didn't truly believe. "Since I've arrived, I've murdered werewolf and fae. I'm heading to an arena where, as much as I'd like to lie to myself and say that I won't have to kill again, I know I will. How can I condemn you for doing the same thing to keep yourself safe?"

His breath caught, and she reached out, pushing back a stray piece of hair from his forehead, her fingers trailing over his skin.

"What are you doing?"

Rune hesitated, her hand resting at his temple. She looked at his eyes, his nose, his lips, drinking him in. "I have *no* idea."

His hand whipped up and snatched her own.

Rune startled, gasping as she leaned back. "I'm sorry," she said. "I thought—"

He pulled her hand to his mouth, kissing the tips of her knuckles, the back of her hand, the top of her wrist. His lips were velvet, and it ignited a hunger within her. Beltran turned her hand over as though it were made of glass and continued what he'd started. When he reached the thin skin on the underside of her wrist, he murmured against it, "We shouldn't be doing this."

She was so tired of that sentiment coming out of his mouth. And when it wasn't from his mouth, he was shouting it with his actions. She slid her other hand under his jaw and pushed his head up to look at her.

"Why?" she demanded fiercely. "Why shouldn't we?"

"So many"—he leaned closer, his eyes flitting to her lips—"*many* reasons."

Grey screamed.

37

Tar-like darkness dripped around the edges of Grey's dream. For the first time, he recognized the incoming vision and bypassed the confusion. While in the nothingness, he told himself he'd be all right, but when the headlight in the distance appeared, rushing at him like a freight train, he ran. Because fear was fear. Grey was caught, picked up, and hurtled through the air.

Don't touch anything. Don't let anything touch you.

He smashed against smooth stone. The floor was cool against his palms and the space deathly quiet. He braced for the overwhelming odor that always came next, but there was nothing. Reluctantly, he opened his eyes and waited as they adjusted to the dark. A bedroom slowly took shape around him.

An oversized bed took up a significant portion of the room, its headboard looming fifteen feet up the wall. A wardrobe stood against the far wall, along with a dresser with a washing basin on top. Grey slowly stood, unable to shake the feeling that he was placing himself in front of a firing squad.

There was a click, and he turned to face the sound. The door opened, and a woman entered, carrying a torch and wearing tight black clothing similar to his own. Her platinum hair was pulled back, and though she looked young enough to be in her late twenties, confidence rippled around her. Grey had become familiar with the look since arriving in Eon—a tangible self-surety worn only by the extremely powerful.

"Ryker," she said. "Wake up."

No!

"What time is it?" a deep, sleep-smeared voice mumbled.

"Early. Get dressed and meet me in the training room."

The sound of his voice killed Grey's disbelief before it had time to settle. Years of pain and fury exploded, roaring in his ears.

Ryker sat up, scrubbing at his face. The covers rolled down to his waist. "I love training, you know I do . . ." He yawned. "But it feels like I just went to bed."

"That's because you did. But this is worth waking up for."

She reached in the direction of a torch hanging near Ryker's bed. Though she was nowhere near it, flames ignited. Magic. With the second torch burning, more of the room came into focus. Ryker was shirtless and exactly how Grey remembered him: bodybuilder shoulders and arms, washboard abs, an angular jaw line, and that perfect face everybody loved.

"Get dressed," the woman ordered on her way back out the door.

Ryker watched her leave, a crooked, half-asleep smile on his face. When the door closed, he threw back the covers and lumbered over to the wardrobe.

It was hard for Grey to articulate what it felt like to see Ryker *here*, alive and covered in Venator markings. There were so many feelings, but louder than anything was pure juvenile resentment. Ryker had ruined elementary school, middle school, high school, and college, and now . . . *now* he was here, in an alternate universe that should've been Grey's new home—his fresh start as the truest version of himself.

But it didn't matter when or where; anytime Grey attempted to grab a measure of joy, Ryker was always right behind, ruining everything.

The little boy in him couldn't stop thinking the same three words on repeat: *It's not fair!*

Ryker was dressed and crossing the room, pulling Grey from his stupor. If he didn't get through the door when it was open, he'd have to either sit in this room until the vision ended or walk straight through it. Which he *really* didn't want to do. Ryker opened the door and then gave the handle a jerk, pulling it closed behind him.

"No, no, no!" Grey dove.

The bottom of the door cut through his ankle as it snapped shut. Wood adhered to bone and ripped through skin. Both muscle and bone moved one way, following the arc of the door, and then snapped back the other. Grey cried out. Then he was free and rolling over large, flat stones. As usual, the pain died once he was no longer sharing the same space as something else; waking up would be a different story. He slapped his palms down to stop his momentum. His head snapped back as he looked for Ryker, who was now halfway down the hall and moving at a fast clip. Grey braced his toes against the ground and pushed into a run.

He couldn't get left behind or caught in another door, which meant that Grey was forced to walk so closely behind Ryker that if he'd actually been there, Ryker would've felt his breath on his neck. He could see the hairs on Ryker's head fluttering with every step and smell the faint odor of stale sweat that floated out behind him. As they walked, everything Ryker had ever done to him ran through his head like a twisted movie reel. It wasn't long before Grey was staring at the back of Ryker's exposed neck and fantasizing about what it would feel like to bury a dagger between two of his vertebrae.

For almost as long as he could remember, Grey had taken whatever Ryker dished out because he was terrified of losing control—worried that, if he reacted, he would tap into what he now knew as his Venator abilities. It was the same reason he hadn't stopped his stepfather when he had the capacity to do so and why he hadn't broken the man's arm and shoved him into a hole so deep no one would ever find him. Grey had taken abuse over and over again, all while trying to protect himself from being discovered.

But they weren't on earth anymore. And he was done being abused.

Grey continued to imagine a number of locations a dagger could go. If not between the vertebrae, maybe the liver or spleen. He could puncture a lung before Ryker knew what was coming. He knew what he was thinking was wrong, and he waited for the guilt to follow.

But it didn't.

There was an acknowledgment, on a logical level, that no matter what Ryker had done to him, contemplating murder should make him feel bad. But even as he tried to force the emotion, his understanding remained cold and distant. The core truth was, the only thing about this entire scenario he felt bad about . . . *was that he didn't feel bad at all.*

They took a series of twists and turns, and Grey realized that Ryker was following a path he'd obviously taken before. Grey stutter-stepped, then played back the events since he'd arrived, eliminating his own emotional distractions from the formula, and frowned. What in the hell was going on? Ryker didn't look like—and certainly wasn't acting like—a prisoner at all. Looking again with new eyes, he realized that Ryker's Venator pants were loaded with weapons.

Ryker started whistling as he stopped in front of a door and pulled it open. Grey moved in so tightly that he was walking on tiptoe. The moment they were through the frame, he leapt to one side, clearing himself from danger. The room was well lit, immense, and completely empty with the exception of a wooden crate large enough to transport an elephant. It was so big that Grey's head immediately swung around to look behind himself, trying to figure out exactly how they'd gotten it through that door.

Ryker wandered forward, oddly at ease. "Zio?"

The platinum-haired woman stepped out from around the other side of the crate. "I assume you brought your weapons?"

That was Zio? Grey had expected someone older, someone less human looking. Someone . . . What? Less attractive?

"You said we were training. I brought everything except my sword and ax—I left those here yesterday."

"I'm thrilled to hear you're aware of your main weapons' location." When Ryker didn't respond, Zio sighed and leaned a hip against the box, crossing her arms. "If I were you, I would get one in my hands."

Ryker jerked straight, as if coming to, and hurried to shut the door, behind which a battle-ax and a longsword were leaning against the wall. He chose without hesitation, hefting the ax.

"I've managed to capture something special." Zio patted the box. "Inside is a creature called the arachneous. They're rare . . . and almost impossible to kill. When I release her, I don't intend to help you."

Ryker grunted acknowledgment and readjusted his stance. His feet were spread wide, and his hands were clasped behind him so the head of the ax hung at the back of his knees.

"The arachneous's exoskeleton is stronger than bone, varies in appearance, and covers the *entire* body. Your instinct will be to hack the legs out from under it. Don't. She's impervious to blades. Be aware: even at a distance, her webbing is dangerous. It's sticky, thick, and, if she aims well, will suffocate you before you can clear your nose and mouth. If she misses your head but makes contact, the webbing will stop you in your tracks, and she will take her time before biting your head off."

"Understood."

"Use the entire space. She can climb these walls as easily as walking flat. Nothing is off limits to her."

Ryker brought his arms forward and spun the ax, using the weight to loosen up his wrists and shoulders. "Sounds like a dream."

"Would you like to know how to kill her?"

"Please." The grin that followed was not gratitude for the answer but excitement for a kill.

Grey's stomach rolled. Ryker didn't care what this creature was, if it could think, or what its desires were. He hadn't even seen it yet. The only thing he cared about was blood. Grey's hatred for him hardened in place, and any doubts on Rune's behalf vanished. Ryker was exactly the kind of Venator that could not be allowed in Eon.

"The arachneous's body tapers from woman to spider," Zio said. "At the transition point, you'll see a split in the exoskeleton. Its purpose is for molting, but it's just wide enough for a blade to slip between. When you strike, drive up and deep. If you do it properly, you'll hit her heart. She'll drop immediately. If you don't, well . . ." Zio tilted her head and shrugged with calm amusement. "You'll likely be dead before you realize you missed. Before I open this door, is there anything else you'd like to ask or do?"

Ryker thought for a second, set his ax down, and picked up the sword instead.

"Correct. Now, to survive this fight, you'll need everything we've been practicing." She sauntered forward, swaying her hips, and ran a hand down Ryker's chest. "Show me that Venator. I want to see him. I want to *smell* him." She leaned in and nipped at his earlobe.

Ryker's breath shuddered. Grey's mouth gaped.

"Ready?" she asked.

"Let's do this."

Ryker stepped away from Zio and toward the crate, raising his sword. Zio positioned herself near the exit. She flicked a wrist, and her lips moved with whispered words too soft for Grey to hear. The lock clicked, and the door swung out.

From within the shadows of the crate, one oversized arachnid leg emerged. The jointed tip smashed down, and the floor shook. There appeared to be the slightest of hesitations—a test to check for danger. When nothing struck at the first leg, the rest followed. One after another they came, faster and faster. A bulbous body lunged forward, ducking its head to clear the lip of the box before straightening to its full height. Bright eyes took in the room in an instant, identifying targets.

Grey could not have been more startled if this overgrown giant of a tarantula had been wearing the head of a pink elephant. The rounded, hairy front of the arachneous's body flowed seamlessly into the upper half of a delicate woman. The black exoskeleton of the spider's body extended around her human form, flowing over the sides of her nipped waist and ribs like armor, then crossing to wrap around her breasts.

He couldn't decide where to look. Her neck was as delicate as a swan's, her lips red and full. Her eyes were wide, with thick lashes that brushed the tops of her cheekbones when she blinked, and the cut of her waist was enthralling. Beauty was the arachneous's bait, and it perfectly entranced him to forget her lower half.

"You know who I am," Zio called. The arachneous's eyes cut toward the sound. "Attack me, and it will be the last thing you do. Your target is the Venator."

The creature's eyes narrowed, and she hissed a series of sounds strung together like words.

Whatever she'd said, Zio understood. "Yes, my old friend. You will definitely die today. But I can kill you now, or you can take the opportunity to try and kill a Venator first."

The arachneous made a sound in the back of her throat, then hissed several more words.

Zio smiled. "A secret between us, I'm afraid. Make your choice."

The spider opened her perfect, red-lipped mouth and shot webbing across the room at Ryker. He cut left, heading in Grey's direction. The arachneous anticipated it and shot more sticky webbing directly into his path. He dropped to avoid it, sliding across the floor on his hip.

With Ryker's body out of the way, the incoming mass of grayish-white web headed straight for Grey. His eyes widened, and he turned, pushing off the wall. But he wasn't fast enough. The edge of the web splattered over his arm and halfway across his chest, pinning him where he stood. Nobody else saw the sticky mass sink into his skin, pressing through organs and veins in its bid for the wall behind him. He screamed just as the webbing slipped between two ribs and sliced though his lungs, changing the cry into desperate gasps for air.

Rune and Beltran raced toward Grey's tent. The nonmagical tents didn't offer much protection, but at least they were easy to find.

Beltran flung an arm out, smacking Rune in the chest. "Stay back!"

He ducked inside, catching his back on the top arch of the tent flap. It bowed and creaked, threating to collapse. From inside, Grey's scream rose again, animalistic. Like a fox with its paw stuck in a trap. Rune's shoulders hunched toward her ears.

Verida shoved out of her own tent, fighting with the flaps at the same time Beltran was backing out of Grey's, dragging the Venator by the shoulders. The second they were clear of the heavy fabric, Beltran sprouted wings, scooped Grey into his arms, and took off. Rune didn't need to be told where he was going. She sprinted toward the river, Verida on her heels.

Ahead, Beltran's dark wings were outlined against the sky. He was nowhere near the river's surface when he let go. Grey's silhouette tumbled freely, fighting the entire way down. He twisted and thrashed, engaged in an air battle with an enemy only he could see. Rune skidded to a stop at the edge of the river moments before he hit the water. Part of Grey's shoulder vanished, from the center of his clavicle to the ball and socket of his arm. The light of a star winked through.

Rune slapped her hands over her mouth to hold back a scream.

Grey crashed down flat on his back. Water sprayed up and around him, blurring the world. Even kicking the way he was, Grey sunk like a rock. Verida and Rune paced the bank, crossing one in front of the other like a set of lions while Beltran flapped steadily above. The surface settled, and the world went quiet, hanging on the same breath that all three were holding.

Seconds moved into a minute, then two.

"Beltran!" Verida shouted. "He's been under too long."

She was right. Grey wasn't coming up.

Beltran didn't look from the spot he'd been staring at. "I don't know what else to do to wake—"

"Get him out!" Rune's fists curled against her side. "Get him out *now!*"

"Those damn wings!" Verida snarled. "He doesn't have time." She leapt, lengthening her body in the air and executing a perfect shallow dive, slipping under the surface of the water like an eel.

Rune couldn't breathe. She couldn't think. Why hadn't she gone in herself, instead of shouting at Beltran as if she didn't know how to swim? What if it was too late? What if they'd lost—Verida burst to the surface, her forearm wrapped beneath one of Grey's arms and across his chest. He'd been deprived of oxygen for so long he should've been gasping for air. Instead, he thrashed and bucked as if his life depended on it.

"Beltran!" Verida spat out a mouthful of water. She tried to balance out Grey's weight by lying back. "A little—"

His arm flung up and over, slamming a fist into Verida's eye and pushing them both beneath the surface. When she bobbed up, she was holding Grey around his middle and sputtering a string of swear words.

"Hold him right there!" Beltran dove, sliding his hands between Verida and Grey and lifting him straight into the air from under his armpits.

When the two were over the bank, Beltran began to change his angle to land. Grey's shoulder went translucent again, allowing Beltran's hand to pass straight through. Grey's body swung to one side, dropping his full weight onto Beltran's left arm, then slipped free.

Beltran shouted. "Rune!"

She ran, but it was too late. Grey smashed into the ground. His body flopped like a rag doll, his head bouncing twice. Rune slid to her knees at his side, murmuring his name on repeat. She reached to roll him over, then stopped. His arm was bent underneath him at such a severe angle she couldn't tell if it was broken or not.

"The ribs!" Verida was hauling herself out of the river. "Hold on to his ribs!"

Rune tried to carefully flip him onto his back without doing further damage, but Verida shoved her aside and roughly pulled Grey onto her lap. She wrapped her arms around his chest and leaned back, using the angle to apply additional counterpressure. Verida was strong, but she was smaller, and she couldn't get her arms all the way around him. Her fingers dug into his chest as she tried to hold her grip.

"We're losing him!" Verida's eyes turned a blazing red. "His heart is stopping and restarting, and it's getting weaker each time. I don't know how much longer he can keep this up."

Beltran fell to his knees. Rune couldn't hear him over the roar in her own ears, but as his hands turned up in a helpless plea, his mouth clearly formed the words, *I don't know what else to do.*

The white noise amplified, and Rune's mind pulled away, leaving her to watch as the scene played out across miles. The boy she'd known since the first grade was wrapped in a vampire's arms. A shifter with giant wings leaned over them both. Pieces of Grey's body were coming in and out of focus. Verida's hand sunk into his chest. Grey was going to die. Right here. After everything Rune had done to keep him alive, he was going to die on the bank of this river, not fighting but trapped in a damn dream!

No! This was *not* happening. Not on her watch. Both she and time rushed forward, catching up to reality.

"Move!"

There was something in her voice that even she didn't recognize. Beltran stepped back without question. She yanked a dagger from her thigh sheath at the same time Grey planted his feet and threw himself to the side, breaking Verida's grip. Rune jumped over the top of him, sitting to straddle his chest. Her hands were dripping sweat, and she readjusted her grip on the knife.

"I'm sorry," she choked out. "I don't know what else to do."

Rune pressed the blade into Grey's bicep.

He screamed and rolled. The handle ripped from her hand, the blade embedded in his arm.

"Somebody hold him!"

Beltran was there. He put one hand against Grey's chest and gripped his wrist with the other, pushing it into the ground. Rune tore the blade free and laid it on its edge. It bit into the first few layers of Grey's skin with little effort, and she dragged it from bicep to wrist. Tears blurred the trail of the dagger, turning the stream of Grey's blood into a sea of red. He still didn't wake up.

"I'm sorry," she gasped, pressing the blade even deeper. "I'm so sorry."

"He'll heal." Beltran's voice finally cut through, and she realized he'd been repeating the same thing over and over again. "He'll heal, Rune. He'll heal. He'll heal."

"Shut up!" she screamed. There was fire in her heart and panic hammering through her bloodstream. "He can't heal if he's dead!"

Grey's eyes flew open. "Arachneous!"

Grey struggled to sit up, pushing at the ground with the same ferocity he'd been using to yank at the arachneous's webbing. It was the feeling of soft grass beneath his fingers that triggered the realization that he was back.

He'd escaped the vision.

Alive.

There was nearly a half second of relief before the excruciating reality of what his body had been through hit with the combined force of multiple jackhammers. His elbows buckled, and he collapsed, gasping for air like a fish on land.

"Rune! Get off his chest," Beltran said.

The pressure against his ribs vanished, and Grey sucked in oxygen. Bones were broken, he was sure. As for the rest of his insides, the pain was so universally spread that his organs could've been soup for all he knew.

"Put pressure on that wound," he heard Verida say. "With as long as it took him to heal last time, he's going to bleed out."

Grey turned his head to look as Rune laid the heel of her palm against his bicep and leaned in, pressing with her full weight behind it. Bursts of light exploded behind his eyes, and everything went black.

When he regained consciousness, the sun was shining overhead, and his body had become one giant ache. He groaned.

"He's awake." Beltran's voice.

"Grey?" Rune said. "Grey, are you OK?"

He licked his lips. The inside of his mouth tasted like an old sock. "Not really."

There was a small rock under his tailbone, and the angle of his knee was sending shooting pains through his entire leg. He gingerly readjusted and pushed up to sitting, swallowing as many of the grunts, groans, and wheezes as he could.

When he was almost settled, he caught sight of his arm. "What . . . ?" He leaned to one side and lifted his hand to examine the sleeve of dried blood. "What happened?"

"Rune woke you up," Beltran said, as if that explained everything.

He considered a follow-up question but decided he didn't want to know.

"Well?" Beltran cocked a brow. "Where did you end up this time, and why were you shouting about an arachneous?"

"I was in Zio's castle. She was . . . younger than I expected."

Verida snorted. "I would maybe let you get away with that if she were human. Care to rephrase?"

Grey blushed. "She was . . ."

"Gorgeous, yes." Beltran impatiently waved for him to get on with it. "All the worst ones are. I'm more interested in the arachneous."

"What do you want to know? It was the most insane thing I've ever seen." He rubbed at his chest, remembering the feeling of its webbing cutting through his spectral form.

"Are you sure that's what it was?" Beltran spoke slowly, as if Grey had lost his mind from one too many visions.

"Yeah," he said dryly. "Bottom half spider, top half woman, enormous, shoots webbing out of her mouth. Does that sound right?"

"Rana!" Verida ripped a handful of grass out by the roots and threw it to the side. "She already has a dragon. The last thing we need is for her to have an arachneous!"

"They're notoriously hard to control," Beltran said.

"So are dragons. And she figured that out without issue."

Grey looked between the two of them, confused. "She was using it to train Ryker. I got the impression that win or lose, she was planning on killing it."

"Ryker!" Rune surged up to her knees. "Is he OK? Did he look OK?"

Grey flinched, wishing that hadn't just come out of his mouth. Rune waited for an answer, wringing her hands and staring at him like all her hopes rested on his shoulders. But how could he possibly tell her what he'd seen? As she looked at him with that naivety that took over whenever her brother was mentioned, the real question took the previous one's place: How could he not?

"Ryker . . . He . . . Well . . ." Grey stammered. He wanted to soften the reality but couldn't see any possible way to do that. He exhaled. "Ryker is more than OK."

Rune didn't see the look that passed between Verida and Beltran.

She blinked. "What do you mean?"

Her blank expression irritated him, and he tried to will her into understanding without having to spell it out. "Rune, Ryker was *fine*."

"How can he be fine? He's being held captive."

"Not exactly."

"I don't understand."

Grey ground his molars together. Of *course* she didn't understand. She *never* understood. And there was nothing he could say that was going to soften the blow. "He was *happy!*" he shouted, with a cruel lack of delicacy. "He's not a prisoner, all right! He's walking around that place freely, with access to weapons, and—"

Rune's blank stare twisted to a thought-stopping scowl that silenced him as effectively as a gag.

"*Oh*," she seethed. "I see. So you mean he's free like us? Wandering around the council house? Training with weapons?" She walked two fingers through the air like a pair of legs. "Cause we were *so* free to head out whenever we wanted."

"No. This was different. You didn't see his face. He was excited to try and kill that thing."

"Grey, maybe that's not—"

"I would know, because it was the same expression he wore every time he was trying to kill me!"

The blow hit, and Rune recoiled. "That's not fair."

The tips of his ears were about the only part of his body not hurting, but with that comment, they started to burn. "Not *fair?* Really?" He shook his head. "What's not fair is that while you're out here worrying about your poor brother, he's up in that castle working on a new conquest. It appears to be going well, because he and Zio are waaaay closer than they should be."

Verida choked on nothing.

Beltran cleared his throat. "If I may, are you implying that Ryker and Zio are . . . ?" He waggled his eyebrows.

"Yes!"

"No," Rune said. "This is ridiculous. I don't know what you saw, but why would Ryker—?"

"Stop it!" Grey worked to get on his feet. He realized how foolish that was the minute he started to move, but this conversation felt like a replay of his entire life, and he refused—*refused*—to take it sitting down any longer. He wrapped one arm around his middle and braced the other hand against his thigh to keep from falling over. "When are you going to open your eyes and see who your brother is? You've spent your entire life making excuses for him and everything he does. I'm done! I'm not going to stand here anymore and listen to you defend him. Ryker is dangerous, and he will do everything in his power to kill me . . . and him"—he pointed at Beltran—"and her"—he pointed at Verida—"the second the opportunity presents itself."

"Grey—"

"No! You don't get to interrupt me. Not today. I've known your brother since the first grade, and any redeeming qualities he had died a long, long time ago. You can lie to yourself all you want, but I'm . . ." Grey took a second, trying to catch his breath while shaking his head. "I'm done helping you do it."

38

It had been two days since Grey's vision. The boy appeared fully healed, and thankfully, they were almost to the Underground. However, the proximity to the entrance made Beltran uncomfortable, and he'd insisted they use Arwin's tents tonight for security.

Waiting for everyone to fall asleep, he stared up through the sheer fabric at the stars and found distraction in a kiss that almost was. He'd told himself that it was for the best—that the interruption had been a blessing. But the more he said it, the less he believed it. He'd caught himself trying to recreate the moment several times, but the last few days of travel had been tense, leaving little opportunity.

Grey's choice to yell the truth about Rune's brother and what he'd seen in his last vision had not gone over well. However, it had increased Beltran's respect for the boy—not that he'd be admitting that to Rune. Tomorrow morning, they would all descend into the Underground, and he'd told Rune and Grey in no uncertain terms that if they cared for Tate's life—or their own—they would put this Ryker business behind them until after the games. And if they didn't think they could handle that, they could stay here with the horses.

Remembering the feeling of Rune's fingers as she brushed his hair to the side, Beltran lifted a hand to his forehead. He rolled his eyes. This was ridiculous. Now he needed a distraction from his distraction. If he didn't leave for the Underground now, he was going to find his way to Rune's tent instead. Groaning, he rolled to his knees and slipped outside.

The land they'd crossed into was dirt and rock, with the occasional small sage bush and clumps of brown desert grass that rustled in every breeze. Knowing he'd be sneaking out later, he'd carefully watched as everyone set their tents up, memorizing where each was placed by the natural features surrounding it. He was passing the last tent when Verida poked her head out from between the flaps.

"Shouldn't you be sleeping?" she whispered.

Beltran frowned. Then, with enormous intention and a heavy dose of the dramatic—because he knew it irritated her—he sidestepped toward the illusion of her floating head. He bent at the waist and looked her in the eyes, stretching out the moment until her nostrils flared.

"I would be keen to ask you the same question, darling, if I weren't so distracted by the fact that this"—he poked at the fabric to the side of her head—"is *Grey's* tent."

Verida's lips pursed. Her arm emerged, and she placed her palm flat on Beltran's chest. She took her time before shoving him back, ensuring her move was equal to his own dramatic reply. When she pushed, he stumbled away, laughing under his breath. It had been so long since she'd engaged with him in any sort of humor; it brightened his whole week. She stepped outside and motioned for him to follow.

They plodded silently closer to the towering mounds of rubble that squatted along the base of the cliffs. He'd chosen this location for camp because it was as near to the entrance of the Underground as he dared get without increasing the risk that they would run into someone or something unsavory. When they'd moved far enough away from the tents that they could speak with normal voices, Verida's steps slowed.

"I've been sneaking into Grey's tent at night to watch him sleep."

Beltran's irritation spiked. So much for all his worrying about the Venator markings not alerting them to any other vampire's presence because of Verida. *She'd* just waltzed around a camp of *invisible* tents while he'd been *awake*, and he'd been so distracted thinking about Rune he hadn't even noticed.

He forced a smile. "Do tell—is Grey as handsome when he sleeps as he is during the day?"

"More." Verida smirked. "I've been watching him to see if there were any tells, any changes that might alert us when he's about to have a vision. If we can learn when one is imminent, maybe we can wake him up before he's in so deep we can't get him out."

"It's a . . . good plan."

Verida's eyes cut to him. "Annoyed you didn't think of it first?"

"Perhaps. Have you watched him the last two nights?"

"Not the whole night. I have to sleep eventually. But yes."

"It *is* a good idea. But why didn't you tell me? Or Rune? We could've helped."

Verida scoffed. "Rune is ready to rip his head off, or haven't you noticed? As for you, I probably didn't tell you for the same reason that we're standing here in the middle of the night."

"Because . . . we have a long and ugly history? You don't trust me? You didn't want to argue? Ah, I know. You miss my kissing and didn't think you'd be able to resist—"

"Rana, Beltran. Shut your mouth."

He did but couldn't resist a suggestive eyebrow waggle.

"I hate you sometimes."

He perked up. "We're down to 'sometimes'?"

"Don't push it."

"Very well. Point taken. We're standing here because we need to work on our communication?"

"Of course. So, anything else you'd like to tell me?"

"I'm headed into the Underground."

He hadn't told her because he was sure she would demand to go, and he wasn't quite ready to reveal his Underground persona just yet. To his surprise, she just nodded, as if him going in alone made sense.

"Are you planning on meeting with your contact from"—she glanced around, making sure they were alone—"the resistance?"

"No. I need to find something to disguise those two with. We shouldn't be walking Venators through the Underground at all. We certainly can't do so openly."

"Agreed. But I'll need a disguise as well. Dracula's prized fighter is in Keir's hands. The more eyes that can testify to where I've been, the more restricted my stories will become. And I'm still not sure how I'm going to get out of this."

"We'll figure it out." He patted her on the shoulder and walked on, sprouting wings.

"Do you really think there's someone in there who knows how to help Grey?"

He twisted, looking around the feathers he needed for tonight. "No. But I'm hoping. Try to get some rest. I'll be back by morning. Have them ready to move."

Beltran took off. He caught an air current and headed straight at the rows and rows of cliffs. The last geological feature before the Blues, the cliffs acted as a warning to travelers. On the other side, the land grew wild with monsters, and the earth was pinched into higher and higher peaks until the tops were no longer visible, surrounded by a halo of clouds and drenched in snow.

Nothing was predictable in the Blues.

But here, the cliffs stood like foot soldiers, lifting the flats of their plateaus across their shoulders. In the darkness, he could barely detect the columns of square and rectangular black stones that lined them. It was a feature Beltran had never seen anywhere else. He'd always thought it looked like someone had ripped the spines out of an entire generation of giants and wrapped the cliff sides with them.

Between two of the plateaus near the top was a vee of empty air where the cliffs rolled in. Tucked neatly within the space, two arching arms of rock formed the vague shape of an eye. The feature was partially obscured by the plateaus on either side and difficult to locate during the day. But tonight, the moon was low, and it shone through the formation like a beacon.

Beltran made some simple adjustments to his face midflight and glided straight through the center of the eye. The rocky world vanished, as did the moon, and he emerged in the center of a natural cave.

He had reached the gates of the Underground.

The Underground had been birthed so long ago that not even Beltran knew who'd started it or how it had come to be here. The cave had no natural entrances. The only way in or out was to step through one of the three doorways scattered across the Blues.

Although Beltran had an odd affinity for the Underground itself, the entrance always sent a chill up his spine. He didn't know how large the cave actually was because the majority disappeared beneath a darkness so complete that the limited light of the ever-burning torches could not penetrate it. But he could feel the space expanding around him, pressing with its own weight and hiding any number of things.

The smell also grated on his nerves. Dirt. It was such a common scent he shouldn't have noticed it at all, but it was so intense that it felt like he'd been buried alive.

As he landed, the powdery dirt of the floor puffed up and around his shoes and pants. Ahead, two flaming rows of torches created a wide path that led to the keeper and the door. Behind the keeper, two ten-foot-tall square pillars had been marked with spell work and placed against the sides of a natural tunnel that ran between the entrance and the Underground itself.

The keeper waited, legs shoulder-width apart and holding a long-handled ax between his hands. "Back so soon?"

Keeper's true name, along with his identity, had been stripped when he was cursed to guard this place—though his fae bloodlines were obvious in the ears that poked through his white hair. His skin, however, was unique. It was mottled gray, green, and white—like moldy fruit.

"So soon?" As he walked down the path, Beltran fluttered his wings out behind himself, ensuring that the firelight caught the rich black color of the feathers. "I think this cave is starting to affect your mind."

"No night, no day. It's possible. Do you have your invitation?"

"Do I ever?"

Keeper grinned like a werewolf whose moon had just risen.

"How many will it cost me this time?" Beltran asked. "Though, before we start negotiations, bear in mind that I'll be back in the morning and will need to buy passage for four."

"A fair price—"

"Oh, and one last quick reminder. These longer flight feathers are not up for negotiation."

Keeper pouted. As he always did. "But those are my favorite."

"I know, my friend. I know. It cannot be helped." Beltran brightened, fluttering his wings to lift Keeper's mood. "So, how many will it be today?"

"Ten."

"Ten? *Today?* I will be paying passage for four in the morning. Surely we can be a little more reasonable tonight."

He rubbed at his chin. "Six."

"Three."

"Five."

"Three."

"Four."

Beltran nodded. "Agreed."

Keeper squeezed his ax closer to his chest in glee, and Beltran turned around, spreading his wings wide. Fingers brushed up and over his feathers until Keeper finally made his first choice and yanked. Beltran winced as a tiny piece of himself was removed. Three more plucks, and they were done.

When Keeper stepped to the side, he was twisting the feathers between two fingers, admiring them. "You may pass."

With those words, the pillars lit up, and Beltran safely crossed between them and into the tunnel beyond. The keeper's responsibility was now done, and he never looked behind. To look was to turn away from his responsibility. Beltran used this to his advantage and made a second shift as he walked through the tunnel. He absorbed both the wings on his back and the hair on his head, grew a foot and a half taller, thickened his forehead, and widened his nose and chin. In fewer than ten steps, the version of Beltran that the Keeper knew was gone. In his place was Beltran's well-known alter ego, Fal. To most, Fal was a fair but gruff slave trader. To a few, he was a member of the resistance.

The tunnel turned, and Beltran stepped out into a world of brilliantly colored debauchery. The Underground was a subterranean city with any amenity you could ask for. There were shops and taverns, food carts and vendors. Outside the main square, streets stretched in all directions with row upon row of homes constructed of cut timber—a building supply that didn't need water or sun to be maintained.

In the daytime, the ceiling glowed with enchantment, and the city was full of silk banners in brilliant colors strung from every cart and home. At night, the ceiling dimmed, and thousands of glowing blue, green, and yellow butterflies flitted freely around, creating both light and ambiance.

The sounds of the Underground changed depending on whether it was night or day. Tonight, the booths were vacant. There was no shouting of prices or wares, and the slave traders could not be seen hauling their prizes through the streets to the lower levels in search of buyers. Instead, musicians played on every corner, creatures danced in and out of establishments, and drunken patrons spilled from tavern doors, riotous with laughter.

Beltran cut through the crowds, turning toward a residential street, but pulled up short. Red. He was surrounded by red. He turned in a slow circle, taking in the main square. The number of prostitutes fanning through the area had easily quadrupled since his last visit. It was then that the first flutterings of desire hit him.

Incubi.

He scowled and pushed deeper into the city, but the incubus magic grew denser with every step. A hand ran across the back of his shoulders, and a fae blinked at him over the top of her sheer face covering.

He grabbed hold of the wayward hand. "Not. Interested."

The moment the words were out of his mouth, the wave of magic intensified, and the already attractive fae looked damn near irresistible.

Beltran leaned closer. "And tell your master that when I figure out who he is, I'm going to teach him a lesson." He shoved her hand away and turned, shouldering his way through the beginnings of a drunken fight.

Prostitutes in the Underground were always easy to spot, as their uniforms were dictated by their masters. The females wore red dresses with high necks and long sleeves. Their sheer face coverings hung from ornate chains that draped over the nose and past the chin. Most distractingly, the fabric of their dresses was cut away below the breasts in an oval to expose the midriff from ribcage to hip bones. The males wore pants in the same color—tailored as tight as a second skin—no shirt, and black half masks to cover their eyes and noses. And working behind the scenes were their masters. The brothel owners—all incubi—sending out their drug-like influence to increase their clientele . . . and pay.

Another hand. This time running across the back of his hips. It wasn't that incubus magic didn't affect him, but he was old enough to have learned self-control. Beltran didn't bother with verbal threats. He grabbed the male's hand and twisted until the vampire dropped to his knees, begging for release.

Beltran turned down one of the many winding streets, leaving the worst of the crowds behind. Seven homes down, Beltran knocked at a plain brown door. Despite the hour, it swung open immediately.

A green goblin looked up at him and scowled. "The master is not at home."

"I'm sure he's not. But if he were here, I would appreciate you letting him know that Fal has stopped by for a visit." He smiled. "I'll wait."

The goblin's lips tightened around his tusks in a downward turn of disapproval. He shut the door in Beltran's face.

Beltran waited, whistling to himself loud enough to guarantee the goblin could hear it through the walls. It wasn't more than ten minutes before the door was opened again, this time by a male with white hair, white eyelashes, and watery blue eyes.

"Hello, Lornan."

The albino werewolf was barely five feet tall and rounder around the middle than most of his kind. The tie on his bed robes emphasized the bulge. "Fal!" he said. "Why didn't you say it was you? I would've gotten the door sooner."

Bemused, Beltran leaned against the doorframe. "I did."

"Ah, so you did. Come in, come in."

"What's changed?" he asked, following Lornan through the front parlor. "There are a lot of incubi working in the shadows tonight."

"You know how it goes. Shax says, 'Jump,' and I say, 'How high?'" He plopped into an armchair. "At least for now. Sit, sit."

Shax made a point of hiding his involvement here. Lornan was always quite agreeable to his demands. And he would remain that way . . . until the day he turned on the incubus. Lornan had climbed the ladders of the Underground hierarchy with his ability to procure things for powerful people and a ruthless streak that put the council members to shame. This wolf had ambition—a fact that Shax either hadn't seen or foolishly ignored.

The goblin reappeared, carrying a tray of small cakes. Lornan selected two. "Now, my friend, I assume you aren't here for a social visit."

Beltran waved the tray away. "Are you implying I don't stop by for social visits?"

"About once every ten years. We're only on, what? Year six? Eight?"

Beltran chuckled, settling back into his chair and crossing his leg. "Now that I know you keep track, I'll be sure to return in a couple more years for a drink or two. In the meantime, I need a favor."

"As I suspected." He took the first white sugar-covered treat and popped it into his mouth.

"I need entrance into the gladiator games."

Lornan threw his head back and laughed. Little pieces of cake puffed out of his mouth and dusted the front of his robes. "Oh!" He brushed at the sugar. "Is that all?"

"Not really, but what's so funny? You *are* the man with the access."

He grew somber. "Not in this case, I'm not. The Underground networks have been buzzing with rumors. Everyone who's anyone will be attending these games. I can't even get myself in."

"Come now, the games are nothing new. These ones can't be that popular. How much do you need?"

Lornan snickered as if they were sharing a joke, but at Beltran's blank stare, his face fell. "You really don't know?" He took his time licking each finger and then leaned forward, resting his arms on his knees. "Rumor has it Tate is returning to the games."

Shit. Beltran had assumed people would talk and that perhaps there would be some rumors in the inner circles, but what he hadn't anticipated was the entire Underground knowing before he got here. Someone had sent out an announcement. But who?

Lornan was staring.

Beltran stalled. "Tate?"

"The one and only." He relaxed back into his seat. "How could you not have heard? You can't walk anywhere down here without over-hearing at least three conversations about it."

"I've been otherwise engaged."

"How long has it been since you've been down?"

"Poke all you want, Lornan. I'm not telling you where I've been or what I've been doing."

"You're no fun, Fal." He pointed a thick finger with an unmanicured yellow nail. "Never have been."

"We both know that's not true. You really can't get me in?"

"Not possible. Not this time. I'm sorry. Next month, sure. But anyone who might be willing to sell a ticket for this event has a price tag not even I would be willing to pay."

Beltran tapped his fingers against his knees. "That's unfortunate."

"It is. I do hate being woken up for nothing."

"I do need a few other things, if that will help to ease your old, tired bones." He winked at Lornan's scowl. "I'm looking for some information, as well as suitable disguises for three—two female, one male."

"As you know, the best disguises are veneers. I'd send you to find Kit, but she's been missing of late. The only other fae in the Underground who's decent with veneer magic can't create one that will last longer than an hour. We'll have to think of something else. It won't be as good, but I can find something." Lornan stood, brushing the remaining crumbs from his robe. "Shall we just put it on your tab?"

"I don't make tabs. But you always try to create one. How much is it going to cost me?"

"Now that depends. What information are you looking for?"

"Beorn's pack. Do you know anything?"

Lornan's expression darkened, and he sank back into the chair. "Fal, tell me you aren't mixed up in all that?"

"I'm mixed up in everything."

He clicked his tongue. "Nasty business."

"Have you seen any of the pack?"

"Of course. They've been in and out, selling slaves and recruiting. Even tried to recruit me." He snorted. "Can you imagine? Most of the pack has moved on, but there are a few scouts still hanging around. Say they're looking for two Venators, if my ears didn't deceive me." He crossed his arms over his belly and raised his chin. "I don't suppose a fine trader like yourself has heard anything about that, now have you?"

"What? *Two* Venators?" Beltran scoffed. "Sounds like the council is trying to play cards they don't have, if you ask me."

39

"Where am I supposed to put these adilats?" Rune asked.

They were the only weapons Verida agreed were small enough to bring. Their outfits, if you could call them that, were bright red, and although Rune was technically covered from the top of her neck to the bottoms of her ankles, a substantial amount of fabric was missing from the center. The hot breeze tickled both her bare stomach and the tops of her hip bones.

"Strap the pouch around your ankle. The loose fabric will disguise it."

Rune crouched, tying it high enough that it wouldn't show while she was walking.

When she stood, Verida was holding out a veil and headdress. "You forgot something."

She wilted. "You've got to be kidding me."

"I wish I was."

The headdress was made of delicate gold chains that swooped down in three perfect rows. The partially sheer veil connected at two points on either side and covered Verida's nose and face, leaving only her eyes and forehead showing.

Rune snatched it and begrudgingly started to pull it on.

"No, stop. You can't go in with your hair like that." Verida took her by the shoulders and turned her, pulling out the braid and fluffing her hair until it fell around her shoulders in waves.

"What?" she asked. "Braids aren't allowed in the Underground?"

"Don't be ridiculous. But braids aren't worn by—"

Beltran rose over the edge of the cliff, holding Grey beneath the armpits. His large, feathered wings sent a wave of fine dust rolling toward Verida and Rune. They turned away, covering their faces with the crooks of their elbows. Setting Grey on his feet first, Beltran landed and folded his wings behind him. "Everything has been done. The horses are happily grazing back at the river, and the tents, supplies, and weapons have all been safely stashed."

Verida pivoted on the balls of her feet, waving away the dust with one hand while using the other to trace a line down the front of her outfit to the missing center. "Was this really necessary?"

He tucked his hands in his pockets, smiling. "You both look lovely."

"Beltran." Verida effectively turned his name into a threat. "Is this where you tell me they were out of cloaks?"

"No. But Shax has initiated some changes down there. You'll blend in better this way. Trust me."

"I try not to make a habit of that."

"Shax is part of the Underground?" Rune asked.

Verida rolled her eyes.

Beltran smirked. "Not officially."

"So, yes." Rune couldn't help but notice Grey's casual disguise of ill-fitting pants and a white tunic. She pointed. "He gets to wear baggy, dirty clothes. Why can't I?"

"I was limited in options. Your markings—"

"Grey's markings aren't covered either." Though his pants were to the ankle and the tunic's sleeves were long, his black Venator markings could still be seen above the loose collar on the shirt.

Beltran pulled a canvas bag from over his shoulder and drew a thick metal collar from inside. "I was going to cover them with this. Sorry, Grey, but down there, my persona is a slave trader. May I?"

Grey's shoulders drooped, but he nodded and allowed the collar to be clamped around his neck.

Beltran tapped at two small screws on either side of the collar. "These bolts are usually tightened to press against the arteries in the neck. It keeps the slave on the edge of consciousness; any exertion raises the heart rate, puts extra pressure on the arteries, and causes them to pass out before they can fight or escape. I'm not going to tighten them, for both of our sakes, but you need to act as if they are. Understood? You are to look afraid. No fighting, no running, no posturing—no anything."

"Got it."

"OK, so Grey's a slave." Rune motioned to her midriff. "Who am I supposed to be?"

"Well . . ." Beltran cleared his throat. "I suppose it's a tad bit similar. That's an outfit worn by the, uh . . ."

"The whores," Verida said. "That's why you can't wear your braid, by the way. Not sexy enough."

"What!"

"Come now, Verida, I quite like the braid. I find it to be—"

Rune's glare cut Beltran off, and he threw out his hands in a plea of protection. "I was out of options, love. If there had been anything else, I would've brought it." His eyes cut to the side. "Besides, *Verida*, they prefer the term *consorts*. Seven hells, would it kill you to employ a little tact once in a while?"

"I understand why you put *her* in it." Verida hooked a thumb toward Rune. "But I don't have markings to cover."

"We have to hide your face. Of the four of us, yours is the one that will draw attention. Slinking around beneath a cloak and oversized hood only makes people look harder, and you know it."

Verida muttered something under her breath that sounded like reluctant resignation.

"Glad we're in agreement. Now, I did a little digging last night."

"I hope you did more than that," Verida said. "We need a miracle, not buried treasure."

"We'll have to separate if we want to blend in and have enough time to get everything done. Grey will be with me. I did verify that Silen still has pack members in there, as we suspected, so watch for wolves. As for you ladies, I expect you'll run into some problems while in the square. Just tell potential clients—"

"—that we already have a job," Verida said. "This isn't my first time in the Underground."

"And if necessary, break their fingers. The incubi have gotten a little aggressive in their tactics. Find out everything you can about the games. People are excited. They should be talking. I tried to get us entrance last night, but . . ." His wings gave a nervous flutter.

Verida scowled. "But *what*, Beltran?"

"I can't get us in. Word has spread that Tate will be fighting."

Verida snorted and looked to the sky. Rune was considering taking a step outside of the vampire's immediate reach when Verida dissolved into hysterics. She laughed until she was crouched on the ground with her head between her knees and her breath coming out in wheezes. Rune stared in shock. When she finally looked to the others, she found that Grey's mouth was gaping and Beltran's lips were twitching as if he couldn't decide whether he should laugh with her or be concerned.

"What's so funny?" Grey finally demanded. "If we can't get into those games, we can't get Tate out. This whole journey will have been for nothing, and Tate will be stuck back in the arena, and it will be all my fault!"

Verida's laughter slowed. "You're right." She stood, wiping tears from her eyes. "It's not funny. But I could either laugh at the insanity that has become my life or take out my frustration on one of you."

"Those were *really* the only two options?" Rune said.

"Only two I could see." Verida worked to smooth out her silken pant legs and straighten her veil. "Has word of Tate's fight spread past the Underground?"

"I don't know for sure, but I would have to assume yes," Beltran said. "With Tate fighting again, demand for attendance has far exceeded capacity."

"Wait." Grey frowned, his eyes flitting back and forth across the ground as if reading words scrawled across the surface. "Tate told us that from the time he was a boy, he was continually bought and sold. Why can't we just . . ." He looked up. ". . . buy him back?"

"Don't you think that if that were an option, we would've thought of that before trekking miles to try and break him out?" Verida snapped. "Even if we could afford the price that Tate would fetch, his ownership lies with my father. And he would no more sell Tate than he would sign over his lands to me. It will never happen."

"But"—Grey's scowl cut deeper into his forehead—"Dracula *gave* him to the council."

"No, he *lent* him to the council for a hefty sum. Dracula has every intention of fighting Tate again in the future. What neither you nor Rune understands is that when my father hears that Tate is back in the games, he will go to Dimitri, who will have two choices. He can admit that he knew nothing of it, which will not end well for him. Or he can fabricate a story about Tate's capture being intentional, claiming that it was a ploy to further the council's goals. Dracula will demand the treasury provide their usual payment, plus any and all fees raised at the games, as well as a hefty penalty to be paid by Dimitri himself for his lack of transparency."

"In other words," Rune said, "Dimitri is going to be pissed."

"Extraordinarily so." Beltran said.

"And when he's done with Dimitri, my father will come for me. I am Tate's keeper."

The reality of Verida's dilemma finally registered with Rune, and the angry demeanor she'd had since they left made a lot more sense.

Beltran reached out as if to comfort her before stopping inches from her shoulder and letting his arm drop. "We are going to figure out a solution," he said softly. "But one thing at a time. Today we need to learn everything we can about what Silen might be planning . . . and figure out how to either buy access to or sneak into the games."

"Sure," Verida said. "Sneak in. Because there won't be a hundred others trying to do the same thing. I give it twenty minutes before some idiot triggers the giants' patrol. After that happens, nobody's getting in."

"If you have a better suggestion, I'm all ears."

"Let's get this over with." Verida marched to the edge of the cliff. "Just keep your hands off my waist. I don't need those clammy fingers on my bare skin."

"I beg your pardon?" Beltran's posture pulled tight, and his wings flared out behind him. "I think I'll take Rune down first." He marched over and scooped her into his arms. One hand wrapped around her waist, and his fingers splayed flat against her stomach.

Startled, Rune looked up.

He raised a dark brow. "Clammy?"

Without waiting for an answer, Beltran ran and dropped them both over the edge.

40

The smell of dirt was overwhelming. Grey stood with Rune and Verida at the head of a path lined by torches, waiting for Beltran to motion them forward. Being belowground again was unnerving, and Grey stretched his neck, pulling anxiously at the slave collar that was already cutting lines into the bottom of his jaw.

It was obvious that a negotiation was taking place between Beltran and a fae referred to as Keeper—a word Beltran used as if it were both the fae's name and his title—but their tones were hushed, and Grey couldn't make out what they were bartering for.

Beltran turned around, wearing a different face, and spread his wings wide.

"What is he doing?" Rune whispered.

Nobody answered.

When Keeper jerked out the first feather, Grey understood the price but didn't understand the value. Keeper continued to carefully choose and pluck, drawing out his selections with care. Beltran stared at the ground, wearing an air of humiliation that Grey had never seen on him before. He wondered: Was it caused by the payment itself or by being observed paying?

After the last feather had been plucked, Beltran snapped his wings tight to his back. "Payment for four. As agreed."

Keeper stepped to the side. "You may pass."

Two glowing stone pillars lit in time with the announcement, and Beltran motioned everyone between and into the tunnel beyond. Grey tried not to stare at Keeper's strange skin as they passed, but the fae looked like a slowly molding pear holding a battle-ax in one hand and a pile of feathers in the other.

The rock of the tunnel was unnaturally smooth on the bottom but rough on the sides and top. Beltran pushed his way around them to lead. As he walked, his wings shrank and vanished into his back while the hair on his head pulled in until he was completely bald. He was still growing taller when he turned around, revealing that he'd adopted a square face with a heavy jawline and thick, protruding lips. His forehead was too large and sloped heavily down to meet a wide bridge, nose, and chin.

"Mother of Rana!" Verida hissed, stepping closer. "Fal? You're *Fal!*"

"I believe we've met before." Beltran's voice was deep and raspy—as if he'd been smoking for years and chasing the nicotine with handfuls of gravel. "I believe you had a problem with my odor, if I remember correctly."

"Your explanation of that was a night in the whorehouse."

"I lied. An entire bottle of cheap perfume. I couldn't have you recognizing my scent and outing me."

"No, of course not." Verida squared up in front of him, planting her feet so they were toe to toe with his. "Tell me, Beltran, how many other times have we 'met'? Hmm?"

"I'm afraid I can't answer that question."

"I cannot handle this place." Rune put one hand on her hip and cocked it to the side. In her Venator clothes, she would've looked annoyed. This outfit put out a different vibe. "Another past history we know nothing about. Only this time, it's with the same two people, who didn't know it was their history or that they were the same two people."

Grey blinked. "What?"

She cut a nod in his direction. "Exactly."

"I always know who I am, thank you." Beltran took a second to scan the tunnel ahead and behind. "Verida and Rune, you exit first so we aren't seen together. Grey and I will come behind in a few minutes. We will meet at the Raven Inn. Tell the bartender you have a meeting that has been prearranged. He'll give you a key. Go straight up to our rooms when you arrive."

Verida stepped around Beltran in a deliberate move that said she wasn't done with him yet. "Let's go. And Rune? Try to walk with a little more sex appeal."

"Wha . . . What is that supposed to mean?"

"It means you walk heavily, don't sway your hips, and are, overall, not the picture of a whore."

"Consort," Beltran corrected wearily. "We've been over this."

Verida ignored him. "Even with the incubi's help, I don't think you'll pass."

"I'm going to take that as a compliment," Rune sniffed.

Verida sashayed away, calling back, "Don't."

Rune's arms flew out, air-strangling Verida from behind; then she stormed after her, her feet slapping the ground as she went.

"Uh, love, when Verida said sway, I don't think that's what she meant."

"Shut. Up!"

"The council dance," Beltran said a little louder. "Just move like that, and you'll be fine."

Grey stepped up next to the shifter. "Council dance? Something else I missed?"

"Rune had to jump through a lot of hoops to get you out of Feena's hold."

The words weren't unclear, exactly, but by the way Beltran watched Rune as he said it, it was obvious to Grey that something had happened at the dance that had had nothing to do with him.

"Keep your eyes down, and stay beside me at all times." Beltran must've decided that the ladies had enough of a head start, for he began to walk forward. "Fal has a reputation, so we shouldn't have any trouble. But if you stray too far without a master in sight, someone will try something."

"What kind of something?"

"Steal you, sell you. Maybe both."

"Seems on par. I've been a slave from the minute I stepped through that gate."

Beltran stopped abruptly. He turned his head so Grey could just see the heavily rounded tip of his chin over his shoulder. "There are worse kinds of slavery than the one you're enduring. Trust me. Now, be on your guard. I know Verida and Tate taught you both a little about resisting incubus and succubus magic, but keep your mind centered and away from whatever desires it might awaken." As they exited the tunnel and stepped into the light, Beltran added, "And try not to gawk."

The reality of the Underground came into focus, and Grey couldn't decide where to look. His steps stuttered, and his head swiveled up and around, pressing against the hard metal collar as he tried to find the source of the light shining down from the roof of the cave.

Beltran reached back and grabbed him by the wrist, jerking him forward. "What did I *just* say?"

Grey mumbled an apology and put his eyes down and to the side, still trying to look at the creatures of all shapes and sizes that thronged around crowded stalls. Shop owners hawked their wares loudly, waving flowers, trinkets, vials, and small bags.

"Place your bets," someone shouted. "Place your gladiator bets here."

They weren't that far out of the tunnel when Grey felt the incubus magic. Sexual energy floated everywhere, growing thicker with every step and plucking at his senses with a strange, multilayered depth—like a whiff of liberally applied cologne. From the few dealings Grey had had with Tashara, he could tell that the individual strands of magic were not at full strength, but there were a lot of them. No matter where he looked, he saw red. Both males and females roamed through the crowd, wearing the crimson outfits of the consorts.

Someone crashed into Grey with enough force that he stumbled backward and tripped, landing on his butt.

"Hey!" Fal's voice shouted. "Watch where you're going!"

A shadow fell over Grey, and he looked up. Although he knew it was Beltran standing over him, he couldn't see anything other than the harshness of Fal's persona.

"Get up," Beltran snarled.

Scrambling to his feet, Grey kept his eyes down and fell obediently into step directly behind Beltran's larger-than-normal shoulders. Around the edges of the market were larger establishments, stores, and taverns. Between those were streets and alleyways where Grey could see the first of rows of homes built with plank wood. Beltran veered toward a crowd that had gathered around a betting booth, stopping near the back. A tall, willowy fae with yellow skin glanced behind him. Upon seeing Fal, he stepped away.

"Waste of money, if you ask me," Beltran said to no one in particular but loud enough that it could've been to anyone.

Several more looked at Fal's hulking figure. All moved away. It wasn't long before Beltran and Grey stood in an oddly conspicuous empty pocket of space—with one exception. A male vampire hadn't moved. He stood a little way off, wearing a heavily brocaded vest, and was watching them with interest. The male shoved one hand in the pocket of his black pants, looking amused while maintaining a specific tangible elegance that Grey had only ever noticed from the vampires.

"Fools. All of them." Fal spat and turned to go.

The vampire stepped closer. "And why is that?"

As Beltran was now facing Grey, he could see the shifter's slight smile and realized immediately that Beltran's choice to walk away had been an effort to get the vampire to come to him, eliminating what would've otherwise been a natural suspicion.

Fal reengaged, first looking around as if to make sure that no one was eavesdropping. "Rumor is, these games aren't going to make it to the final match." He spat again. "Didn't even have to search that out—heard it three times since last night—and these fools are out here throwing money away."

"Three times, you say?"

"In one night." He shook his head. "I've got better things to do, like sell this one."

"Hold on." The vampire's brown eyes were glittering with amusement. "Fal, correct? Help me out. I'm usually well connected, so you can understand that I'm dying to hear what I've missed."

"Sorry. My lips are tighter than those I drink with."

"I thought, maybe . . ." The vampire pulled a coin from his pocket and twisted it in the light.

"A bit less than I'm accustomed to, but . . ." Fal snatched the coin into his meaty hand. "You'll hear it for free by this evening anyway. By the looks of it, Tate has a new owner. With Dracula out of the picture, imaginations are running wild, wondering how much that Venshii is worth and how to get their hands on him. There are rumors of a group effort to take down the wards."

The vampire made a scoffing sound in the back of his throat. "I assure you, Dracula has not sold the Venshii, and whoever is making these claims will likely find his head mounted in Dracula's main hall."

"Then make your bets. I thank you for your coin."

"Next time you hear those rumors, you should let the teller know that those wards are not going anywhere."

Fal threw his head back and laughed. "Why not? Supreme faith in the wizards?"

"Wizards die as easy as the rest—a fact they themselves are also aware of. In that regard"—the vampire held out his hand—"I have a tidbit of information for *you.*"

Fal chuckled, a raspy billowing of air. "What's your name?"

"Anton."

"I like you." He pulled the coin from his pocket and slapped it back in the vampire's hand.

"I have no doubt the match will proceed as scheduled, because they've moved the wizards out of their old boxes in the stands and beneath the arena. Between the wards and Sarley"—he neatly tucked the coin into the small pocket of his vest—"those wizards are untouchable."

"Well, then." Fal smiled broadly. "Maybe I'll place a bet after all."

"Now who's the fool? The odds for Tate are so high you'll barely make your money back."

"Maybe. But Tate's been gone a while. Maybe he's grown soft."

Anton gave Fal a nod. "Maybe. Nice chatting with you."

Beltran grabbed Grey by the arm and hauled him away. When they were well out of Anton's earshot, he let loose a lengthy stream of swear words. "I had *one* plan for how to get Tate out of that arena, and now it's shot all to hell."

When Beltran had instructed them to break fingers, Rune had thought he was being facetious. But when an older male with partially shattered ram's horns and pale-green skin put his hands on her waist for the second time, she lost it.

She whirled and ripped his hand free, squeezed three of his fingers so the knuckles ground against one another, and bent them backward. Rune both felt and heard the pops as multiple bones broke. He dropped to his knees.

"I *said* we've already been paid for. Touch me again, and I'll break something else." She threw his hand back at him and stomped off.

Verida was waiting a few steps away. "Nicely done."

"He's lucky I didn't have a dagger on me," she growled. "I would've shoved it through his eye—"

The monster of her inner Venator agreed and was crawling up her throat. She leaned over her knees, taking deep breaths and trying to clear her head of both the Venator desires and the incubus magic that was taking advantage of her distracted state.

"Rune? Rune?" Verida grabbed her by the shoulder and shook. "Rune!"

"I can hear you just fine," she said through clenched teeth. "Can we *please* just get to wherever we're going? I don't know how much longer I can do this."

They'd been wandering around the stalls and listening to gossip for at least an hour while trying to navigate the host of very interested parties, some of whom were more persistent than others. Being around the paranormal didn't trigger her Venator like it used to, but the touching, the leering—it had pushed her past her limits.

Verida linked her arm through Rune's and dragged her toward a tavern. "Listen," she said in Rune's ear. "There are only two people I trust down here. The one we're about to visit asks too many questions. Keep your mouth shut."

"Isn't that what you always tell me to do? No matter where we are?"

Verida took the single step up to the door. "So it is."

"And why are we talking to him if he asks too many questions?"

Verida grabbed the door as she looked over her shoulder to Rune. "*Because* he asks too many questions."

The inside of this tavern was very different from the first one Rune had visited after arriving in Eon. This clientele was of a higher caliber, well dressed and wanting to be seen. The tables and chairs were of fine wood and upholstery. The staff was well dressed in crisp shirts and dark pants. In the corner, an elven male with long chestnut hair played a strange-looking version of a piano.

As they hovered near the back, Rune worried that they would stand out, but the tavern was awash in red. There'd been a distinct spike in incubus magic when they walked through the door, and she suspected there was one somewhere in the room. Consorts were settled on or near almost every patron, with more looking for a mark.

"How does nobody realize they're being magically manipulated?"

"They do. They just don't care. It feels good, so they lean into it, shell out enough coin for the whore, and enjoy their day." The door opened, and a tall, extremely handsome vampire walked in. "Ah, perfect timing. That's who we're looking for."

The vampire wore an ornately embroidered black and gold vest that emphasized his broad chest and tapered waist. He was alert, taking note of the activities in the room with a perpetual twinkle in his brown eyes. Rune lost herself for a moment in admiring him, the incubus magic swooping past her defenses, muddling with the things she was already feeling.

"Pull yourself together, Rune."

She jolted, and her cheeks burned. "Don't act like you haven't noticed how pretty he is."

"Everyone notices Anton Pietrala. Including himself."

Verida made a beeline through the room, cutting between tables and chairs. The male in question had stopped at the bar and was speaking to the bartender. She tapped him on the shoulder.

When he turned, the smile in his eyes vanished. "I don't care what you have to offer, how you can make me feel, who you belong to, or why you're here; for the last time, leave me the hell . . ." He trailed off and sniffed the air. "Verida?"

She held her finger to her lips. "Can we talk somewhere private?"

He leaned one hip against the bar and took his time undressing her with his eyes. "That look doesn't suit you at all. Still, it's hard not to appreciate it."

"Anton."

He winked and gave the room a quick once-over, his eyes landing on Rune. "And who is this one?"

"She's with me."

He crooked a finger. "My office."

Anton ushered them behind the bar and through a door into a small but exquisitely decorated back room. The richness of it reminded Rune of Dimitri's quarters, but Anton's were comfortable. The furniture was overstuffed. The books didn't appear to have been straightened nightly with a ruler, and the desk had papers spread across the surface instead of evenly stacked one on top of the other. Verida pushed Rune toward the love seat and immediately positioned herself between Rune and Anton. Apparently, Rune wasn't to be heard *or* seen. She swallowed her annoyance and sat.

He leaned against the desk, crossing his ankles and then his arms. "Verida, it's been a while. You look . . . ridiculous."

"I'm aware." She tore her veil off and tossed it to Rune. "But thank you for the unsolicited assessment."

"Anything to assist House Dracula." He leaned to the side, looking around Verida. "Who are you trying to hide back there? She could pass for human, but she doesn't smell completely human." He frowned. "In fact . . . she smells very similar to a prisoner I passed by earlier."

"She has an odd odor. I try to ignore it."

Anton must've seen Rune's annoyed twitch at Verida's description because he smiled at her. "I think you smell quite nice, actually."

His teeth were perfect, even with the fangs, and Rune nodded an uncomfortable thank-you. She then thumbed through every disgusting memory she could access to keep herself from betraying how attractive she found him. Stupid incubus magic. Stupid vampire senses. She felt very, very human at the moment, and it made her want to punch something.

"You bring a stranger into my private office, and you really aren't going to tell me who she is?"

"Look, Anton, I'm sure it won't be long before you figure it out. When you do, send me a message, and we can have the discussion I'm purposely bypassing. At this exact moment, I don't have a lot of time, and I need your help."

"Is this about Tate?"

"*Of course it's about Tate!* Why else would I be wandering around the Underground dressed like this?"

"You actually did manage to lose your father's most prized gladiator." He chuckled and shook his head. "Oh, Verida, you're in so much trouble. Your father doesn't love you this much."

"Thank you for yet another fact I'm acutely aware of. I need to know everything you've heard about who's running Tate in the games."

Anton settled in further, readjusting his arms and leaning his weight fully against the desk. "His name is Qualtar. At least, that's what he's listed his name as. I'm sure it's an alias. I've never heard of a Qualtar of any consequence, and yet we're getting reports that there's an army of fae—rumored to be his—camping as near the arena as they dare while avoiding the giants' ire, in broad daylight and in full battle gear. Curious, wouldn't you agree?"

Rune couldn't see Verida's face, but there was a long pause before she responded. "An army. Just . . . sitting there?"

"That's what I said."

"That doesn't make any sense."

"No, it does not." He kicked himself off the desk and took a crystal decanter and glass from a shelf, pouring himself a drink of amber liquid.

"When did you start drinking?"

"I didn't. It's for the lady."

"No, she doesn't need—"

Anton stepped neatly around Verida, smiling his award-winning smile, and bent at the waist to hand Rune the drink, breathing deeply as he did.

"Uh, thank you." Rune took the glass, because anything else would've led to more words than the three she'd already uttered, and she'd probably already broken some etiquette law she was unaware of.

"Anton!" Verida snapped. "Stop smelling her. I have to get into those games. Can you help me or not?"

He straightened but kept staring at Rune. "No. Unless you've got enough money to buy out a ticketholder, there's no getting in. Normally, that wouldn't be an issue for you, but I'm assuming you aren't in a position to ask your father for money."

"How much are they going for?"

"It doesn't matter. Without your family money, it's well out of reach." He finally released Rune from the pressure of his gaze and stalked back to Verida, putting one hand in his pocket. "So, tell me, was Tate stolen from the council? Or from you?"

"You know I can't answer that."

"Ah, Verida." He reached out with one elegant hand and brushed a thumb along her jawline. "You always have taken more than you give."

Her tone softened. "Not always."

"I really thought that when you joined us it would be different, but then they moved you ahead of me, and—" His eyes grew wider. It was slight, barely perceptible.

Verida reached for him. "Anto—"

He was faster. He blocked Verida's arm, pushing her one way while he went the other. Rune knew something was wrong, but there wasn't time to figure out what was happening before he was on top of her. Anton grabbed her and pushed her onto her side, digging his knee into her ribs. The glass she'd been holding flew from her grasp and shattered against the floor. He pressed her face against the arm of the love seat and pulled her hair to the side, jerking down the high neckline of her disguise. The three buttons popped off and landed amongst the glass.

The monster was out. Rune roared, and it was a sound not even she'd ever heard come out of her mouth. She twisted, put her hands on Anton's chest and her feet on his stomach, and shoved back with all her might. He flew up and out, slamming into the back wall. Books tipped and smashed to the floor. She ripped the adilat pouch from her ankle and leapt for him.

Anton was back on his feet, but not before Rune had the tip of her adilat shoved against his jugular.

"Rune, stop!" Verida shouted.

She was breathing so hard that it pulled the fabric of her veil tight over her mouth and nose, cutting each breath in half. With the amount of adrenaline pumping through her system, she should've been shaking, but she held her weapon steady. A born assassin.

Anton's eyes were red, but his glare was for Verida. "You brought a *Venator* into my establishment! Holy mother of Rana! What the hell is wrong with you?"

"Lower your voice!" Verida grabbed Rune's elbow and pulled her away, jumping between the two of them. "Rune, put your weapon away."

"He attacked me!"

"Yes, he did." She looked back at him. "Because he's an *idiot* who has clearly forgotten not only what Venators are capable of but also his manners. You owe her an apology."

Anton smoothed his vest, barking out a laugh. "That is not going to happen. *You* owe her an apology. If you had just told me what I was inviting into my office, I wouldn't have been forced to figure it out for myself." He put his hands on Verida's shoulders and gently pushed her away. He circled Rune with a wide berth, taking slow heel-to-toe steps. "So . . . It was the resistance, then, not the council, that brought the Venators back."

Rune's head snapped to Verida.

"Oh," Anton said. "Our Venator doesn't know either. Rune, was it? How interesting."

"What is he talking about?"

Verida's eyes matched Anton's in color, and her breaths were coming out short and tight. "Something he shouldn't be."

"No matter how many times all of your secret keeping bites you in that adorable little ass, you never learn your lesson. The Venator will see that soon enough."

"I came here for your help."

He motioned to Rune. "Is this what that looks like? You need a lesson on how to ask for favors."

"I don't need a favor. I just need to know whatever you can tell me about what Silen has been doing here and whether there have been any movements in the Black Forest."

"The Black Forest? You're checking on Zio?" Anton dropped into a chair and crossed one leg neatly over the other. "I must start being more careful with whom I associate. Everywhere you go, chaos follows."

"Can you help me or not?"

"For payment, I'm sure I can."

Verida closed her eyes and took a deep breath. "We're working on a payment basis now?"

"After what you just did? Today we most definitely are."

"Fine. What do you want?"

"I want to see her markings in action."

"What? No!" Rune tossed the adilat to the couch, aware that stalking him down like she was about to with a weapon in hand would not be a good idea. Standing over his chair, she glared. "You *attacked* me, and I don't care what Verida did or did not tell you, you can't just grab people and half-rip their clothes off."

"I can't argue with your moral outrage, and somebody does owe you an apology. But for the information Verida is seeking, the price has been set, and I'm afraid it's the only thing I'm interested in."

"I can think of something else." Verida dropped onto the love seat, picking up one of Rune's three buttons from beside her and tossing it to the floor with the others. "How long has it been since you've heard from Kasove?"

Anton's bright, casual demeanor dropped. He looked up at Rune, gave her a tight-lipped smile, and put an arm out, pressing it against her hip and nudging her to the side. "Excuse me, dear." He leaned over his knees. "My brother? After he called me a traitor and threatened to out me to Dracula if I ever showed my face in my family home again? We haven't spoken. Why?"

"He's dead. And I really think you'd like to hear how."

412

41

Beltran's alter ego, Fal, had seen someone he recognized—another slave trader—and was having a rather loud conversation about selling Grey to a werewolf pack. Halfway into the talk, their voices lowered; Grey heard the name Silen dropped once but couldn't make out much more. When the two were finished, they shook hands, and then Beltran and Grey were moving through the crowd again.

"Sounds like Silen is buying up as many slaves as he can, planning to turn them and boost his numbers with forced loyalty."

Grey had to ask all his questions by turning his head in Beltran's direction while looking at the ground and speaking half under his breath. "Will that work?"

"Wolves who are turned instead of birthed are always at the bottom of the pack hierarchy. They'll have the best chance of survival by staying within the pack that created them, so yes. Most of the werewolves that are run as gladiators are not natural born. They were either turned and sold or turned and chased out of their pack only to find themselves landing here."

Grey was bumped into for what felt like the thousandth time. It was like the collar made him invisible.

Beltran headed toward a stall that was smaller than the rest. An old woman sat behind it—a human, by the looks of it, which struck Grey as strange because he didn't think he'd seen another human in the Underground. As he thought about it, he realized he hadn't seen a human who looked over the age of fifty since he'd arrived. The old woman's cart was strung from top to bottom with unidentified pouches of all shapes and sizes. Cut and polished stones were laid out in open boxes, feathers hung on leather cords, and a variety of bird skulls were neatly displayed next to small metal cages full of insects and rodents.

The booth currently had only one customer, a female whose coloring was nearly identical to Omri's—white hair and skin so black it was like coal in firelight—and whose long, delicate ears poked through her hair. Because of her similarity to Omri, Grey would've assumed she was elvish. But just like when he'd come into the council house for the first time, he could distinguish the difference. She didn't feel elvish. She felt fae.

"Blinding powder," the fae was saying to the shop owner. "Just one dose."

The woman behind the cart got slowly to her feet, moving like her joints were riddled with arthritis. She pushed her wrinkled hand through a mass of hanging pouches, fussing and fumbling until she found the right one and plucked it from its hook.

The fae handed over payment, and the merchant woman squinted at the coin in her hand. "This is very generous."

"I'm always generous when I want to be forgotten. But a warning: I have a habit of returning when the memory of my face remains."

"In return for your kind payment, might I suggest the burning dust as a better choice? No extra charge. The blinding powder is not a strong brew."

414

"A better choice," the fae repeated. "How very presumptuous of you."

The old woman dipped her head and clutched the coin tight to her chest. "My apologies. Please forgive me. I was only looking to provide the best value to a most valuable customer."

The fae sneered and tucked the pouch under the blue cloak she was wearing. Turning to go, she came face to face with Fal and Grey. "Out of my way, you . . ."

Grey glanced up to see why she'd stopped speaking and found the fae looking directly at him. He hurriedly looked away. Remembering Beltran's description of the collar's use, he swallowed and blinked his eyes, trying to appear dizzy.

"That is a fine specimen you have, slaver. How much?"

"He's not for sale."

"Everything is for sale." The fae put a slim, pointy finger under Grey's jaw and lifted his face. She gripped his chin and turned his head from side to side. "Oh, yes, I will take him."

"Perhaps I should've been clearer." Beltran removed the fae's hand himself. "He's not for sale because he's already been sold. I'll be delivering him tonight."

"Then I'll take the matter up with the new owner. What is the name?"

"My client demands privacy."

Grey felt her finger on him again, inching under the metal collar and starting to pull back his shirt. He'd been ordered not to fight or yell. He wasn't supposed to do anything but stand there. But another couple of inches and she would catch a glimpse of the markings on his back.

Beltran's slaver hand clapped down over the top of the fae's fingers, pressing them flat onto Grey's shoulder. "I don't know who you are, but this one has been sold. *Find. Another.*"

"No." She smiled and jerked her hand free. "You don't." The fae's voice dropped to a whisper. "But I have a sneaking suspicion of who you are. Tell me, slaver, what did you say your name was again?"

The cadence and sound of her voice was suddenly eerily familiar. Grey couldn't place it, but unease tingled up the back of his neck.

"Fal."

"F-a-l." She repeated it slowly, emphasizing every letter as if it were wrong. "And who is this?"

"Still none of your concern."

"Fal!" The name came loud and clear over the crowd.

Beltran ignored it, staring down the fae.

"*Fal!*" The voice shouted more insistently.

"Fal, someone is desperate for your attention." The fae moved away but kept her head turned, watching Grey with every step. Then she slipped into the crowd and was gone.

"Bloody hell. What was that about?" Beltran asked, more to himself than anyone. He turned to the shop owner. "Who was that?"

"I don't know, and I'm afraid my memory of her face is fading quickly. What can I do for you this time, Fal?"

Beltran pulled Grey tightly up to the front of the booth, keeping one hand wrapped in his shirtsleeve as he leaned closer to the old woman. "I need to speak to the scorpion."

"She doesn't speak to just anyone."

"Tell her it's about her favorite topic. She'll know."

"Fal, *Fal!*"

The old woman leaned back in her chair. "You have company."

Whoever was doing the shouting, they were getting closer.

Beltran turned around, grumbling, "Blood of the saints."

"Fal!" A man with broad shoulders, a hooknose, and overly muscled arms shoved his way through the crowd. Grey assumed he was

416

a werewolf by the muscle distribution. "Fal, thank the stars. I've been watching for you."

Whoever this wolf was, Fal did not look happy to see him. His lips pursed. "What can I do for you?"

"I have something to deliver. It's important."

"I'll pick it up the next time I'm around. Thank you."

"No." The male's face went very hard. "You will take it now. I'm afraid I must insist."

Beltran sighed and gave the wolf his back, handing the old woman a coin. "Where should I wait?"

"If she decides to see you, she'll find you."

"Thank you." Fal grabbed the man by an arm and Grey by another, dragging them both away. "This had better be important."

"It's from the wizard."

An unspoken code passed between Beltran and the wolf, and then they were moving. Beltran dragged Grey through the crowd, pushing and shoving until they reached the stairs of a small establishment. There, he released his hold as he ducked around a colorful piece of fabric that had been hung in place of a door. Grey followed right behind, pushing the fabric aside and running into the chests of two very large men with blue skin and ram's horns. The guards crossed their arms and pushed forward, shoving Grey back.

"He's with me," Beltran said.

The two guards were silent. They straightened, took one step back, each of them in time with the other, and cut to the side, opening a path between them.

The inside of the building they'd just entered looked like a regular home, full of nothing that would require guards. There was a seating area that flowed into a small kitchen with a black kettle hanging over a fireplace and a simple table with two chairs. That space transitioned into a bedroom, where a small bed was dressed by one thin and tattered blanket. On the back wall was a large tapestry that looked like it had been around as long as the blanket. Small, moth-eaten holes disrupted the pattern.

The werewolf pulled the tapestry back with one hand and placed his palm on the center of the blank wall. He pushed, and a door that Grey hadn't been able to distinguish by looking at it hinged inward. The wolf slipped through.

Beltran turned abruptly and placed his hand on Grey's chest. "If I *ever* regret letting you in here, I swear I will shift into something quite capable of delicately and slowly ripping your intestines out through your nose."

Grey swallowed. His Adam's apple rubbed against the collar. "That sounds excruciating."

"It is. I'd leave you out here, but I don't trust the guards enough to risk it."

On the other side of the door, the room was drastically different. Maps covered the walls, push pins dotting their surface. Single shelves had been hung here, there, and everywhere with no apparent rhyme or reason. Strange trinkets had been arranged on those shelves, interspersed with piles of weaponry. Parchment letters were strewn across the desk and weighted down by orbs that looked like the one Tate had used to familiarize Grey and Rune with the council members before they'd arrived at the council house.

Once they were inside, the door shut behind the three of them, and Beltran charged the wolf. He slid his forearm against the male's neck and slammed him against the wall. "How many bloody times do I have to tell you not to approach me in the marketplace? Especially while *shouting my name?*"

"I'm sorry," he croaked, clawing at Fal's bulky arm. "I wouldn't have done it if it wasn't important."

"Important. Important? And *how* would you know it was *important* unless you opened the letter—*again?*"

"Because . . ." The croaking was now wheezing. "Fal—"

"Uh . . . *Fal*," Grey said. "You're going to kill him."

Beltran stepped back, and the wolf fell forward, gasping for air. "I didn't open it, I swear. But he hand delivered it."

"Who hand delivered it? The wizard?"

He nodded. "Yes."

"He was here?"

"I never saw his face, but it was him. The scroll is enchanted. I couldn't have opened it if I tried."

"Hand it over. And Maken, don't think the fact that you knew the scroll was enchanted was lost on me."

Maken scurried over to the desk and picked up a piece of rolled parchment from the back corner. Beltran held out his hand, but the wolf paused, grasping the scroll between both hands.

"What are you doing?"

"It's not actually for you." Maken tilted his head. "I think it's for him. Are you . . . Grey?"

Beltran snatched the scroll and passed it over his shoulder. "Open it."

As soon as Grey touched the parchment, it recognized him, turning from pale yellow to white. He unrolled it and began reading lines of flowery handwriting.

"Who's it from?" Beltran demanded.

"Uh, it's—" He scanned to the bottom and read the name twice. "Tashara."

Beltran gave him an irritated roll of the hand to hurry him up.

Grey went back to reading, and as he did, words seemed to jump off the page.

Veneer.

Dead.

Games.

Black skin. White hair.

When Grey was done, his mouth was bone dry. The parchment turned back to yellow, the magic apparently dissipating after completing its task. He handed it to Beltran, who hurriedly scanned it.

"Bloody saints." Beltran stared at him over the letter. "That fae in the marketplace. That was—"

"Ambrose."

42

Verida and Rune walked briskly down a side street lined with single-story wooden homes. Once Verida spotted a door with three talismans hanging to the right-hand side, she grabbed Rune's elbow and yanked her into an alley. "We're almost done, but I need you to stay—"

"Sooo . . ." Rune fell back against the wall. "*Anton.*"

"Seriously?" She craned her neck, checking the street for anyone they might need to be wary of. "You want to do this now?"

Rune stubbornly crossed her arms.

"Fine. Yes. Anton and I had a history. I was close with all the brothers. And then we finished growing up, and loyalty to my father—or lack thereof—took us all in different directions."

"Sounds like you and Anton went in the same direction, actually. What did he say about you 'joining us'?"

"Anton should've kept his mouth shut."

"But he didn't. What is the resist—"

"Quiet!" Verida stepped in, slapping a hand over her mouth.

Rune glared, and the words she grumbled in response were muffled.

Looking skyward for strength, Verida dropped her arm. "What?"

"I *said*, 'I will bite you.'"

"You can't just blurt things out! Just because it looks like we're alone doesn't mean we are."

"How convenient," Rune drawled. "There are always listening ears in the shadows whenever you or Beltran don't want to talk about something."

She looked out to the street again. They needed to get this over with so they could get back to the inn. "I'm sorry you're upset."

"Are you?" Rune pushed off the wall and stepped in front of Verida, forcing her acknowledgment. "I don't like feeling *used,* and even though you are the moodiest and most perpetually angry person I've ever met, you were one of three people in this whole damn world who never made me feel that way. Turns out I'm just an idiot for not seeing what was actually going on."

Verida grabbed her by the shoulders and stepped in a small circle, switching their positions. "I can't do this now." She pointed over her shoulder. "That's where I'm going, and you have to stay here. We can't have another incident like Anton."

"I didn't do anything wrong at Anton's! Why can't you just be honest? You're not bringing me because you're worried they might say something you don't want me to hear."

"You can think whatever you want about my motivations, but you're going to do it from this alleyway. Alone." She backed out before Rune could continue objecting, talking all the way to the corner. "Don't follow me, and don't make eye contact with anyone until I come back."

Verida straightened her veil as she hurried across the street. It was a risk, leaving Rune out here by herself, but the girl had been right. There were questions she needed answered about Beltran and his involvement in the resistance—answers she couldn't risk Rune overhearing. But when Verida knocked on the door, it creaked open, and the familiar smell of incense wafted out.

As she stared at the crack between the door and the frame, the hairs on the back of her neck stood on end. Sutree was diligent about locking every door and window in the house at all times. Verida pushed at the door with one finger, and it creaked open further. Assessing the latch and frame, she looked for signs of damage or forced entry but could see nothing of concern. She slipped inside.

The room was awash in a fog of scented smoke. Verida's eyes watered, and she coughed into her sleeve. "Sutree?"

Sutree always burned incense to ensure that unwelcome visitors with heightened senses of smell couldn't easily pinpoint her location. But today it seemed like every incense bulb in the house had been lit.

"Sutree?"

There was no answer. A nearly full cup of tea sat on the table. She brushed her finger over the side—still warm. Verida cautiously stepped through the room, past the sitting chairs and wardrobe, placing one foot silently in front of the other. The artwork that normally hid the entrance to the study was sitting on the floor and leaning against the wall, indicating that Sutree was inside.

This door was also cracked open. Verida pushed, and it swung wide. The room appeared empty, but as she stood in the threshold, scanning the piles of books and papers, she could hear two heartbeats. Sutree always kept at least two servants on staff, so that alone wasn't odd, but where were they? It sounded like she was right on top of both of them. Verida took one step in, then another, looking around the corner before realizing what was off. This room, too, had been completely overwhelmed by incense burning on every open surface—yet this was the one place in the house where Sutree never used the stuff.

The door slammed shut. Verida spun.

Leaning causally against the exit was a vampire. She was tall and thin, with hair as blonde as Verida's, blue eyes, and blood-red lips that had been painted to further enhance them. Her breasts spilled over a tightly corseted top. Thigh-high boots added sex appeal while a flat heel ensured practicality in a fight.

The vampire smiled with her mouth, her eyes chips of blue ice. "Hello, sister. Should we hug? It's been a while."

"*Vega,*" Verida snarled. "What have you done with Sutree?"

Vega's hand rose from her waist, as if pulled by a string held by a puppeteer. She pointed a finger.

Nervous to take her eyes off Vega, Verida slowly craned her neck, flipping her eyes up only at the last second. Sutree's squat, motionless figure was suspended above, wrapped so tightly in rope that it could've been a funeral dressing. The goblin always kept her tusks filed down to nothing, which had allowed Vega to wrap her entire head, leaving only her eyes showing. If it hadn't been for the heartbeat, Verida would've assumed she was already dead.

"I will never understand your friendship with that thing." Vega stalked toward her, managing to look—as always and forever—both alluring and deadly. "She is weak and ugly. But once I got word, I figured you'd show up here eventually."

Verida readjusted her weight, ready to dodge an attack if necessary but not prepared to make a move that would initiate a fight with her father's pride and joy. She was already in enough trouble as it was.

Vega scoffed at her posturing. "Sister dearest, you always play at bravery in the most ridiculous of situations."

"I have no idea what you're talking about." Ignoring the chill running through her, she raised her chin. "What did you get word of?"

"I've heard a great many things recently that I ought to rip your throat out for." She smiled tightly. "You know, of course, that I'm referring to father's Venshii. My source tells me Tate is fighting."

"Playing spy doesn't suit you. Tate is on loan from father . . . and none of your concern. This is council business."

"Odd. My source found no connection to the council at all."

Verida shrugged. "As I said, reconnaissance is not your strong suit. In fact, *my* sources have told me that you do your best work flat on your back. Perhaps you should stay there."

She shouldn't have said it, but Verida's hatred of Vega always overruled her senses. Vega lunged forward. Verida moved to protect her ribs—her sister's favorite place to attack. Vega punched her in the stomach instead. The force doubled her over, and she dry heaved.

Vega grabbed her by the hair, yanking her head back. She leaned closer, baring her teeth. "For the record, I am rarely on my back."

She wrenched Verida the rest of the way up and shoved her to the side. Verida stumbled, cursing the misstep. When she straightened, she wanted to wrap her arms around her throbbing middle but, determined not to show weakness, instead lowered them to her sides and faked a casual laugh. "Not on your back? Oh, sister, I am so impressed with your standards."

"It's not a standard, you imbecile. It's control."

"You're wasting your time. Father knows what the council and I are doing, and if he hasn't seen fit to share it with you . . ."

Vega reached down the front of her corset with two fingers, withdrawing a small roll of parchment and holding it up. The seal of House Dracula, pressed in red wax, had been broken open.

"You didn't," she breathed.

"Of course I did." Vega unrolled the parchment with relish. "I was curious as to why father would allow a victor's purse to go elsewhere. Had Tate been registered under a member of the council or one of their known aliases, perhaps I wouldn't have questioned." She held it out. "Would you like to read it?"

When Verida reached for the scroll, Vega snatched it away. "On second thought, I do so love to read aloud.

"*'Vega, pull your sister's reins. Inform Verida that I will expect her explanation in person by the next moon.'*"

The world spun. Castle Dracula. She could not go back. Not yet.

"Oh, Verida. You look even more pitiful than normal." The parchment snapped as it rolled closed. "I take it you don't have an explanation for father?"

"Of course I have an explanation. And it's council business, which is above what you've been cleared to know. I'm happy to tell father what we've been up to, but the new moon will be a problem. There are things in play that need to be taken into account."

"You've never been a very good liar."

"We both know that's not true." Verida jerked her head toward Sutree. "You've delivered your message. Release her."

Vega tucked their father's note back into her corset. She strolled forward as if she might actually do what Verida had requested, then veered to the side instead, making a wide circle to cross behind Verida's back.

"This again?" Verida sighed. "You've been playing this game since we were children. Haven't you tired of it?"

"I never tire of what works. I can hear your heart picking up even as you mock me."

"I'm not turning around. You don't scare me."

"You can release your little friend yourself after I'm gone," Vega said. "But first . . ."

The blade went straight through Verida's spinal column.

She hissed. Her eyes flooded red as she lost feeling in the lower half of her body. Her legs crumpled, and she dropped. Her sister withdrew the blade and shoved it in again at the base of her neck. Verida's entire body went slack, and her head cracked against the floor. She could neither feel nor move anything from the neck down.

"You are pathetic." Vega leaned over her, leaving the blade where it was to prevent Verida's body from healing. "You don't think I heard about your little stunt? Giving those werewolves my name like I was some common whore. Cost me a payday and a piece of my reputation, you bitch. Consider this your warning. If it happens again, I'll kill you."

"Father would—"

"Father would mourn, and I would mourn right beside him, railing against the monster who did such a thing to my poor little sister."

"You"—it was getting hard to breathe—"deserved it."

Vega stepped over her like she was a rolled-up rug and crouched down, resting her hands on her knees. "Still not over *it*, I see."

"I will *never* be over *him*."

"You are such a child. I saved you from yourself."

"The only thing you saved was your precious reputation!"

"Why father puts up with you, I will never understand." Vega stood. "If you aren't back to Castle Dracula by the full moon, I expect father will send me to retrieve you."

"Then perhaps I'll miss the deadline on purpose, because next time I see you, I'm going to slit you from nose to navel before you can open your mouth."

"Exercising such bravado while paralyzed on the floor is . . . well, it's pathetic. Honestly, I'm embarrassed to call you family."

"The feeling is mutual."

"New moon, Verida. And bring the Venshii."

She watched, unable to move, as her sister's boots walked out of sight. With the blade in her back, she was unable to heal, and though the weapon itself was slowing the bleeding, she was still losing blood. There wasn't anything she could do but wait for someone to find her.

Verida thought she could still smell her sister, but with the cloud of incense, it wasn't possible. It was just her mind remembering. She closed her eyes and let past and present collide, reliving the moments that had brought she and her sister here.

"Verida?"

Standing in the doorframe, her hands trembling, was Rune.

The parchment slid from Beltran's fingers to the floor. That black-skinned fae had been Ambrose, wearing a veneer. Beltran replayed every moment of their encounter. She'd *seen* Grey. And during that strange conversation—where she'd said she suspected she knew who he was—he hadn't for a second thought she actually knew him as *Beltran*.

He looked up. "Get out."

Maken looked to Grey first but quickly realized it was meant for him. "But this is my—"

"I said get out!"

The werewolf shuffled past them, snatching an orb and two rolls of parchment off the desk, then had the audacity to bend down and pick up the message Beltran had just dropped.

"Stop." He held out a hand. "Not that one."

Maken huffed and slapped the parchment into Beltran's waiting palm. "Be quick about it. I have others to meet in here." The door swung shut behind him.

Grey looked as numb as Beltran felt. "Ambrose saw me."

"A problem that is going to be hard to lie our way out of. What is she doing in the Underground?" he fumed. "I knew she'd be at the games, but not down here, not now. This place is not Ambrose's style. She doesn't lower herself to this."

Beltran prided himself on many things, one of which was the length of his temper. But that wick had been burning for some time, and he'd exhausted his stores of wit, charm, and patience. He kicked the back of a chair. It slid across the room and crashed into the wall.

"Bloody hell, what is she doing! And *why* can't I figure it out?" He crumpled the parchment in his fist. The noise brought him back. He opened his hand, peering at Arwin's letter and then at Grey. "Why is Tashara sending you messages? Grey?"

The boy's spine was stiff, and his hands hung loosely at his sides. Though he was staring straight at Beltran, his eyes were wide and glassy. Whatever he was seeing, it was not in this room. Beltran moved closer, looking for any signs of awareness, worried that Grey's visions were starting to take hold while he was awake. But Grey's form was solid, and he wasn't crying out in pain.

"I know what she's doing. I know what—" The words cut off abruptly as Grey gasped and reared back, sucking in mouthfuls of air as if someone had been holding his head underwater.

That same parchment crumpled again as Beltran's hand clenched. *"What did you just say?"*

"What? I, uh—oh . . ." He scrubbed a hand over the back of his neck and laughed—at least, it was supposed to be laughter. It sounded more like something trying to breathe while having the life choked out of it. "I don't know. I guess I kinda just zoned out there for a minute. What were we talking about?"

It was a pathetic attempt at nonchalance, and if the situation itself hadn't already piqued Beltran's interest, that performance alone would've put him on the scent like a bloodhound.

"We were talking about Ambrose, and you said, 'I know what she's doing.'"

"Huh, that's weird." Grey swallowed and tried to smile.

Beltran shook his head in warning. "Don't. Don't lie to me. You just saw something, and you're going to tell me what it was."

The two stood face to face, staring, each pressing their own silent desires. Grey's eyes begged Beltran to drop it. Beltran's demanded answers. Grey yielded first, his eyes fluttering closed as he took a slow breath in through his nose.

"You don't understand what you're asking. It's not safe. Rune can't know. Nobody can know."

"I need information. We can't walk into this any blinder than we already are."

Grey's jaw clamped shut, but Beltran knew he'd won. He could see the truth bubbling just behind those lips. All it needed was a little nudge. "Listen very carefully. There are too many blind spots. If you don't tell me what you know, what happened out there with Ambrose is just the beginning. Somebody is going to die! Could be me, might be Verida, maybe Rune."

The truth blurted out with the force of a volcano. "I know what Keir demanded as trade from Ambrose for the key to Kastaley."

Air lodged in Beltran's esophagus. When he could breathe again, he took one step, then two. He shoved Fal's oversized hands, along with Arwin's message, into his too-small pockets. Although he wanted to ask what the trade would be, the more pressing question was, "*How?*"

There was a beat, then a blink, as Grey executed the most painfully obvious stall Beltran had seen in a while. "I overheard Feena talking when she had me in her courts." The story was cold, his words flat. "She thought I was asleep."

"Really."

"Really." Grey offered a strange half smile, then gave Beltran his back and perused the maps on the wall as if the last minute hadn't happened.

What Beltran wanted to do next was remove that slave collar and wrap his hands around Grey's neck. But he knew a sensitive situation when he saw one. He measured both his words and his tone. "The morning after I threw you in the lake, we discussed Ambrose and what her plans might be. You didn't say a word. You knew nothing, if I remember correctly, but now, minutes after we accidentally run into her, you have all the answers?"

Instead of responding, Grey stepped to one side, moving to the next map on the wall and clasping his hands together behind his back.

"All right, fine. Tell me, then, what is this wager?"

"Ambrose bet her council seat against the key to Kastaley."

Fal's mouth started to form the sentence, *She would never*—but of course she would. Ambrose would do almost anything for that key. More to the point, when she made the wager, she'd been in possession of the top fighter in the games and certain she would win. Implications and understandings—regarding what might happen during these games, his past, and multiple versions of the future—crashed around Beltran like the freezing waves of a stormy sea, ripping through his mind, upending, solving problems and creating new ones. His legs felt strangely weak, and he pushed himself onto the desk, haphazardly shoving an orb out of the way and not caring what papers he was crumpling. Maken probably had them all memorized anyway.

"You're sure?" he asked.

Grey was still staring at the map, showing only his profile. He gave a short half nod, his chin stopped by the slave collar.

The question was unnecessary. He'd seen the moment Grey had remembered. The truth of it had been written all over his face. But . . . Beltran frowned. *Remembered* wasn't the right word. Nobody looked like someone had struck them upside the head with a sledgehammer when they *remembered* things.

"Just so I understand. You're telling me that you overheard Feena talking while you were hooked into her wall of flowers, and you just now remembered it?"

A muscle in Grey's jaw ticked.

"That's what I thought. But if you didn't overhear, how could you possibly know?"

Beltran had spent time in Feena's court. He knew what happened down there and with what frequency. Grey would've been Feena's new favorite pet, as he'd predicted to Rune. She would've tapped into him multiple times during his short stay, desperate to see his past, to experience all those feelings of his.

Beltran inhaled sharply. "Bloody hell—you could see into Feena's mind. Couldn't you?"

With the truth now floating in the room, Grey's cold disregard dropped like rain and puddled on the floor. He gripped at his scalp as if he could tear the memories out by the roots. "Rune can't know. If *anyone* finds out what happened, every one of us is at risk."

He wasn't wrong. But Grey was at risk from far more places than he realized, including a certain shifter he'd just taken into his confidence.

"Why did you admit to the council what Feena had done? They had no idea what she was doing with those vines, and now Ambrose is suspicious of what you might have seen. Did you see her face in the council room? Because I did."

"I had no choice. I had to make them believe I was loyal to them if I wanted them to let us out of there."

"How much did you see?" Beltran pushed. "What else can you remember?"

"That's the problem. Linking to her mind was traumatic—the fae think so differently." Grey put the heel of his hand against his temple. "Everything hurt. I have huge chunks of missing time."

"When you remembered a minute ago, it didn't look like a memory. It looked like a vision."

Grey started to pace, shaking one wrist as if the movement would somehow help him explain. "There are some things I saw clearly, and I can remember every detail. But there are other things, like this, where I don't know that I know until someone says something that triggers a memory. When that happens, thoughts and feelings flash forward, and I suddenly recognize places or people. They present like my memories, but with Feena's emotions attached."

"That was how you got out of her court. I wondered."

"Yes. I didn't know what to do next until we got there, but then I would see something and would remember which paths to choose and which to avoid. Even with that, I didn't have enough notice before the memories came, and there were holes, things I couldn't see. We almost didn't make it."

"Didn't Verida and Rune find it a little strange that you just 'knew' what to do?"

"Of course they did, but we didn't have time to sit around and talk about it. Rune just informed me that after the battle"—there was a hiccup in his step, and he rolled his neck—"I died. Which explains why they stopped asking questions about our escape."

A fist pounded on the door, and Maken yelled a muffled, "Fal!"

Beltran pushed off the desk and opened the door as the werewolf lifted his fist again. "Breathe. Your face is the color of a beet."

"I have business to attend to, Fal. I cannot have you commandeering my residence all afternoon."

"Grey, I think our presence is no longer welcome." He stepped back and waved an arm. "After you."

Beltran fell in behind Grey and stared down Maken as he exited. "Don't think I missed the fact that you tried to walk off with the wizard's message. You are treading on treacherous ground."

If—when—Tate won the match, Keir would become the new fae council leader. This was bad for the Venators. After what they had done to Keir's mother, he would be out for their blood. For Beltran, the implications were no less serious. It was possible that Feena had told Keir how to prevent Beltran from shifting, which was bad enough. But once Keir arrived at the council house, he would need to gain the support of the others—he would need a hand to play. Passing on the knowledge of how to cripple Beltran would do the trick.

They passed between the watchful eyes of the two guards.

It was conceivable that Beltran's secret had died with the queen—Feena didn't share everything with her son. But that was not a risk Beltran was willing to take. Once he'd realized what Keir was trying to do, he'd quietly toyed with plots capable of eliminating the new king prior to him claiming the fae council seat.

But now . . .

Beltran stared at the back of Grey's head as they walked.

Now he could not ignore the possibility that tucked somewhere within the folds of that Venator mind was a large, pulsating mass of a secret, dropped unwittingly by Feena, waiting for the proper trigger to bring it surging to the surface.

43

Verida hadn't moved in well over an hour.

When Rune found her, Vega's knife had been embedded in flesh, muscle, and bone. To create enough leverage to pull it free, she'd had to place both feet on either side of Verida's spine and lean back. The sensation of metal grinding free of the spinal column vibrated through the handle, leaving Rune's hands gritty with phantom bone dust.

The injury was severe, and Verida's ability to walk hadn't fully returned fast enough. Rune had half-carried her across the Underground, listening as she haltingly relayed the story of how she'd ended up with a dagger in her back, then helped her up the stairs to their dark, windowless room at the inn and into bed. With nothing to do but wait, Rune sat at the two-person table and watched the unnaturally still vampire. But staring at someone so motionless that they looked like a corpse didn't exactly help time move faster.

Rune's nervous energy continued to redouble on a constant loop. Beltran and Grey hadn't arrived yet, and even though she hadn't heard a sound, she kept checking the interior door between their rooms, hoping that knob would turn. She tapped her fingers against the table, sighed, took off the pouch of adilats, tapped some more, and finally resituated her body weight in the chair, purposefully grabbing the seat and jerking it forward so the thin legs scraped against the floor.

Verida finally blinked. "Could you be any louder?"

"You're alive—er, I mean, awake."

She rolled her head against the pillow, her lips pursed but paler than normal. *"Alive?"*

"I had to keep checking to make sure you were breathing. I was getting nervous. Are you hungry? Can I bring you something to eat? You lost blood."

"Are you offering to coax some dinner back to the room with you?" When Rune didn't argue, Verida chortled. "I'd like to see that. You'd have to make sure he's handsome, though. I'm not in the mood for an unappealing dinner."

Relieved at the normalcy, Rune smiled and relaxed back into the wooden chair. "I didn't realize you were picky about looks."

"I'm not. But I'm in a bad mood."

"Should I request a certain handsome vampire? Or find someone less acquainted with you?"

"You're getting funnier. I'm starting to enjoy it."

The pride Rune felt at that statement was comically inappropriate for the situation.

"Although"—Verida pushed herself up, groaning as she swung her feet around to the floor—"Anton wouldn't be an ideal meal. Vampire blood isn't terribly nourishing."

"Huh, interesting." Rune made a mental note. "How are you doing?"

"I didn't lose enough blood for you to start panicking, if that's what you mean."

"It's not. I mean, how are you? You know, after seeing your sister?"

"Is that how we're referring to the situation? 'Seeing my sister.' I'm doing fine, now that I've thought of a hundred ways to kill her using the knife she left in my back." Verida slid a hand under her pillow and retrieved the blade. Leaning over her knees, she held the dagger with the blade lying flat against her forearm and stared at the handle. "My father gifted me this years ago to help me remember one of his favorite sermons. I left it in that damned castle on purpose."

After having to remove it from Verida's spine, Rune was well acquainted with the knife. It was wide and flat with a thick channel down the center of the blade, but Verida's attention was on the handle. Fashioned from bone or antler, the pommel had been carved into the head of an eagle and set with a winking ruby eye. The beak's tip was wickedly sharp and in just the right position to let the wielder use both blade and handle as weapons.

Verida stood and stretched, twisting at the waist and rotating her shoulders. "I feel almost back to normal." She pulled out the chair across from Rune and dropped into it, slamming the dagger point down into the table. "I hope Beltran and Grey did better than we did."

"We got some good information on Silen," Rune pointed out, trying for optimism. "And Sutree said she might know someone who would be willing to sell some tickets . . . after I got her off the ceiling."

"Useless. Those short on money have already sold their tickets, which leaves us needing to catch the attention of the rich. The fact is that we don't, and won't, have the funds to tempt anyone into selling." She jerked the blade back out of the table and went to work jabbing at the wood with short, aggressive pops. "We aren't going to be able to walk through the gates. My father is going to make the last punishment I received from Dimitri look like a gift." Verida's nose scrunched, and her lips pulled over her teeth in distaste. "And the thing that's making me the *most* upset is that I made a *Venshii* a promise, and I didn't keep it."

Rune reared back. "A Venshii? Why are you talking about Tate as if he's some sort of disease?"

Verida glanced up, her fangs outlined clearly beneath the skin of her upper lip. "Seeing my family always brings up old habits. I'm not proud of it. In my household, Venshii were lower than dogs. To care for their feelings or needs was ludicrous." She returned to using the table as a training dummy.

Pop, pop, pop.

"That's part of why I chose Tate. I knew my father would assume he wasn't capable of thinking for himself." She shook her head bitterly. "I promised Tate that if he helped me, I would keep his family safe and away from the games. I sold every piece of jewelry and family heirloom I had to buy Ayla and Brandt. Tate held up his end of the bargain, but I didn't hide his family well enough to keep mine."

"You own Ayla and Brandt! But that means you can get them out."

"I would prefer if you would ask questions instead of assuming I'm that stupid." She readjusted her grip on the blade. "I gifted them their freedom." *Pop. Pop. Pop, pop, pop.* "A lot of good that did any of us."

"Oh." Rune cleared her throat. "That's a pretty big favor. What did Tate help you do?"

The blade stopped a centimeter above the wood. "It's not important."

"Just like the resistance isn't important?"

"Mother of Rana, I should've stayed in bed. You didn't ask me questions over there."

"I was letting you heal."

She brought the knife down. *Pop.* "I think I'm still feeling twinges of pain."

"Verida! How am I supposed to trust you when I know you're keeping things from me?"

"Knowing isn't always better."

"Are you seriously trying to make a case for ignorance? Because I've seen how you react when Beltran doesn't share things with you."

"This is not about me and Beltran."

"No, this is about me and you. And all of us together. And walking into a gladiator arena in two days and knowing I can trust you!"

Verida jerked the blade free of the wood and dropped it flat on the table. It clattered and rocked from side to side on the uneven cuts in the eagle's feathers. "I know we don't always get along, but that doesn't mean you can't trust me."

"How am I supposed to trust people who have a secret agenda?"

"The same way you expect me to trust you. Get off your moral high ground and think. You withheld information about that nixie bubble in your arm, you still haven't explained the orbs you took into Feena's lands, and I suspect Omri didn't suddenly start believing in no-strings-attached gifts. I also don't know what you're planning to do if that brother of yours shows up at the games, but I'm nearly certain you're not going to ignore his presence. You hold your secrets as tightly as the rest of us."

"Ryker, he . . . It's my—"

Verida held up a hand. "I'm not asking you to talk to me about your brother, but I *am* asking you to try to understand. I've sworn to keep this secret until instructed otherwise. The timing is for your own protection. And mine. And Grey's. Sooner or later, you'll know, I promise. But it's not safe right now."

"You said you had a plan."

"I said I *thought* I had a plan. I'm still mulling." Beltran pushed Grey into an alley between two inns. After they left Maken's, they'd seen something extremely interesting in the square. "You're sure that crate was the same one you saw in your vision?"

"Positive. But why is the arachneous still alive? Maybe Ryker couldn't kill it, and Zio had to intervene?"

"Maybe. Or maybe it was just a test, and she never meant for him to kill the arachneous at all."

Or maybe it was something else entirely.

Grey gestured toward the square. "But how did it get out there? That thing was huge! And Zio's castle isn't within walking distance." He paused. "Right?"

Beltran almost laughed. "Right. And 'How did it get here?' is a much better question than 'How is it alive?'—and one that I don't like the implications of. Especially after that portal I watched Amar make the first time I saw him."

"You think that they—"

"I don't know, and until we do, we aren't going to worry about it. I'll keep my eyes and ears open for anything strange. But as far as the arachneous goes, let me be the one to tell Verida. I'm still working out a few details in regard to the plan. Here." He handed Grey a cloak.

The Venator removed the slave collar and pulled the wool cloak on, buttoning it at the top and using the folds of the hood to hide the markings on the back of his neck. He rubbed at the red marks on the underside of his jaw. "Couldn't we have just started with this?"

"No, because then you would've been my associate. We would've been asked for introductions. As it was, you were invisible."

"Almost." Grey kicked the collar into the shadows. "Except when it mattered."

Beltran considered responding but couldn't talk about it right now. For one, he was distracted, trying to finish creating the plan he'd already mentioned. And two, his default nonchalance was unavailable, because he was also still wondering what it would take to figure out whether Grey knew how Feena kept him from shifting or not. Trying to discuss Ambrose would likely result in him punching a wall and fracturing his own damn hand.

He shouldered the bag full of food and clothing he'd purchased in the market. "Don't forget, no sudden moves once we get inside. Those markings cannot be seen."

"I'd planned on waiting until we had everyone's attention and then whipping off the cloak for a grand reveal. But, I mean, if you'd rather me not . . ."

The sarcasm surprised Beltran, and his smile spread slowly. "A good plan in theory, but then I'd have to pretend not to know you, which means I'd have no choice but to help the bar patrons kill you, and then I'd have to explain what happened to Verida and Rune. Then *I* might die—"

"So we should stick to the first plan?"

"You're the Venator. Whichever you'd rather."

Beltran had chosen accommodations he was comfortable in. This inn was neither the least expensive nor the most, and the establishment as a whole worked to be nothing more than average. The front served food and drink and was full to the seams tonight. As they stepped inside, the hum of conversation bordered on a roar, muting the constant squeals of chair legs and the clanking of dinnerware.

Beltran led, weaving around the tables and chairs and stepping up to the bar. The incubus pouring drinks recognized Fal's face immediately and stepped away to slap a key on the counter.

"The two consorts are already waiting for you in your rooms."

"Thank you." He dropped a coin on the counter. "We aren't to be bothered."

"Of course. Would you like a mood set?"

"I think we can handle it just fine on our own." Beltran let the incubus hold on to his assumptions about what activities would be taking place tonight. It was a better cover story than anything he could offer anyway.

Most of the staff were under the impression that he'd reserved two rooms. In truth, he'd reserved all the rooms—the entire top floor of the inn—under several different names. If anyone else set foot up there, Beltran wanted to know it, and he couldn't risk writing off a potential threat as just another guest.

At the end of the hall, he reached for the door on the left without hesitation. Verida always went left if the option was open, though he'd yet to figure out the why behind the habit.

The room was empty.

"Huh." He pocketed the key. "That's interesting."

"Where are they?"

"That way." He pointed to the interior door. "I'll be right behind you. I need to change my face."

Grey burst out laughing. "Nobody's ever said that to me before."

Beltran winked. "Honored to be your first."

"And on that note . . ." Grey gave a quick knock and headed into the adjoining room.

Beltran slowed his steps, buying time to absorb Fal's heavy muscle mass. The strength and intimidation factor were bonuses when acting as a trader, but the form changed the way he moved through a space, limiting his flexibility. Beltran preferred the smoothness of his usual, more limber human form.

He'd shifted in front of Grey before, but it wasn't something he enjoyed doing in public—in part because he didn't care for the expressions on the witnesses' faces. It was like walking around naked while everyone stared at you in a way that said they couldn't decide whether they were impressed by what you had to offer or horrified. It was also self-preservation. As he'd told Rune, the more someone knew, the more they looked for.

Holding on to the mystery was always the better choice.

As he crossed through the threshold, he reached into the bag at his shoulder and tossed Verida and Rune a ball of white fabric. "I thought you two might appreciate something else to wear."

Verida pushed back from the table. "Thank Rana! Get me out of this outfit."

As she got up, his eyes fell on a dagger. He'd never seen the particular piece before, but given its proximity to where Verida had been sitting, the eagle's head on the pommel piqued his curiosity.

Rune shook the fabric and held it out. "A slip?"

"A nightdress. But if you'd like to stay in what you're wearing, I won't complain." He traced the curve of Rune's waist and hips with his eye, hoping to elicit a scowl or a few choice words. Instead, her cheeks pinked, and he lost himself in the moment.

Grey smacked his arm, pointing in the opposite direction.

"Wha—?" Beltran turned and inhaled sharply. Verida's silk consort costume was ripped and covered in dried blood. "What in the bloody hell happened to you?"

"My sister paid me a visit. She summoned me to Castle Dracula and then nearly severed my spinal cord."

"Oh."

"That's it? *Oh?*" Verida was working at the three top buttons. She stripped off the ruined silk. "You have nothing else to say?"

Grey's face went scarlet, and he turned away so fast his cloak swung.

"'I'm sorry' came to mind first, but you hate when I say that." Beltran headed back to his room to grab two more chairs, calling back, "I assume it was Vega, then, who gifted you the dagger on the table."

"Regifted, actually. Lucky me, I received it twice."

When he returned, Verida had changed and was tossing the destroyed clothing into the corner. Rune hadn't moved. He dropped the chairs next to the table. "What's the matter, love? I thought you'd be in a hurry to get out of your present attire."

"Well, I—"

"Ah, yes. Sorry. Take my room, but hurry. We have a lot to talk about."

"I hope you two had a better day than we did," Verida said.

"Darling, you had a knife shoved in your back. That's not terribly hard to beat." Beltran started unloading food from the bag onto the table. They'd been eating dry, tough packed food for days, so he'd stocked up at the vendor stalls. Bread, cheese, fruits, tarts—every-thing he could get his hands on. "Did you manage to learn anything useful?"

Verida sat. "I'm told that Beorn received some news recently that caused most of the pack to withdraw from the Underground and move on to the Blues. I assume we know what that news was."

"The massacre of Ransan's pack. Where is—?" Beltran looked around. Grey was still standing where he'd been, staring at the wood-paneled wall. "Grey, Verida's dressed. Sit down and eat."

"Beorn still has a few wolves here"—Verida's eyes tracked Grey as he joined them and attacked the food with fervor—"trying to buy up candidates for new pack members. But current events should slow down his plans for a takeover. The other packs will be wary."

"Of course. Side with Beorn, and your entire pack might be wiped out. It'll make them all think twice."

"Did you bring us real food?" Rune's voice came from behind.

"Yes, but hurry." Beltran motioned. "Grey might not leave anything."

"You bought enough food for an army," Grey said, not bothering to look up from the turkey leg he was demolishing.

"We're all running on a deficit, and we're going to need all the energy we can get over the next few days. That goes for you, too, Verida."

"I am well aware of my needs, thank you. Rune already offered to lure dinner back to the room for me."

Rune went straight for a tart. At Beltran's surprised expression, she shrugged. "I was worried. I didn't know what else to do."

"You offered to find Verida blood?" He whistled. "That must've been quite the wound Vega gifted." He grabbed the eagle-head dagger and a block of cheese.

"Don't cut it with that!" Rune dove across the table, reaching. "All she did was wipe it off on her pants."

Beltran leaned out of Rune's reach but held up the dagger, looking closer. It was marred by smeared remnants of blood. He crinkled his nose and returned it to Verida. "Lovely, darling."

"Squeamish?" She smirked. "It's just a little spinal fluid and blood. Might improve the flavor of that cheese."

"And bone dust." Rune added a gagging sound. "Can't have cheese without bone dust."

"I think I'll just use my fingers." Beltran tore off his piece of cheese. "I do have some bad news to share. Ambrose is wearing a veneer and, as of this morning, was in the Underground."

Verida looked from Grey to Beltran and back again. "How would you know that if she was wearing a veneer?"

"Grey?" Beltran spoke around his food. "Would you like to expound."

He wiped the grease from his mouth with the back of his arm. "Not really, but I don't think you're asking."

Beltran tipped the tart he was holding toward him in a mock toast. "Clever boy."

Rune shook her head. "You're such an ass sometimes."

"Well established, love. Grey?"

Grey sighed and tossed the cleaned bone to the table. "Tashara had Arwin deliver a message to me detailing what Ambrose's veneer looked like."

"And then you just happened to see her?" Verida asked.

"Not . . . exactly."

"Oooh, no." Beltran squeezed every ounce of faux excitement he could into the words. "See, we saw her *first*. It was wonderful. This strange fae was rambling on about how she knew who Grey was and then proceeded to say she was pretty sure she knew who I was. I ignored the lunatic. And *then* we got the message."

Verida kicked the leg of the table. "Ambrose saw you!"

"She knows we're here. And in that vein, there's one more thing."

Grey's head snapped up, his eyes wide as saucers. Beltran ignored him but made a mental note to have a little talk with the boy about the importance of nonchalance when someone was about to lie for you. "Arwin included a note for me as well. He has reason to suspect that Ambrose may have bet her council seat on this match."

Verida laid her forearms across the table. "Where did he hear that?"

"He didn't say. But I trust the information. Arwin never passes on hearsay unless there's good reason to pay attention to it."

"If Tate fights . . ."

"She's going to lose that council seat to Keir. Which is less than ideal."

"Why is Keir worse than Ambrose?" Rune asked. "They're both insane."

Beltran and Verida both twisted to look at her as if she'd suddenly sprouted an additional eye in the middle of her forehead.

Grey answered around a mouthful of bread. "Rune, we killed his mother."

Verida tapped her finger to her nose. "Please, will someone just tell me that you found a way into the games."

"In a manner of speaking," Beltran said. "I saw someone else I recognized in the square today."

Verida swung the dagger out, pointing it straight at Beltran. "If it's Dimitri, I don't want to know. Do you hear me?"

"Relax, darling. It was a werewolf." He put a finger on her wrist, pushing the dagger back the other way. "But it was the very same wolf I followed through the forest after I found the massacre of Ransan's pack."

Unsurprisingly, Rune caught the scent immediately. "The one who used the portal? Zio's wolf?"

"That's an assumption we're making. Don't mix assumptions with what we know."

"But if we're right, it could mean that Zio will also be at the games."

The hope in her voice made it very clear that she wasn't talking about Zio at all. She was hoping for an appearance by Ryker. Grey's scowl was so deep it looked to be working its way through his brow bone.

"It's possible." Beltran quickly changed direction. "This wolf was in the middle of the square with the same crate that Grey saw in his vision. He just sold an arachneous to the games."

"So Zio didn't kill it," Verida said to herself. "This is bad."

"No, it's wonderful! Because now I know how to get us into the games and how we're going to get Tate out." He spread his arms wide. "You're going to sell *me*." All three stared at him in total silence. He dropped his arms back to his lap. "A little enthusiasm in the face of brilliance is always appreciated."

"Sell you?" Grey said. "As what?"

"A manticore."

He could see Rune's mouth starting to open, no doubt to ask what a manticore was, but Verida slapped her palm against the table.

"No! Absolutely not. There is only one member of this group who can move completely unseen. How is having you locked under the arena helpful?"

"I'm glad you asked." Beltran swiped the heel of bread that Rune had left and stood. "I originally thought that if we could get inside the arena, I could use my gifts to eliminate the wizard responsible for holding the wards between the audience and the gladiators. Knocking those out would've allowed Tate to climb into the audience and out one of the exits, or it could've given us access to the arena floor, depending on the situation we found ourselves in. But today I learned that the wizards have been moved belowground. The only wizard not beneath the arena is the one in charge of the wards around the owner's box."

He put one foot on the seat of his chair and started to gesture with the bread. "Now, the only way to get Tate out is to bring down the wards when Sarley is too distracted to stop him. Considering the strength of the spell casters, we will have to use physical force. The wizards block magic use, but my shifting is biological. I can sneak into the room as something small and take down the wards from the inside. Once they drop, I could be in some trouble, so it'll be up to you three to make sure Tate gets out of there."

"But why do we have to sell you?" Rune asked. "Can't you just sneak in as a bug or something?"

"Sure. But we don't need just me in. We need all of us in. For that, we need money, and a manticore is worth a bloody fortune."

"It's worth a fortune because everyone wants to see it played," Verida said. "What are we going to do when they put you in a match before it's time to take the wards down?"

"Glad you asked. If we wait until the day before to sell me, the schedule will be set. And if they're debuting their arachneous, they won't play the manticore until the next games. Creatures like those don't come into their hands often. They'll spread out the appearances to garner excitement for the next event."

"But if we sell you, you'll be beneath the arena the night before," Rune said. "Let's make a plan to get Tate out before the games start."

"Getting him out has always been the core problem. The games master is a siren. Sarley's song will stop both of us in our tracks before we're halfway to the exit. Breaking Tate out of his cell was never a thought. But if the wards were to go down midbattle, the noise of the crowd should diminish Sarley's song enough to take the sting out. And that's if she arrives on the arena floor quick enough to sing at all. I suspect she'll be tied up dealing with some angry wizards."

Verida pressed the tip of the dagger into her pointer finger, twisting as she thought. "It might work."

"Not the enthusiasm I'd hoped for, but I'll take it." Beltran ripped a mouthful of bread off and dropped back into his chair. "It better work. It's the only plan we've got. Oh, and Verida—when you sell me, I would suggest maintaining ownership and taking the smaller payout in conjunction with a monthly percentage of profits. Demand a wizard's guarantee for my safekeeping. In writing."

Verida's breath caught in her throat, and her eyes held a little bit of hope for the first time since he'd entered the room. "Because when they lose you—"

He grinned. "And they will."

"The payout will be substantial."

"And, I imagine, enough to cover what Dimitri will owe Dracula. You might even impress them both with your ingenuity. My contact said he could find someone who will be willing to sell us entry stones if we have enough. I'll let him know where and when to meet you."

Verida was nodding, but the up-and-down motion slowed until she was still and staring at the table. "No."

"Did you have a better idea? Because I'm pretty damn proud I came up with anything at all at this point."

She tapped the blade across the flat of her palm. "My father knows Tate is here . . . I wouldn't be surprised if Dimitri knows. If we want to make any part of this disaster look like something besides an accident, I can't . . . I can't go *skulking* in through the backdoor cloaked up like a common criminal. No. Rune, Grey, and I will use House Dracula's box."

Beltran wasn't sure he'd heard her correctly. "Everyone will see you. You'll lose all deniability. And if Dracula doesn't put out a death warrant on you, Dimitri will."

"Losing deniability is exactly what I have to do. Instead of buying entry, I'll use the manticore money to place a few bribes. I'll open the games with the announcement that my father is offering a spectacle match with everyone's favorite gladiator as a generous gift to the people."

"Tate's fighting under Keir," Rune said.

"The games will be announced using whatever aliases they have chosen, and those in attendance don't know what deals have been made behind closed doors. Ambrose won't be able to say anything to contradict me without revealing her identity, and Keir won't be able to object unless he's prepared to publicly admit that he's stolen Dracula's property prior to winning himself the power that he surely intends to hold between himself and my father."

Beltran rolled his eyes. "Not that a council seat will be enough to soothe Dracula."

"Something Keir will figure out soon enough. Regardless, both Ambrose and Keir will already be in the owner's box and unable to leave until Tate's match is over. If we succeed in our plan and get Tate out, I'll announce that we intervened because the wards failed and it was necessary to retrieve my father's valuable property. But if we fail to get Tate out and he fights to the end of his match, Keir is almost guaranteed to win the council seat. At that point, everyone will know who he is and what the bet was. My announcement at the start of the games will create a rumor that Dracula *lent* Tate to Keir to manipulate the situation. Since the people know that Tate has been working for the council, the assumption will be made that the council either agreed to or turned a blind eye to the match, giving the people what they want. That will leave everyone except Ambrose in a position of power. Which by default puts us in the strongest position we could hope for."

"It's a risk," Beltran said.

"It's the only card I have left to play."

"Grey? Rune?" Beltran looked at both of them, gauging their reactions. "No matter what we choose, it's dangerous. Are you both on board with Verida's plan?"

They both nodded their agreement, and Verida's shoulders lifted. "Good. Beltran, I need you to fetch Rune's and Grey's clothes, cloaks, and weapons. Tonight."

"Their *council cloaks*? Verida"—Beltran sputtered—"All right, yes, by giving them those cloaks the council took the first step to claiming them, but we were supposed to be delivering a summons! This . . . this is different. If we end up with a full Venator reveal at the games, in front of some of the most powerful families in the land, without permission, clearly labeling them as council representatives in an official capacity, it will very likely undo any benefit you could gain from claiming Tate."

"I need them in those cloaks to validate the story I'm feeding the audience. And if something goes wrong, we can't send them into battle without weapons and wrapped up in some costume. Besides, from the moment we decided to come after Tate, there was always a risk that they were going to be revealed."

Beltran backed out into the hall on his way to retrieve the clothes and weapons from where they'd hidden them in the rocky inclines of the plateau. He softly pulled the door shut and turned on the balls of his feet. The barely there flames, flickering on only two sconces, did little more than outline a figure waiting at the far end of the hall, their identity obscured by a floor-length cloak and oversized hood.

His weight dropped back to his heels. There shouldn't have been anyone on this floor at all. But the fact that they appeared to be waiting just at the top of the staircase—ensuring they would be out of range of Verida's senses—was concerning. The other party withdrew their hands from the pockets of their cloak and held up a key pinched between two long, delicate fingers. She wore a thick gold band on her middle finger that was connected to a chain that ran over the back of her hand. She gave Beltran a nod of acknowledgment, then slid the key into the nearest lock and disappeared inside, leaving the door open.

Beltran followed, stepping into the unoccupied room and closing the door behind them. "It unnerves me how easily you always find me, Amaya."

"You assume because it was fast that it was easy. Besides, you *are* always lacking in humility, and I find pleasure in gifting it to you as often as possible." She pushed back her hood, revealing dark brown skin, round black eyes, and a thick braid of shiny ebony hair that hung over her shoulder and ended at her waist. She raised her chin, managing an expression of looking down at him despite the height difference. "Take off that ridiculous face. I can't stand having a conversation with you like that."

She clasped her hands and waited. There was no use arguing. Beltran did as he was told.

"Better. Now, what was so important that you decided to risk the cover of our stall owner?"

"It's in regard to our Venators."

The room was identical to every other on the floor; she moved to the table in the center of the room, pausing to run a finger across its surface. "I assumed. As you stated, it is my favorite topic." She examined the dust, rubbing it between her fingers.

"Grey has begun to exhibit some strange abilities."

"This is what you called me for? All Venators have special gifts and talents pulled from whatever other bloodlines were dropped in during the creation of their lineage. It is neither new nor surprising."

"I am familiar, and Rune is progressing as I would've expected. She's showing promising mental acuity. With training, she'll be a fine diplomat, a formidable warrior, and, without doubt, someday a general for the cause. But Grey . . ." He rubbed at the back of his neck. "Grey is having visions."

Amaya's chin jerked to one side, like she'd misheard him. When a correction wasn't forthcoming, she walked to the bed and pulled her cloak tightly behind her, sitting on the edge. "Explain."

"Grey's exhibiting the abilities of a traveler. So far, he's only visited present events, and what he's seen has proved accurate, but—"

"He's not responding well."

"It's like nothing I've ever seen. His body actually vanishes in spots. You'll be holding on to his arm, trying to wake him up, and then your hand will slip straight through as if he's not there at all. His ribs flex outward with enough force that Verida has to throw herself over him to add counterweight to prevent them from shattering. Grey's body is being torn apart from the inside. I suspect the fact that he's not yet visited the past or the future is the only reason he isn't dead."

"It's his human body."

"It's not compatible. I know. I came to you because what I don't know is how to stop them. These visions are completely unpredictable, and it's getting harder to wake him up. The last time, Rune had to carve open his bicep with a dagger."

"But he's healing? After the visions?"

"Slowly. It's a full day before he appears fully healed, and I suspect it's taking longer. I think he's hiding the severity of his injuries. If I don't figure out a way to stop this, we're going to lose him."

"There's never been a case of this before."

"At least not one recorded. It's possible that it's happened but the Venator didn't survive."

Amaya's full lips twisted in thought. "I can think of only one place that might have the answers you seek."

"I can think of one as well. I was hoping you had a second option."

"You'll have to visit the three sisters. Their source may have the answer."

Beltran pressed his fingers into his temples, digging at the tension. "I was afraid that's where you were headed. That visit isn't likely to go well."

Amaya looked at him wearily. "I heard a rumor about your last visit to the sisters. I had hoped it was another one of those exaggerated stories that always come up whenever your name is mentioned."

"My stories are awfully hard to exaggerate."

"You stole one of their baskets?" At his wincing expression, she took in a slow, deep breath through her nose.

"I still have it," he said. "At the council house."

"Then I will suggest you put some thought in during your trip there and be prepared to make some heavy and thoroughly convincing amends. Returning the basket will not be acceptable. You've desecrated it."

Beltran couldn't do much more than nod.

"The resistance has waited too long and worked too hard to lose these Venators now. When Zio succeeds in tearing apart the council from the inside, we need them to stand with us against her. One will not be enough. There must be two. We need a balance of strengths and weaknesses for each to keep the other in check."

"I was at that table when we came up with the plan. I'll do everything I can to fix this."

"I know you will. I will do research as well, and if I discover any other options, I'll send word." She got to her feet and pulled the hood back over her head. "Good luck. With everything."

She was at the door when he stopped her. "Have you heard anything else since we last spoke?"

She turned her head, but all he could see was the edge of her hood and the long braid spilling out. "We've been unable to ascertain the limits of the spell holding Elyria. I'm sorry."

His heart constricted. "I had to tell Verida, by the way, of my involvement in the resistance. She doesn't know where I am in the hierarchy or who I answer to, but she has the persistence of her father."

This time Amaya turned back to face him. The shadows of the hood hid everything except the flash of her teeth as she spoke. "Verida of House Dracula will control herself, or I will send a reminder."

"Of course. And what of the Venators? When will you tell them their true purpose here?"

"You have a great many questions for an emergency meeting."

"I'm an opportunist. It's why I'm good at what I do."

"I had hoped to give the Venators some time before we revealed our existence, to ensure that their loyalties are not tied up with the council. But . . . things are changing fast." She stepped closer. "Arwin tells me he has great hope for them, but what do you think?"

"I think they will struggle here. They're adults who have been raised on earth. Their humanity is as ingrained in them as the blood of Eon that runs through their veins. But the more I watch, the more I think it will be their humanity, not their Venator nature, that saves us."

45

Tate's official return to the games was less than a day away. The air in the arena hung heavy with dust and vibrated with the ring of weapons. All around Tate and Dalbor, warriors of every species and gender dodged, lunged, and parried, with blunted weapons in hand, while others practiced their hand-to-hand grappling. Around the perimeter walls, guards watched the practice session for any problems, their spears at the ready.

Tate and Dalbor had been in the arena longer than normal. As champions, they could choose their hours, and they used their extended time to put the final pieces of their plan into place, sharing details as they danced closer together, weapons clashing in the center.

Sweat dripped from their noses, and both their off-white shirts were soaked through. Tate finally held up a hand. "Five minutes."

"Thank the stars." Dalbor leaned over his knees, showing the white and gray streaking through the top curl of his ram's horns. "I thought I was going to have to admit I couldn't keep going."

Tate was well accustomed to fighting matches to the death, as was Dalbor, but it had been some years since he'd been paired with anyone approaching his skill level. Pairing top gladiators in a match to the death was a financially foolish decision and only ever done for reasons that had nothing to do with money. Such as what was driving Keir.

Keir didn't actually own Tate and was thus unconcerned with what his death would cost Dracula. The new fae king was counting on the fact that because the games were publicly outlawed, financial grievances related to the arena were not eligible to be reported to the council and Tate's place as a gladiator would not be recognized by council-represented channels.

It was foolishly shortsighted. Tate's status as a gladiator, and his worth, would be defended by House Dracula and recompense demanded. A threat that Keir had gravely underestimated.

"Ready to go, old man?" Dalbor hefted his ax.

Before Tate could respond, three guards marched into the arena from the cells below, leading a new group of gladiators. These were brand-new warriors—Tate could always tell by their wide-eyed looks as they stepped out onto the sand. It wouldn't be long until they no longer noticed the size of the oblong arena and the rows of empty benches. The only thing that ever mattered was staying alive. And when you had been in those cells long enough, you stopped seeing anything besides the way back to them at the end of the day.

Sarley followed behind the group, wearing a cropped leather top and her braids piled on top her head as she watched for any runners. Once they'd cleared the shadows of the benches above, she instructed them to stop.

Dalbor took advantage of Tate's distraction and leapt, his ax up. Tate's eyes flicked to the side. Dalbor's horns were blocking out part of the sun, and his pale-yellow eyes glinted with childlike glee. Without turning his head, Tate lifted his shield a moment before Dalbor's weight crashed into him.

Tate took two steps back and looked over the edge of his now-dented shield. "That was cheap."

"No, that was smart. You got lucky."

Tate had been the one who'd taught him to always take advantage of distractions, so there was nothing to argue about. He reset his stance, ready to finish the bout, but his attention was still drawn to Sarley as she paced back and forth, giving the same required speech that Tate had heard her give a thousand times about loyalty and honor and other qualities that barely existed in the arena.

Dalbor dropped and swept Tate's leg out from underneath him. He crashed flat on his back. Sand flew over his face and stuck in the lines of his sweat. Dalbor chortled the throaty laugh that was so uniquely his.

"What's got you so distracted today? You look like you're wanting to march over there and tell those poor fools the truth."

"Why would I want to do that?" Tate let go of his shield to regain use of his hand and pushed up, simultaneously blocking Dalbor's next attack with his sword. "Their hope will be stolen soon enough."

"You think they have hope? Did they start buying up gladiators from a hole in the bottom of the ocean? They know what's coming for them."

Tate circled, resetting his grip on the hilt. "They know about the games, but every one of them is still holding on to hope that they'll survive."

The odds of living through the first few matches were low. The new gladiators were always paired against stronger, more experienced fighters or added to the exhibition death matches with the beasts. At least half of that group would be dead by tomorrow.

"Samwell," Sarley yelled from across the arena.

Dalbor's head snapped up in response, and Tate took advantage of the loss of focus, charging.

"Samwell!"

Dalbor stepped to the side without engaging. "Hey, *Samwell*, I think she's talking to you."

Tate grunted. "That was a nice side step."

"Thanks. I'd compliment your attack, but it looked a little like you were falling."

"I truly thought you'd grow out of that bravado at some point."

"I decided to grow into it instead." He winked.

Sarley marched up, her hair shining blue black in the full sun. "Forget your name again?"

"Didn't," Tate said. "Just decided not to answer to that one."

Dalbor's throaty laugh returned. "Liar."

Sarley smiled, but it quickly faded. "Are you two prepared for tomorrow?"

Dalbor rubbed his massive green forearm across his face, wiping off the sweat. "We'll see if the old Venshii can keep up with me, but we've gone over it so many times, I'm sure I'll be walking through the steps in my sleep tonight."

Sarley nodded her approval, but her lips were pursed and her shoulders tight.

"What's going on?" Tate stepped closer, lowering his voice. "Is there a problem with the plan?"

"No, everything's in place. But . . . something is off. I can't explain it, but I feel it. Here." She patted a fist against her belly. "I had an interesting creature come in yesterday. An arachneous."

Tate could do little more than blink. They were not only rare but vicious and almost impossible to get close enough to kill. "How?"

"A new trader that we've never worked with before—werewolf, although not purebred, by the look of him—showed up in the Underground with a giant crate stuffed with one nasty arachneous. The wizards, as you can imagine, are excited to feature her tomorrow."

"That's . . ." Dalbor looked to the wall as if he could see through to the animal cages on the opposite side.

"Strange, suspicious. Use whatever word you want. They all end with me saying that I don't like it. The wolf took a smaller payment in exchange for a portion of the profits until someone finally manages to eliminate the thing. Not unusual, but he also demanded three entry stones as a part of the payment. When they offered to put him up in the private box next to House Dracula, he declined, insisting that he be given regular seats instead."

Tate frowned.

"Is that an insight I see on your face?" Sarley asked.

"Not exactly."

Which wasn't *exactly* true. Entrance for three, the wizards walking their strange new creature straight past all their protective measures and into the heart of the arena . . . He suspected Beltran.

Sarley sighed. "That's unfortunate. I have my orders."

Dalbor was looking over her head at the arena full of gladiators. "'Orders' means an exhibition match with an arachneous."

"Which means that she'll be choosing sacrifices today," Tate added.

Sarley moved one hand to rest on her trim waist. "I never did care for your vocabulary, *Samwell*."

Tate shrugged. "It's the truth."

"There's a way to speak the truth without building a bonfire around it. Remind me why I missed you again."

"I've asked you the same question."

"It's his sparkling personality." Dalbor reached out and tapped Tate's shoulder with the hilt of his sword. "The smiling and general spreading of good cheer. Makes everyone feel all warm on the in—" He cleared his throat. "Sarley, you have company."

One of the new gladiators had peeled off from the group and was heading straight for them, his eyes fixated on Sarley's back. He was of average size for a human, which meant he was undersized for the arena.

The guards nearest them stepped forward. Sarley stopped them with a hand.

"Is he armed?" she asked mildly, not turning around.

Tate scanned. "Only with the look in his eye."

"Idiot. I heard them talking earlier."

The gladiator rushed the last few steps. He slid one hand around Sarley, grabbing a handful of her breast, and placed the other flat against her stomach to pull her against him. Sarley seized the hand at her waist and bent his pinky finger down and out. It snapped immediately. She then elbowed the young man in the gut, whirled, grabbed his head with both hands, and brought her knee up, smashing it into his nose. The would-be gladiator collapsed, cradling his arm against his waist.

The sound of fighting around them dropped off as his nose freely bled, dripping onto the sand. When the last bout stopped, the final two joined the rest in staring at the fool who'd attacked a siren.

"Congratulations," she said, breaking the silence that shrouded the arena, "on volunteering to be my first contender for the arachneous bout tomorrow. Would anyone else like to join him?" She looked straight at the group he'd come from.

Not a one would look her in the eye.

"Get back to training!" She motioned to the guards, who picked the man up off the ground and hauled him away.

"What got into him?" Tate asked.

"They were plotting their escape, loudly. I stood down the hall and listened to the whole thing. Once they came to the inevitable realization that escape wasn't possible, they concluded that death at my hand would be a more pleasant way to go. Their words were that they wanted to die 'blissfully unaware.'" She snorted. "I'll have you both know that I always stop singing before I kill someone. If they deserve to die, they deserve to feel it."

"Still . . ." Dalbor's head tilted from one side to the other, appearing to weigh his options. "I'm a little upset I didn't think of it. Trading a few moments of fear for an actual battle isn't a bad plan."

"Care to join him in battling the arachneous?"

"I might. My odds may be better."

"Tate and I have made you a promise. I'd say your odds are pretty good." She straightened out her top, tugging on the bottom while she peered at Dalbor. "Go get a drink. You look parched."

He shouldered his ax and grinned. "I'm feeling fine."

Tate chuckled.

"Fine. Dalbor, go away."

"As you wish."

She waited until he had strolled away but was still within earshot. "I've never had a gladiator who thought he was so damn funny."

He called back, "Thinking and knowing are two different things, Sarley."

She laughed, then moved closer to Tate, giving the guards her back.

Tate kept his eyes up, giving the impression that they were looking over the field of gladiators. After what had just happened, it was probably assumed that they were busy picking contenders for the arachneous. "I take it there's more."

"In addition to the arachneous, we just received another arrival. A manticore. Strange, don't you think?"

Sarley's concern bled over to him. "Very."

One of them had to be Beltran. The odds of both creatures arriving right before the event were miniscule. But which one was the shifter, and which was the problem?

"There's an army of fae camped outside of the walls, and we have an arachneous and a manticore inside. Since all of these events coincided with your arrival, I hoped you would be able to share some insight."

"I don't have any answers for you."

"I'm concerned, Tate. I can't control what I can't see, and surprises keep coming."

His mouth went bone dry. She wasn't talking about the matches or the new creatures. "We had a deal."

"I know. And I will keep my end. Everything's been arranged. The poison is ready, and the name you gave me to reach out to has responded with the meeting place. The forged sales documents have been drawn up, and payment will be delivered within the hour. It could not have gone smoother, but with every new variable, I become more uneasy that I'm not seeing something I should." She glanced up at him, crossing her arms. "You know I would do almost anything for you, but I'm not willing to die for you."

"Promise me, Sarley, that no matter what happens, Brandt and Ayla will not be here once the bidding starts. If they lose their freedom, nobody will *ever* give that back to them. I swear on my life, the documents will hold up, the arena will be paid, and you won't be held responsible. That nixie bubble of yours will stay put."

"You never did tell me who bought their freedom for you."

"Her father would be most unhappy if I did."

She humphed. "Verida. That is interesting."

"I never said that."

"No, you did not." She turned to look at him. "There was a time when I dreamed of the day I would escape this. I would lie in bed and think of all the things I would do once I got my freedom back."

"Me too."

"Hmmm . . ." She smiled softly. "Well, then. You got your freedom. Ayla and Brandt got theirs as well. Twice, it seems. Maybe one day it'll be my turn."

46

Beltran had needed the manticore to seem wild enough that, on the off chance the wizards decided that playing both creatures in one event was a good idea, he would appear too dangerous to remove from the cage.

He may have oversold it.

The spears had started coming in from all sides in such rapid succession that he couldn't avoid them. Spearheads gouged the sides of his lion-shaped body and ripped through the muscles that wrapped over the hips and thighs of his back legs. One guard actually managed to impale the head of his scorpion tail. After that, Beltran's attempted bites and the snaps of his stinger were no longer for show.

Once within the arena walls, no one attempted to remove him from his cage. They placed him as far away from the commonly used paths as they could, covering the cage with a thick tarp to prevent him from shoving his scorpion tail through the bars. If he hadn't been poked full of spear-sized holes, he would've offered himself a little self-congratulation. He'd managed to land exactly where he'd wanted to, as effectively as if he'd said, *Please place me in the furthest corner and make sure to cover my cage so that no one notices when it's suddenly empty.*

Waiting for everything to go quiet, Beltran settled down to heal. He rested his head on his paws, cursing every one of the guards as he dozed off. When he woke, the sounds of gladiators sparring were gone, and he was surrounded by the snuffles and rustles of the different creatures in the cages around him as they bedded down.

It was time.

He needed to find Tate. But first, Beltran intended to check out a hunch. He shifted into a mouse and nudged at the bottom edge of the tarp until he'd pulled up just enough to wiggle his small frame through and slip to the ground.

The outer enclosure shared one wall with the main arena and was shaped like a horseshoe. It housed everything from the goats and sheep they slaughtered to feed the gladiators, to the large mountain and jungle cats, to the more deadly competitors, like the newly added arachneous and manticore. In order to keep the animals healthy and the smell down, it was open air and depended on several wards placed by the wizards to protect against theft.

Beltran scampered around unnoticed until he found the arachneous in the furthest cage to the east—no doubt placed in proximity to the gate she would be entering through in the morning. The creature was sitting in the back, partially draped in shadow, with her eight legs pulled in tightly and a muzzle locked around her face to keep her from spitting webbing through the bars.

Before approaching, he cut between the cage and the wall, using the darkness to hide as he shifted into the new form he'd strategically chosen: a female fae with copper skin and long black hair.

The sound of voices came. He waited, perfectly still, as two guards strolled by. When he could no longer hear them, he stepped closer and wrapped his female hands around the bars. "Elyria?" he whispered.

The arachneous stirred and pushed up to standing. When her large eyes took him in, Beltran swore he saw recognition. Emboldened, he continued to speak as she inched closer. "Elyria, please, if it's you, give me a sign."

A low, threatening rumble sounded, but her forward movement stopped. Beltran's heart skipped in his chest. He was within range—a fly wandering freely into her web. A real arachneous surely would've attacked by now.

For years, he'd been tracking Elyria's movements as best he could by, for starters, making note of unexplainable appearances of council members—reports that claimed they had been in one location when he knew them to have been in another. Her actions during these times were always out of character. When he combined that with her inability to escape, it became clear that she was somehow being controlled both in and out of Zio's presence.

"I've been working for years," he said, "trying to figure out how Zio's controlling you. I've never given up, but I can't find anything. Please, tell me what to do! Tell me how to help."

There was no response.

Beltran took in a slow, shaking breath and voiced his worst fear. "Can she control what you say? Is that why you haven't reached out to me?" He ached to hear the sound of her voice again, and the current silence was killing him. Wearily, he leaned his forehead against the bars. "Saints, I've missed you so much."

The arachneous moved so fast that Beltran only had time to raise his head. A leg rushed past him on one side. The jointed appendage twisted and pressed against his back, holding him tight to the bars. The other went straight for his shoulder. Though it wasn't a claw, it was sharp enough to puncture both skin and muscle. Beltran gasped. The arachneous's eyes grew bright with excitement, and the edges crinkled, telling of a smile hidden under the muzzle. She withdrew the leg from his shoulder, the small spines catching the edges of his wound like a saw blade. She reared back, ready to strike again, but this time she was aiming for his eye.

Beltran pulled his feminine legs up, planted his feet against the bars, and pushed back with everything he had. The momentum rolled him over the leg pressed against his back and tilted him into a backflip. He landed too far forward and fell to his knees, but he was out of her reach.

He put a hand up to stanch the bleeding from his shoulder. Behind the mask, the arachneous hissed what sounded like a series of warnings. He was angry at his own stupidity and bitter for daring to hope. Of *course* Zio would send the real one. Why would you slaughter a creature like that when you could count on its nature to mercilessly kill, enabling you to collect a small fortune in royalties to finance other plans all while leaving the more versatile, intelligent, and completely controllable shifter to work elsewhere?

The arachneous chattered as she ran one leg across the bars.

"Yes," he seethed. "Not Elyria. Message received."

Beltran had a hole in his shoulder—and what felt like a new wound in his heart—and now he had to bloody shift again. Swearing profusely, he began to shrink, realizing as he did that he'd ripped himself apart more times this month than he had in the last decade. Returned to mouse form, he ran across the enclosure, aiming for the partially raised roof of the champion's hall. The windows were at ground level, allowing dust and dirt to blow in constantly, but it was the only section with a measure of fresh air—a reward for surviving, he supposed.

Choosing the first window, he peeked over the edge, his whiskers brushing against the bars. The drop to the floor was longer than what was acceptable, but there were no other options. He went head first, digging his claws into the natural pits of the brick, grabbing hold in some places while skidding in others. It was less of a descent and more of a controlled fall. When his front two paws hit the ground, the wound in his shoulder burned like a hot brand had been shoved against it.

Blasted arachneous. He'd been embarrassingly unprepared for the attack. Because that's what happened when you allowed feelings to be involved in . . . anything. He supposed he should be grateful that it hadn't gone for his eye the first time.

He scampered past the first cell, only to turn around. Sitting on the end of the bed was a large blue Venshii, the white scars on his neck and arms shining brightly in the limited light. Beltran ran straight into the corner of Tate's cell so he could shift without being seen from the hall.

When he was full size, Tate murmured, "I've never watched you perform a full shift."

"I try not to make it a spectacle, although the last few days have been one reluctant reveal after another."

Tate stood and walked to the door, putting his arms through as he leaned on the crossbar to watch the length of the hall. "Are you the arachneous or the manticore?"

"The manticore. The arachneous is, unfortunately, exactly what she appears to be."

"How is everyone?"

"As well as can be expected, I suppose." He didn't think mentioning Grey's visions was necessary at this exact moment, so he proceeded to explain the best-scenario sequence of events they'd planned to get Tate out of the arena. Beltran hadn't reached the end before Tate interrupted him.

"No."

He waited for a second, as if he'd somehow misheard the unmistakable single syllable. "I'm sorry, what do you mean, 'No'?"

The Venshii's shoulders were taut, and he shifted his weight from one foot to the other.

"We've all risked our lives to get you out of here." Beltran lowered his voice again. "And we've discovered that Ambrose bet Keir her council seat for the key to Kastaley."

Tate turned his dark eyes to Beltran. His voice rumbled. "I *said* no."

"I heard you, but *you're* not hearing me. Putting Keir in the same house as the two Venators that killed his mother will not end well for either of them. Your match has to be stopped. Not to mention, if Verida doesn't get you back—"

Tate's arm flung out. He grabbed Beltran by the throat and slammed him against the wall. If Beltran could've rolled his eyes, he would've, because the odds of this happening twice in ten minutes were obscenely low. As it was, he was otherwise occupied with trying to work his fingers between Tate's and his own neck.

"You will not stop my match. Do you understand?" Tate's hot breath washed over him. "And you will tell Verida that if I even *think* that any of you are interfering, I will shove a blade through my own heart."

"What is—the matter with—you?" he gasped, still clawing at Tate's oversized fingers. "We're trying—to—*save* you."

"And what about Ayla? What about Brandt?"

"We'll get them out too."

"Don't lie to me." Tate dropped him. "You haven't made a single mention of my wife or my son since you crawled in here. You can tell Verida that I've taken matters into my own hands. The arrangements are made, and I will not allow any interference. If that means Keir gets exactly what he wants, so be it."

"Perhaps next time we could start with the mention of your arrangements. Seven hells, Tate!" Beltran rubbed at his neck, trying to catch his breath. "All right, tell me your plans, and let me work backward from there."

"I don't know if I can trust you."

"I can't blame you." He held his arms out wide. "But this is where we're at."

Tate's lips pressed together.

"Listen, old friend. You're right. I didn't talk about Ayla and Brandt—"

"We're not friends."

"But it appears that you're going to be in the arena while . . . whatever is going to happen happens. Which means you've left yourself out of these 'arrangements.' Let me in on the secret, and maybe I can help get you out as well."

At Tate's unmoved expression, he crossed his arms. "Or you can go ahead and keep everything to yourself and watch Ayla and Brandt go free while you end up stuck here as Dracula's property. Both ways end with your wife and son regaining their freedom, but the only way Ayla still has a husband and Brandt has a father is if you let me help."

Tate pulled a deep breath in through his nose, and on the exhale, the Venshii's shoulders slumped. "Ambrose bet her council seat?"

Grey and Rune traveled through a series of tunnels and caves, wearing their Venator clothes beneath the council cloaks with their hoods up and tied at the front to obscure their markings. They both had grown more comfortable with their weapons, having trained with Verida and Beltran on this trip, and each had a sword strapped to their hip. The specially lined pockets and sheaths in their pant legs were filled with smaller daggers, adilats, and throwing stars.

Unfortunately for Grey, Verida didn't want to give advance notice of her attendance, which took any conventional methods of arrival off the table. Their passage to the arena consisted of a bribe, a well-obscured tunnel, and a cavernous tube of rock that cut straight to the surface with an old, rickety ladder attached to the side. Grey wasn't claustrophobic, but the ascent up that ladder had nearly been enough to convince him otherwise. He crawled out of the death tube onto yet another dusty cave floor and finally stepped out onto the side of a mountain and into the sun.

The air was crisp and sharp—the unique chill of high altitude. He was grateful for his heavy wool cloak. The sun was just rising, and the rays that broke over the peak behind them were bright orange, turning the dew on the bushes into kaleidoscopes of color.

Verida motioned for them to follow, and they began their descent down a barely marked trail slick with loose gravel and pockmarked by the entrances to a variety of burrows. While Grey and Rune were obscured as nameless representatives of the council, Verida had dressed for her role as the daughter of Dracula.

Her boots were similar to those Grey had always seen her in, calf height and black—although the heel had been mitigated to a small wedge instead of the spikes she'd preferred at the council house. The pants were skin tight, with carefully placed rivets and stich lines emphasizing every curve, while her corseted top was laced with blue satin in the front and back.

She'd painted her lips a dark red that was almost black, slicked her blonde hair back with oil so that it shone in the sun, and lined her eyes in kohl. Verida claimed to have borrowed the necklace she'd returned to the inn with, but the string of rubies around her neck looked like they'd been borrowed from the queen of England.

As they came around the mountain's face, Grey caught his first glimpse of the arena. Far below and set into a natural bowl between three mountains was an immense oblong structure straight out of ancient Rome. There were throngs of creatures around the perimeter, waiting to be allowed in, and giants guarding the gates.

Verida stopped, staring out across the valley.

Grey came up next to her. "What is it?"

She pointed. Between the forest in the distance and the natural incline that led to the land the arena sat on was a small army. It was too far away for Grey to make out all the details, but he had a fairly good idea of who the warriors belonged to.

Keir.

Zio had instructed Amar to procure entrance to the games and then to find somewhere safe to wait until she arrived. He didn't know how Zio used his blood to open portals straight to him, but he imagined it was a similar process to what he'd done to create portals leading to her. Not that he understood either bit of magic in the least.

It had taken some doing, but he'd finally found a quiet location outside the curving back wall of the animal enclosure. As there wasn't an entrance on this side, it was the only place outside of the wards where there weren't any crowds or guards. Amar patted his pocket, checking for the hundredth time that the entrance stones he'd been given were still where he'd left them.

There was a flash in his peripheral vision, and Amar turned to face it. A glowing portal hung in the middle of the air, doubling in size every second. When it grew to size, Zio stepped out, followed by the Venator, both wearing long black cloaks. Amar dipped his head in respect as the portal shrunk and then closed behind her.

Zio looked around. "Risky position, Amar."

"There was nowhere else, I assure you."

Zio pinned him with her violet eyes, using a look that he never could determine the meaning of. It straddled the line between surprised approval and intense disapproval and had meant one or the other depending on the situation.

She reached beneath her cloak and pulled out a leather satchel that was nearly identical to the one he'd buried in the cave near Ransan's borders.

He took it from her outstretched hand. "What's this for?"

"Find a seat at the very top of the arena, east side. Make the first circle under the bench before the games start. When the barrier goes down, finish the ritual, and open a portal."

"Where am I going?"

"It's not for you. Just open it."

Amar clutched the bag to his chest. "Of course. But . . ." He hated questioning her, always worrying that he would ask one question too many. But it seemed that she always offered just short of what he needed to know. "How is the barrier coming down?"

"Elyria has her orders. Just watch, and be ready." Zio turned, her cloak swinging as she raised one hand and crooked a finger for the Venator to follow. "And then, Amar, if I were you, I would get out of the arena."

The Venator—what had she called him . . . Ryder?—glared at him, looking him up and down as if he were covered in dog shit before turning to follow. Amar bristled. From within the walls, the deep booms of barrel drums played, and a sparkling wall of magic rose up and over the arena.

It was time.

47

Tate had been shackled by his ankles and wrists, escorted to the center of the wagon wheel, and placed beside Dalbor, who was wearing matching restraints. Two guards stood in front of them, two more behind. All six were waiting on Sarley.

Tate could hear the roar of the crowds gathering outside the arena walls and feel the vibrations of the giants' feet as they paced in front of their gates.

Sarley emerged from one of the side tunnels, dressed and ready in her game-day attire: tight black leather pants and a blue presenter's jacket that buttoned to her chin, with long sleeves and a hood that hung down her back. "It's that time again. Let's move."

He tried to catch her eye, needing to verify that everything was still in place. But she would not look at him.

Their group took the same tunnel that Tate had followed on his way in. When they emerged aboveground, the sounds amplified, and the excitement of the crowd buzzed in his ears like a nest of angry wasps. Sarley led them along the outer perimeter of the stands, then turned before the main doors and walked up a ramp that led to the first landing of the arena's interior.

Two wizard's barriers had already been erected and were clearly visible, sparkling here and there like a net of stars caught in the early haze of dawn. The first was draped over the entirety of the arena to prevent attendees from magically interfering. A second, smaller one bubbled up around the sandy floor like the top of an overbaked roll, protecting the audience from anything that might happen inside—flying pieces of viscera and bone, attempted escapes by the gladiators themselves, and, for today, webbing from a particularly angry arachneous.

The steps rose steeply, putting ample room between each row and the one below it, ensuring that all would be able to the see the gore they'd come to witness. Along the upper rim were large boxes owned by the most powerful families in the region, each identified by bright pennants emblazoned with their family seals. Dracula's box was located on the south side, dead center, and lined up exactly with the owner's box half an arena below.

The stands were empty, with the exception of the witch waiting by the owner's box. She was tall and lean, with fair skin, brown hair, and no defining features of any sort. If it weren't for the wizard's robes announcing her power, she would've been utterly forgettable.

As they grew closer, Tate could make out the expression on her face. The witch looked annoyed, scowling—as if Tate and Dalbor had arrived late to sign their own death warrants and their lack of urgency in the matter displeased her.

He leaned his head to one side and murmured to Dalbor, "I think she wants us to be more excited to die."

"Sometimes I am, my old friend. Sometimes I am."

Tate understood. Even with a need to survive, there had been days and nights in which the hell of the situation was so intense that the tranquility of death looked appealing.

When they reached the box, the witch ushered them in, then leaned to the side and raised a hand to someone unseen across the arena. A small door opened on the east side, and the two owners entered.

Even at this distance, Tate recognized Keir immediately. Ambrose, on the other hand . . . Tate squinted. He couldn't make out distinct facial details, but her skin was obviously still black and her hair bright white. He couldn't understand it. Beltran had told him that she'd been wearing this veneer, but it should've been stripped away the moment she passed underneath the arena's barriers.

Ignoring one another, the two owners walked through the stands under the distant, watchful eye of the witch. Ambrose arrived first, followed by Keir, and the witch ushered them into the box, then stepped in behind them and closed the door. Though it had been invisible in the sun, the roof of the owner's box shaded them so that Tate could see the sparkling sheen of magic that surrounded the witch like a second skin.

In order for all of this to work—for the barriers to prevent magic while still allowing the wizards to maintain control and place spells as necessary—the wizards had to maintain the ability to do magic themselves. He'd never seen the spell work performed, but he'd heard that the wizards began preparing days in advance, wrapping both their magic and the prevention of others' magic into one giant spell that required multiple witches and wizards to support.

Keir had never been in the owner's box before, and it was obvious. He gawked at the space with his soulless black eyes. The box was situated midway up the arena for prime viewing in both proximity and height. And it was luxurious. Chaises, chairs, and sofas were spread around. Ornate buffets sat along the back side, already full of fruits, wines, and an assortment of other delicacies. Because one should experience the finest life had to offer while watching others suffer and die.

Ambrose ignored the finery and walked straight to the swearing table near the large window open at the front. It was a small, circular thing made of glass that had been set on the back of a stone gladiator, his foot resting on the face of one who'd fallen. Tate hated this box. He'd been in here more times than he cared to count, because every count was another dead at his hands, haunting him every day like the inescapable brands across his skin.

In order to start the ceremony, the witch had to request that Keir join them. Ambrose sneered at his ignorance. The table was now surrounded by the circle of participants—some willing, some not. Tate, Dalbor, Ambrose, Keir, the witch, and Sarley as witness. The witch waved a palm up over the altar. "Place your items on the table."

Keir reached beneath his vest and pulled out a rose gold key, which glowed with elven magic that lit the colored jewels inlaid beneath. The witch's eyes went wide. Sarley did a double take. Tate had never seen such an obvious reaction to a wager.

The witch cleared her throat. "And you?"

Ambrose pulled out a ruby pin in the shape of a four-pointed star. Her hand, veneered dark, extended over the table, and she dropped the piece from a distance. It hit with a bang and rattled against the glass, tipping from one point to the other.

The witch's head snapped up at this, and she pinned Ambrose with her gaze, eyes brimming with suspicion. "Is this yours to give?"

"It is."

"Then I will have verification of your identity, or we cannot proceeded. I will not induce the council's wrath or force their hands over these proceedings."

Ambrose smiled, a lazy, catlike expression. Even with the new face, Tate recognized her smile. The silken robes she wore had been tied at the sides, showing off her waist, and when she unbuttoned the top, the fabric spread wide. The black skin stopped in an abrupt line below her collarbones, giving way to green skin that was flecked with the same darker markings that normally surrounded her eyes. The pattern cut across her sternum and over the swell of her breasts. "I am Ambrose. Queen of the fae of Salandria, council member, and wielder of wind. I will be invoking the protection of the games and demand that my name be announced as it is written."

"But"—the witch stammered, searching for words—"a veneer cannot hold here. This is not possible."

"I paid well for the possibility, and I will leave you to unravel your new problem after the games. If you'd like a demonstration of my power for further verification, let down your wards, Yasmina."

At the mention of her name, whatever doubt the witch had had vanished. She gave a short nod. "The name will be announced as written."

Keir sneered. "When you lose your seat, they will all know your identity."

Ambrose turned her head slowly to look at him, rebuttoning her robe. "You should hope that I win, Keir. Because neither the council nor my people will ever accept you."

"The council will have no choice. The arena is out of their jurisdiction, and the magic of the rite will ensure it. Your seat is given here today of your own free will, and what is bound by blood and magic is done. As for those of Salandria, I would be more concerned of what they will think of *you*." He tsked. "Their queen, who so carelessly tossed away all they sacrificed to place her on the council seat?"

"Enough. You two may bicker while the games unfold. We are here to swear the oaths." Yasmina adjusted the key and the brooch so that they sat in the center of the table, perfectly in line with each other. "Your wagers will remain on this table until the match is over and a winner is declared. You will not leave this booth at any point during the match. The doors and windows will be protected by me, and the wards won't be brought down for any reason until the match between Tate and Dalbor has reached its conclusion. Once the heart of the loser has beat its final beat, it will be the magic, not I, that will allow the winning owner to remove both items from the table." She touched the surface with her pointer finger and whispered a series of spells. The tabletop began to glow a deep purple. "Keir, son of Feena, you place on the table the key to Kastaley. Do you freely give this?"

"Yes."

"Ambrose, queen of the fae of Salandria, you place on the table the fae council seat. Do you freely give this?"

"Yes."

"Now, the gladiators."

There was never a question as to what those who were about to die would freely give.

Tate and Dalbor stepped closer, bringing up their bound hands. The wizard took a small, thin blade from her cloak and pressed it into first Tate's finger and then Dalbor's. Their blood dropped onto the table, spattering across the jewels of both items. The wizard whispered two more words and withdrew her hand. The table flashed and glowed red.

48

The farther down the mountain they descended, the hotter it became, and the cloak that Grey had been so grateful for near the peak was now stifling. Sweat dripped into his eyes and down his back, and by the time they finally approached the arena, the wool was damp and starting to smell.

In front of them, the enormity of the structure sprawled across the mountainside. The similarity to the Colosseum was uncanny, and Tate's words rolled through his head: *Your familiarity implies Venators took that tradition home too. Shouldn't surprise me. After the gates closed, I'm sure the Venators' thirst for blood needed an outlet.*

By the time they arrived, the outer doors had already been opened and the guests allowed in, but the arena was still surrounded by hundreds. Grey, Rune, and Verida pushed their way through creatures of every shape, size, and color—most of them too excited to pay any attention to who was cutting between. But anyone who noticed the council symbols emblazoned on their cloaks took a closer look at Verida, then proceeded to move to a new location.

"If they can't get in," Rune asked, ducking her shoulder to avoid crashing into a tall, thin fae, "why is everyone still here?"

"Most are hoping to be part of it by listening and trying to picture for themselves what's happening inside," Verida said. "But inevitably, there will be someone who tries to sneak in, and the giants will force the crowds to disperse. It never fails."

A squat, round male with two nubs on the top of his head that looked like they might've been horns at some point and a fat tongue lolling out the side of his mouth ran into Verida.

She shoved him and hissed. At Rune's expression, she demanded, "What?"

"Nothing." Rune shrugged. "The hiss seemed like an unnecessary touch, but what do I know?"

"Not a whole lot," Verida bit off as she marched ahead, leading the way to the main gates.

Grey looked up at the faces of the two giants as they passed between them. Both were highly attentive but nervous. Their beady eyes scanned the crowd for signs of trouble while their hands continually readjusted their grip on their weapons.

Next to the open, gilded doors was a younger man dressed in wizard's robes.

"Verida," he said warmly. "We were unaware you were coming. Will you be using your family's box today?"

"Unaware? Surely you received the missive yesterday announcing my intentions."

"No, we—"

She handed him a bag of gold.

"Ah, yes. I did."

"Good. Then you also remember that my father requested that I be allowed to announce our gladiator. Tate."

The wizard hefted the bag and slipped it beneath his robes. "Of course. I will ensure Sarley is aware of the change in plans." He eyed Rune and Grey. "And these two are?"

"My guests and representatives of the council."

"It is an honor to host all three of you." He welcomed them in.

They stepped into a space between the outside and the arena. Stone walls rose on both sides of them, and shining marble pillars, three across, ran in rows as far as they could see in either direction, throwing shadows over the tiled stone floor and following the curved lines of the arena out of sight.

The noise was so overwhelming that Grey barely heard the wizard at the doors shout. What he heard clearly was a bellow that struck the fear of God into him. He and Rune both ducked and spun, reaching for weapons and trying to locate the threat. From outside the wall, screaming erupted.

"As I said," Verida yelled. "It was only a matter of time before someone tried to sneak in."

Rune straightened and looked at Grey with a spark of excitement in her eyes. She took off running back to the main doors, lining herself up behind the wizard and looking out.

Verida rolled her eyes and motioned. "Well, go on. I assume you're curious as well."

He was. Grey jogged back. Rune grabbed him and jerked him tight to her side. "Look!"

He had to do so twice. If he hadn't seen the transformation happening for himself, he never would've believed it. The first giant was already unrecognizable and on the rampage, bending at the waist to swing his wooden mallet inches above the ground. Creatures scattered. One elf held out her hand, but whatever magic she'd been trying to use couldn't beat the speed of the mallet. It smashed into her and sent her flying.

The other guard was still midtransition, and Grey couldn't take his eyes off him. The giant's skin was bubbling, as if massive beetles were crawling beneath it. His back arched, growing larger both up and out. Muscles bulged, teeth elongated, and black spikes exploded up his spine and down his arms. It was like watching a transformation between a werewolf and a puffer fish . . . and the Hulk. Once the second giant completed his transformation, he joined his companion, attacking the crowd without mercy or discernment.

Verida strolled up next to them. "Mindless buffoons. They won't be any good after this. The stress on their bodies is so much that they'll have to bring in replacements to let these two recover."

"First time seeing a giant rage?" the wizard said, as if it were a joke.

"The council keeps these two under lock and key." Verida patted Grey and Rune on the shoulders. "And no one has been dumb enough to attack the council house in some time."

The wizard now turned his head, looking them over and obviously wondering what kind of monsters they'd have to be for the council to lock them up. Grey had the urge to throw his hands up and shout, *Boo!*

A mallet came straight down, obliterating a male and female who had been running away and almost out of range. Grey flinched. "I've seen enough."

Verida met his eyes. "I'm sorry."

"For what?"

"This isn't going to be easy for you." She tapped Rune on the shoulder and jerked her head. "Let's go."

They followed the pillars, passing by two ramps that led into the stands before taking a third. At the top, the arena floor stretched out below, and stone steps with rows of wooden benches rose all around them. The space was full to the brim with spectators. Some had already taken their seats, while others sauntered about between benches, talking and laughing.

There were two barriers that Grey could make out: one over the arena floor and another that stretched over the entire stadium. On the floor below, several humans were busy raking the sand into a smooth surface.

"Try and close your mouth," Verida said. "We will be passing by the owner's box on the way to ours. Keir and Ambrose will already be inside. You can look, but do not stare or draw attention to yourselves. Ambrose may know you're here and who you are, but Keir doesn't, and I'd like to keep it that way. Put those hoods up, and keep them on unless I say otherwise."

As they walked up the steps, Grey didn't have to be told which box was the owner's. It sat in the center of the south side of the stands, the hinged shutters pushed wide open, allowing everyone to see in. The black fae that Grey had met in the marketplace was standing at the front. Her eyes went immediately to Verida and her two council representatives. Keir was stretched out on a chaise, his arm thrown over the back and his legs crossed. All that was missing was the whip that Grey had never seen him without.

Grey moved to the side so he could whisper near Verida's ear without being obvious. "I thought the arena had barriers to prevent magic. How is that veneer still working?"

"A question I intend on asking Arwin the next time I see him." She put her hand on his back. "Walk faster."

The top rim of this side of the arena was lined with boxes that looked nearly identical to the owner's, different pennants hanging along the top edge of each, displaying what Grey was sure were family crests. For something that was supposedly forbidden by the council, there seemed to be no attempt to hide the identity of those who frequented the establishment.

The box that Verida led them to lined up directly with the owner's box below. She opened the half door and ushered them inside. A wooden roof kept out the sun, but the front was completely open, save for the waist-high wall that had been built to mark off the space. Grey ignored the plush furniture spread throughout and walked to the front, resting his hands on the ledge.

From this angle, he saw what he couldn't before. On the side of the owner's box opposite the stairs they'd taken was a small metal cage, and inside was a female wearing wizard's robes.

Grey pointed. "Why is she locked up like that?"

"For her own protection. That is the only witch they've left aboveground, and she's powering the barriers on that box. The cage has been protected to prevent anyone from killing her in an attempt to bring the wards down around the owner's box before the match ends."

"Just out of curiosity . . ." Rune meandered around behind them. "Is there anything *not* surrounded by a barrier?"

"Not exactly. Difficult to have a fair match when magic is involved."

A beautiful woman with dark skin and piles of blue-black braids on the top of her head approached Dracula's box. She stopped outside, speaking through the open window. "Miss Verida, I just received word that you had guests. My apologies. Had I known you were attending, I would've had the box stocked earlier. Will you require . . . *nourishment* for all three of you?"

"No, Sarley. Thank you. Standard fare for two only."

"I will send someone up at once. I have also been informed that you will be introducing the games. The names of the owners are written here." She handed over a folded piece of parchment.

"Thank you."

The two women looked at each other, unspoken words passing between them.

"Enjoy the games." Sarley turned to go but stopped, twisting her shoulders to stand in profile. "Also, I was happy to see that you and your sister are on speaking terms again. She should be up within the next few minutes."

Verida sighed. "Thank you."

"Of course. Anything for House Dracula."

Verida didn't argue Sarley's assessment because she was reasonably sure it had been less of a statement than a warning. "I'm going to need both of you to stay in the shadows until I get back."

"Vega is here?" Rune asked.

"Apparently. I shouldn't be surprised. Keep those hoods up, and if I have to return with her, you will both remain completely silent. Do not answer her questions or ask me any. Not a single sound. No matter what she does."

"The last time we had this conversation, it didn't go well," Rune said. "What if she puts another knife in your back? Can we speak then?"

"No," Verida snapped.

"*Rune.*" Grey shook his head.

"What?"

Verida turned her attention to the flow of attendees, narrowing her focus to the ramps nearest the box. It wasn't the blonde hair that gave her sister away but her distinctive swagger as she moved through a sea of everyone else's flurried, excited movements.

Verida leapt the half gate and shoved her way through those still coming up, meeting Vega just before she made it to the stairs. Her sister wore a corseted top of deep maroon, and each finger dripped with heavy gold and jeweled rings.

Those rings Vega wears . . . What would you wear?

Verida imagined wearing the lovingly carved ring that had been waiting for her in the Venator tower on her own finger . . . and saw red. But revenge had to come later. If she hoped to avoid the imminent disaster that was allowing Vega up to that box, she couldn't show even the slightest objection to her doing exactly that.

She stepped off the last rise and in front of Vega, cutting her off. "What are you doing here?"

"Well, well." She smiled, resting one hand on her hip. "Aren't you looking recovered this afternoon. Who did you find to dig that dagger out of your spine?" A female fae bumped into Vega. Her arm flew out, grabbing the fae by the wrist and twisting so hard that she dropped to her knees. "Watch where you're going."

The fae's face twisted in fury until she recognized who had a hold of her. "Lady Vega." She dipped her head. "My apologies."

Vega released her hold and smiled a thin-lipped warning at Verida as the fae scrambled away. "Shall we visit the box?"

"If you're prepared to sit next to me for the next few hours, I suppose we shall."

Vega laughed. "So agreeable. Are you hoping it'll be enough time to take your revenge?"

"The thought would never cross my mind."

Anton stepped out from the ramp behind Vega, looking dashing in a high-collared white shirt with his sleeves rolled up to the elbows. His brown eyes were the color of rich honey in the sun, and Verida did a double take.

What in the name of Rana and all her saints? If Vega hadn't been staring at her, she would've had a number of choice questions for her old friend. She swallowed them all.

Anton stepped around and to the side, hovering between the two sisters and half-blocking the already overcrowded aisle. "Vega," he said brightly, tilting his body just enough to give Verida a clear and intentional cold shoulder. "It has been far too long."

Although highly annoyed that Anton had failed to mention he had entrance, Verida knew an answer to a problem when she saw one.

She crossed her arms and frowned in a way that she was sure looked embarrassingly petulant. "Hello to you too."

Anton barley acknowledged her, giving her a shrug and a smirk. "Oh, Verida, I didn't see you there."

The pouting combined with Anton's snub delighted Vega, and she smirked, pushing her hair over her shoulder as she stepped closer to him. "Last I heard, your brother had told you not to come back."

"He never did have a very good sense of humor."

"I can relate."

"Hmmm . . ." Anton bravely ran a finger along Vega's exposed collarbone. "It has been so many years. I would say I'd forgotten how exquisite you are, but there is nothing that could wipe your beauty from my memory."

"Nothing?"

"*Nothing.*" He brushed his thumb over her lip, then tucked his hand into his pocket. "You know, darling, there are still hours until Tate fights. We could pass the time in more comfortable accommodations if you'd like."

"Rana!" Verida didn't need to feign her disgust. "I'm standing right here, you two."

Her sister placed a hand against Anton's well-defined chest, lifting her chin. "Verida, exactly how many hundreds of years old will you need to be before you stop acting like a child?" Still wavering, her eyes flicked to the owner's box.

Ambrose was hidden with her veneer, but Keir was now standing at the front, with no attempt to disguise himself. The idiot. Fae pride and new royalty were a dangerous combination.

"Which one is Qualtar?" Vega asked.

"No." Verida stepped between her sister and Anton, breaking their contact. She grabbed her sister by both shoulders and pulled her closer, pressing her cheek against Vega's. "I told you, I'm working for the council. Qualtar is the name that Keir, son of Feena, used when he took a piece of rope that wasn't his to borrow. And now I'm going to let him hang himself with it. Do me a favor: when you pass that information along to Father, please let him know that it was his childish daughter who made the noose."

When she stepped back, Vega's eyes were cold slits. "We shall see whose noose you've made soon enough." She grabbed Anton's hand. "Let's you and I get reacquainted."

As Vega dragged Anton away, he pulled something from his pocket and held it over his shoulder. He waved it at Verida, then glanced back as he tucked the glass vial away.

A measure of tension bled from her shoulders. She didn't know what drug that vial contained, but unless Anton suffered a major misstep, Vega would not be rejoining her this afternoon. She mouthed, *Thank you.*

He gave a short, upward jerk of his chin and mouthed in return, *You owe me.*

That she did.

It was time. Rune stood at the front of the box on Verida's right, Grey on her left. She stared down at the arena floor, wondering what would come first, trying not to think about what could come last, and desperately working to ignore how hot she was under this cloak. At least Verida had allowed them to remove their hoods.

The audience's excitement had increased to an impatient energy that seeped into Rune's bones and caused her to shift her weight from one foot to the other.

"Hold. Still." Verida eyes remained forward, her lips barely moving. "You are a representative of the council, not a nervous child. Back straight, head high. Today, you stand above everyone. Look like it."

Zio had gone ahead, leaving Ryker to wait near the railing until she was ready for him. He didn't know what she'd said to the two strange-looking creatures that had been sitting directly in front of the thing Zio called the owner's box, but they had gotten up and moved without argument. Once she sat, he followed, as requested.

She'd been clear that he was to observe everything he could about the owner's box, its inhabitants, and the table at the front. But he was struggling to focus, because right before she'd walked away, Zio had also pointed out Dracula's box. And now that was all he could see.

Even with the distance and the cloak and the shadows, he knew it was his sister up there. Which meant the male on the other side of the vampire was Grey Malteer. Ryker's heart was pounding, and he couldn't keep his fists from clenching and unclenching at his sides. The fact that his inner Venator was going crazy as he stepped over fae and elves and werewolves on his way to Zio wasn't helping.

As he passed directly in front of the owner's box, his view of Rune was obscured, and he looked inside. A black-skinned fae stood next to a glowing table with a key and a large ruby on it. The fae stared back at him, her eyes narrowing on his face before sliding over the rest of him. He no doubt looked as murderous as he felt—which was an obvious departure from Zio's instruction to appear forgettable.

He took his seat on the wooden benches next to Zio. She'd removed her cloak—a choice he was denied due to his Venator markings—and was wearing a pair of tight black pants and a black linen shirt with a hood. She'd left the hood up to cover the platinum hair she'd pinned back, and she'd applied so much kohl around her eyes that it completely changed the look of her face. Still . . .

He leaned to the side, talking under his breath. "Are you sure no one is going to recognize you?"

"Very few know what I actually look like. I've been careful to keep my face hidden from the council members. It will be enough. Why are you shaking? We knew there was a chance your sister would be here."

"It's not my sister. I'll get through to her. I know I will."

"You'll get your chance at Grey. But for now, you must focus. All that matters is this box behind us. That blade that I mentioned has to fall today, and we are here to ensure things go as planned."

"Ryker," Rune whispered.

Verida twitched. "What did you just say?"

She pointed. "My brother. He was right there."

"Are you"—Verida pressed her arm down—"sure?"

"I . . ." *Was* she sure? It was so far away, and she'd seen his face for only a spilt second before he'd disappeared. But he had been looking right at her. Or had he just been looking up? "I think so? It was fast, but I swear . . ."

"Where did he go?" Grey asked.

"In front of the owner's box. I don't know. Maybe I'm going crazy."

"Maybe," Grey said, but Rune felt herself stiffening at the amount of venom he'd infused into the word . . . and the equal amount speared into the daggers he was glaring at the back of the owner's box.

"We'll deal with it later." Verida laid her hands on the ledge. "The gate is going up."

A hush fell over the crowd, and Rune heard the heavy clinking of chains being ratcheted as the west gate lifted. When it reached the top, it cracked into place, the chains squealing under the tension. From beneath the jagged metal teeth, Sarley emerged onto the field, the silver buttons of her blue jacket glinting in the sun.

Everybody in attendance launched into a rolling cheer, their shouts rising higher with each of her steps until the sound was deafening. Once she reached the center of the arena, she held up both arms and spun in a slow circle. The roar had been fast in coming, and the crowd was reluctant to release it. She waited, stepping and spinning, demanding silence, until it was so quiet that it felt as if they were all hanging on the same breath.

When her body was lined up with Dracula's box, Sarley stopped. She brought her arms to the front, palms up, hands side by side, directing every eye toward their announcer.

Verida pulled in a breath. "As a representative of my father, I would like to thank you all for coming." The acoustics were spectacular, and her voice rang clean and clear across the stands. "We have many things planned today, and I've even heard rumors that we may have an arachneous in play?"

She held a hand out to Sarley in question as another collective cheer went up around the arena. Sarley nodded affirmation and motioned again for quiet.

Verida continued, "My father has heard your complaints and, to illustrate his concern and listening ear, has generously decided to lend the Venshii Tate for a match today." The arena exploded with excitement. Verida waited for the sound to dip just enough that she could shout over what remained. "The final match of today's games is to honor you, the people!"

The crowd went wild. Sarley strolled off the field, and a group of gladiators ran on.

50

The sound of weapons clashing was buried by the excitement of the spectators.

"This is the exhibition," Verida said. "It demonstrates the caliber of contenders for today's game and allows the gladiators to loosen up their muscles before the matches."

"I don't see Tate," Grey said.

"The main event's contenders will warm up belowground."

"Why are there no shields?" Rune motioned toward the field in disgust. "Or armor?"

The males were wearing the equivalent of a loincloth, while the women were granted the addition of a leather top that covered their breasts and part of their rib cage.

"The games are a test of skill in battle, and that includes avoiding your enemy's weapon. You will see a few competitors with shields once the matches begin, but they're only allowed as compensation—to equal out a lack of healing in one gladiator compared to his opponent. If the healing capacity is equal—even if that is none at all—no shields are allowed."

A new group of gladiators ran in, and the first group ran out. As the new warriors began sparring, it was obvious that these were more skilled than the first. Verida scanned the rows of muscular bodies until her eyes fell on a young male competitor with dark brown skin sparring with a tall woman whose stately frame she would recognize anywhere—Ayla.

Brandt had been so small last Verida had seen him she had been sure she wouldn't be able to recognize him. But even had his mother not been next to him, Verida would've known. The resemblance to Tate in his shape, his presence—even the way he held a sword—was so uncanny it rolled off the boy, announcing his heritage as effectively as a banner.

She kicked the edge of the box, swearing every combination she could think of.

"What's the matter . . . ?" Grey followed her gaze. "That's Ayla and Brandt."

"Where?" Rune asked.

As Brandt and Ayla sparred, they couldn't help but stand out from the rest. It wasn't their power but their prowess. The smoothness of their combat was hypnotizing, both moving like dancers, their weapons extensions of their arms.

Verida swallowed. "There will be a bidding war after the games. Tate will never forgive me for this."

Beltran used his scorpion tail to poke at the tarp that covered his cage as both guards and slaves scurried around, preparing the participating beasts for their matches and moving cages to the eastern gate. He jabbed with his stinger, clawed at the tarp, and threw himself against the bars, snarling—a few quick reminders that this cage was to be avoided.

He waited through Verida's announcement, continuing his vicious charade until he heard the first official match begin. Beltran settled down and listened—waiting in case someone decided to risk a peek at the resting manticore—then shifted into a mouse and used his nose to push up the bottom edge of the tarp for a quick look around. With the game preparations complete, the area immediately around the manticore's cage was clear of witnesses.

He slipped out and scampered down the same path he'd taken last night, unable to keep from looking toward the arachneous cage . . . and the piece of his hope that had died there. But she was already gone, moved to the eastern gate.

Bloody unfortunate for the warriors who were about to be shoved into the arena with that monster.

He made his way straight to the same window he'd used to gain access to Tate last night, cutting between the bars and digging his nails into the porous stone to slow his fall. Tate's cell was empty. The Venshii had already been taken to the holding cells near the west gate in preparation.

As Beltran scurried down the hall, he was careful to behave exactly as a natural mouse would, sticking to the sides and ducking in and out of cells to avoid notice. Although he had a general idea of the layout, he still didn't know where they'd decided to house the wizards. But, last night, Tate had identified one hall that he'd never been down in all his years here.

It stood to reason that both the guards and Sarley would have quarters located on the premises, and that hall was the most likely choice—which made it Beltran's first guess as to where the wizards would be stationed as well.

Approaching the center of the wagon wheel, Beltran slowed and pressed his body tight against the wall, mapping out the space before him. Each hall around the wheel's center was blocked by a line of guards, their battle-axes crossed. The open space between was full of gladiators. Some were pacing like wild animals, stretching their arms and rolling their necks. Others curled in on themselves like paper under heat.

Beltran slipped between the wall and a boot, running toward the hall in question. His whiskers brushed against the perimeter, and he cut toward the entrance, dodging another guard's boot as he read-justed his stance. And then Beltran was in.

Slowing, he scanned the area. This hall was much tighter, the walls closer—obviously not built for transporting prisoners. The first door he came across was solid oak, reinforced by iron bars that crisscrossed the front and a heavy lock secured through the latch. A protective measure in case of a prisoner's escape, he assumed.

Beltran darted around door after identical door, listening against the bottom edges until he finally heard the whispers of spell work slipping beneath. He tucked himself into a shadowed corner opposite the door at the end of the hall and looked over the new obstacle. Although the lock didn't appear any different than the rest, this one was glinting too brightly in the low light. Enchanted.

Overhead, the crowd roared—at least he was positioned to hear that. If he could make out both the announcer and the cheers, he might be able to time this right.

Maybe.

Beltran huffed, and the fine particles of dirt in the corner flurried around him. It was madness, trying to time a jailbreak blind and half-deaf. But ... . his beady mouse eyes rolled back to that glinting lock. None of that would matter unless he figured out how to open that door without getting himself killed.

The matches kept going and going . . . and going. It hadn't taken long before Rune left the front of the box and migrated to a chaise in the back, sipping on a glass of water and trying not to look.

Grey had yet to leave the railing.

It wasn't that he wanted to watch. He did not. But it felt like a duty. His job to stand as someone who clearly saw how wrong this was, to witness and respect what these men and women had been relegated to, and to honor the sacrifices they were being forced to make. There needed to be at least one voice, one set of ears, and one thudding heart in the arena today that did not enjoy what they were seeing.

The emotional cost was high, but each time he thought he would crack, he reminded himself that the price he was choosing to pay was less steep than those fighting below. And no matter what, he would bear it.

Verida stepped up next to him. "You're going to break off that railing if you don't let go of it."

"Sorry." Grey flared his fingers out, relieving the pressure. "This is a lot."

"You know"—she stared down at the sand below—"there was a time in my life when I enjoyed these."

"What happened?"

"It wasn't a what. It was a who."

Grey glanced over to her proud profile. "I assume that's all I'm getting in regard to that."

Her smile was a whisper, and she drummed her fingers against the railing. "You are correct."

The female gladiator currently in the arena had arching yellow ram's horns, and as her male vampire opponent ran at her, she raised her round wooden shield. The male ran straight into it. The female bent her knees, her toes digging into the soft sand, and held her position. The momentum of the vampire's speed flipped him up and over the top. She lifted her head as he flew past, turning her neck so that the vampire's arm would slide between her horns. She then twisted and threw her head toward her knees. The vampire's shoulder lodged into one of the curls of her horns and was yanked and then dashed to the ground. She stepped through and over his body, twisting again, taking his arm with her. The shoulder and forearm bulged and broke as she simultaneously brought her sword around, stopping at the vampire's neck.

Grey swore. "What was that?"

"*That* was impressive. She's just made a name for herself."

"Is that a good thing?"

"Depends."

Sarley emerged from beneath the gate, holding her forearms up in an X. Everyone in the arena held their breath. She pulled them back to her chest, still crossed. Not a death match.

The sounds were disappointed at first but quickly followed by a cheer for the victor, who shook her horns free and helped the vampire to his feet.

"How many of these matches are to the death?" Grey asked. They'd yet to see one.

"It varies. They have to mitigate the deaths with supply and demand. If they're overcrowded, there will be more death matches, and less if they're not."

The two contenders passed beneath the gate, and then a group of males and females were being shoved into the arena by a line of guards. Grey leaned over the ledge. He'd never seen anyone enter at any slower than a jog, but these contenders were leaning back, pushing against the guards and their battle-axes.

The guards extended their weapons, holding the twenty or so males and females at bay as they stepped back. The gate lowered and slammed shut. One male ran and threw himself against it, gripping the iron squares and shaking, his mouth open in a scream that Grey couldn't hear. Through the holes, swords were thrown out onto the sand. The unarmed gladiators rushed to pick them up.

Grey didn't understand. "What's happening?"

"I suspect Sarley was asked to hold off on the death matches because of what's coming next. Look." Verida jerked her head toward the slowly opening east gate. "That side is used for the beasts. They butt the cages up to the opening to release them straight into the arena."

The first of eight gigantic spider legs stretched out into the light, met by the excited screams of Eonians. The creature unfolded, leg after leg, until the top half emerged, the female part of its body wrapped in both flesh and darker stripes of impenetrable exoskeleton.

"*Oh my God.*" Rune reappeared next to Grey. "*That's* what you saw in Zio's castle?"

Unable to get any words out, he nodded.

The arachneous stepped fully onto the arena floor, taking in the environment, its eight legs carefully dropping as she walked deeper. Her large eyes washed over the group of terrified males and females huddling around the western gate. She stopped and rolled her neck, tracking the barrier that extended over the top. The stuttering sound from the stands communicated the audience's confusion at the creature's behavior. The arachneous turned away from her would-be victims and cut instead toward the south side of the arena, stopping in front of the owner's box. She stared, unblinking, with those large black eyes for an uncomfortably long time.

"What is it doing?" Rune asked.

Verida slowly shook her head. "I have no idea."

The arachneous opened her mouth, red lips stretching wide. She spat her first mouthful of web not at the victims on the other side of the arena but at the box. It splattered against the barrier, sticking as fast as a wad of gum to a railing.

The creature squealed and stumbled backward, the womanly hands crossing over its abdomen. It shot a glare toward the box, then thrust into action, scuttling straight toward the arena wall. It ran up not only that but the barrier itself. Zio had said that the arachneous could run up walls as easily as it could floors; apparently, this applied to magical barriers as well.

The gladiators realized what it was doing and scattered, each of them running in different directions. The paltry number of weapons that had been thrown out was useless against something like this, and they knew it.

The arachneous crossed above what was likely a human, based on his speed and size. She released a wad of webbing. It landed on his head and left shoulder, pressing him to his knees. He frantically reached up, trying to tear off the sticky mass that obscured his nose and mouth.

The creature continued on, scurrying across the barrier upside down, spitting attacks from above. When nearly half of the contenders had been secured, she dropped to the ground and continued the same pattern—chasing them one at a time and, before they could turn to fight, tying them up in masses of webbing. There was a vampire who gave her a bit more trouble, but eventually, he made a wrong turn, and she plastered him to the arena wall, his feet kicking helplessly and his arms pinned fast.

Once she'd secured all twenty, she swung her attention to the body nearest her and picked up the still-struggling woman. She lifted the woman up and, while holding the body aloft with her two spindly legs, took the head between her hands and twisted it *off.*

"Holy shit!" Rune gasped, stumbling backward.

The webbing absorbed much of the blood, but because the creature had removed the head using brute strength and torque, the skin hung in jagged pieces, and part of the spine dangled in what looked like the most terrifying horror-movie prop Grey could've imagined. The arachneous threw the severed head straight at the barrier, knowing it was there and surely expecting that the webbing would stick but that the weight of the head would pull it down. The arachneous grinned wildly as the macabre pile slid down the barrier like condensation on a glass of water.

Grey finally had to look away, covering his mouth.

While the arena was distracted with the horror before them, one gladiator had freed himself and run to help another. He was hacking at the sticky mass with his sword, but the arachneous's head turned, quick as a whip, and she rushed for them. She picked up the first as she ran by, took him between her humanoid hands, skidded to a stop, and brought his back down over a leg like she was breaking a stick over a knee. And he did break, bending in two on his way down and landing in a twisted pile at her feet.

"Why," Grey said, through heaving breaths. "Why would they do this? No one had a chance. They can't even—"

The arachneous turned slowly, then burst into motion, tearing across the arena like a bull seeing red. She impaled gladiators with her legs, tore off arms and legs, threw them against the barrier. She bit and broke and ripped until there was hardly an inch of sand or barrier that was not splattered with blood and gore.

51

Beltran couldn't tell what was happening above—the cheering had dropped off, but he hadn't heard a new announcement. It was too early for Tate's match, which was good, because he was stuck in the same bloody corner, staring at an enchanted lock and trying to determine if he could shift into something capable of tunneling beneath the door or if the wizards would've protected against that too.

He was flipping through his memories, searching for something of use in regard to enchanted locks, when the approaching slap of feet interrupted him. From down the hall, Sarley appeared, flat-out running in his direction. Her shoulder crashed into the wall as she tried to stop in front of the wizard's door. She fumbled the key, working it against the lock, hands shaking so badly that the key's metal tip slid to the side and over the wood twice. She swore under her breath, each word an exclamation between gasps of air, as she tried a third time. When she finally managed to line up the metal teeth of the key, the lock clicked, and she threw the door open. She didn't bother to close it behind her as she ran in.

Confused, but not one to question when fate fell on his side, Beltran rushed through the door on Sarley's heels. In mouse form, he was too

504

near the ground to properly evaluate the layout of the space, and necessity demanded that he focus instead on what he could quickly make out. A rapid scan revealed multiple pairs of feet, the dusty edges of wizards' robes brushing against the ground, thick table legs, and, to his right, a dresser with the perfect amount of clearance for him to slide beneath.

"Bring it down," Sarley shouted. "Bring the overhead barrier down *now!*"

Beltran laid himself flat and peeked out from beneath the dresser. The wizards were standing in the center of the room, sipping from crystal glasses. Something was off.

"What are you talking about?" a wizard sputtered, his round face turning red as he set down his glass. "You aren't supposed to be in here!"

"The arachneous used your barrier as a weapon. The entire thing is covered in blood and who knows what else. We can't clean it."

The same wizard blustered past her, slamming the door. "And what do you expect us to do?"

"The arachneous is locked up, and we've secured all the gladiators below. Bring down the center barrier for a second and then restore it." At their incredulous expressions, she pointed. "It's a mess out there. We can't continue like this. The spectators can hardly see the arena floor."

A witch with wrinkles cut so deep across her forehead they looked like ancient riverbeds waved a hand. "We'll take care of it. Get her out of here." When the door had shut behind Sarley, the witch looked to the other two wizards. "Hurry."

The third was younger than the rest, but half his face was covered in ropey burn scars. He reached beneath his robes, pulling out a piece of jewelry on a silver cord that glowed bright green. What in the seven hells was that? Beltran inched forward, trying to get a better look at the stone, but froze as the reason behind the wrongness that he'd felt in this environment hit him upside the head.

He'd attended gladiator matches before. The wizards were normally outside in their protected cages, within full view of the arena, chanting and waving their arms. By the end of the games, they were often dripping in sweat and leaning against the metal bars, too exhausted to stand on their own. But here, there was no urgency, no appearance of difficulty. When Sarley barged in, the chanting had stopped, and yet . . . no concern was voiced that the barrier may have dropped. These three had been relaxed, sipping their drinks as if they were attending a casual dinner party.

The young wizard ducked his head, pulled the silver cord of the necklace over his head, and reached out, preparing to lay the piece on the table. The amulet now swung in clear view. If Beltran had been standing, he would've needed to reach for a chair. He'd seen that amulet before, and it shouldn't have been here. It shouldn't have been anywhere.

The glowing amulet was framed with silver metalwork twining around the convex piece of wizard's glass in a pattern meant to mimic Venator markings. The spell work was old, laid down by the same wizard who'd erected the barrier around the Venator stronghold, and capable of preventing magic in those near it. It was one of the many things that the Venators had used to tip the scales—increasing their deadly effectiveness against the fae and elven armies.

Beltran had heard rumors that the amulet didn't affect wizards. Which . . . He supposed that creating something like that without any precautions to ensure that the Venators didn't turn around and bite the hand that had fed them made sense. After the war, a group of wizards had sworn the amulet had been destroyed. Instead, they'd managed to harness its power and amplify it into something new. Something lucrative as opposed to battle ready.

Beltran had been concerned from the moment he realized the wizards had been moved, knowing that in order to keep the barrier down and get himself out alive, he'd likely have to kill all three. The situation would no doubt have proved problematic. But . . . He smiled as wide as his little mouse mouth would allow. There was only one reason the wizards would've gone through the trouble of finding a spell to redirect the amulet's power.

Because they'd *required* it.

Everything had been for show. The waving, the exhaustion—all of it a diversion to stop anyone from looking at what was really powering the barrier. And *that* was why the wizard in charge of the owner's box acted differently than the rest. Because that poor sap was the only one actually holding an entire spell and had to bloody concentrate!

The wizards placed their hands on top of the amulet and resumed chanting. It all came together, and Beltran wanted to laugh. They hadn't moved belowground for their own protection. No; they'd grown tired of the production and decided to work their magic far from probing eyes.

Beltran peered up at the green glow emanating from the table. The good news was he didn't need to kill three wizards. All he had to do was figure out how to destroy that magical amulet.

After the barrier dropped and immediately reappeared, there were three more matches before Ayla and Brandt entered the arena. Neither carried shields, but each had a sword strapped to one hip and a long spear in hand. The eastern gate reopened, and a wild cat stepped onto the field.

The feline had the coat of a leopard but the height and width of a saber-toothed tiger. It postured, opening its mouth to expose oversized teeth, its roar rumbling through the arena like that of an entire pride of lions. Grey's shoulders drew tighter to his ears. After watching the arachneous, the thought of Ayla and Brandt in the same arena as that made his heart race out of control.

Verida placed a hand over his. "Don't worry. This is as good as we could have hoped for. Ayla is known for this. She's showy, survives, and doesn't kill the animal."

"Isn't that the point? To kill it?"

"No." She withdrew. "If you kill every exotic beast you find, you run out of them. The goal of this exhibition is to push the animal until it's too exhausted to attack. The process increases the risk for the gladiator and thereby the excitement for the audience."

"Because the longer they're trapped in there together," Grey finished, "the higher the odds that something will go wrong."

Brandt and Ayla separated, stalking the cat from two sides. Out of the corner of his eye, Grey thought he saw Verida frown. The beast watched as the gladiators approached, flicking its tail in aggravation. When they were within striking distance, Brandt shouted, pulling the cat's attention, and Ayla darted closer, jabbing her spear into the cat's hindquarters. It snarled and spun, batting at her retreating figure. Brandt jumped in and lodged his spear into the top of the cat's foot.

The audience booed.

"What are they so upset about?" Rune asked. "That was amazing."

"They aren't supposed to work as a team. It tilts the advantage, and gladiators who don't follow the rules are punished." Verida's brows cut over her eyes like a dark shadow. "If they aren't careful, they could end up volunteered for the next match with the arachneous."

Grey tracked every movement happening below. "Why would they risk that?"

"It's Brandt's first match." Verida closed her eyes and shook her head. "She's protecting him."

The teamwork continued, mother and son darting in and out of the cat's focus, one jabbing and slicing while the animal turned to deal with the other. The boos grew louder as the cat started to waver, blood pouring down its flanks. Ayla stuck her spear near the ribcage, keeping it close to the surface and dragging the point down, cutting a long gash through the cat's hide.

The cat snarled in pain, but this time, instead of turning toward her, it anticipated and spun to Brandt, who was already lunging in. With the animal now coming at him, Brandt tried to redirect his momentum but landed off balance, his ankle rolling. He sprawled across the ground, the spear wrenched free of his grasp.

The cat leapt, paws extended. Brandt rolled onto one hip, trying to pull his sword while pushing his body backward through the sand with his feet. The weapon was caught in the scabbard, likely by the angle he was trying to use to pull it free, but the extra few feet Brandt had gained prevented the cat from landing directly on him. Still, it was too close, and the beast stepping almost lazily over Brandt's prone body, spreading its jaws and leaning in for the kill.

"No," Verida breathed.

Ayla ran, her limbs moving as fluidly as any supernatural creature Grey had seen. She leapt onto the cat's back, dropped her knees on either side of its shoulders, and slammed her spear into the base of the neck. The cat bellowed, thrashing its head. Ayla threw herself free. Brandt rolled, then scrambled to his feet, pushing himself clear a second before the animal stumbled and collapsed.

The boos were deafening.

Ayla placed herself in front of her son, her spine straight as she glared at the crowd as if daring them to come down and challenge her themselves.

Grey looked around at the sea of angry faces. "What did they expect her to do? Let Brandt die?"

"Yes," Verida said. "Those are the rules of the game."

Tate and Dalbor were secured and side by side in the holding cell, waiting for Sarley to escort them to the match. She would be bringing with her a vial of moreatum—the poison she would dip one of Dalbor's blades into. After that, it would be Tate's responsibility to draw out the match long enough for Sarley to transport his family to safety. And then, when Tate gave the signal, Dalbor would stab him.

The moreatum on the blade would slow Tate's heart, creating the illusion of death. Dalbor would be declared the winner and therefore get to live. The spell would be finalized, keeping Keir out of the council house and away from the Venators. As long as Sarley returned in time, she would be able to administer the antidote to restart his heart. Beltran would bring down the barrier, allowing Tate to escape. He could then help present Verida's version of events to Dracula—hopefully putting him back in his position with the council and keeping Verida alive. And finally, it would reopen the possibility of him someday reuniting with his family.

Dalbor sighed and leaned over his knees.

"It will work," Tate murmured. "Don't worry."

"And if it doesn't?"

"Then today is my day to die. My concern has only ever been Ayla and Brandt."

Dalbor grunted, examining the filth stuck beneath his fingernails. "You know, I'm not saying that I'm not grateful you found a way around killing me. But either way, I stay here. As Ambrose's pet champion."

From beyond the bars came the telltale clomp of boots and the jingle of keys. Tate shuffled forward, expecting to see Sarley, but their armed escort was one member short. The siren was nowhere to be seen. Two guards sidled up to either side of the door, spears at the ready. "It's time."

When Tate and Dalbor arrived in the armoring area, two other gladiators were passing through, being escorted back to their cells. Both had been brutally beaten to the point that Tate couldn't tell who was the victor.

"Tate," one called. "Your wife and son took a little revenge." He grinned, his mouth coated in blood from a newly missing tooth. "Killed that cat." They both laughed. "We'll be toasting them tonight!"

Dalbor stepped up next to Tate. "You didn't tell her, did you?"

"No," he mumbled.

Tate had not told Ayla any of his plans outside of their escape. The plan to momentarily kill him was risky, and she never would've agreed. The problem with a dead cat was—

"Sarley!" The shout floated down the hall right on cue. "Where is she? Sarley!"

Tate couldn't hear what was being said. No doubt Sarley was trying to soothe the owner, but he heard the male's response.

"An accident? An accident! It didn't look like an *accident* from where I was sitting! Those two Venshii worked together. She killed that cat on purpose!"

Dalbor looked to Tate, the look on his face a silent question, asking what they were going to do.

She'll be here. Tate eyed the weapons wall. *She has to be here.*

He hefted the shield he was allowed as compensation for Dalbor's minor healing abilities. Dalbor joined him, buckling on two leather straps that crisscrossed his bare chest and sliding a dagger into a sheath on each. He then strapped a sword at his waist and grabbed his preferred weapon, the ax. Tate chose a sword as well, a dagger secured around one bicep, and a staff with a blade at each end. He preferred to fight without a shield, but he held on to it anyway—just in case he lost his staff and Dalbor was still in possession of that ax.

"Move!" Sarley came barreling toward them, shoving guards out of the way and swearing with every footfall. Her hair was falling out of her topknot, and tiny braids framed her face, sticking to the sweat that dripped down her temples. She positioned herself between the guards and Tate and Dalbor.

"I didn't think you were going to make it," Dalbor said under his breath.

"Never doubt me. I might want to burn this entire place down today, but I hold to my word." She reached into her pocket and pulled out a small clay vial, holding it at her waist to hide it from view as she popped the cork.

"Dalbor, those daggers need sharpening," she announced loudly. "Choose two others."

It wasn't uncommon for Sarley to demand a weapons change, so no one looked in their direction. Dalbor pulled out the daggers and chose two new ones from the wall.

"Let me see." She held up one of the blades, eying it to ensure it was ready for battle. "Much better."

She lowered the dagger, carefully lining it up with the lip of pottery, just as two of the nearest guards burst into laughter. One shoved the other, who lurched to the side and stumbled into Sarley's back.

The vial of poison flew from her hand. Tate jerked to catch it but was too late. The pottery shattered against the stone floor. He stared as his future seeped into the cracks, disappearing as rapidly as his hope.

Sarley whirled, raging against the guard who had caused the disaster. But nothing mattered anymore. They were out of time. Sarley's words were lost beneath the sound of feet stomping in the stands. A rhythmic *boom boom*, *boom boom*. The audience was demanding their finale.

Sarley turned back to Tate, her palms up in apology and her eyes filled with sorrow.

He took her hands in his. "It's all right. You know what matters to me."

She nodded and pulled him in for a rare show of affection, wrapping her arms as far around him as she could. She stretched up on her tiptoes, whispering in his ear, "I swear on my life."

She pushed back and motioned to the guards. "Get them out there."

The stomping rattled the wood beneath their feet, and Rune leaned against the edge of the box as if the simply built half wall would be of any assistance if the stands collapsed.

"Be ready," Verida said. "Beltran should be bringing the barrier down any minute. We don't know what route Tate will have to take to get out, but he's going to need us to help clear a path."

Applause thundered, and the stomping puttered away. Rune reluctantly turned to face the western gate. Two male gladiators were striding across the sand, dressed only in loincloths. Rune's heart dropped into her gut.

The gladiator Tate was fighting had been announced as Dalbor. He was taller, with green skin, arching ram's horns, and biceps so large they didn't look real. Next to him, Tate appeared almost . . . small. It wasn't the size difference, however, that had stolen her ability to breathe. It was the exposure of their brands.

She'd seen the scar tissue on other gladiators scattered here and there. Dalbor had branding marks present on almost every part of his body. Too many to count with him moving. But Tate . . .

Rune couldn't help but remember their conversation—it hadn't been long ago. Tate had been in the library at the council house with her and Grey when he'd revealed what his white scars were from. She could almost hear Grey's strained response: *That's not so many.* And she clearly remembered the dark look Tate had given him as he pulled back his collar. *There are more.*

One brand per kill.

Tate was covered in so many brands that the natural color of his skin had been obliterated. His body was dominated by the raised white scar tissue. *My God.* There were so many that they'd been layered one on top of the other, creating sections of scars that stood gnarled and knotted above the rest. Tears welled in Rune's eyes, and her chest jerked. That was why Tate was always covered. He used clothes to cover proof of the nightmare that had been his life.

Verida put a hand on her shoulder and pulled her away from the edge. "In these boxes, we show no remorse for the fate of the gladiators. Do you understand me?" She pointed. "Go. Stay in the back and out of sight until you can pull yourself together."

Beltran had heard the stomping of feet, the announcement of the final match, and the cheers. All that was left now was to guess the timing of this whole blind fiasco. He peeked out from beneath the dresser.

The wizards had completed their most recent chant over the amulet and resumed relaxing, glasses in hand. Beltran shook his head as he moved toward the back of the dresser. He should be used to surprises like this—absolutely nothing in Eon was ever what it seemed. But he hadn't even suspected something might be off about those barrier spells.

Beltran positioned himself between the dresser and the wall, intending to shift fast enough that he could use both the increase in size and his feet to propel the dresser across the room and into the wizards. It wouldn't be a lengthy distraction, but it should keep them occupied long enough for him to break the amulet and get out.

Tate's and Dalbor's attacks were dizzying, each warrior's blows raining down so hard it looked like it would be the end for the other. But the sparkle of the barrier didn't waver.

"What is going on!" Grey demanded.

"I don't know." Verida's eyes flicked back and forth, taking in the arena. "But we can't wait any longer. We're going to have to anticipate." She waved at Rune to rejoin them. "I'm going to move to the north side. Rune, you take the east. I want you midway up, positioned with a clear view of what's happening. Grey, you'll stay on the south side. I want you near the bottom of the stairs, between the owner's box and Tate. When that barrier drops, Ambrose and Keir will get their magic back, and they will not be happy that someone interrupted the match. Grey, stay out of their way, and make sure Tate does too. If he starts heading for you, turn him around. I'll get him out the north entrance."

Dalbor swung the long-handled ax down, overshooting the edge of Tate's shield by a few inches. Tate leaned his head away from the glint of silver. The ax caught on Tate's shield like a grappling hook, and Dalbor jerked, pulling him forward and pressing the two of them together.

Tate was familiar with this move, which was why he'd allowed it. This was the first part of one of Dalbor's favorites—a sequence of three steps that would have him disarmed in two more seconds. But Dalbor didn't move. He just held him there, glaring over the shield.

"What are you doing?" Tate shouted. "Kill me, damn you!"

"No." Dalbor kneed him in the groin and shoved away. "You're going to fight me."

The crowd booed.

Tate grunted, bending slightly at the waist. "What do you want?"

Dalbor circled, his feet carefully crossing, always ready to change directions. "You really are blind, old man. You have a family waiting out there. Do you know what I have?"

Dalbor attacked, swinging his ax in a downward arc. Tate almost didn't block, almost let it come, but instinct and the undeniable will to live drove his arm, lifting the shield. The ax thudded into the wood. Dalbor wrenched it free.

"Is this where you tell me you have nothing?" Tate said, walking closer, putting himself within range. "As if breathing is of no consequence to you?"

"Worse than nothing." Dalbor grabbed a dagger from the leather strap around his chest and whirled, flinging his arm out. "I have an *owner.*"

Tate held still this time. The blade sliced across his bicep.

Dalbor looked at the blood on his dagger and snarled. "You let me take that. Do it again, and I swear I will fall on my own damn sword and end this match right now."

"Don't you dare."

"Then fight! You know you can beat me."

"I won't. All of this is my doing."

Dalbor bellowed and descended in a flurry of movement.

Tate let him come.

Verida was waiting on the north side of the arena, cursing Beltran's name and coming up with a lengthy list of the things she would do to him if the barrier didn't drop, when she heard a high-pitched screech and then a crash.

She stilled, turning her body in the direction of the animal pens. She knew that sound. Verida took the stairs three at a time, hitching against the upper edge of the arena just as the arachneous darted free across the compound. It scuttled toward the arena, ripping the doors clean off and throwing them behind herself—the same doors that led to the gladiators' cages, to the wizards holding the barrier, and eventually to the gate to the arena floor.

Verida's mouth went dry, and a cold sweat broke out across her palms. Tate was trapped and battling his way across the arena floor with no idea what was headed his way.

Dalbor kicked Tate's knees out from behind him. Tate went down. His shins had barely hit the sand when he felt the kiss of Dalbor's dagger against his neck.

It had been a lengthy battle, longer than he ever allowed them to go, and his chest was heaving, body slick with sweat. But a moment earlier, Tate had seen the flash of silver buttons as Sarley stepped closer to the gate, ensuring he witnessed her return.

Ayla and Brandt were safe.

Dalbor would not die for Tate's mistakes.

He was at peace.

Tate raised his head, taking in the surroundings of his final moments. After all this time, he was finally going to die the way this world had always expected him to. Dalbor had brought him down facing the owner's box, and he looked into Keir's face. It was twisted in fury.

The screams within the arena rose to a crescendo as they anticipated the death blow. Dalbor leaned closer, yelling at his shoulder to be heard. "This is *their* doing. Look at them, watching as we fight their fights for them. Using our blood to further their goals. I had years to listen to the stories of how Dracula would treat you. The horrors he put you through. Hear me, Tate, when I say *Ambrose is worse.*"

Dalbor withdrew, slicing the knife up Tate's cheek, cutting a clean, shallow line. Tate hissed, and then Dalbor was in front of him, pushing the tip of the dagger beneath his chin and forcing him to lift his head.

"Before you walked back into this nightmare," Dalbor said, "I would lie awake at night, deciding whether I was strong enough to kill myself. I wasn't sure, but I am now."

Tate spoke through clenched teeth, the blade nicking the soft skin beneath his chin. "You said you didn't want to die; that's what you said to me when I returned."

Dalbor dipped his head, eyes flashing. "No, I said I didn't want to kill *you*. I don't live, Tate. I breathe, I *exist*. *You* are the only one of us who has ever managed to live. I know the worth of that, and I refuse to take it away."

"You are young, you don't know—"

Dalbor jerked the dagger up Tate's other cheek and promptly returned the blade beneath Tate's chin—using the blood to placate the screaming crowd. "After this match, I will be dead no matter what steps I need to take. I will no longer be Ambrose's pawn. I am begging you for the honor of a champion's death. If you ever cared for me at all, you will disarm me. *Now!*"

There had been too many "mistakes," too many "close calls." He hadn't made up his mind, but Tate could not let this moment drag on. He grabbed Dalbor's wrist and forced it out, twisting until the dagger fell to the ground. Dalbor stumbled away, retrieving the ax he'd dropped. Tate surged to his feet, wiping the sweat from his palm and readjusting his grip on the sword as he stalked toward Dalbor.

The stadium was a mix of boos and cheers.

"Listen to them," he shouted. "They know you've thrown this."

"Go with your family. Live, love. I can't survive another day under Ambrose's thumb. There is only one way I escape. Please, Tate, *please*." Dalbor's yellow eyes burned bright, and though Tate couldn't make out his last two words, he saw them on his lips.

Save me.

Tate's eyes blurred with tears, and he lunged.

The two gladiators moved across the arena, parrying and dodging, dancing in the first real bout since they'd entered the arena. It wasn't long before Tate relieved Dalbor of his ax and felt the advantage tip.

Dalbor felt it, too, and he smiled as he pulled his own sword. "I want to see her face as I die. That's all I ask."

Anger rang through Tate's ears—at the reality of this life, this moment. "Dalbor," he yelled, knowing he would never be heard by the frenzied crowd, "I will never forgive you for this."

"Yes, you will." Dalbor gripped the pommel with both hands. "When you kiss your wife, remember me, and know I'm happier than I was when I lived."

Tate swore, screaming his agony into the sky as he maneuvered himself toward the center of the arena and put his own back to the owner's box. Dalbor charged straight at him. To anyone in the stands, it would appear that he was attacking with deadly intent, but Tate saw the hole. Dalbor's sword arm was held a little too wide, leaving a clean opening for a weapon to enter. Tate bent his knees and lunged, driving the blade into Dalbor's belly and angling up, cutting through enough organs to negate his healing ability.

Dalbor fell forward, his sword dropping soundlessly to the sand. "I can't see her. Tate," he gasped. "I can't see her."

Tate's throat was so raw it felt swollen shut, but he pushed the blade in deeper, lifting up so that Dalbor could lean against him, could use his legs to remain standing.

"Ambrose's face. You should see . . . Thank you." Dalbor relaxed, resting his head on Tate's shoulder. He wheezed out a bout of laughter. "Thank—" He choked, shuddered, and was gone.

Deadweight fell against Tate, and he bore it, not wanting to lower Dalbor to the sand, not wanting to see the gore on his sword. The crowd's shrieking and stomping were so loud they'd become a roar of silence. He stood, motionless, grieving Dalbor's loss while his friend's blood ran down his back.

53

While those around the arena focused on Tate, cheering their champion, Zio twisted to look behind her, her knees pressing against Ryker's. With the match complete, the wizard released the barrier over the owner's box, stepping out of the cage and wiping the sweat from her face with the sleeve of her robes. Inside the box, the spell that protected the two items on the table turned clear, indicating it was time for the winning owner to reach through and claim his spoils.

Keir's grin stretched from ear to ear, maniacal in proportion, as he strolled toward the table. The magic flexed around his hands, verifying his identity before yielding to the victor. Through the barrier, he raised his chin, chest full to bursting as he wrapped his long, thin fingers around the key to Kastaley and the pin to claim his new council seat. Keir's eyes fluttered shut for a moment, the smile twisting into pure glee as he withdrew his spoils.

Beltran's shoulders bulged out, his tail extending, stinger forming. He pressed two lion paws against the back of the already tipping dresser, sending it flying across the room. There were shouts and then thuds as the heavy chest of drawers barreled into the three wizards, knocking them to the floor. Crystal glasses shattered, a waterfall of tinkling accompanying their cries.

With nothing standing between him and the glowing amulet, Beltran leapt, covering the distance in one bound. The wizards were struggling to free themselves, and he heard the first shout of warning as someone caught sight of the manticore in the room. Beltran lined himself up with the table and brought the stinger over his head, smashing the tip into the center of the amulet.

The glass made a ting like the ring of a bell, but his stinger harmlessly slid off, scratching a deep line into the tabletop. He repeated the action again and again, throwing every bit of strength behind the attack, changing the point of impact. It didn't matter. The pendant glowed on, unmarred.

To his right, the dresser exploded. Bits and pieces of wood flew across the room, impaling walls and floor with tiny spearheads. Beltran was to the side of the main spray, but a large shard of wood embedded itself deep in the top of his hip. He snarled and used his tail to pull it free as three very angry wizards got to their feet.

Beltran took a step back, mind racing—reformulating. The only course of action he saw was to take the amulet and run, but the beginning of an incantation was already on the lips of the scarred wizard. With no idea what spell the man was about to throw, he couldn't anticipate a countermove. He had to stop him before he completed it. Beltran lowered his center of gravity, pushed with his back legs, and catapulted across the room. His body unfurled in the air as his stinger whipped forward.

From behind came the screeching of metal.

The scarred wizard looked past the airborne manticore, and his lips stopped moving, blood draining from his face. All three wizards ducked, covering their heads with their hands. Beltran couldn't look—he was midattack—but he felt the wrongness in his gut a moment before something massive struck him from behind. The force whiplashed his head and shoved him off target. He flew sideways, smashing into a wall and sliding to the floor. There was another crash as whatever had hit him impacted the back wall.

Beltran gasped for air, struggling to get up but unable. His limbs were weak, and his paws slipped and slid, landing him back on his belly. He opened his eyes, trying to deduce what had happened, but there were three versions of the room swimming in front of him. Then two. He blinked hard, and his focus tightened.

He'd expected the wizards to be on top of him by now, but they weren't even looking at him. If they were unconcerned by the manticore, what could possibly . . . ?

He reluctantly followed their gaze.

The door to the room was missing—that had been what hit him. The hinges were gone, their location marked by splintered wood and the door itself thrown by the nightmare squeezing itself into the room one spindly leg at a time. The arachneous. An exquisitely crafted woman's face appeared, her body slumped at the waist to clear the doorframe. Once in the room, she drew herself upright, though her neck remained bent due to the low ceiling.

The wizards' hands were all moving in tandem, each speaking the same words, crafting a stronger spell than they'd intended to use on Beltran. An oversized spider's leg flipped out, burying itself in the abdomen of the witch, who gasped. The arachneous's eyes were bright as she withdrew, and the witch dropped to her knees, tipped to the side, and was still. The other two stepped back, their faces masks of shock.

Fools.

Arwin would've already come up with a plan, but these two were inexperienced. They'd been conduits for horror all these years but had never been on the receiving end of it. The arachneous surged forward. She reached down with her feminine hands, grabbing them both by their heads and knocking them together. The crack of skulls reverberated, but not nearly loud enough to suggest permanent damage. They both fell to the ground, unconscious.

It gave Beltran pause. Why would she show mercy? Why now?

The arachneous shook her head as if trying to clear it, then hissed, curling over at the waist and clutching her hands against her abdomen in pain. None of it made any . . .

She snarled, whirling back to face him.

Beltran braced, but her eyes grazed over him as if he weren't there, falling instead on the amulet. He was beyond confused but did not intend on making the same mistake the wizards had. Using her distraction, he made a run for the door, fully expecting to hear the click of those spider legs falling in behind. But there was nothing.

He was almost out when he couldn't help but look over his shoulder midstride. The arachneous picked up the amulet and slammed it onto the table. The initial snap of glass was followed by more cracks, the sound like the spiderwebbing of a mirror. She exerted so much force that the table itself groaned and split down the middle.

Beltran burst into the narrow hall. He elongated his body, pulling all four legs together to propel him forward. He wasn't even halfway to the center of the wagon wheel when he heard what he'd been waiting for: the dreaded tapping of the arachneous in pursuit.

The barrier dropped.

From within the box, Ambrose's head snapped up, and she watched as the sparkling cover receded to the edges. A deviousness twisted her lips and lit her eyes. Keir was too busy admiring his spoils to notice. Zio pushed her cloak from her knees to the ground, her muscles primed for action. Ambrose dove for Keir, smashing into the unsuspecting fae king and knocking him backward onto a chaise.

"Find your sister!" Zio shouted to Ryker as she leapt through the unprotected opening into the owner's box.

Ambrose had her magic, but she was preoccupied. Zio grabbed her by the hair and ripped backward. The fae queen swung around, the key to Kastaley clutched in her hand. Zio pulled a blade, positioning herself between the two fae. Ambrose flung out her free hand, and a pile of white powder billowed out. It would've fallen short had Ambrose not followed it with a gust of wind that drove the powder into Zio's eyes. She hissed and recoiled, rubbing at her face. Burning powder. It had been years since she'd felt its sting.

The room was blurry, but her limited sight would have to do until the effects wore off. Ambrose had used the distraction to change, and her physical form was vanishing as she prepared to escape as a tunnel of wind.

"Keir, get to your army," Zio shouted, grateful she'd thought to instruct him to bring his people in the first place. She looked back at him and noted the confusion on his face—they'd never actually met—but she saw recognition take hold just as quick. "Take the safest route, but get to the council house as fast as you can. Do not delay."

Keir grabbed his whip and the pin and jumped through the window into the crowd.

Ambrose's wind tunnel ripped the door off the box, and she slid into the stands, moving east. Her winds were weak enough that they spared the owner's box and most of those nearest it, but the farther she moved, the larger she became, and it wasn't long before a tornado was ripping through the arena.

Though the barrier was down, there was a reason Ambrose led— her power was above most of her species. With no wizards in sight and no time for the spectators to coordinate an attack, there wasn't anything to do but run. Those not already caught up in her power screamed out warnings, and the northern stands stampeded toward the exits. Those unfortunate enough to be trapped in Ambrose's path were picked up and thrown, their bodies breaking over benches and flying over the top of the arena.

Zio had anticipated a great many things; the extent of Keir's stupidity was not one of them. She gripped her dagger so tight that the muscles on her forearm bulged as she helplessly watched the fae queen escape with the key to Zio's future clasped in her abhorrent little hands.

A spark flashed in her peripheral vision, then another, followed by the telltale glow around the arena's edge of the magical barrier rising. That had not been part of the plan. Something had gone wrong—a colossal mistake that Zio would not usually be apt to forgive. But every now and again, plans failed at the most opportune times. The wizard that had been in the cage by the box was gone—no doubt she'd run to help the moment the protection went down.

Which was absolutely *perfect*.

Ambrose's wind tunnel lifted to the sky. The barrier picked up strength, arching over the center of the arena.

There was a commotion on the south side, and as Rune looked to the owner's box, she swore she saw Ryker sitting just beneath. But then the door shattered outward, and it wasn't long before there was a tornado tearing through the stands. When she looked back to search for her brother, the crowd had erupted into motion, running for the exits and blurring any sight lines she'd had.

With the barrier down, signs of magic started appearing elsewhere. A section of seating cracked and shattered. On the arena floor, Tate was lowering Dalbor's body to the ground when the sand began to lift and swirl around them, battering Tate with virtual arms.

Rune was bumped and shoved as more creatures joined the exodus, pushing past her. Needing to get closer to Tate, she joined them, running down the stairs. From behind, there was a loud hiss and a pop. She was so preoccupied that she barely noticed it, but her subconscious did. Rune flashed back to earth—to her dormitories, St. Louis, the Arch.

She looked over her shoulder, and what she saw made her miss the next step. Rune crashed and rolled down the stairs, coming to rest at the bottom. Someone stepped on her hand, and she yelped, pulling it in as someone else kicked her in the stomach. She jumped up before she could be trampled to death. At the top of the arena, a portal glowed, and leaping out of it were vampires whose eyes were lined with thick black trails.

"Tate!" Verida screamed, waving her arms. It was useless. "*Tate!*"

He had to get out; if that arachneous decided to make its way to the gate, he would be dead. She would be dead. Everything would be over. But that bastard was still down there, letting himself be bested by a pummeling of sand formations as if the world itself were not collapsing around them.

"Get out. The barrier is down. Get out!" She was still screaming—but there was no point. She could barely hear herself.

She never should've separated the group. She didn't know where Grey and Rune were, but Ambrose's magic was destroying the south side of the arena, and a portal had appeared at the top of the east side, bodies leaping from it.

Overhead, there were signs that the wizards were working to reset the barrier. Given what was happening around her, it should've given her a little peace. But an *arachneous* was coming, and she couldn't leave Tate down there alone and trapped.

Verida ran down the stairs and vaulted over the railing.

The barrier rolled overhead, snapping into place as she landed in a crouch. The sand fists that had been pummeling Tate separated into individual grains and rained harmlessly to the ground. Verida slowly stood, craning her neck to look at the barrier above. It was working—otherwise the sand magic wouldn't have dropped—but something was wrong. The barrier was crackling, and across its surface, misshapen holes were forming and then closing again.

54

The whirlwind dissolved, and Ambrose's body free-fell, her silken robes twisting around her. She crashed in the swath of empty stands. Zio watched, her smile restrained, as the thrill of the hunt wound its way through her veins, the sensation a giggle bubbling up from her toes.

It had been so long since she'd felt it. She'd been stuck in that castle for *years*, making due with reports and the retelling of stories, having to watch her plans play out in an amulet through the eyes of her dragon.

She hopped from one bench to another, savoring the feel of the wood as it gave slightly beneath the soles of her boots. Stalking her prey, long dagger in hand, body humming with dark energy.

"Ambrose!"

The fae queen was on her feet and moving. She whirled at the sound of her name.

"You and I have some business."

Ambrose lifted her chin, looking down her nose. "Who are you, and what do you want?"

The imperiousness was such a part of her mannerisms that she'd probably forgotten how to speak any other way, regardless of circumstance. But today, Zio was the one standing at a comfortable advantage.

The fae and elves were reasonably skilled with weapons and formidable when wielding magic, but Ambrose had neither.

"I've come to collect the key you've stolen."

"What key?"

Zio stepped off the bench onto the stone walkway. "The key to Kastaley, of course. I know you aren't going to give it to me"—she smiled, rolling her wrist so that the blade flashed in the sun—"and I'm immensely looking forward to taking it."

The superiority that was the constant mantle of the queen slid from Ambrose's shoulders, pulling her frame lower with it. She turned and ran.

Grey had been shouting for Tate when the panicked flood of escapees swept over him, pulling him down the ramp and to the outer door before he could manage to fight his way back through. Inside, he grabbed the rail.

What was happening?

Not only was the barrier back up, but Verida was down on the arena floor with Tate.

"Grey!"

Even with the chaos around him, he *knew* that voice. There was no place, no alternate universe, no dream or jacked-up vision where he would not have recognized it. Keeping his grip on the rail, he twisted his shoulders, looking over the heads of those still streaming by. The stands themselves were nearly empty now, but standing on a bench in front of the owner's box, a black cloak draping over his broad shoulders, was Ryker.

Darkness twisted in Grey's gut. A snake, coiling in his belly. His inner Venator was demanding to be let out, roaring for justice. In the beginning, he'd been scared of Rune's Venator—of the blinding fury it created that stood in the way of her seeing reality. As such, he'd been determined to keep control of his own.

But as he stared at Ryker, the burn of righteous indignation flowed down his legs and over his arms. It didn't feel blinding—it felt good. It was power and ease and surety. And he made a choice.

Grey let the beast loose.

The inner Venator slithered through him, and Grey directed his unfolding anger at the true abomination he was now facing. It wasn't the paranormal he hated—magic didn't make him uncomfortable—and acting on universal hatred based on species was absurd. But if something in this world did deserve to be eliminated, it was a Venator with a core so rotten that disease spread wherever he landed.

And besides . . .

He and Ryker had a debt to settle.

Tate glared at Verida, pointing at the barrier with his sword. "That doesn't look *down* to me."

"There was plenty of time for you to get out, you big blue oaf. Instead, you were down here swinging at . . . at *sand!*" Verida snatched up Dalbor's ax from where it had fallen. "I have never hated you more than I hate you right now."

She eyed the west gate and then turned to the east, walking backward, craning to see into the stands. "I need to find Grey and . . ."

She spotted Rune at the top of the east side. Her cloak was missing, the black Venator marks on her arms clearly visible, and sneaking up from behind was what looked like two vampires.

"Behind you!" Tate shouted.

Verida was sure Rune couldn't hear him, but as the vampires jumped, Rune fell flat to her belly, dropping out of view between the benches. She reappeared behind her attackers. A dagger in each hand, she lifted both arms over her head and slammed them into the vampires' necks—much like the move Vega had used on Verida the other night. The vampires dropped.

"Where did she learn that?" Tate asked.

"Let's just say she witnessed the aftermath of a very effective demonstration." Verida scanned the arena. "How do we get out of here?"

"We don't."

"We have to. There's an arach—"

Beltran exploded into the arena from beneath the gate, his wings tucked tightly to his human body. He was midtwist when he shouted, "Look out!"

A wad of webbing shot by, barely missing the corner of his wing and splattering into the sand. That was followed by a guard thrown from beneath the gate, his neck already broken.

"The arachneous?" Tate yelled. "*This* is your rescue?"

55

The flow of those trying to escape had thinned, the stands almost empty. Grey shoved his way across traffic and took the first step. Ryker grinned. He unhooked the cloak he was wearing and pulled his sword. Grey freed his own cloak as he climbed, letting it pool on the steps behind.

"Good to see you again. You ruined my life." Ryker took the hilt in both hands, rolling his wrists and spinning the sword. "And now I'm going to kill you for it."

Grey saw red. *His* life? *His life*? But as he stepped up onto Ryker's bench, he smiled at how light he felt. It was probably a combination of factors—experience in battle, the inner Venator, opening up about his past, finding a place where he didn't have to pretend he was something he wasn't—but whatever the cause, Grey was missing a whole lot of things as he pulled his sword.

Fear.

Worry.

Uncertainty.

Insecurity.

Grey advanced.

"Oh-ho." Ryker's mouth twisted into a sneer Grey was all too familiar with. "What's this? Playing brave today?"

"I'm going to let you in on a little secret," Grey said. "I played brave *every day*."

Ryker's brows pulled together.

"That's right. Because what I'm about to do to you now, I was capable of doing every time you beat the shit out of me. But I'm done, Ryker." He held his arms wide. "I'm done caring about what happens to you. You are worthless. A fraud. A scared little boy wearing a man's body."

With every word and every step he threw down, Ryker's sneer faded a little more. Grey took the first move. He launched into action, shouting as he swung his sword in an overhead arc. Ryker barely blocked, and as their blades crashed together, Grey heard a startled grunt.

He leaned in, pressing. "What's the matter? Don't know what to do when your victims decide to fight back?"

Ryker roared, shoving him clear, forcing Grey to take several steps to maintain his balance. "You kidnapped my sister and left me to rot."

As Grey reset his stance, he barked a laugh. "Is that what you think happened? Let me tell you about that night." There was a particularly vindictive joy blooming in his chest, and he maneuvered backward, making space to ensure he had time to finish what he was about to say. "I found your sister in the hall, crying. Because of you. When she came to talk to me, she asked if we could hide in my room—to get away from *you*. Seeing a pattern? But the best part was when, given the opportunity to walk through a portal in a wall, away from *you*, she came willingly." He cocked his head to the side, grinning with an expression that he didn't think he'd ever worn before but that his Venator was enjoying. "In fact, *she didn't say a word about you* . . . until it was too late to go back."

Ryker charged—as expected. Grey held. At the last second, he stepped off the bench onto the stone between, ducking away from Ryker's blade, then jackknifing straight and swinging his elbow back, driving it into the base of Ryker's spine.

Ryker stumbled forward, going down on one knee, but was quickly back up. "That was cowardice."

Grey jumped onto the next bench and higher ground. "A word you're familiar with."

"You don't know what you're talking about."

He pulled a throwing star with his left hand and flicked it at Ryker's feet. It stuck into the wood between his boots.

"You missed."

"Did I? Cowardice is shoving a boy who doesn't fight back into a locker. Or deciding to have your entire football team come after the same boy. Or there's the hands-off approach you liked. Rumors and lies." He checked his grip, centering his weight and still wearing that same strange smile. "I'm not a coward, Ryker. I'm just the kid currently kicking your ass."

Another vampire was approaching, his focus locked on Rune. The black veins were unsettling, but the feral *blankness* in his expression was worse. Rune pulled a dagger in preparation, quickly glancing down to verify that the two vampires she'd already hit with adilats weren't moving.

When the barrier went back up, it had cut off the magic powering the portal. Although only a few vampires had made it through, their eyes matched the ones who'd obliterated an entire werewolf pack. *A pack.* She was just one Venator . . . and alone. Speed and strength were not going to be enough.

But . . . Rune didn't need to be faster or stronger.

Just *smarter*.

The vampire surged toward her, and she turned, jumping downhill and landing three rows below on the stone walkway between benches. Rune dropped to her hands and knees and rolled beneath a bench. Feet smashed down in front of her, just below where her elbow rested. She whipped a hand out, using the dagger to slash through the Achilles tendons on both legs. He collapsed, falling face forward over the bench.

Rune scrambled out, stood, and raised her dagger, lining up the tip with the upper part of his spine. As she brought the blade down, the vampire pushed up with his palms and twisted to the side, grabbing her by the wrist. Her eyes widened. The male's strength was obscene. He twisted so hard she cried out, the dagger falling from her hands.

He yanked her closer. Rune tripped over his useless legs and tipped off balance. The vampire took over what gravity had started and yanked her flat next to him. The edge of the bench pushed painfully into her spine. He let go, but she had time only to lift her head before he used his hands to push himself into the air and came down atop her.

His body pressed into hers, and he stretched his mouth wide, those black-veined eyes staring at her neck. She grabbed him by the throat, but he was so strong. He inched closer. Rune grunted, rolling her head to the side and working with her other hand to wiggle an adilat free.

As Beltran was approaching the gate, worried that one of the guards would try to impale him before they realized what was chasing him, he'd seen that Tate was still in the arena. He'd decided right then and there that if he survived this bloody attempt to save the Venshii, he was going to kill him! What was Tate waiting for? An invitation? And then . . . Beltran saw that Verida was also in the arena, and although he had questions, he considered applying the same sentiment to both of them.

After making it through the gate and shouting his warning, he pulled straight up, intending to take to the sky. He needed to be out of reach from the arachneous and gain a bird's-eye view if he was going to figure out what in the seven hells had gone wrong.

"Left!" Verida shouted.

He didn't question; he rolled left. A sticky attack slid past and arced its way back toward the ground.

"Bel—"

He saw the shine of the barrier with only enough time to pull his arms over his face before he collided into what felt like a wall. His head and neck rolled, and his chin smashed into his sternum, the tips of his wings splaying in awkward angles. His forward motion stopped, and a squeak of breath eked out of him before he was falling.

There was no time to roll over and stay airborne. No time to do a full shift midair. Beltran did the only thing he could and pulled his wings back into his shoulder blades before he shattered every bone in them.

As he shifted, air rushed past his ears, and he blinked at the sparkling magic above. Why was it still up? He'd seen her crack the amulet. Heard it shatter. Directly in his sight line, a hole opened in the barrier, ragged around the edges, then resealed. He braced for impact.

The amulet wasn't destroyed, just defective.

And the arachneous had left two wizards alive.

The vampire was inches from Rune's face. Though she was barely holding him back, it was with her left hand, and she'd crossed it over her body. Between that and his angle, she couldn't move her right arm, rendering the weapon she was clutching in her fist useless.

She had one shot, and it was going to suck.

Rune relaxed.

The vampire fell on her, sinking its teeth into her neck. She screamed, and the inner Venator roared in her ears, tunneling her vision. She rolled to the left, as if trying to pull away from the bite, then brought her other hand up and over and slammed an adilat straight into the hollowness at the base of his skull. The male went slack. Deadweight fell against her.

Rune frantically pushed him away, but while his jaw muscles were loose, his teeth were still embedded, and they tore gashes down her neck on their way out. She sat up, gagging, as the vampire slid to the ground.

Her neck was burning, and she clapped a hand over it, but her heaving breaths soon turned to laughter. She'd done it! She'd . . . A flash of silver caught her eye from the west side of the arena.

Her laughter dropped off as she watched her long-lost brother swing his sword at Grey's neck. Grey arched backward, the blade skimming too close to be anything other than what it looked like.

"Ryker, no!" Rune screamed, already running.

56

Sarley stepped out from around the corner she'd dodged behind when the arachneous came through. Out of the ten guards who had been near the gate, five were dead on the ground, one body was lying out in the sand, and the other four stared at her, mouths wide and weapons held loosely in their hands.

The beast was in the arena. She ran to shut the gate but stopped short. The winch was coated in arachneous webbing so deep she couldn't see the gears. Outside, Tate held a sword and shield, watching as the arachneous climbed up the barrier. The creature spat. Tate's shield came up, taking the sticky mass.

"Get them out," Sarley said softly, then again with force as she faced the remaining guards. "Get them all out."

They stared blankly. One spoke. "What?"

She rubbed a hand over her nixie bubble. "Our job is to protect the owners' investments. Get the gladiators out of their cells and take them into the mountains before that thing comes back through this gate."

"You think they're going to just . . . walk with us?"

"Let them know this is their one chance at life and that I'll be coming right behind you. Go!"

Sarley armored up with as many blades as she could carry and stormed down the only tunnel without any gladiators. She didn't give a rat's ass at this point if those wizards lived or died—frankly, she thought a run through the arena would do them all good—but she needed a favor. And saving a wizard's life had to be worth something.

57

Ambrose was running flat out—Zio doubted she'd done that in some time. The fae queen was out of the arena and nearing the second set of doors, almost on the other side of the magical barrier, and within feet of regaining her magic. Because Zio had allowed it.

She wanted to see hope on Ambrose's face before she ripped it away.

Zio lunged, grabbing the collar of Ambrose's robe and jerking her to the right, whiplashing her into one of the stone pillars. Those still looking for escape parted around them. She seized a handful of silk from the front of the robe and pulled Ambrose forward, then slammed her back again, making sure her head cracked against the stone.

As Ambrose's head spun, Zio stepped in, using her body weight to keep the fae pinned. She pressed her left forearm over Ambrose's chest, rested the blade of a dagger against her neck, and dug a knee into her leg.

"Where. Is. The key?"

Ambrose struggled, calling out to a young male fae who was running past. The fae looked briefly but moved on.

Zio laughed. "That little veneer trick is impressive, but it just cost you. He has no idea who you are."

"Why are you working with Keir? He's a pretender. Whatever he's giving you, I will promise you more."

Edging closer, Zio whispered, "I'm not working for Keir. Keir is working for me." When she pulled back, Ambrose had gone very still. Zio could see her wheels turning.

"You're not fae."

Her lips turned up at the edge, and she shook her head. "No."

"You're not human."

"No. This is a delightful game. I'll make you a deal. After you hand me the key, I'll let you know what I am. Although . . ." She clicked her tongue. "I will have that key either way."

Zio changed the angle of the blade. It didn't take much, and Ambrose's clear blood bloomed around it. Her mouth gaped, and her eyes rolled, looking for help that wasn't coming.

"You have two choices, *Your Majesty*. I can take the key and be on my way . . . or I can take you elsewhere. Somewhere we can have a little more time together. I would love to see how deep this veneer goes. If I take off a few layers of skin, will it be black . . . or green?"

"Stop." Ambrose's blood was pooling between her chest and Zio's forearm. "The key. It's . . . tucked in . . . the . . . front."

Zio pursed her lips. "There. That wasn't so hard." She leaned in with her hips as she removed her arm from across Ambrose's chest. "I wouldn't move; this blade is dangerously close to your windpipe." She wiggled her hand down the front of Ambrose's robe, sliding it between her breasts, and withdrew a rose gold key. Zio smiled and tucked it in her pocket.

"What will you do with such a prize?" Ambrose said. "It is useless to you. Let me pay you for it, anything you desire."

Zio took a step back, steadily changing the position of the blade until the tip was over Ambrose's voice box. "You cannot begin to imagine what I will do with this, because you have forgotten our history.

There is a wealth hidden in Kastaley that neither you nor Omri knew to look for."

Ambrose's eyes were blazing now, and the edges of her nostrils flared. "You have the key. Our deal is complete. Now tell me, what type of creature are you?"

"Why do you want to know? So you'll have somewhere to start looking for me?" She smirked. "I'll do even better. You and the council refer to me as Zio, but—"

At that name, Ambrose's eyes widened. She opened her mouth.

Zio clucked her tongue, shaking her head. "Wait . . . wait. You'll want to keep listening, because my birth name is the important one. My parents once called me . . . Calah."

It had been so long since Zio had said that name aloud that it felt strange on her tongue, like coming home to a place that had decayed away.

"That's impossible," Ambrose spat. "I don't know where you heard that name, but . . ."

The words died as she started to see the similarities. Zio knew she would, and she followed the path of the queen's eyes. "Same nose, yes. Ah, same cheekbones. The eyes used to be brown, hair black. That's right."

Ambrose looked over the rest of her.

Zio shrugged. "And that's . . . almost the same, isn't it?"

"But . . . you . . . you're—"

"Dead? Not yet. Despite your very best efforts."

Zio dropped her arm, letting the blade at Ambrose's throat fall away while pulling a second dagger. The transition was smooth; the first blade stopped at her side as she raised her other arm and slammed the dagger into Ambrose's chest, purposefully aiming an inch from her beating heart.

The fae queen clutched at the hilt, dropping to her knees.

Zio strode closer, her words ice over her tongue. "*That's* what it feels like to have absolutely everything ripped from beneath your fingers."

She bent at the waist. There was more to say, but the barrier collapsed again. Ambrose breathed in, her back arching as her magic returned. In one slick motion, Zio slit her throat wide open.

The barrier returned. She rolled her eyes at the timing and straightened, wiping the blade on her pants. "I thought you should know."

Ryker had obviously been trained well, and he'd survived the arachneous—assuming Zio hadn't assisted once Grey was pulled from the vision—but he'd yet to be in battle. Grey had fought werewolves, fae, and a damn dragon. He leapt, using his Venator strength to propel himself into a flip, up and over, landing on the opposite side of Ryker.

"Cute trick," Ryker sneered, turning.

Grey dipped down, bracing himself with one hand, and swept Ryker's leg.

There was a grunt of surprise as he fell, his sword clattering free. He cracked his head, and his body slumped awkwardly between two benches in the shape of a C. Grey jumped on top, drilling a knee into Ryker's chest as he brought the tip of his sword against his throat.

Ryker was breathing heavily, and the movement caused the blade to nick the thin skin of his throat. "Please," he ground out. "You don't want to do this."

"I do." Grey's lips formed carefully around each word, feeling the truth of them even as he knew he could never come back from this. "More than I have ever wanted anything."

His inner Venator had merged so completely with his past trau-mas that Grey could see nothing other than *this* path. It was better this way. It was the only way. Ryker could not be allowed to stay in this world, and Rune was too blind to see what a monster her brother was. It had to be him. It had to be now. He raised his center of gravity and leaned over the sword.

"Goodbye, Ryker."

"*Grey, no!*"

He jerked up to see Rune dashing around the owner's box.

58

When the barrier vanished, the arachneous had fallen straight to the ground like a rock, but it had barely gotten its legs in order before the magic was up again.

Beltran, Verida, and Tate were huddled beneath Tate's shield, using it to block the attacks. When it got too heavy, Verida would pop out and use an ax to scrape the bulk of the goo away.

"What is going on?" Verida demanded. "How did we go from getting rid of the barrier to . . . to . . . *that?*"

"Turns out the wizards were using an amulet to power it," Beltran said absently. "I thought it was broken, and it obviously is, but not completely." He cocked his head to the side as the arachneous resumed climbing the barrier at a . . . well, leisurely pace. "Does anyone else find it odd that she's being so passive?"

Verida scowled. "You call the number of gladiators she's ripped to shreds today passive?"

"No, but the number of attacks she's conveniently dropped right on this shield strikes me as odd."

Tate grunted, but before he could say anything else, the barrier vanished *again*, and the arachneous landed in another splay of legs.

Determined to take better advantage of the mishap this time, Beltran shoved Verida and Tate. "The gate, hurry. Before she's up."

They ran, but the arachneous recovered faster this time. She hissed and screeched at their escape attempt. Beltran looked over his shoulder to see her running on the side of the arena wall, parallel to ground. She pushed off, those long legs helping to spring her further across the arena, and dropped right between them and the open gate.

They skidded to a stop, and Tate moved to the front, holding up the shield. The arachneous stepped closer, chattering a series of sounds that sounded like speech. Beltran had no idea what she was saying, but something had changed. The eyes were different, harder . . . more intense? He couldn't even explain to himself what he was seeing. It was indefinable—just the awareness of a difference and the distinct feeling that while they'd been in some danger before, they were in very real danger now.

"You're both going to need swords," Tate said under his breath as the arachneous scanned its three choices of victim. "Dalbor's is by his body, but the rest are on the other side of the gate."

"Or we could try to escape over these walls while the barrier is down, like we originally planned," Beltran said.

Verida shook her head. "I don't think that's going to work. You should've seen that thing earlier. She has excellent—"

"Aim," Beltran finished, his brows pulling together. "Yes . . . I was just thinking about that."

Except what he was actually thinking was how many times she'd *missed*.

Him in particular.

"Here we go." Verida spun and took off in the opposite direction, running toward Dalbor's body at full vampire speed. The arachneous darted after her. Tate dove to the side—out of the way—then pushed up and ran to help Verida.

Beltran used the distraction she'd offered to make his own run for the gate. He bent, taking the first sword he saw off the dead body of a guard, but as he stood to rejoin the others, something clicked.

This was the second time Beltran had seen the arachneous's strange transformation. In the room at the end of the hall, she'd left two of the wizards alive and ignored his presence entirely. Then something had changed, and she'd come after him like the crazed wild thing she was. In the arena, she'd been acting like she was biding time, but now . . .

Beltran's eyes slid up to the place where the barrier had been moments before, wondering.

Tate rushed for the front of the beast, shield up. She twisted, one leg out, clobbering the shield and sending Tate soaring through the air. He smashed into a wall and dropped. Before the arachneous could advance for the kill, Verida dove in, acting as a distraction. She barely managed to roll out of the way before a long black leg punched a hole through her chest.

"Grey!" Rune screamed again, her pitch driving up with panic.

Grey leaned back, and Ryker pushed him off his chest and into the bench behind them. And then she was there, dropping to her knees, reaching for her brother.

Ryker shoved her away, yelling as he scrambled to get out of the position Grey had pinned him in. "He's a maniac!"

Rune sat back on her heels, face red, looking between the two of them. She scowled, and her focus swung back to Ryker. "What did you do to him this time? Huh? I watched you almost take his head off! How much do you think he's supposed to take before he fights back?"

Grey wasn't quite sure he'd heard her right.

Ryker's jaw dropped, and he stared at his sister as if she'd committed a heinous betrayal of the worst kind.

"Don't look at me like that, Ryker. I saw you from over there. You attacked him. What did you expect him to do? Stand there and not defend himself?"

"Verida, hold on!" It was Beltran's voice, bellowing across the empty stadium.

Rune jackknifed to her feet, scanning the arena floor. Grey followed. Below them, Verida was being picked up by her ankle, grasped in the human hand of the arachneous. She swung herself up, grabbed the arachneous's elbow, pulled back a fist, and punched the outside, hyperextending the joint. The beast hissed and released.

"Come on!" Grey grabbed his sword as Verida dropped to the ground. He bounded down the stairs. "They need our help."

Rune hesitated, watching her brother haul himself to his feet.

This was all wrong.

It wasn't how their reunion was supposed to go.

She'd planned to hug him, tell him how sorry she was, how hard it had been for her to keep going while knowing he was locked up with some crazy villain.

Rune held out a hand. "Ryker, help us."

His jaw set, a bright flush across the top of his cheekbones. "Us? You mean Grey?"

She sighed. "I can't do this right now. They need my help. I'll be back soon. Just . . . don't move."

He seized her wrist, his hazel eyes bright. "Don't leave me."

"Ryker . . ." Her voice cracked as she turned to look down at the mash-up of species that had been her friends and family since crossing over. "I can't do this with you right now. They're in trouble. I have to go."

Grey vaulted over the railing and dropped into the arena. He'd barely cleared the edge when the glow started and the barrier rushed back into place. *No!* She'd been so desperate to see her brother, frantic to find him. And now he was standing right in front of her, and she wanted to kill him!

She twisted, punching Ryker in the shoulder. "What have you done?"

"Rune. Rune, stop!" His eyes flicked around, checking to make sure they were alone. He put his hands on her shoulders and pushed her to the bench, sitting beside her. "We probably don't have much time. I need you to listen."

Her eyes slid past him, to the arena—to her friends. The arachneous tipped to the side, falling, but she couldn't see who'd managed to knock the legs out from under it.

Ryker leaned, placing his head in her field of vision. "I didn't think I'd ever see you again."

Tears welled up in her eyes, and she sagged. "Me neither. God, Ryker, I'm so glad you're OK."

"I am. I'm safe. I'm perfectly safe. It's you that I'm worried about."

"I'm . . ." She frowned. "What?"

"Zio told me all about the—"

"Zio! Ryker, no, Zio is horrible. She's—" Rune tried to stand, but Ryker still had a hold on her arm, and he gently pulled her back down.

"How did you escape?" she asked.

"It doesn't matter. Please, just listen to me for five minutes."

Rune jerked her arm free, pointing toward the arena floor. "They might not *have* five minutes!"

And then he started talking, his intensity pinning her in place. About the council and the Venators of old. How the Venators had protected earth and how the council didn't want that anymore. How they'd tried to exterminate the Venators to gain access to the portals between worlds. And how now that everyone had forgotten the truth about Eon, the council was actively working in secret to reopen the portals and return to earth to take their revenge and control of that world.

"Wait." Rune held up a hand. He'd repeated most of the stories she'd been told, but with the opposite twist on each piece. "You're trying to tell me that the council is trying to *open* more portals to earth?"

Last she'd heard, they'd been trying to keep them closed.

Ryker nodded solemnly. "The council wants to bring all of this"—he motioned wide—"to earth. It's what they wanted to do before, when the gates were open, and the Venators stopped them. And now it's up to us. Don't you see? Zio isn't evil. She's the only thing standing between the council and earth. She's working to prevent them from reopening the portals."

Rune shook her head.

"*Think about it!* What if these things were in our home? What if there was a vampire after our parents . . . or *that* god-awful thing"—he pointed at the arachneous—"wandering down our streets and knocking down our doors?" He took her hands between his. "You have to come with me. I can keep you away from the council, away from all of this. And then it'll be you and me." He smiled brightly. "The Jenkins twins, saving the world."

Her head hurt. She didn't know what was true anymore. And if he were right—if those portals opened and this world intermixed with hers . . . She *could* imagine the hell that would follow.

Ryker read her indecision as consent, and he smiled, reaching up to muss her hair—the way he'd done since they were twelve. "I love you, little sis. I told Zio you wouldn't let me down."

A screech of pain ripped her from the moment, and she surged to her feet. The barrier was gone—how had she not noticed? The arachneous had one leg through Grey's shoulder, and his legs were flailing as she lifted him into the air.

"Rune?"

She picked up her sword and stepped past her brother. "Don't go anywhere, Ryker. I mean it—*don't move*. I love you, and . . . and I'll be right back. We can finish talking then," she shouted as she ran. "*I'll be right back!*"

"Rune!" He screamed her name with an undercurrent she'd never heard from him before.

It echoed around her, piercing her heart, and she felt his pain. Rune almost tripped as she stopped on the edge of a stair, turning to look at her brother.

Ryker's face was red, and he was shaking, his hands balled at his side. He seethed with a fury that he'd never directed toward her. "You *will not* pick Grey Malteer over me."

Grey cried out, and Verida shouted orders.

"Ryker," she pleaded, desperate for him to understand. "I love you. I'm not *choosing* him—I'm saving him. I will not stand here and let him *die!*"

Zio waited unseen on the ramp leading to the stands, her head just below the top edge where the seating began, listening as a series of events too perfect for her to have hoped for unfolded.

She could've stopped the fight between Ryker and Grey, intervened and killed the boy. She could've overpowered Rune and brought her back to the castle to appease Ryker. They were all so wrapped up in emotion that the attack would've been easy.

But she was waiting for Ryker to break.

It was the only way he was going to let go of his insistence that they find his sister. Until Rune became something other than the saint he'd made her out to be, Ryker would never fully belong to Zio.

He screamed his sister's name. Zio smiled at the pain in his voice. Feet came pounding down the stairs, and she rolled her head, watching as Rune entered her vision, jumped over the railing, and disappeared again from view.

Zio waited, counting out seconds, then straightened and walked the few more steps into the arena. Ryker was in the stands, still staring at the place his sister had vanished with dull, hard eyes, anger and devastation writing their presence across his shoulders. He was, as she'd hoped, broken.

"Ryker?" Zio made a show of looking around, as if she didn't already know they were alone. She ran to him. "What's wrong? What happened? Are you all right? Did you find Rune?"

He didn't look at her, staring instead at the arena floor. "You were right," he said, his lips barely moving. "Rune picked Grey."

"I'm so sorr—"

"Did we get what we needed?"

"We did."

"Then let's go." He walked around her and headed down the stairs.

"But your sister—"

"She made her choice!" Ryker turned and descended down the ramp, never looking back.

Zio's smile was serene, her fingers brushing against the outline of the key in her pocket. "And you've made yours."

59

The barrier sputtered out, and Beltran shot straight up, rushing to take in the bird's-eye view he'd been needing to create an escape plan. Far outside the arena walls, he spotted a line of guards and gladiators trudging into the mountains.

Sarley had ordered them out.

Of course she had. There was an arachneous running free.

That was good news. The tunnels were unguarded and without their siren. But as long as that thing was still alive, it would follow wherever they ran. They had to kill it. And their attempts at that were going . . . well, so far.

Below, Verida was working to free Tate from the webbing wrapped around his legs. Grey was on the ground, blood coming from the wound in his shoulder and lucky to be alive. But it looked like the arachneous was coming around for another go. As it neared Grey, Rune came sprinting across the arena, running straight under the arachneous's legs.

She was too close. Beltran's heart lodged in his throat, and he cut into a steep dive, knowing he would never make it in time. Rune emerged. The arachneous reared. Rune slid to a stop, turned, bent one knee, and swung the other leg, using the inside edge of her boot to send a pile of sand flying.

The majority fell short, but some arced high enough, spraying across the arachneous's face. She hissed, pulling away, rubbing at her eyes with the back of her arm.

Rune was on to something.

He pulled up, toes skimming the ground, and scooped up a pile of webbing, holding it well away from his body.

The arachneous had already refocused and lunged toward Rune. Beltran flew over, wrapping his hands over the creature's head and smashing the mass across her face. He tried to let go, but it was so sticky that, though his wings pushed him forward, his hands remained adhered, and his feet flew over his head. Finally, the combination of momentum and his body weight yanked him free, and he spun away, crashing into the sand.

Beltran hurriedly pushed up onto his hands. The arachneous had stopped, her eyes and mouth covered in the sticky substance. She reached up and scraped it away as if it were water. He deflated. Of course she could handle her own webbing without getting caught in it.

The barrier returned.

The arachneous turned its attention to Rune, who was helping Grey run toward Verida and Tate, ignoring the more obvious target sprawled in the dirt in front of her. *Again.*

Beltran set his jaw and took to the air.

He smashed down in front of Rune and Grey, planting his feet against the charging beast and wondering when exactly he'd started testing theories with his life.

The arachneous skidded to a stop.

Dust and sand billowed around them as Beltran slowly looked up. She towered over them, breathing heavily, her head ticking to the side as if trying to escape someone whispering in her ear. From behind him, Beltran could barely hear Grey muttering instructions to Rune. A moment later, she shoved past his wings, sword drawn, aiming straight for the small split in the exoskeleton.

Beltran's eyes followed the path of the blade. She was going to make it. He saw the twitch of movement in the legs as the arachneous realized what was coming and prepared to escape, but there wouldn't be time.

And then, he saw *it*.

Settled against the black exoskeleton, camouflaged by its matching color, was an obsidian pendant. Identical in shape to the ones in the random reports he'd read about possible shifter activity.

"No!" He leapt forward, shoving Rune off balance. She tripped and sprawled across the ground.

The arachneous hissed and raised a leg, ready to impale her. He threw himself across Rune's body, folding his wings around them. He cringed, waiting, but as before, no attack came.

"Beltran?" Rune gasped.

"All right, love," he whispered in her ear. "I need you to trust me. I'm going to lead her away. Once I'm gone, tell the others to take the tunnel to the main entrance. Tate will know it. I'll meet you in the cave at the top of the mountain."

He pushed up, staring down the arachneous as he helped Rune to her feet and nudged her toward Grey. Beltran walked backward, slowly, wanting to make sure the arachneous would follow before leaving Rune. But her large eyes slid away from Beltran and toward the group. She hissed, opening her mouth.

"Seven hells." Beltran lunged, snatching a dagger from Grey's belt. "Not another step!" He held the blade against his carotid artery, backing away. "I don't know how much blood a shifter has to lose before his heart stops beating, but I'm willing to test it today. Walk with me, or I stick this through my neck."

The arachneous swung around, following obediently.

"That's it," he murmured. "Come on."

Rune relayed the message. She could see the same questions on the others' lips as were on hers, but now was not the time to sort them out. As they ran for the gate, she veered to the side, craning her neck to see over the sidewall and into the stands, hoping to see Ryker.

But he was gone.

Part of her had known he would be.

Her throat grew tighter, and her lungs burned, but her tears were missing. She would cry later—when she found them in the wreckage of what this day had cost her.

They ran under the gate, and Rune made sure she was at the back of the group. With directions from Tate, Verida sped ahead, listening for anything or anyone that might stand between them and freedom. Rune moved slower and slower, putting distance between them. When nobody noticed she'd fallen behind, she stopped and went back the way they'd come.

Beltran's mood grew more and more somber as he walked. He'd planned on taking the arachneous as deep in as they could go, but they weren't that far down a tunnel before she stopped and refused to move.

He stared at her. Her eyes drifted up. His followed. If he were to guess, she'd stopped on what was the edge of where the stadium towered above them. The line where the magic of the barrier stopped.

"It's the wizard's magic, isn't it? It's interfering with the control Zio has over you . . . Elyria."

The arachneous started to shrink and shift until Elyria stood before him, wearing her favorite form. Pointed ears barely stuck through her long, straight black hair, and her copper skin lacked its brilliance in the low light.

Elyria's eyes were pinpricks of pain, and beads of sweat were breaking out over her forehead.

"I don't understand what's going on," he said.

She laughed, but it was strained. "You saw more than she did. She said the barrier couldn't . . . couldn't . . . affect—"

"Zio doesn't know you have your will back?"

"I don't have . . . it . . . all." She groaned, clamping her teeth together as she tossed her head back, the muscles in her neck straining. "I can't . . ."

She fell to her knees, and Beltran surged forward, dropping in front of her. He set down the blade, gathering her small, delicate hands into his. "Talk to me. How is she controlling you? What can I do?"

Her head snapped back up, eyes cutting to the blade on the ground. Beltran watched as the same indefinable switch happened and the Elyria he knew vanished. She grabbed him by the neck, jerking him closer.

"Can't kiiiii—" She squeezed, digging her nails into his skin. "Can't kiiii—"

Beltran wrenched free, rolling away and grabbing the dagger as he did. On his knees, he held it to his throat, breathing hard. "You can't kill me. Got it." He rolled his eyes at the mess they were in. "Seven hells."

Elyria flopped onto her back, writhing, her hand clawing at her chest. He didn't know what was going on or how to help. The obsidian pendant around her neck slid to the side, resting on the ground. His eyes narrowed. Whatever Zio had done, he was going to bet it originated from that. He carefully angled toward her, holding the blade in place, his fingers brushing the obsidian.

"No!" Elyria screeched, rolling in on herself, wrapping both her hands and her body around the pendant. She tried to form words but expelled only mouthfuls of empty air.

"I'm sorry. I'll stop. I'll stop!" Beltran backed away until he hitched against the tunnel wall.

What was he supposed to do? He needed answers, but the questions were killing her. He reset the blade, racking his brain and probing at the problem from every direction.

"Elyria," he began, hoping, "can you tell me what color your eyes are?"

"Green."

His eyes cut to her. She was sitting up. Her breathing had returned to normal, and her eyes were shining with pride.

"And where did we live?"

"Mage's Circle."

"Why are you here?"

Gasping.

"What are you orders?"

Gasp, a croak, more clutching over her heart.

His chest was tight, his eyes swimming. "Damn it!" He banged his head against the tunnel wall. The force knocked the tears free, and they ran down his cheeks. "If you take it off, it kills you. It you talk about your orders, it kills you. If you disobey the orders, it kills you." He looked at her, wiggling the hilt of the dagger. "But why this?"

"I'm very happy with Zio." A strange smile stretched across Elyria's face—stiff . . . drawn on. "You should come with us. Leave the council."

He peered at her, then slid down the wall. "That's what I thought. You aren't allowed to kill me because you're supposed to bring me back. I assume she's got another one of those fabulous pendants waiting for me."

He closed his eyes, not wanting to see Elyria try to answer. He couldn't watch her mouth gaping like a fish while she clutched at her chest. When he opened them, she was sitting on her heels, her hands folded on her knees.

"*I* would *love* to have *you* with me. Zio will treat us well." The emphasis had been clear enough.

"I love you too." His voice cracked.

She pressed her lips together, fighting the next words as they came out. "We could be together again."

"I hear you." He sighed. "We will be together again someday. Back in the Mage's Circle."

Elyria's shoulders relaxed.

The sheer quantity of emotions breaking free inside him was so intense he didn't know how to process them. Being here, with her—it was too much. In this moment, Beltran was a boy again. And he was lost. A sob rattled its way free, then another. They refused to be contained. Careful to keep the blade at his neck, he leaned over his knees and cried.

"Mother," he croaked through his sobs. "I don't know what else to do."

"*Mother?*"

Beltran jerked his head up so fast at the third voice the blade nicked his skin.

Elyria snarled. "Venator."

At the mouth of the tunnel, a female form was silhouetted, blurred by his own tears. He blinked, hard. As Rune came into focus, time spun away.

She knew.

Rune had heard him name Elyria as who she really was to him. *Mother.* In order to maintain freedom from a world that always wanted

560

to use them, it had to appear to their enemies that there were no strings to pull. No pressure points to leverage. If Zio realized . . . With the level of control he'd just witnessed, he would expect his mother's torture to be public and horrific and to last until Beltran walked into Zio's castle of his own free will.

Elyria was already shifting, legs growing, fur exploding. In seconds, a wolf was tearing down the hall. She leapt, punching into Rune's shoulders and knocking her flat.

With Rune in imminent danger, he felt all over again what it would cost him to lose her. Something new broke inside, and for the first time in more years than he cared to count, Beltran made a choice with his heart alone. He ran down the tunnel, shifting into a wolf as he went, not a single reservation trailing behind him.

Rune screamed, turning her head to the side, away from the teeth that were inches from her face. She kicked and pushed, trying to pull herself free, her sword just out of reach from her stretching fingers.

Beltran leapt and kicked off the wall, coming at Elyria from the side. He smashed into her, and they rolled, snarling and biting, evenly matched. Elyria pulled free, shifting back into her elven form. Beltran followed her lead.

"Leave her alone!"

Elyria's eyes went straight to his empty hands. She stepped forward, grunting as she tried to resist.

He swore and picked up the sword Rune had dropped. Sticking it beneath his chin, he raised a brow. "Better?"

"She knows!" Elyria shouted, jabbing a finger. "She has to die."

Beltran's eyes fluttered closed, needing to say the word but dreading it. "No."

Elyria rushed to shove past him. He cut to the side and extended the blade, pressing the tip over his mother's heart. "Has Zio ordered you to come back alive?" When she didn't move again, he relaxed.

"How magnanimous of her. Remind me to say thank you next time I see her."

"What have I taught you?"

With those words, he saw his mother again as she'd once been. It made it worse. "I remember, and I have done *all* of it. I have sacrificed everything to protect us. *Everything.* And I will *never* stop trying to free you from Zio. But I will not—" His voice wobbled, and he swallowed. "I will not allow you to kill Rune."

She shook her head. "This cannot be."

"It is. If you try to hurt her, you will have to go through me."

She took one step backward, then another. And Beltran didn't think he'd ever be able to forget the pain on her face. "You choose a Venator?"

He started to shake his head no, then yes. What was he supposed to say? What did he want? What did Rune want? In the end, he said the thing he'd been aching to. "Mother, I've missed you so much."

Something passed over Elyria's face. He recognized it immediately.

"Rune," Beltran said. "The barrier's down. She can't help herself. Run."

Elyria started to shift.

"*Run!*"

60

Rune tore down the tunnel, arms pumping, as the sounds of a battle exploded behind her. Growls, roars, and bodies smashing into walls. And it didn't sound like Beltran was winning, because despite her speed, the sounds were getting closer.

She burst into the wagon wheel, scanning the tunnels that shot off in every direction. Which one had Tate taken? She had no idea. They all looked the same. From behind her, something or someone smashed into a wall so hard she felt the vibrations under her feet.

Beltran's voice, strained. "You're under orders now, Elyria, and I'm the one Zio wants." There was a grunt, a female screech, another bang into a wall. "If you're going to bring me back with you, you're going to have to catch me."

Every swear word in the book ran through Rune's head, her eyes flicking across her options. *Which one, which one, which one!* She heard the flap of leather wings and looked over her shoulder.

It didn't *matter* which tunnel as long as it wasn't this one!

She ducked into the nearest option, shoving her back against the wall. But she was breathing so hard it sounded like she was wheezing into a damn megaphone. She leaned her head against the wall, trying to dull the sound as best she could.

Beltran cut through her view, flying across the wagon wheel in a blur and whoosh. Elyria was right behind, white-feathered wings stretched wide. Rune poked her head out just as Elyria disappeared down the only tunnel she recognized—the one leading to the arena floor.

The barrier's down.

Beltran was leading Elyria on a chase out of the arena and away from the rest of them.

Rune stepped out, her knees weak. She stared at the darkened tunnel they'd vanished into, replaying the scene she was never supposed to see over and over again in her head.

If you want her, you're going to have to go through me.

You choose a Venator?

The sound of feet startled her, and she whirled, patting her pant legs to see what weapons were left. Tate burst into the wagon wheel. Seeing her, he exhaled.

"Rune! What are you doing? Where's Beltran?"

"He's gone." She pointed. "The barrier's down. He got . . ."

Rune almost said, *His mother.*

Two minutes. That's how long it took for her to almost spill his secret.

She knows, Elyria had said. *She has to die!*

Rune cleared her throat. ". . . the arachneous to chase him. They're probably in the stands by now."

"He's leading it away." Tate let out a sigh that turned his body to liquid. "It's over. Come on."

They hadn't gone far before Tate stopped, staring at a burning torch. He snatched it and walked on without a word. When they emerged aboveground, the bottom framework of the stands extended above them, large support beams crisscrossing from the ground to the upper levels.

Tate crouched next to one of the beams. He jabbed the end of the torch into the dirt, leaning it against the wood. "I never said it aloud, but I always told myself that one day, I was going to burn this place to the ground."

Wearing a loincloth, his past branded across his skin, Tate stepped back and watched in silence as the wood blackened and the flame caught.

Sarley trudged through the empty underbelly of the arena, a quietness surrounding her that she'd forgotten the feel of. Only the lingering stench made it feel like home. She'd escorted the surviving wizards to freedom, and the gladiators had been taken out of harms way. The nixie bubble hadn't moved, which was *grand*. She must've adhered closely enough to her orders.

It had taken a very long time, but she'd finally reached the end of her rope. Her parents would never free her from this, and if she couldn't figure out a way to leverage a favor from the wizards, well—perhaps she'd find a way to end her own misery.

Heading for the exit, Sarley breathed in the fresh air. Sunlight filtered through the stands. She stopped, staring. Ahead, a torch had been wedged against a beam. Flames were licking up the side, but the trail was still weak—thin and no more than a couple feet in length. Some dirt, her jacket, and she could easily snuff it out before it spread to the stands.

Nibbling the edge of her lip, she took one step, then another, glancing at the bubble in her arm. One more. Her back was now to the growing flames.

She'd never been instructed to protect the arena itself, now had she?

Sarley smiled, putting one foot in front of the other and humming as she abandoned her prison to fend for itself.

61

Verida was still in the Underground, finding food and clothing. Grey was sleeping as his body worked to heal his shoulder wound. And Tate leaned against a wall, looking particularly broody. The cave was stuffy, smelled like dirt, and was still missing Beltran. Rune was pacing like a caged animal when Tate finally suggested she take a walk.

She didn't go far—partway down the mountain path they'd followed this morning—before she sat, letting her legs dangle over the edge of the mountainside as she looked across the valley. The raging inferno that had been the arena illuminated the night sky with reds and oranges. Finally alone, her mind jumped through the events of the day, poking at each like a loose tooth. Feeling the pain and then moving to the next.

Ryker had been right there—trying to kill Grey, but *right there*. The look on his face as she left him had been . . . awful. The feeling of looking up into those stands to find them empty . . . had been worse. An all-too-familiar guilt sat heavy in her chest.

And as far as Beltran was concerned . . . She didn't even know where to poke.

He'd stood between her and his own mother. And though Rune didn't totally understand what it all meant, the things that had passed between the two of them in the silent spaces in between had been breath-killing, throat-closing moments where feelings floated tangibly. So though she didn't understand the details, she *understood*.

Rune scrubbed at her face. From above, the smell of roasting meat wafted down, and her stomach rumbled so hard she felt it.

"Yeah," she muttered. "All right, all right."

Rune scanned one last time, watching for the outline of Beltran's wings. But the sky was still empty. She got to her feet, brushing the dirt off her pants as she walked, dirt and gravel crunching beneath her boots.

She came around a bend and stopped short.

Beltran was standing in the middle of the path, no wings. His head was down, shoulders rolled forward, dejectedly human in appearance.

Rune was scared to speak. She took another step. He lifted his head, hair falling across his forehead as he stared at her from beneath his brows.

The pain in his eyes held her in place.

They were only feet apart, and everything in her longed to run for him, to wrap her arms around him. But something in his presence had built a wall between them, one that she didn't know how to penetrate.

"Did you tell them?" His voice was raw and broken.

"No."

"Why?"

He didn't ask it under the assumption that she'd made a mistake, as if maybe what had already almost slipped out had. He was *asking*: What would motivate her to keep his secret? Why hadn't she run and sold him out to the highest bidder?

A spike of anger drove home, mitigated only by the broken way his lips were trembling, the way his fingers were brushing against his pants in nervous repetition. She took a breath, letting her feelings rise to the surface as she looked him square in the eye. "Beltran, you know you don't need to ask me that question."

He huffed out a breath, and his body lurched forward, moving as if someone were physically holding him back. The sky was glowing red and orange around them, painted like a dream. Beltran took the final step, the toes of his boots even with hers. Rune could smell sweat and smoke, see the track marks of old tears on his ashen face. And his eyes were poring over her as if he were starving and she was life.

Rune wanted him, *needed* him. But she feared if she moved, she would shatter the moment, and he would be gone.

Beltran reached for her face, painfully slowly. Rune held her breath, tried not to panic at his hesitation. Then his fingers were brushing across her cheekbones, soft as feathers.

She trembled, her teeth chattering.

"Are you cold?" he whispered.

"No," she breathed.

"Have I ever told you I love your freckles?" He tilted his head to the side, tracing his finger over the bridge of her nose.

Rune couldn't form words. She shook her head.

"From the first time I saw you, I loved them. And every day since, I've wanted to touch them. To lie next to you and run my fingers over your skin and count every single freckle until I knew for sure just how many of them there were."

His hand cupped her jaw, sliding toward her ear. His green eyes burned with desire, and they latched onto hers, searching.

Searching.

Beltran leaned forward, and his breath skittered across her skin. His nose brushed hers. A whimper lodged in the back of her throat.

"I thought I was going to lose you today," he whispered.

"Me too."

His hand slid to the back of her neck, and he pulled her close, pressing the length of his body against hers. She lifted her chin. His lips were right there, flushed and pink in the orange glow. She could feel his chest heaving against hers and the fluttering of his heart.

The whimper she'd tried to hold back escaped, and then he was there, his mouth open, lips capturing hers. Rune's limbs went fluid, and she folded into him. His lips were hot, and he kissed with the firmness of desperation. He pressed and brushed and nibbled, and as their tongues danced, she wrapped her arms around him, sliding her fingers up the back of his neck and into his hair.

Beltran groaned and slowed the kiss, gently pulling away. Before she could object, he pressed his forehead to hers, his thumbs rubbing tiny circles against her cheeks.

"Rune, I—" He shuddered so hard his knees buckled.

She grabbed his elbows to steady him and leaned back, looking him over. "Are you all right?"

Trembles ran through him one after another.

"Saints and demons, no," he breathed. "I am *not* all right. I should not have done that."

"But—"

He shushed her, gently kissing the tip of her nose, her cheeks, and then her lips. "Rune, I can't lose you."

"You won't."

"You don't understand. I lose everything. It's my fate." He stepped back, his hands sliding from her skin and falling to his side. "I can't do this. Not to you."

The pain was so intense that she couldn't find words. She wrapped her arms around herself, the sudden separation from him feeling like she'd been ripped out of bed on a cold winter's night.

"Please." Beltran held his hands out, palm up, despondence leaking from every part of him.

Tears pooled, his form blurring out. "*Please* what? God, Beltran, what do you want from me?

"Tell me," he croaked . . . the words cutting off. He swallowed. "I need you to tell me to leave you alone."

She shook her head. "No. I won't do that."

They stared at each other, both shivering, the air between them sparking. Beltran moaned again, the sound coming from so deep that he bent at the waist. And then he was rushing forward, grabbing her, pressing a hand into the small of her back. As her mouth parted, the stars seemed to spin. Rune tasted the salt of their combined tears on his lips, and the world faded away. No sound existed outside of their own rushed breaths melding to move as one.

Every touch and every brush of his lips exploded through her with an intensity she'd never experienced before. She couldn't get close enough. Rune nipped his bottom lip, and he gasped, running a hand through her hair as his other trailed down her back.

She'd listened to every vague objection he'd held between them. More importantly, she'd seen the panic in his eyes at the thought of what they were doing right now. She'd be lying if she didn't admit that it had lodged a sliver of fear in her as well. But her heart was bursting in this moment with the rightness of it all. They fit. In every way.

That realization sent a new tear trickling down her cheek. There were so many unknowns, so many secrets and questions. His past was a giant dark hole hinted at only with warnings.

But it didn't matter. Because he was hers now.

She was his.

And *she was lost!*

When the kiss inevitably ended, the spell that held them apart from the world broke, and she found that they were still standing on the side of a mountain, serenaded by the singing of crickets.

Beltran's cheeks were flushed, his eyes wide.

"What?" she asked, scared of the answer.

He shook his head, a bitter smile on his face. Looking to the sky, he reached for her, pulling her against his chest. He wrapped his arms around her as if he could hold her tight enough to stop the march of fate itself.

"Hey," she said gently. "I'm not going anywhere."

He set the softest of kisses on her nose, her cheeks, her lips. "I don't know how I'm going to stop touching you."

"So don't."

He sighed, resting his head on hers.

Rune closed her eyes, breathing him in. "Beltran?"

"Hmmm?"

"What are you thinking?"

He jolted. "Seven hells, Rune, you don't want to know."

She shrugged as much as his grip would allow. "I might."

"I was thinking . . . about . . . how afraid I am."

"Why?"

He pulled her tighter still, nestling his lips into her hair as he mumbled, "Because, Rune Jenkins, you will be the end of me."

ACKNOWLEDGMENTS

I always feel overwhelmed trying to write this section. There's always the worry that I'll callously forget someone. The worry is more so this time; 2019 left me reeling for many, many reasons, and I'm not sure that my cognitive functions have recovered. So, here goes nothing.

First and foremost, to Milli and Tom at Brown Books, thank you. Sometimes others see so much more in me than I'm able to pinpoint within myself. This is one of those times. For your faith in me as a person and as an author, I can't thank you enough. And beyond that, for your belief and faith in this world of Eon and its characters. Thank you for not only publishing it but continuing to push it, pitch it, and believe in it.

My husband has sacrificed more for me than should probably be asked. He affords me the opportunity and privilege to do what I do and take the roads I'm traveling. At times those roads leave me a little lost, and I fear he thinks his sacrifices are for nothing. Because the reality is that all he ever wants is my happiness. Zack, I love you. Sometimes happiness hides under tears. I'm so grateful for what you've done and continue to do. And although tears seem to be programmed into my system, I can't imagine being happier with anyone else or doing anything else.

To Erynn Newman, editor and friend. I'm truly sorry that commas are utterly elusive to me. And thanks for offering to lie to me when I asked if I was starting to wrangle the little devils properly. I appreciate not only your eye but your patience and pep talks.

Allen Johnson. You have popped up in this section again! Your expertise is invaluable, and I am so grateful for the video tutorials with the weapons and full-size battle dummies . . . that you just happen to have in your office. As I said to Zack while watching said demo—you can't buy friends like this! Thank you for always being there.

To my beautiful, smart, capable children, I think I'll quote the inscription on our yearly Christmas ornament this time: "It was rough, but we made it." I'm proud of you both, and I hope that out of this craziness comes belief in yourself. You can do hard things. You've watched me cry, and you've watched me get back up. Trust me when I say you're both strong enough to *always* get back up.

To the team at Brown Books. I can't decide if I should say sorry or thank you, so let's do both. I try not to be too much of an "artist", but dang it, sometimes it just comes flying out. So sorry. And for all your hard work on every front, thank you.

Finally, to my fans and readers. I wish I could make you all understand how utterly amazed and grateful I am for every last one of you. Thank you for the belief, the love, and the support. For every friend and relative you introduce to this world. For every library where you've requested Venators. For every message you've sent me. Thank you.

I hope I can offer you all art and escape for many, many years to come.

DEVRI WALLS

Devri Walls is a US and international best-selling author. She specializes in all things fantasy and paranormal. She's best known for her uncanny world-building skills, her intricate storylines, and the ability to present it all in an easy-to-digest voice. Devri loves to engage with her loyal following through online sessions organized for her readers and social media. Devri lives in Meridian, Idaho, with her husband and two kids. When not writing, she can be found teaching voice lessons, reading, cooking, or binge watching whatever show catches her fancy.